THE SATURDAY EVENING

READER OF

WESTERN STORIES

Edited by E. N. Brandt

D0031045

DOUBLEDAY & COMPANY, INC., GARDEN CITY, NEW YORK, 1960

All of the characters in this book
are fictitious, and any resemblance
to actual persons, living or dead,
is purely coincidental.

CONTENTS

Outlaw Trail, *by S. Omar Barker*   11

May the Land Be Bright, *by Sigman Byrd*   24

Law of the Lash, *by Prentiss Combs*   40

Stage to Yuma, *by Marvin DeVries*   52

Fiddle-Footed, *by Cliff Farrell*   69

The Lady from Red Gulch, *by Michael Fessier*   84

Test by Torture, *by Williams Forrest*   96

The Marriage of Moon Wind, *by Bill Gulick*   109

A Widow of the Santa Ana Valley, *by Bret Harte*   122

Dead-Man Trail, *by Ernest Haycox*   137

Dakotahs Coming!, *by MacKinlay Kantor*   154

How Mr. Hickok Came to Cheyenne, *by Alfred Henry Lewis*   183

The Hasty Hanging, *by Morgan Lewis*   195

The Fool's Heart, *by Eugene Manlove Rhodes*   211

Top Hand, *by Luke Short*   237

Guest's Gold, *by Stewart Edward White*   250

Fast Gun, *by Robert Patrick Wilmot*   269

The Gift Horse, *by Owen Wister*   284

NOVELETTES

The Devil in the Desert, *by Paul Horgan*   306

Smoke over the Prairie, *by Conrad Richter*   333

PREFACE

There are many Wests—the West of the explorers, the West of the Mountain Men and the Indian Wars, the West of the wagon trains, the gold seekers, the homesteaders, the ranchers, and the cowboys. Each one has had its faithful chroniclers, and it is to them and their painstaking research that we owe our knowledge of the West's colorful past. Not only in such fine novels as *The Virginian* and *The Covered Wagon* but in many splendid short stories these chroniclers have preserved and passed on to us their love of the country and their understanding of the men and women who first braved it, fought it, and finally won it. To these chroniclers we owe a debt that we hope will be partially repaid by publishing in book form some of their tales of those days that might otherwise be lost or forgotten.

E. N. Brandt, Senior Editor

THE SATURDAY EVENING POST

THE SATURDAY EVENING POST
READER OF WESTERN STORIES

OUTLAW TRAIL

by S. Omar Barker

The kid was rawboned, red-necked, straw-headed, small for sixteen and a long way from Arkansas. His name, if it mattered, was Elnathan Calhoun. The stump he sat on was the hip-high relic of a fallen patriarch, genus cottonwood. It was located in the noonday shade of a considerable *bosque* of its own glossy-leafed descendants, on the sunward side of the one-legged street of Bosque Largo, Territory of New Mexico, more or less U.S.A.

Old breast-yoke rings triple-stapled onto the top of the stump and hoof-trampled earth around its base bore witness to its sometime utility as a hitch rack. But there were no horses shading there now. There was only Elnathan Calhoun, who had judiciously cached his mount off up the draw and was now carelessly ensconced between hitch rings, blowing a soft whimsey of melody through a six-inch mouth harp. The tune was a tender ballad of hill-folk vintage called Barbara Ellen, and it had a lonesome sound.

That the rider dust-jogging up the road from the southeast was a pilgrim seemed evidenced by a lightly packed bed horse. Distantly viewed, he looked to be tall in the saddle, weathered in the hat, and adequately armed. His calling name, if it mattered, was Tonk Mc-Spadden, and Texas lay six days behind him.

That the nearer rider approaching from the opposite direction was no pilgrim was betrayed by the undusty spruceness of his garb and rigging, from burnished black boots to brim-broad black sombrero, including the gleam of a six-shooter's mother-of-pearl handle in between. His calling name was Pete Hadlock; he wore a deputy sheriff's badge, and he rode his sleek sorrel proud and prancy, like a man who doesn't much care who's watching him, just so it's somebody.

He was within ten feet of the hitch stump when Elnathan Calhoun took a sudden notion to see what a sorrel horse would think of a train whistle, with no train in sight. What the *whee-oo-whee-whee-oo-oo* of Elnathan's mouth harp lacked in steam, it made up for in surprise. The sorrel did not think well of it. He promptly, as the cowboys say, "swallered his head," and his equally surprised rider sailed off over it.

"Mister," said Elnathan Calhoun with the friendliest of grins, "you couldn't have flew off purtier if you had wings!"

For a moment Deputy Sheriff Hadlock sat in the dust calling a wrathful roll of swearwords. By the time he arose from disgrace and advanced upon the person of Elnathan Calhoun, he was beginning to repeat himself, and the boy's Arkansas grin was half an inch wider.

A brawny hand gathered up a fistful of Elnathan Calhoun's shirt front and hoisted him ungently off the stump.

"You think spookin' horses is funny, huh?" said the burly bucka-roo-deputy. "Darned if I know whether to slap your face, kick your pants or throw you in jail!"

From the way he drew back his right hand it was evident that Deputy Hadlock aimed to try the slapping first.

Six days' ride from the Texas line, two weeks from the scene of a bitterly lost love, and headed for hell-don't-care, Tonk McSpadden arrived just in time to mind his own business—but didn't. Approaching unobserved, he flicked a midget lass-rope loop over Hadlock's ready-to-smack arm and yanked.

"I do declare," he remarked with a dryness not wholly due to a dusty throat, "if it ain't ol' Pearl-Handled Pete!"

Hadlock whirled around.

"Tonk, you damn Injun!" His greeting smacked only a little of brotherly cordiality. "What you doin' in New Mexico?"

"Right now I'm takin' a census—countin' the growed-up men that come it big over kids—and it looks like you're number one." Tonk obligingly let out enough slack for Hadlock to slip the noose off his arm. "Somethin' rile you, Pete?"

"My train whistle spooked his bronc." Elnathan Calhoun's grin widened again at the memory. "He couldn't have flew off purtier if he'd had wings. But I don't need no thirty-dollar help, cowboy."

Tonk McSpadden stepped off his horse and stood between them.

"Tonk," said red-in-the-face Hadlock, "I'd just as soon wallop you as the kid. And I kinder think I can do it!"

"Someday when you ain't got on your big behavior maybe I'll accommodate you. Right now I don't hate nobody but myself. Besides you look over-het and I'm over-dry. If that sign yonder don't lie, I'll buy you a beer and let you tell me your secret of success."

"There's two things," declared Hadlock, preening his brown mustache, "that tally big in this Territory, Injun: straight pistol-pointin' and crooked politics. You're lookin' at a he-wolf expert in both. There ain't been a holdup nor a horse stole in Tuloso County since I hired out to the law. Nor there won't be. Not even with Curly Jack Marcotte and his wild bunch rendezvousin' not a hundred miles north, and the sheriff away."

"If I could admire myself thataway I wouldn't speak to nobody but me—and that only on a Sunday." Elnathan Calhoun batted his crockery-blue eyes and grinned engagingly.

The grin appeased Pete Hadlock not at all. "Buster," he said, "this is one fair city where bums ain't welcome. You've got just ten minutes to start goin' someplace else—or to jail as a hobo!"

"And me without no watch," sighed Elnathan Calhoun. "Just good looks and money." He tossed a silver dollar—his last—in the air, caught it, returned it debonairly to his pocket, and addressed himself to Tonk McSpadden as if Hadlock no longer even existed.

"I can't buy you no beer, mister—my daddy was a pure-water preacher and he'd ha'nt me. But let's you and me go cut a can of pork and beans. I got the money to pay for it. We can talk about robbin' banks, shootin' sheriffs and huggin' purty girls."

"I'm a crackers-and-sardines man myself, Buzzsaw," said the black-eyed cowboy. "Let's go."

The patched kid from Arkansas and the part-Tonkawa-Indian cowboy from Texas sat on the steps of Ike Bamberger's store spooning pork and beans and sardines onto crackers with their pocket-knives. Cooling tomatoes they slupped direct from the can.

Elnathan Calhoun's silver dollar now reposed in Ike Bamberger's cash drawer, but Elnathan didn't care. Tonk's letting him stand treat for the grub gave him that precious grown-man feeling. Pete Hadlock's horse now stood hitched in front of the Bosque saloon.

"I could have whipped ol' shiny-boots if you'd have let me," Elnathan complained mildly. "I make a big show with my fists, then kick 'em in the groin."

"That's as good a way as any to get yourself shot," said Tonk dryly. "But there ain't nothing wrong with Pete except he fancies himself. Him and me went up the trail together. He drifted out here and finagled him a badge. Me, I went back to Texas, but things had changed some, so I lit out for new country."

"Meanin' your girl had went back on you?"

"You finish them termaters, Buzzsaw. I'm running over. You aiming to get out of town like you was told? You've done used up twenty of your ten minutes."

"Tonk," said Elnathan Calhoun earnestly, "I'm goin' to tell you a secret. I never had no girl go back on me, but I got plumb wearied of my stepdaddy's whippin's. I've been a month gettin' this far. From what I hear, it ain't much farther." Elnathan Calhoun lowered his voice. "I'm fixin' to join up with that Curly Jack outfit and be an outlaw!"

For a long moment Tonk McSpadden sat silent, feeling a resurge of lonely bitterness within him—the bitterness that had ridden with him every foot of the long miles from a homey little town deep in the live-oak hills of Texas. When finally he spoke, his tone was short and abrupt. "Outlawin' is a risky business, kid."

"Bug on a buzzsaw!" retorted Elnathan Calhoun scornfully. "You think I ain't got the guts?"

Again Tonk took a long time to answer. "I hate to see a man afoot," he said finally. "My bed horse is packed light. You reckon you could straddle him behind the pack?"

Pete Hadlock's horse was still hitched in front of the saloon when they rode out of Bosque Largo. A mile out, Elnathan Calhoun slid off the pack horse.

"I've got another secret, Tonk," he said. "You wait here."

With a gangling gait not unlike that of a loping jackrabbit, the boy hurried into a dense *bosque* of young cottonwoods. He emerged a few minutes later astradle a bony red mule, without a saddle, but with an ancient six-shooter belted around his skinny middle. Before him on the mare mule's high withers he carried a bundle rolled in a rusty-black preacher's coat. A crudely fashioned rope hackamore served for bridle.

"Kid," said Tonk, "it ain't polite to mention it, but I left my good manners in Texas. Hiding out that mule and gun while you went into town could smell to a man with a long nose like maybe you stole 'em."

"I bought the pistol and a piece of rope from a Mexkin with—with my next to last dollar. The mule just follered me."

"It's a habit mules have got," commented Tonk dryly, "specially with somebody leadin' 'em."

Elnathan didn't answer. As they rode on, he got out his mouth harp and tenderly revived Barbara Ellen.

"I knew a gal that used to sing that tune," said Tonk sharply. "Play something else or shut up!"

"Tonk"—Elnathan Calhoun put away the harmonica—"are you goin' with me to join up with ol' Curly Jack?"

"Might." The cowboy pinched out his half-smoked brown cigarette and threw it down. "Me and Curly Jack growed up together, back in Texas."

"Bug on a buzzsaw!" exclaimed young Mr. Calhoun. "That makes it a cinch! I was scared Curly Jack might suspect I was a detective out to betray him to the law. Thisaway he'll know it's all right, won't he?"

Tonk McSpadden didn't answer. He and Curly Jack Marcotte had been friends before Marcotte took to the outlaw trail. It had been strong in Tonk's mind that they could be friends again out in the wilds of New Mexico. The thought had been a sort of salve to the soreness of his heart—and of his pride. To hell with untrue women, to hell with honest wages, to hell with Texas, to hell with everything.

Word of the bold bravado of the Curly Jack Wild Bunch had drifted as far away as the Texas Hill Country—apparently also all the way to Arkansas. It was a savage purpose in Tonk McSpadden's heart that more of the same word, his name with it, would one day come to the ears of the blue-eyed girl he had meant to marry—just to let her know that he didn't give a damn. Of such bitterness of heart, in those hard horseback days, was the fabric of outlaw character all too often woven.

Tonk McSpadden rode with a six-shooter at his hip, a short

thirty-thirty in his saddle scabbard, and he knew how to shoot them. What Curly Jack had learned to do, Tonk McSpadden could learn. So could a buzzsaw kid from Arkansas—and who would there be to care?

They camped together that night in a draw twenty miles from Bosque Largo. For an hour after they had eaten, the wild, weird howl of coyotes played intermittent accompaniment to the tunes of Elnathan Calhoun's mouth harp—none of them, this time, Barbara Ellen.

The kid had no bedroll. Tonk unspooled his own for double.

"You don't need to bed me," said Elnathan. "I'm used to sleepin' wild."

"Suit yourself," said Tonk shortly, and turned in.

He was still awake an hour later when the kid came crawling under the bed tarp.

"A mite chilly out there," he apologized. "You ain't been asleep anyhow, have you, Tonk?"

For answer the cowboy made a brief, grunting sound. Tonk had seen stray dogs take up with a man after no more than one kind word, then stay with him whether he liked it or not. Already the kid seemed to consider them pardners in adventure—which, in that day and time, meant considerably more than if you pronounced partner with a "t." Whatever the nature of the attachment, there was admiration in it that made Tonk uneasy.

"Tonk"—Elnathan spoke timorously in the darkness—"you reckon that deputy sheriff suspicioned where we're headin' for?"

"My reckon machine don't work after dark. Now shut up and go to sleep!"

Samuel W. Loftis, long on hard luck and short on cow savvy, was having bull trouble—big trouble for a granger with only a slim fourteen-year-old daughter on a work horse for cowhand help. On money borrowed from the so-far-unrobbed bank at Tuloso, county seat of the same-named county, Loftis had ventured a small start in the cattle business: thirty crazy-quilt cows and one rangy bull of ungentle temper, which Janie, with a young girl's whimsey, had christened Sir Roanyred.

Now, still five miles from home with the cattle, the bull had sulled on them. He had put both Loftis and the girl on the skedaddle, then waded out into a cattail marsh from which neither hurled rocks, cuss words nor sweet persuasion could budge him.

Topping a nearby rise, Tonk McSpadden appraised the situation thusly to Elnathan Calhoun:

"When you ride the outlaw trail, Buzzsaw, you don't help nobody's bull out of a bog. You pull your hat down real low and ride 'way 'round 'em, Shep, hoping they won't notice you."

"Bug on a buzzsaw, Tonk!" Elnathan pocketed his mouth harp. "The little one in overalls looks like a girl!"

"For a lad of your tender years," said Tonk, "you've got mighty growed-up eyesight."

Instead of "riding 'way 'round 'em," Tonk made spur-jingling entry upon the scene, the boy close behind him. At their approach Janie Loftis ducked behind her horse, plainly bashful about being seen in two-legged clothing.

"Mister," Tonk addressed the harassed homesteader, "you look right pestered."

"Just purt' near pestered enough to borrow your pistol and shoot the dang-dratted critter!"

"Dead bulls don't daddy no calves," observed Tonk. "Too bad my rope won't reach him from solid ground or I might drag him out for you."

"Tonk," said Elnathan Calhoun, sliding off his mule, "you git your rope ready!"

Without further powwow, the boy struck out into the marsh, leaping from one grass hummock to another. By the time he got within ten yards, Sir Roanyred's front hoofs were slinging mud. His tail was up and his neck was bowed.

"You better watch out!" Janie called out shrill warning. "He's on the fight!"

From ten feet away Elnathan Calhoun's handful of mud splattered Sir Roanyred smack between the eyes. There may be more provocative methods of insulting an angry bull, but Sir Roanyred wasn't choosy. With a big whoosh of wind he lowered his sharp-horned head and charged.

With hardly a six-foot safety zone between bull's horns and boy's behind, Elnathan headed for solid ground.

"Here come us wildies, Tonk!" he yelled. "Git ready with your doggone rope!"

Slogging almost knee-deep in muck, neither boy nor bull could make much speed, but the race was evenly matched.

Six yards from solid ground Elnathan hit a deep spot. A dagger-sharp horn tip ripped his shirttail within an inch of live meat. As the bull's massive head swung for another gouge, Tonk's loop snugged suddenly around the base of his horns, jerked tight, and yanked Sir Roanyred over on his side.

In response to this further insult, the roan bull lurched on out of the bog in a head-on charge at Tonk's horse. But that wise Texas pony had side-stepped belligerent bovines before. As the momentum of blind rage carried the bull on past, Tonk squalled his wildest cowboy squall, grabbed and bent his tail in such a painful kink that the anguished animal kept on going.

Tonk ran him a few yards, flipped the rope over his high hindquarters and fair-grounded him so hard they could hear all the wind whoosh out of him as he hit the ground. Tonk waited, let him get up, then wind-busted him hard again.

"Texas cure for big behavior," remarked Tonk. "Buzzsaw, will you kindly slip my rope off before the gentleman ketches his wind? I do believe he won't give these good folks no more trouble."

The cowboy believed right. Sir Roanyred lurched up and high-tailed it to the other cattle without even looking back.

"I sure am obliged to you!" The granger sounded like he meant it. "My name's Sam Loftis. This is my daughter Janie. Time we get these cattle home it'll be comin' on night. We'd be mighty proud to lodge you boys, Mr.——"

"Smith—John Smith. No, let's make it Bill Jones. Too many pilgrims ridin' under John Smith's hat already." Tonk said it soberfaced. "My pardner here goes by the name of Cadwallader Casanova when the sheriff ain't after him, so maybe you'd better call him Johnson. And we thank you kindly, but us owl-hooters like to ride by night, don't we—Johnson?"

"Bug on a buzzsaw, Tonk!" exclaimed Elnathan. "You gone plumb crazy?"

A troubled look came into Sam Loftis' eyes. In it suspicion and fear battled with stubborn good will—and lost.

"Boys," he said evenly, "I don't take you to be the kind that have to hide behind fake names. You come to my house for the night—and welcome."

"I sure wish you would," put in Janie timidly. "We don't ever have no company any more. With that Curly Jack Marcotte and his outlaws terrifyin' the country, ma's plumb scared to let a stranger step inside the door."

"Hush, child!" said Loftis gently.

Here it is again, thought Tonk. *Curly Jack . . . a name to be whispered in fear; a shadow of dread across a sunny land. And what the hell do you care, Tonk McSpadden?*

Aloud he said: "You see, Buzzsaw? We fooled 'em. All right, let's get on with the man's cattle—and see if this little junie-bird's ma makes good biscuits!"

She did. With fresh fried ham and eggs, Mrs. Loftis' biscuits were manna and ambrosia, and her look of suspicion relaxed when Loftis and Janie took enthusiastic turns telling her and three wide-eyed littler girls how the bull came out of the bog.

"He purt' near got Buzzsaw—I mean Mr. Johnson, ma!" Janie favored Elnathan with an admiring smile. "Scared me purt' near to death!"

"Shucks"—Elnathan buttered another biscuit like a man who trusts his own capacity—"that's the way I used to toll wild razorbacks out of the brush back in Arkinsaw. They're a heap dangerouser than bulls. Anyhow, I knew Tonk's rope would ketch him before he yamped me."

"He plays the mouth organ, too, ma—real pretty."

"Well, now!" Mrs. Loftis' smile was warm and motherly. "Maybe he'll play some for us after supper. Pass Mr. Jones the biscuits, Janie."

While Janie and her mother washed dishes, Elnathan Calhoun sat on the woodbox breathing tender mountain melodies through his harmonica, and now not even Barbara Ellen had a lonesome sound.

In the cool dark outside, well out of kitchen hearing, Tonk McSpadden meshed mixed strands of inner torment into firm resolution and spoke his piece.

"Mr. Loftis," he said, "of course you know my name ain't Jones. What it is don't matter. What does matter is that this kid has took to me like a stray pup—and it ain't good."

"I doubt that, young man."

"Put it this way, Mr. Loftis: when a growed man gets his hair ruffed the wrong way, the trail he picks to get away from it is his own business. But this young Arkansas stray is a good solid boy, except he's got some wild and venturesome notion and he don't know which from 'tother about the whys and wherefores. What I'm asking is for you to home him in off the rough trail right here and now. Work him. Feed him. Daddy him what you can. It could turn out someday he'll do you for a son."

"You puzzle me, young man." The granger's answer came slowly. "But I'll do what you ask—if the boy will stay."

"Work it this way: bed him in the house tonight if you can. Tell him I can't stand his infernal kickin'. Time he wakes up in the morning, I'll be long gone from here. Thanks, Mr. Loftis, and I wish you good night."

"Hold on, Jones, Tonk, or whatever your right name is." The homesteader's tone turned suddenly stern. "I'm no hand to pry, but one thing I want to know: are you scoutin' for Curly Jack Marcotte —or ain't you?"

"You're smart enough to know that if I was I wouldn't tell you."

"If Curly Jack should clean out that bank at Tuloso," Loftis went on grimly, "it would ruin me and some other honest folks around here."

"From what I hear, no bank is plumb safe with Marcotte around," Tonk said dryly. "As for me, Mr. Loftis, let's just say I'm a bug on a buzzsaw. Whichaway I jump ain't nobody's business but my own."

The homesteader's shrug was a gesture of bafflement. "So be it," he said. "But I know which way I'm fixin' to jump all right: I'm going in and draw what savings I've got out of that bank while it's still got a chance to be there—just in case."

Half old in sun-browned adobe, half new in sun-warping pine, the village of Tuloso, Territory of New Mexico, couched itself peacefully and with some prosperity in the embrace of rimrocked mesas gapped widely by a two-way valley whose green embroidery of tule marshes gave the oasis its name.

Leaving the Loftis place, Tonk had first thought to give all settlements a wide berth. He had foxed his trail and camped last night among remote rocky hills, hoping thus to lose the Buzzsaw Kid if that misguided youngster should try to follow him. Now that he seemed to have succeeded, the cowboy had re-estimated the hazards of an empty grubsack and was riding into Tuloso to replenish it.

Looking down on the placid settlement, Tonk remembered similar hill-country villages in faraway Texas, and tried hard to clamp down on the nostalgic pang under his ribs.

How far must a lonely man ride to rid himself of bitterness, how far harden himself to callus his soul against old hurt? That he had managed to turn the kid aside on a better trail was good—much as he missed him. As for himself, close ahead lay the outlaw trail. By tomorrow night he would reach Curly Jack Marcotte's reputed hideout—and for better or worse, the die would be cast.

"Hey, Tonk!" The red mare mule brought Elnathan dusting up beside him at a gangling gallop. "Bug on a buzzsaw, Tonk! If I'd knowed you aimed to sneak out on me, I'd have hobbled you instead of the mule! Maybe I'm a cuckleburr in your tail, but wherever you go, I'm goin', Tonk—and—and nothin' can stop me!"

"For two cents and a ticket to hell," Tonk told him dryly, "I'd turn you over to Pete Hadlock for stealing that mule!"

Elnathan's only answer was an ingratiating grin. In a mutual stubbornness of silence, they rode into Tuloso together, hitched their mounts in cottonwood shade and started up the street toward a sign that said GENERAL MERCHANDISE.

Across the street Tonk recognized Sam Loftis' team, hitched to a rickety buckboard, dozing at a hitch rack. Evidently the homesteader had come to town after his money, just as he had threatened. Straight ahead in front of the Tuloso County Bank, a whiskery man with a six-shooter in one hand stood holding the reins of five saddled horses with the other. Nearby, a second black-shirted *hombre* had two men and a woman backed up against the wall, held there, their hands high in the air, by the threat of his six-shooter.

The man holding the horses waved his gun warningly at Tonk and Buzzsaw as they approached.

"Face to the wall and hands high, boys!" he ordered in a tone of insolent confidence. "Curly Jack's in town!"

It was sound advice—but wasted.

A shot sounded inside the bank. Three men came rushing out. Two carried loot-laden gunnysacks. The third shoved a valiantly kicking and clawing Janie Loftis along beside them, a shield against possible attack.

The outlaws' sudden rush excited the horses, making them hard to hold.

"Hang onto the gal till we get mounted, Cuff!"

To Tonk McSpadden the leader's voice had a familiar sound that somehow sickened him, and suddenly he knew whose side he was on. Grimly his hand dropped to his six-shooter.

"You skedaddle, Buzz!" He spoke with quiet urgency back over his shoulder. "Hell's fixin' to pop!"

This, too, was sound advice—but wasted.

Quick as a cat, Elnathan Calhoun had already darted in among the lunging horses, harmonica in hand.

"*Whee-oo-whee-whee-oo-oo! Whee-oo-whee-whee-oo-oo!*"

At the train-whistle screech of the boy's mouth harp, the outlaws' already nervous horses went crazy-wild. One lunged against the man holding them, knocking his gun off aim so that his quick shot at Tonk McSpadden flew wild. The whirled-around rump of another bumped into the outlaw who held the girl and knocked him down.

Thus abruptly freed, Janie wasted no time. Grabbing the fallen outlaw's gun, she hit him over the head with it just as Elnathan Calhoun's big old pistol, having failed to fire, dealt a like cranial wallop to another one. A third outlaw went down with one of Tonk's well-aimed bullets through both legs.

Two of the outlaws somehow managed to mount and take off down the street. The last bullet in Tonk McSpadden's wheel tumbled one of them. The other ran head-on into a new arrival galloping in from a side street. Arriving late, but not too late, Deputy Sheriff Pete Hadlock was not on prancy-parade this time—and he knew how to shoot.

In the strange brevity of swift violence, the battle was over and Curly Jack Marcotte's last bank robbery foiled, with the grim tally of one outlaw dead and four safely captured, three of them wounded.

Janie Loftis paused to give Elnathan Calhoun a hasty squeeze, then ran to her father as he came limping out of the bank between two white-faced tellers, bleeding from a bullet wound in his leg—his reward for trying to balk the robbery.

Tonk paused to stare briefly down at the lifeless face of a curly-haired outlaw leader he had once known as an honest cowboy.

"Well, Buzzsaw," he said, deep-down soberly, "now we know about outlawin'!"

"Injun," said Deputy Sheriff Hadlock, and there was no bluster in it, "it looks like you and the kid saved the bacon. If either of you wants to kick me for my big behavior the other day, I'll bend over for it."

"Bug on a buzzsaw!" Elnathan Calhoun managed a faint grin. "Wouldn't I look purty kickin' a law officer, and me with a stole mule I've got to take back before I can start over sure 'nough honest!"

MAY THE LAND BE BRIGHT
by Sigman Byrd

From the Journal of James Holston, Capt., Commanding Co. K, 1st Reg., Missouri Cavalry, Army of the West, USA.

Wednesday, 19th Aug., 1846.

Yesterday we occupied Santa Fe without a shot fired. Raised the Stars & Stripes over the Palacio, whence Gov. Armijo & cohorts had fled towards El Paso at our approach.

This morn. Gen. Kearny addressed the People in the Plaza: "We come amongst you to take possession of New Mexico in the name of the Govt. of the United States. You are now become American Citizens. I am your governor; henceforward look to me for protection."

The People shouted Huzzas; many wept for joy.

This day has healed the scars of 5 yrs. back, when I 1st entered this Capital with high hope, & with other brave comrades departed in Chains for Mexico City.

Were I a Man of Letters, & not a Soldier, might recount here how I met the most beautiful woman in the Dept. of New Mexico. I recollect——

In those days, Texas was a proud free nation with a chip on her shoulder, led by the impetuous dreamer who had succeeded Sam Houston, the soldier. So, being one of her few blue-eyed native sons, and being on a foolhardy secret mission besides, I rode into Santa Fe, at once arrogant and cautious.

I had come with Amos Deckworth's wagons from Independence, where I had joined the train as bullwhacker, mule skinner and Indian fighter. We had been obliged to cross the swollen Arkansas by buffalo boat, and at the Cimarron we had lost two men and a week's march in skirmishes with the Comanches. Now it was September, and I should have been in Santa Fe a month ago.

As we rolled over the last crest and saw the town, looking like a handful of dice spilled at the foot of the mountains, Deckworth rode up beside me. He was a noble-looking man, with a short black beard and graying hair, and the clothing he had put on when we nooned five hours back was made by the best tailor in St. Louis. His pale gray eyes lifted to mine, and he smiled, showing milk-white, gold-filled teeth.

"This is trail's end, Haskins," he said. "But I've been thinking. You came West for adventure. How'd you like to take a train to Chihuahua for me?"

"Being a trader wasn't what I had in mind," I said. "That's why I left New Orleans." I had to curb my pony and raise my voice then, for the wagoners had begun shouting and firing their rifles, saluting our achievement in pushing our freight across prairie, river, mountain and desert to this fabulous land where the hills were veined with gold and turquoise. "Maybe I'll hunt buffalo or trap beaver," I said.

He looked sidewise at me. "You don't strike me as a hunter or a trapper. There are, I admit, adventures to be had in Santa Fe. You may not know it, but Mexico is about to lose this department."

"You mean to Texas?" I asked.

He gave a snort that startled my horse again. "The Texians will be cat's-paws. I mean to the United States. You speak Spanish?" I said I did.

"Then come with me tomorrow night. Don Rafael Castelar always gives a dance the second night after I arrive. You'll meet the gentry and maybe find more interesting game than buffalo."

"Thanks," I said. "I will."

"You know," he said, "I can't get over the notion I've seen you twenty, thirty years ago. But that's impossible. It could have been your father."

"Could have been," I agreed. "He's a native Missourian, tall and fair like me. I was born a year after he settled in Louisiana."

"Haskins." He shook his head, frowning. "I have a remarkable memory for faces, and usually for names. But that wasn't this man's name."

He rode on. It seemed scarcely possible that he had known my father or could know that my father had gone to Texas from Louisiana. I had been warned not to trust Americans, and I had deliberately avoided friendships on the trail. That had been difficult, for these were the sort of men I had marched across Texas with behind the runaway scrape, five years ago when I was a beardless lieutenant under General Houston. We had stopped running at San Jacinto, a cannon shot's distance from my birthplace. And there we Texians who were from Texas and from Tennessee, Kentucky, Louisiana and Carolina—and even from Mexico—had turned and fought with guns and knives until the bayou ran blood and we captured the dictator himself and made my country free.

I remembered that as we rode into Santa Fe de San Francisco, the last Missouri train of that tragic year, 1841. *But I am Captain James Holston of the Texas army,* I argued. *This is enemy country, and I am a spy. The United States Government wouldn't lift a finger to save me. It might even help hang me if it became known at Fort Leavenworth that I had a rendezvous with a force of misguided patriots who hoped by luck and a coup d'état to raise the Lone Star over Governor Armijo's palace.*

At a distance, Santa Fe had taken some color from the late sun lowering in the mountains. But as we came into its streets and smelled its filth and saw the mud-gray adobe walls, I thought with pride of the gracious avenues of Houston and the clean pine houses on my father's plantation.

Santa Fe was a barren town. Cactus was taking its blighted cornfields. The dusty cottonwood trees seemed stunted. Dogs yapped at the hoofs of our horses and oxen. Naked children fled before us to dark doorways to peer from behind the skirts of languid-eyed womenfolk. The women smiled and waved to us, calling their indolent men from the houses.

"The Americans!" they cried in their high, flutelike voices. "Behold! Behold!"

I was one of those men who orient themselves easily. I engaged a monastical room at the Mesón de San Esteban, kept by Baldo Parral, a stout, swarthy fellow who spoke excellent English.

When I had seen my horse stabled and fed, the landlord conducted me to the kitchen. Here the fat, pock-faced Señora Parral served us a supper of *chile guisado* and goat's cheese, with a bottle of Pass wine.

"What do you think of our country, señor?" asked my host.

"I've just arrived," I reminded him.

"Well, one hears wonderful things of the United States and its magnificent cities. Ciudad Méjico is a beautiful city also. It was there I learned English from an Irish padre. But this Rio Arriba country is wild and cruel."

"So I hear," I told him. "Do you know an American named Jason Webster?"

Don Baldo, about to raise his cup, put it down and watched me with beady eyes. "You are his friend?"

"I don't know the man," I said in all truth. "I have a letter for him."

"The reason I ask, señor—Don Hysone is in the calaboose."

"What's he done?"

"Who knows? Once it was for getting drunk and fighting. Again it was for stealing a rooster. He may be accused of cheating at cards again. I could take you to the jail when you have eaten, señor. The guards might let you see him. Again they might not."

I said we would try, then. When the meal was over, he parted the curtains at the kitchen doorway and bowed me out.

We turned into the plaza, and Don Baldo paused at the entrance of the palace, pointing to a festoon of shriveled cup-shaped objects strung overhead. "Those are ears, señor. Indian ears, but they might as well be ours. The Navajos call us their shepherds, and when they burn our villages and steal our flocks, they leave a few ewes and scalps, so there will be increase."

"Why don't you make war on them?"

"We in turn enslave the Navajo maidens and pay bounties for the ears of their braves."

"Are the braves better fighters than your soldiers?"

He shrugged as we moved on. "Our soldiers do not fight Indians; they fight the poor Mexicans. The gentry live in Santa Fe, protected by fat soldiers, or at ranchos surrounded by the homes of the poor. When the Navajos or Apaches come, it is the poor who sound the alarm and lose their lives, while the wealthy saddle their sleek horses and ride to the capital. When we make war, the poor lead the attack with bows and arrows, and the military follows to claim the victory or sound retreat. And for this we are beaten, despised and taxed to degradation."

I was about to speak of rebellion, but Baldo Parral talked too well for one of the poorer class. I would ask Webster about him first.

"Here is the jail," Don Baldo said.

Two soldiers leaned on their guns at the entrance to a long adobe building. Don Baldo explained our mission in fluid Spanish and stood waiting. Deliberately, one of the soldiers drew his sword, then suddenly slashed Parral across the face with it. He staggered, dropped his hat and pressed his hands to his face. Blood ran to his chin. My hand moved to the butt of my Colt, but Parral fell against me, pressing the pistol against my hip with his great stomach.

"No, no," he whispered. Aloud he said, "Do not worry, señor. My cousin, Don Rafael, will boil these two."

The soldier put his sword away. "Don Rafael will boil you, pauper, for using his name. Let the American speak for himself."

I dropped my hands, and Parral moved away. It was not pity for him that made me ache to lay the barrel of my revolver across the soldier's jaw. I simply wanted to see pain and fear on the arrogant face of a hated enemy.

"You heard," I said in Spanish. "I want to deliver a letter."

The swordsman said he would take me to the commandant, and I followed him into the building. The commandant, a lieutenant, was seated on a threadbare mattress in the middle of a room with a barred window. A soiled Mexican flag hung on the scaly white wall behind him. He was eating a portion of lamb shoulder, holding the bone in his hands and tearing the meat off with his teeth. He placed the shoulder in an earthen bowl on the dirt floor, then stood and wiped his hands on his breeches. He had a low forehead and cunning black eyes. He offered me a cigarette, but I declined and stated my business.

"You may see the prisoner, señor," he said, "but the letter must be examined. That is"—he raised his eyebrows—"unless you wish to pay his fee for brawling."

He had me there. Buying Webster's release would weaken my denial that I knew him. If I declined to leave the letter, I invited suspicion against us both. The letter itself was harmless, a device to cover my contact with the informer. It merely asked after Webster's fortunes and purported to be from a friend in New Orleans.

I told the lieutenant that Webster's liberty was no concern of mine, handed him the letter and said good night. Outside, the guards closed the door behind me and became shadows. Night had fallen, but the stars were bright.

Just off the plaza, a shadow moved toward me. It was Parral.

"Your eye is bad," I said. "You should not have waited."

"It is my left—the weak one. You saw Don Hysone?"

I told him about the interview.

"A brawl," he said. "Yes, Don Hysone is a drunkard. A pity, for he also is one of us. He is a Texian, like you."

I froze. To have been discovered so easily was disarming. Don Baldo gripped my shoulder. "Do not worry, friend. Your secret is safe with me. Don Hysone told me you were coming. There are a few of us who itch to rise against that goat, Armijo, and we await only the coming of the Texians."

"He should have told no one," I said.

"He is a man of poor judgment, who refuses to believe he is suspected. One does not believe all he says."

I clutched the collar of his shirt in my fist. "Listen, Parral. If you're not on the level, do you know what will happen to you when the Texians come?"

"Yes, señor." He smiled. "They will put out my other eye."

I let him go. "No, they'll hang you."

In the kitchen of the inn, the stolid Señora Parral cleansed his gashed cheek while we sipped wine. The woman wrapped a bandage around her husband's head and went to bed, and Baldo and I sat talking until dawn.

The long-overdue expedition from Texas, I learned, had been sighted approaching the narrows of the Red River, and Santa Fe was a barrel of gunpowder with a lit fuse. But it was Governor Armijo and not the advancing Texians who had applied the spark. The Texians had been painted as bandits and despoilers of women, and all the rabble east of the Rio del Norte were eager to fight the invaders.

It was fantastic that President Lamar had believed such reports as those of the reprobate Webster, who had promised the populace would welcome the liberating Texians. General Houston, who had won Texas' claim to these lands, had opposed the venture. But Lamar dreamed of a Lone Star republic reaching from the Gulf to the Pacific, and my orders were a thread in the fabric of that dream.

To my commanding officer, Brevet Brig. Gen. Hugh McLeod,

had gone the assignment of bringing New Mexico into the pattern. He had been given five companies of mounted infantry and one of artillery, saddled with about forty merchants, politicians, and other civilians, and sent out across the unblazed prairie to install Texian democracy in these mountains, formally surrendered by Dictator Santa Anna after his defeat at San Jacinto.

First he was to present proclamations offering the New Mexicans Texas citizenship and the protection of the starred tricolor. If that failed, he was to fan the embers of rebellion innocently believed to be smoldering in Taos and Santa Fe, and occupy the department by force of arms. Or, as a last resort, if force appeared unwise, the merchants were to be convoyed to the markets to open friendly commerce.

"Who is this Don Rafael you mentioned?" I asked Parral.

"Don Rafael Castelar," he said sadly, "is the bastard son of the wanton sister of my sainted mother. He is also the governor's chief political scavenger and military adviser. The soldier spoke truly; Don Rafael despises me."

"He is my host for tomorrow evening," I said, and told him of Deckworth's invitation.

"Good! You may learn much there. You will also meet his niece, Doña Serafina, the most beautiful woman in the department of Neuva Méjico."

I shook my head. "I have no time for women."

He laughed bitterly. "Doña Serafina is the widow of Don Xeres de Vera, slain by Don Rafael's traitors in the insurrection, and the only person he fears. No moment with her will be wasted, señor."

The talk I heard the following day in the markets and the American stores confirmed Parral's estimate of the temper of his people. Orders a week old, posted at every corner, had mustered the rural militia, and these troops, numbering a thousand, together with six hundred soldiers of the regular army, were said to be encamped near San Miguel. My duty was becoming clear. Tomorrow I must ride to meet General McLeod's less than three hundred dragoons and report that Lamar's good-will proclamations would become bonfires and there would be war.

Late in the afternoon, visiting the cafés and gaming casinos, I had my first glimpse of the silver-studded gentry of Santa Fe, and I guessed there would be treachery too. Armijo, a foppish caballero

told me proudly, had risen from sheep thief to governor by his sly-
ness; if he could not repel the Texians by arms, he would trick them
to their deaths.

I wore black broadcloth that evening when I saddled my pony
and rode to Amos Deckworth's store. His clerks were still conduct-
ing a brisk trade in calico, knives, lead and powder. Deckworth
greeted me cordially. He wore a plaited straw sombrero with a silver
band, and around his waist was a wide blue sash with a derringer
thrust into it. He said the Castelar hacienda was half an hour's ride,
and we mounted our horses and rode along the *Calle de San Francisco*, past the haymarket and out into the scraggly countryside.

The Castelar hacienda was beautiful, but too Moorish for my
taste. Yuccas bloomed in the patio, where torchlit water splashed in
a fountain and gaudy macaws drowsed in great withe cages. A handsome baggy-eyed man with gray hair and a face as cold and smooth
as yellow marble met us at the entrance to the hall and conducted
us inside.

Dancing had already begun, and the great beamed room was
ablaze with hundreds of candles. I had not expected such elegance
and grace in the enemy capital.

Don Rafael shook Deckworth's hand, then clasped mine and
bowed. "Welcome, señor," he said in English. "Don Amos tells
me you have journeyed from the Paris of the New World. Do you
speak French?"

I thanked him and said I did not.

"But you know Spanish well, I hear." He smiled, but there was
no warmth in his paunchy eyes.

"New Orleans is a cosmopolitan city," I said. "I have engaged in
transactions with many of your countrymen."

A servant brought wine in crystal glasses.

"My own vintage," Castelar said, handing glasses to Deckworth
and me.

The wine was excellent. Deckworth excused himself for the company of two army officers. Don Rafael waved a plump hand toward
the dancers.

"A charming picture, is it not, señor?"

I agreed.

"Exotic to you, perhaps. You see, ours is an older, wiser civilization than yours, despite our more recent changes in government. We

build walls around the fair and the good, while you build trails in search of the beautiful and the perfect. I think we will survive when you have spent yourselves."

"One of those trails leads here," I said bluntly. "Are your walls strong?"

The pouches under his eyes tightened. "You have been listening to our friend Don Amos. Yes, the United States may claim this land one day. But the scene will not change. We will only send taxes to Washington instead of Ciudad Méjico."

"I was thinking of the Texians," I said. "I understand you are about to go to war against a party of merchants."

"Merchants, señor! Our scouts report the Texians have five companies of dragoons and one of artillery."

"Possibly," I said. "The plains are full of Comanches. The New Orleans and St. Louis newspapers spoke of the party as a trading expedition. Would an army of invasion bring wagons of merchandise?"

His smooth cheeks flushed. "A foul Texian trick, señor! Even if they came in peace, trade with Texas is not desired, by us or by the Americans. But there can be no peace with those Texians. You shall see their ears hanging at the palace." He finished his drink and smiled. "But forgive me for mentioning war. Let me find you a young and charming partner for the dance."

He conducted me about the room, introducing army officers, politicos and their wives. When the dance ended, he led me to where three girls were seated on a blue-blanketed couch. He mentioned my name and theirs, but I heard only one. "My niece, Doña Serafina."

I had seen pretty Mexican girls in San Antonio, but never had I seen a face as lovely as hers. Her skin was golden and flawless, except for three small spots of vermilion painted on each cheek— a New Mexican custom I had until now found in bad taste.

Her eyes, black and lustrous, met mine intimately, I thought, through a wisp of tobacco smoke.

She wore a close-fitting gown of black and white lace, and she was smoking a brown cigarette which she held with a little pair of silver tongs. Before that day I had never seen a young woman smoke, and the full red curve of her mouth made me ache to take the cigarette from her lips and kiss them.

I bowed and was led away to another group of vermilion-flecked girls.

As Don Rafael named them I heard the laughter of the three behind me, and Doña Serafina's was like music and a knife.

"Can your Creole belles match their beauty against ours?" my host was asking.

I was about to answer when something small and brittle struck the top of my head as gently as the touch of a hand. Cold liquid spilled over my hair and trickled down my face and neck. I smelled perfume and tasted the sweet, bitter stuff on my mouth.

Laughter filled the hall. Don Rafael smiled indulgently. "It is a Rio Arriba custom, señor. When a girl breaks an eggshell filled with cologne on a man's head, he must try to catch her before she returns to her seat. If he succeeds, he may kiss her."

That spun me about, laughing too. I had no way of knowing which of the girls had drenched me with scent, but I shook the eggshell from my hair and reached for the hand with the silver tongs. Doña Serafina had fled only at the last possible moment, and she fled slowly.

Her friends were tittering when I overtook her and caught her wrist.

"It was you!" I exclaimed, drawing her to me.

She tilted her white mantilla and looked at me with laughter in her eyes, then lifted her mouth for my kiss. I brushed her lips lightly with mine and felt my heart shaking me.

"Will you dance with me?" I said in Spanish.

"With pleasure, Señor Haskins."

The musicians played a waltz, not too fast. I scarcely touched her, but my arms were tensely aware of the firm, warm body moving with mine.

When we had circled the room once, she whispered, "Take me into the patio. There is something I must tell you."

There was alarm in her voice, but I could not think of danger. At the doorway we slipped out into the cool night. She walked quickly through the patio, leading me out into a grove of cottonwoods.

She stopped me with fingers tight on my arm. "You are in danger here, señor. You must leave at once and ride to Taos."

"Why Taos?"

"You will find friends there. You are Texian, are you not?"

"I am a friend of Amos Deckworth," I said guardedly.

"He is not your friend, for I heard him tell my uncle you are a spy. He is an American agent. Believe me, señor——"

The sound of footsteps interrupted her. "They are coming for you. Please go!"

I was aware of the danger, but I could not leave her. Then it was too late. Don Rafael stood before us. "Señor Haskins, I have two other guests I wish you to meet. Will you come with me?"

Doña Serafina walked ahead of us to the patio and did not look back as she entered the hall. Her uncle led me to another door, opened it and bowed stiffly.

I entered a sitting room filled with European furniture, very old and fine. A thick, woolen carpet covered the floor, and Spanish tapestries hung on the calcined walls.

Two men in military uniform rose from chairs at either side of the inner door. One was the lieutenant I had interviewed at the jail; the other was a captain with parted chin whiskers.

Don Rafael introduced them. "Captain Rosete, Lieutenant Quintero."

I bowed slightly. The lieutenant took an envelope from his pocket. "I am unable to deliver your letter, señor. The prisoner Webster is dead."

"You need not have ridden here to tell me," I said. "I told you I did not know the man."

Captain Rosete said, "But he knew you, señor. He was shot while trying to escape, but he lived long enough to say he had expected you."

I was caught. To gain time, I turned to my host. I was not surprised to see the undisguised malevolence in his eyes, nor to see Amos Deckworth just inside the door, aloof and stonily amused.

Deckworth said, "I just remembered the man who looked like you, Haskins. His name was Holston, and he was bound for Texas."

The captain said through his whiskers, "That is the name Webster mentioned. You are Captain James Holston, of Texas."

I looked him in the eye and laughed. "That will be hard to prove to the satisfaction of the United States consul."

Don Rafael snorted impatiently. "Arrest him, captain!"

I had my fingers on my Colt when two soldiers with leveled carbines appeared at the door I was facing. Turning, I saw two more guns at the patio door. I dropped my hand, and the lieutenant lifted the pistol from my belt.

To Don Rafael I said, "Better see they don't shoot me while attempting to escape. Neither the United States nor Texas likes to have its citizens murdered by Mexicans."

His face grew mottled. He raised his left arm and slapped me across the cheek with the back of his hand. The blow had scarcely landed before my own right was swinging. My fist caught his jaw, and he went down with a moan. The captain took my right arm; the lieutenant, my left. The soldiers moved in, and someone began hammering the back of my head with a gun barrel. I felt three blows before I lost consciousness.

I woke when the rising moon reached the high barred window of my cell at the jail and shone into my aching eyes. I lay on the cold earth floor, and chinches crawled on my ankles and hands. Pain filled my head from ear to ear, but remembering that I had blundered hurt worse. I got to my feet and cursed the cold mountain moon. I remembered Serafina de Vera and swore again. She had warned me, yes, and I should have left her and ridden eastward to meet General McLeod. But under the bewitchment of her eyes I had walked into the deadfall set by Deckworth and sprung by the Mexicans.

Dawn came, and someone pushed a plate of beans and a pitcher of water through a trap in the cell door. I drank the water, tasted the beans and spit them out. In the afternoon I heard chains rattling, and my door swung open. A soldier with a bayoneted rifle stood at either side, and into my cell swaggered Rosete.

"You rested well, Captain Holston?"

"My name is Haskins," I said.

"So your passport says. But it could be forged. Ordinarily we would determine that by communication with the consulate at New Orleans, but there is little time. The Texians are at our borders and are moving on Anton Chico."

I suppose the surge of pleasure in me must have shown in my eyes. "Do not think your comrades will find us at siesta, captain," Rosete said. "Already an advance scouting party of four have been taken. One is dead, and two are held at San Miguel. The fourth——"

He spoke to one of the soldiers, and in a moment a figure that filled me with pride and despair was pushed into my cell.

It was Timothy Barton, a lieutenant on General McLeod's staff. His uniform was torn to rags and his right arm hung in a dirty sling. The right shoulder was stained with dried blood and his face was blue with bruises.

"Why don't you salute your superior officer?" Rosete said.

Timothy blinked at me. "This man? Who is he?"

The whiskered captain scowled. "You deny he is a Texas spy?"

"I never saw him before."

"You!" he growled at me. "Do you know this man?"

I shook my head.

"Then you won't object to witnessing his execution." He spoke again to the soldiers, and one came in and aimed his rifle at Timothy's heart. I could not believe he would shoot, but Timothy knew better.

"Long live the republic!" he said, smiling at me.

The cell echoed the deafening report and filled with the stench of powder. "Long live the republic!" I said as he fell.

Rosete leered at me. "Your viva gave you away, captain."

"I spoke in tribute to a brave man," I said. "If he was your enemy, I say, long live the Texians."

Rosete flushed. "I would shoot you now, captain, but I prefer you convict yourself. I leave you the body of your comrade. Perhaps he can persuade you to confess."

The soldiers chained the door behind him.

No one else approached my cell that day, even to bring food. I composed Lieutenant Barton's body and closed his eyes. Then I prayed for his soul and mine. When I had finished, I searched his pockets for a possible weapon, but they were empty. Chinches filled the room that night, and I wore a trail across the floor, listening to the intermittent calls of the sentry in the patio. Five minutes had passed since the last call, when I heard my name spoken.

I stepped to the window and chinned myself on the ledge. "Señor Haskins!" It was Baldo Parral. "Is the body of the Texian officer still with you?"

"Yes," I whispered.

"Then listen. Doña Serafina de Vera is at the inn with a horse for you. When I have gone, you will call the guard and demand a priest. You understand?"

I said I did, and he was gone.

It was another five minutes before I heard the guard's call. I shouted to him, demanding a priest. Timothy was a Protestant, like me, but I said he was Catholic.

The guard grunted and went off. It seemed an hour before the door was thrown open and a heavy robed and hooded figure, carrying a lighted candle and a censer, was admitted. The door closed. It was Parral. He put the candlestick and censer on the floor and began removing the robe. The bandage was gone from his head, and the wound was not healing.

"Make haste," he said, holding the robe for me. "The real padre is coming."

"What about you?"

"I am dying," he said. "Feel my brow."

It was burning and dry. "Sickness of the blood," he explained. "The doctor says I cannot live. You must live, señor. Tell the Texian commander to trust no one, to beware any pretended friendliness and to expect no organized aid from the poor people or the Pueblos. To overthrow Armijo, he must defeat two thousand regulars and provincials."

I got into the vestments and he pressed my hand. "Long live the revolution," he whispered.

"Long live liberty," I said.

I picked up the candle and censer and kicked the door until it opened. I had the hood pulled forward, and when I passed the guards I could see only straight ahead down a long dim passage. I walked unhurriedly, swinging the heavy copper censer beside my right knee.

At a turn I almost collided with Lieutenant Quintero and a priest. Before either could find his tongue or his wits, I thrust a candle into the padre's hands and pushed between them. Quintero drew his sword then, but I had the censer swinging backward, and I completed the arc with the chain gripped in both hands.

The cup caught the lieutenant square on top of the head, and he went down like a sack of wool. Over my shoulder I saw the soldiers coming with leveled bayonets. I hurled the censer at them, lifted my skirts and ran.

Ahead of me, a door opened into the night. I stepped out and an indolent sentry jerked to attention. "Good evening, padre."

I walked rapidly and darkness enveloped me. I slunk through the shadows, skirting the plaza and approaching the Mesón de San Esteban from the stables. My horse was gone. But where the corral opened into the patio a Mexican pony was tied to a mesquite tree. I whispered gently to him and touched his shoulder. His skin twitched. He wore a Mexican saddle with a deep tree, and there was a scabbard with what had the feel of a good rifle. A leather pouch hung from the high pommel, and in it my fingers found powder, caps and lead.

I went to the kitchen window and peered through the crystal pane. A woman sat alone by the fire, her back toward me, a black reboso over her head. She was puffing a cigarette, held between small silver tongs. I opened the door and stepped inside. Doña Serafina rose and threw her cigarette into the fire and stood looking at me. She was dressed like a countryman's daughter, in dark red skirt and a loose white chemise that had fallen from one lovely shoulder.

Again all sense of danger slipped from me. She looked like a young girl now, but her eyes were those of a woman capable of strong love for a man or a principle.

"Why did you do this for me?" I asked.

Her eyes were calm on mine. "I wanted you to live. You are too young and tall and fair to die in a dark and alien land."

I came to her and took her hands. "That will change. A few men will die, and those who live will find life better. If I live——"

"If you live, I will be waiting."

Her arms circled my neck as I embraced her. Our kiss was fierce and brief, for I knew that until Timothy Barton and Baldo Parral were avenged, I could not look at her again.

"Go with God," she said.

I said farewell and went out without looking back. The night was still, but I knew I had yet to escape the town and then ride hard and far, and there was no certainty that I could find General McLeod's columns in time to warn him.

But I had a horse and a gun, and somewhere to the east were more men with horses and guns. Men of whom some would one day see this land proud and free, like mine.

——I recollect the night I left her to ride toward San Miguel. Left the road at dawn, followed a Canyon by day

& hit the trail again at dark. That night saw our campfires nr. Anton Chico & was challenged by one of our Sentries.

It ill becomes me to question Gen. McLeod's use of the intelligence I brought. We advanced, on his order, amidst false assurances of friendship by a Mex. Military Escort, were led into a trap & disarmed. Those of us not deliberately murdered took up the long march to Perote Prison. When we fell from cold, hunger or beatings, our captors cut off our ears for tally & left our bodies on the ice.

The American Legation secured our release at last, & we came home in good time to see our Beloved Texas enter the Union. When the Spring planting was done, I rode to Missouri to join Col. Doniphan's Volunteers.

This afternoon sent a Detachment of Co. K to Galisteo Creek to graze our horses, but kept the best-fed mount at Camp. Rode him this eve. to the Castelar Hacienda. Found the House deserted except for its Mistress & 2 aged Servants, Don Rafael having fled with Armijo.

Doña Serafina de Vera received me in her Sitting room. She wept a little, as women do at such times. Saw the Priest late tonight. Tomorrow Doña Serafina becomes Mrs. Jas. Holston.

LAW OF THE LASH
by Prentiss Combs

Padraic Conmaire was a man with his feet on a road. And a man must follow a road chosen to its end. Boggy or dry, rocky or smooth, level or steep, nor can a man turn from it. He may change his name, his clothes and the place he lives, but the road has a chancy and frightening way to it of appearing beneath a man's feet, no matter what path or highway he walks.

Padraic Conmaire was out of Ballyshannon. A sweet, blond lance of a man, his hair a deep gold and his eyes sea-washed green. He sprang from kings and his smooth face was given the strengthening arch of a high nose, thin and sensitive as a prophet's. He was a maker of songs, and all his songs were of Deirdre, pale and golden, loved and loving, named well for an ancient princess. She was the light of Ballyshannon and all the world to Padraic Conmaire and the lodestone that drew him ever back from the reaches of the land, and he coursing and questing, seeking a kingdom for himself and his queen.

But the face of Ireland lay under the great gray cloak of the bad times and many there were with the deep daft that settles on a man, and he with small ones starving slow before his eyes, and his woman thrusting an empty breast to a small sick face. Every eye in Erin wept, and finally, in all the land, there was no place left to look.

So Padraic whispered a great tale into the lovely ear of Deirdre, "It's to America, then. Three months there and your two fair hands overflowing with the gold I'll send. A short year, no more, and it'll be Squire Padraic Conmaire, plug hat and fine clothes, riding his acres on a blooded horse, and his beautiful wife, Deirdre, clad in jewels, velvet gowns and the mantle of her own man's true love."

It was a thundering tale. Deirdre believed, and worse, so did he. America was not like the tales told. It was a kick here and a curse there and the rough side of every man's tongue for the Irish. Padraic Conmaire was only one of the many had left the sad land. The weak stayed in cities. But the proud and the driven went west to lay the shining tracks across the mountains and plains. It was the railroad. Hard and tearing work for small pay, but a man had to make a start. The black fit fell on many, and many died, but there were always more.

Now Padraic was a proud man. Could a proud one write to tell his queen that gold didn't lie in the streets? Could he say it would be a year before he had one cent to call his own? He could not. He could no more than clutch his emptiness to himself and work.

On payday there was wild drinking at the way station, and Padraic wet his throat, no more. But there was a huge hulk of a Sligo man with the forward curve to his neck and shoulders like a fighting bull. He fleered his pig eyes at Padraic and gave him the bad word.

"I'll take a fall out of you," he said, "and you not running."

Padraic laughed. It was a fine day, with Deirdre's money in his pocket.

"Ah, you killer," he smiled, "and most of your dead home drinking their victory while you pick yourself up."

"So, that's the way it is," the Sligo man said, stripping his shirt.

"Now, let's see the way of it," Padraic answered reasonably, and off with his own shirt. He stripped clean, with bosses of muscle defining lean and ropy under his golden skin.

The Sligo man was big and quick, and Padraic's back marked the sod more than once. But he rose quickly, smiling palely, and he was skilled. In the end, Padraic fetched him a terrible clout and then closed his eyes in quick fear to see the big man's skull slap one of the rails.

So Deirdre's money went to pay the Sligo man's hospital bills, back at the city. The small bit left, Padraic spent in dark drinking.

Just before the next quarter and payday, a work train came. The last to get off was Michael Noolan, of Ballyshannon. A sad man, ever sour-rinded and thin, his tongue bitter with the acid of his sadness. He was stake thin and his eyes were deep pools of something bad.

"Michael Noolan," Padraic shouted to him in his ringing voice, "you've brought me word?"

"Aye, Padraic Conmaire, I've a word." He said it thinly, his eyes fixed on Padraic.

And as Padraic came near, Noolan's blue eyes filled and spilled, and the sound came from him, torn and thin, like the cries of the crones at the wakes, and he said the word, and with the word put the curse on Padraic Conmaire as surely as if he'd been an old warlock.

"Deirdre!" came the word and all the meaning in it.

"Ah, my heart, not dead?" cried Padraic.

"Killed," said Michael Noolan, flatly and remotely, patting the curse. And Padraic had never before dreamed that little Michael Noolan had loved Gold Deirdre. When he went on, Padraic knew that Michael had held her as she died and that Michael was having a triumph.

"Who?" asked Padraic, the madness rising in him.

"The slayers were three, Padraic. Sorrow was one, hunger was the other, and the last was proud Padraic Conmaire. Never a penny, proud Paddy. Never a scratch from a pen and never a penny."

Padraic's face froze to stone. Seeing it, Michael Noolan turned with a sour smile and spat upon the ground. He'd waited long for the day.

Padraic wheeled and started to walk. He walked to rail's end and on to the last of the ties, turning then on his empty road, across the vastness of the plain. By dusk he was no more than a small moving thing almost over the rim of the burning land. He walked on into the night at the same steady pace. By sundown of the next day he was down clawing at the dirt, with his tongue too big for his mouth.

Next, there was the sweetness of water in his mouth, a hand gentle beneath his head and a voice crooning in a strange tongue. Padraic looked up into a face with great sad black eyes and a huge scar running over a ruined nose. He was dark as a Spanish tinker. In a half circle about him were eight or ten horsemen dressed crazily in big hats and much silver. Heading them on a great black stud was a man with the mark of power and evil stamped on him as with a hot iron. Padraic felt a stirring in him and knew this man had a finger in his life, that his name was in the mouths of men, and no word of it good. He was a giant, his length of leg stretching below the black stud's barrel. In his black eyes danced a wild, flickering light. His face was wide, and the bosses and planes were deeply pitted with pox. He snorted as he smiled down at Padraic, as if his strength were too great to be borne still, as a nervous horse must fret and snort.

"Get up and walk, gringo," he said, his voice thick with accent. Padraic slowly shook his head.

"I'll make you, then."

It was a fine whip. It lay dark and oiled and gleaming in wicked coils over the pommel of the strange saddle. He lifted it off, stroking it through his big hands. He moved the horse back one pace by some trick of his knee, and the whip became a thing alive in his hand, making a big streaking S through the air. The lash licked Padraic's left ankle and then the right. The big man's teeth were yellow and long as he laughed. Padraic, proud Padraic, obeyed the lash, taking four, six, eight steps before he fell. The next blow of the lash came down like a hammer across his face, pounding the lifting arch of his nose and crumpling the ridge. He didn't stir.

He woke dimly with the thrust of a horse's hind leg against his face. He was face down across a horse in motion. A gentle hand patted his back and the same voice crooned. Daylight sometimes, and at others dark. Water forced in his mouth, and him muttering and weeping with his fever.

He awakened in bed. There was a buzzing quiet outside. There was a clay jar of water beside his bed, and he drained it. He slept some more, and when he awakened he was hungry with a healthy hunger.

He walked unsteadily out onto a long, cool corridor. There was a great green square where water ran from a fountain and where there were cool trees, and somewhere the gentle clang of a bell.

Behind him a deep, kind voice spoke, and he turned to see a priest.

"Greetings, Lazarus," the priest said in English. "You have risen, then, from the grave."

He was a tall, thick man, his stomach pushing out his cassock, his brown eyes crinkling in kindness and his thatch of white hair springing wild from his head.

"Is it good to be alive?" the priest asked with a smile.

And Padraic drew a breath and found it was.

"Where am I, and who brought me?" Padraic asked.

"You are in La Misión San Gabriel. Little Eusebio wrought the miracle."

"A small dark man with a scar, he would be."

"Yes. The scar is El Sátiro's work. Some call him El Fuete. He's well called. He's Satan himself with whip or women. Eusebio risked his life to bring you in. El Sátiro left you to die."

"Is there no law here, then?" Padraic asked.

"This is Mexico, my friend. Here, El Sátiro is the law."

The priest looked at Padraic and probed with his kind eyes and asked a question, "Are you hunted?"

Padraic shook his head slowly. "Can a man find himself?" he asked.

And the priest answered the strange question sadly, guessing its meaning, " 'Follow me; and let the dead bury their dead.' "

So Padraic Conmaire took up his life at the mission. His strength came back quickly, but his nose was ruined, and his eyes had changed from the laughing, glimmering eyes of a man of dreams. Now they lay ageless and beyond caring. No formal vows made, no oaths taken, but the fine fire in him had died. The fight with the Sligo man had killed Deirdre as surely as if he had stabbed her. Deep within him was the knowledge that he could never again strike a man in anger.

The months passed easily as they worked and slept, speaking seldom. If El Sátiro came to the mission village to drink wine in the night, Padraic left his cell-like room to sleep the night under the stars on the plain. He would fight no man. There went with him, trembling and troubled, little Eusebio, who had held Padraic's life in his hand. Lying there, Padraic looked at the stars and remembered he had never thanked Eusebio.

The mission life moved at an easy rhythm. Mexicans and Indians with light work, long sleeps in the heat of the afternoon, guitars at night stirring old embers and singing. The father was one of those with the understanding heart. He would lay his hand on Padraic's shoulder at these times. Bit by bit, fragment by fragment, he had the story from Padraic. He was a patient man, and he started obliquely and cannily to make Padraic into what he felt him to be.

"Lázaro," he said, calling Padraic the name the village put to him, "I will ask you a favor. Down in the bend of the river there is a bit of land. It is fallow and waste. Would you and Eusebio build a small house there and plant the land to corn and beans?"

Padraic looked at him with his flat eyes and nodded. "All things are the same to me, father."

The preparing of the soil, the planting of the seed, the wonder as it swells to bursting, the deep singing in a man as he reaps. It can cure many things. There's a demanding thing about becoming a part of the great cycle of the land.

To build a house is a warm thing too. Especially a house made of adobe—mud bricks with straw to bind. Each brick receives the pat of a man's hand. Padraic made the bricks, patting them and molding them, and they dried in the sun. He laid the courses, one atop the other, and as the wall grew, something lifted inside him. The house finished, he and Eusebio made their furniture from willows and rawhide. In the gently lowering dusk the two sat there, smoking and watching the slow rhythm of the life around them—the winking fires, the children playing, the pat-pat-pat of the tortilla makers. It was a balm to Padraic.

The father came in the evenings to smoke a pipe with them, talking slow about small things.

It was not unusual for girls to pass. Mothers sent daughters past the house of Lázaro. He was handsome, for all his scarred face, and a worker. But Padraic did not look, ever.

But one evening a girl passed, she was a slow-moving poem. She walked with an olla of water balanced on her head, her bare feet taking that small, smooth step necessary for carrying burdens on the head, straight as a saguaro, breast ajut and her face as still and lovely as the morning.

The father sighed windily. "Ai, Dios," he said softly. "Sometimes being a man of God is a hard thing. That poor orphan, there, driven from house to house, beaten and despised. Nobody cares but me. El Sátiro put his hands to her on his last visit, and next time he will take her. Take her for a few weeks and then toss her as a scrap to one of his savages. And what can I do?"

He shook his head and fetched that sigh again, and Padraic's fine head raised a trifle on his neck. Deep within, a hackle raised.

The next evening she passed again, and the next; and the father, wrenching his sighs from inside him, shook his head and moaned for her, and her so alone.

Padraic raised his head full, followed the honey-sweet figure of her down the path and asked quietly, "How is she called?"

"Maria de la Luz. Mary of the Light," the priest said quickly. "Her mother was blessed on her christening day, for no other name would suit her. She's the sun to her own day. To think of her in the paws of that beast." He brought out another gusty sigh, filled his cheeks and stole a quick glance at Padraic.

"If some man would wed her, the whole thing would be taken care of. Certainly even El Sátiro would feel respect for marriage vows. Ah, the poor, poor small thing."

He grasped Padraic by the arm quickly.

"A Christian favor for charity, Lázaro. Take her into your house. Let the vows be but a farce if need be. But help me keep her from him."

And Padraic shrank. "Father," he said thickly, "and me no more than half a man."

"It's only for charity, man."

And Padraic, not understanding the strange yearnings in him, agreed. It was a wedding with no feasting. As they left the church to walk to Padraic's small house Maria de la Luz fell in behind him, as was meet with women.

Padraic stopped, took her gently by the arm and made her walk beside him. Her smile was shy and gentle and a thing of deep joy.

That was how Padraic Conmaire followed a strange road winding, and took Maria de la Luz into his house. She had a man to protect her, and Padraic had a gentle woman to cook his meals. But there were small things to do for her and to be grateful for, and so it was that he did not spend the day thinking of himself only.

One evening the father went to that house and found something there to make him smile a slow, deep smile. He had not dreamt it would happen so soon. For there was a rhythm and a joy in that small house like deep music. It was not until he saw Padraic lay his hand gently on her shining head that he was really sure. Here was a house with love. Somewhere in the dark softness of a night they had found themselves. The poor, poor things had found the wondrous gift of love. There was a quiet shining about the both of them that was a wonder to see. They were one, and yet the father did not feel unwanted.

Padraic had sworn no vows, had taken no great oaths, but still his deep feelings against violence started to spin a slow winding web, and his feelings were as oaths.

An Indian came into his cornfield and stole corn, and Padraic said no small word. Lazy Emeterio let his cows come in to trample the squash vines and beans, and Padraic said nothing. Antonio borrowed his horse once, and then again and again, taking the animal from the corral and abusing it as if it were his own, and Padraic cast his eyes down and held his peace. A small shadow began to grow in the back of the gentle eyes of Maria de la Luz.

El Sátiro came thundering into the village one evening, drink-taken and spirits raging. Little Eusebio was caught in the plaza and the little man was chased from corner to corner, crying as El Sátiro howled with laughter and chewed pieces out of him with his whip.

Padraic and Maria de la Luz stood in the shadows.

"Your friend needs help," she said softly.

Padraic's body set up a trembling, and he turned his back, covering his eyes.

El Sátiro caught sight of him there, and he kicked his stud over the low wall and laughed down at them.

"Come closer, gringo. Are you growing brave? Why are not you in a hole?"

He laughed, the high, fleering, half-mad laugh, and flicked out the lash.

"Run, gringo. Find a hole. Run! Run!"

Padraic stood rock still, his hand covering his face and let the lash bite him. Maria de la Luz stood and watched while the whole village saw her man humiliated.

"A little wedding present from El Sátiro." He laughed, coiling the lash. "If I want you, little pigeon, I take you," he said to Maria de la Luz, showing the red point of his tongue.

"And you, whom they call Lázaro, another christening." He spat down upon Padraic's bowed head. "Your new name is Gringo Mouse."

Now the whole village knew that the bandit was a madman and a cruel killing beast. But still, they said, a friend is a friend, and pride——

"It would be better to die," some said boldly. It is easy to say such things. But now they no longer called Padraic the affectionate

Lázaro, he who had risen from the dead. Some turned their heads and spat as he passed. Small boys, with their great capacity for cruelty, galloped by him, cracking imaginary whips, and the bolder ones shouted the name El Sátiro had put to him.

So Padraic's fine little house became like a coffin to him. Little Eusebio came to him, drawn by the ties between them, and Maria de la Luz ran from the house, refusing to hear Eusebio beg forgiveness for her husband's cowardice, her shame making her heart a stone. When she went to market, she hurried, with head cast down. Her life had been so good, and now it was a rock in her breast and ashes in her mouth.

The days passed, and they were sad. Padraic kept to his house and his fields, and sometimes he looked up at the sky and trembled. His eyes sank in upon themselves and a line was drawn from the bitter curve of his nostril to his mouth.

It was a time of waiting. And the waiting was over one day. El Sátiro jumped the plaza wall on his big, foaming, black stud and made it rear in the plaza, roaring for the priest.

"*Olé*, man in skirts!" he bellowed. "Roast a fatted calf and bring wine! You are going to have a wedding! El Sátiro will take a wife!"

The priest looked up at him, pale. "Who?"

"The little pigeon of the Gringo Mouse," he laughed.

"She's wed," the priest answered, smiling grimly.

"A widow within the hour," El Sátiro promised, patting his gun.

The father sent a small boy pelting to the small house by the river to tell Padraic the words of El Sátiro. The small boy, spent and gasping with excitement, saw the two turn toward each other.

"Will I go, then, my man?" Maria de la Luz asked calmly.

And Padraic bent his head and looked at the floor and around him at what had been the peace of his life.

"We will go talk to him," he said finally.

Maria de la Luz bent her own small head and went to pack.

"What are you about, my heart?"

"Taking from this house the things with which I came."

"I said I would talk to him."

"If that is what you will do, then I will need these things."

And Padraic again bowed his fine head, and they went out together, through the rows of their planted fields where they had worked together, and into the mission, and finally they stood in the plaza before El Sátiro.

He saw them and laughed and licked his lips with his red tongue. He tossed out the lash so it curled about the small waist of Maria de la Luz. He drew her to him, awkward in the clutch of the lash, up against his leg.

His mad black eyes looked down at her, and his tongue again went out over his lips as he said, laughing, "A man, eh? You will like to be with a man for a while."

She took the lash from her waist and turned proudly to look at Padraic Conmaire and asked one question. "Shall I bring your son back to you, husband?"

Padraic heard her. His smile at her was a thing of great gentleness. He lifted his pale face and answered, speaking remotely, almost to himself, "You will not go, my heart. You gone, and I'm a dead man. What are fears and feelings to a dead man?"

He filled his chest with a deep breath, looking up at the big, dark man on the stallion, and there was the same flickering light behind his eyes that was in El Sátiro's. He was smiling palely under his broken nose.

"You've been long in dying. Let us let blood, then. Two killers. My oaths broken and fears gone, and you a dead man." His voice was a kind of singing.

The madman on the stud cut the lash through the air, seeing Padraic changed before him, and he said, "A killer? A mouse. I christened you. I will spank you."

Padraic nodded his head, still smiling. He moved closer to the bulk of the horse.

"Ay, dead man. Me beaten and you dead on the ground with my hands frozen at your throat." Deep inside him was the singing of a man released from all things, and the old sickness wiped from him and the whetting sound of a keen blade sharpened.

He trembled with the power of it, and the dark man, seeing it, spoke again. "Only a small beating now. Don't tremble."

The lash went whirling out, cutting a piece of Padraic's ear, and that man reached one hand up in a kind of wonder and saw the blood on his hand. The singing in him sent to a high, rending scream of wildness, and when the lash came next time, he caught it in an iron hand. One quick flash, like catching a fly. The lash in his grip, the sudden rending twist, and the bulk of the man out of the saddle.

El Sátiro's hand was at his belt as he fell, rolling, and a small twisting figure ran out from the crowd, and little Eusebio, his ruined face smiling eagerly, picked his spot carefully, kicked the wrist and knocked the gun flying. He picked it up, squatted, panting a little on the fringe of the crowd, and let the barrel waver over the bellies of El Sátiro's men. With the fingers of his free hand he felt the seams of the scar on his nose.

So they faced each other. Two men, half mad. One mad with the ancient berserkers keening and wailing inside him, giving him the strength of ten men and they all mad. "Blood," the ancient voices wailed, and Padraic moved in, face frozen into a terrible smile, to still their singing. The dark one, evil from his spawning, never beaten, eager to rend and to break to still the wild singing of his own blood lust.

They came together with a shock, and the dark giant felt the smaller man hold firm, and as they gripped each other, trying first this and then that, the black man laughed softly, for this man was strong and the pleasure would be deep.

As they walked around, thighs ridged, loins locked with effort, Padraic smiled coldly, his face frozen and his voice brazen, speaking things softly from the cold bronze trumpet gripped deep in his throat. He spoke the things that men tell men whom they will kill. He held the dark man in his hand and he knew it with a terrible strength of certainty.

Some of the people moaned as they watched the struggle. Some yelled hoarsely as they became animals caught in its ancient grip, and some turned their heads away.

They fought as animals—kicking, kneeing, butting, biting and hitting. There was blood on the ground, and when they grew weak from fighting, they fought on their knees, and when they could no longer stand on their knees in the blood and sweat, they crouched like two snapping, snarling dogs, their teeth naked, their eyes dripping.

Finally the big black man slowly felt fear rise in him. He came to know that no matter what he might do, the little man would still be there, and he remembered the words before the fight began, of how Padraic's fingers would be at his throat and he dead. He knew, suddenly and in a panic, that if he reached with clawed hands and plucked the heart from Padraic's body and held it pulsing in his hand, Padraic would not know it at all, but would go on rending and hacking.

Padraic caught the man's huge arm in a cruel lock and bent it, arching the bow of his back into the effort. As the giant's arm snapped loud in the silence of pent breaths, the Satyr screamed and rolled free. Padraic crawled toward him with his fingers locked into steel hooks and his glazed eyes fixed on the man's pulsing, swollen throat, and there was nothing but the dread certainty that he would strangle, and who was the man with the courage to tell him no or to put out a hand to stop him?

He reached him, the big man's eyes wide open and the mouth agape to scream, and Padraic raised his red hands and stopped the scream as it started. The hands sank into the throat, and Maria de la Luz came from the crowd and sank beside him. She pressed her lips close to his ear and whispered and crooned, and one small hand tugged at his wrist.

"Come back to me, heart of my heart and love of my love, and don't kill the swine. As I love you, I beg you. His corpse will be a thing between us, and I yearn to bear your son so he will be all there is between us."

Padraic's frozen face wavered, his breaths came in great torn gasps, and he turned to look at her without loosening his terrible grip. Maria de la Luz looked full at him, and all her love and gentleness shone there in her eyes. As El Sátiro's eyes bulged and his face became black, Padraic Conmaire knew his wife from the depths of his madness and his grip relaxed.

He rose to his feet, straightened, looked around at his new world, and then fell with a terrible weariness, and she had his head in her arms and his ruined face against her breast and her crooning in his ears before he hit the ground. She stayed there, her lovely face reflecting the agony of the terrible game she had played and won, and there was a peace, too, on Padraic's face.

They were beautiful to see. It was the end of a road for Padraic Conmaire, and he had ended his coursing and questing for he had found his kingdom.

STAGE TO YUMA
by Marvin DeVries

The reek of trouble reached Tate Ibsen as soon as the stagecoach entered the gorge. He couldn't give it a reason. His searching eyes swept the high rim and the broken walls, and touched nothing but glare and tumbled rock, but he had the feeling there was more up there than he could find. Until he could point it out, however, he wouldn't mention it, but words were on his lips, so he said a few about the heat, something they were all already miserably aware of.

"Just like I imagine hell is going to be. Don't you think so, Miss Quimby?"

Miss Quimby must have heard a lot of blunt talk during the past few days, but it still shocked her. "I—I really don't know," she said, struggling to be civil and critical at the same time.

This was the route to Yuma. Tate Ibsen was one of six passengers. Ordinarily, he would have taken a horse. He didn't like stagecoach travel. Usually, there were soppy children or ladies with the vapors to contend with. But this time he had business aboard and had to face the discomforts.

There were no soppy children, but there was little Miss Quimby, with her faded parasol and reticule, surely good for one vapor, and there was doc, sagging at the seams and bleary-eyed with booze. Doc, nipping from a fancy bottle, sat next to Ibsen. Miss Quimby, taking no more room than a stick, was in the far corner. Watts, a deputy marshal, and Deuce, his prisoner, who had a stiff leg, sat straight across from Ibsen. The sixth passenger, a Mexican boy dressed up in his best bib and tucker, sat upstairs with the driver. Occasional bursts of barnyard Spanish drifted down from them into the coach. The boy was on his way to a mission school in Faraway, which was Miss Quimby's destination. Ibsen put two and two together, and added it up as one pupil and one teacher.

Waves of furnace heat poured up and invaded the coach. Miss Quimby wiped her gritty cheeks and red eyes with a wadded handkerchief. Doc took another nip. Ibsen could see him considering passing the bottle, but finally deciding against such reckless generosity. The deputy took off his hat and wiped the sweatband with his elbow. The handcuffed prisoner moved his stiff leg and bumped it against Ibsen's boots.

"Sorry," Ibsen said.

Deuce glared and started to say something. The deputy gave him a hard poke and told him to shut up. "Don't bother the passengers."

"I don't," Deuce answered. "They bother me. That big fathead——"

"It's my fault," Ibsen said mildly.

"The hell with it," Deuce flared. "Kick the leg off for all of me. I don't care, leg or no leg. Go ahead."

"No, thanks," Ibsen said. "You might need it more than you think."

"Yeah, on a rock pile."

Miss Quimby bent forward so she could get a good look at the prisoner. "What did you do, my boy?" she asked in a sympathetic voice.

Deuce leaned across toward her and whispered, "Murder." He raised his handcuffed hands and drew a finger across his throat. "You know—zzt!—with a knife. But I didn't do it."

"At any rate," Ibsen said, "you have a sound reason for coming this way. You can't help yourself. The rest of us, I reckon, just don't have good sense. Doc, what brings you this way, if I may ask?"

Doc twirled his heavy gold chain around his finger and gave the question consideration. A small flush showed on his face. "I'm looking around for a place to locate," he said finally. "A little tired of the usual, you know. How about yourself?" The question was a boomerang his pride had taught him to throw.

"I'll be as honest as you, doc," Ibsen said. "I have a friend in Yuma pen and I'm going to try to bust him out." He turned his sardonic eyes on the deputy for an answer.

"Nobody gets nobody outta Yuma pen," Watts told him.

"Still," Ibsen said mildly, "some try, for friendship's sake."

Deuce wanted to smoke, and Watts, with elaborate consideration, rolled him one, but when it was finished he kept it for himself and blew smoke in Deuce's face, grinning at his audience. "I always say nothin's too good for a man who's bound for Yuma pen. My heart bleeds."

"You have quite a sense of humor," doc told him. His voice sounded as though he honestly admired the deputy, but his eyes rebuked him.

A speech of some kind budded on Ibsen's lips, but he kept it back, and turned his curiosity on Miss Quimby. "I understand you're a schoolteacher."

Miss Quimby nodded. The feather on her bonnet dipped and threw off a spray of dust. "I'm going to teach in Faraway."

"So I heard." Ibsen knew the place. It was a small ragged settlement of stealthy folks, and he believed there weren't more than a half-dozen children in the whole district. The poor woman probably had no idea, and he wanted to prepare her a little. "Even in a little place like that," he told her, "you'll probably find someone who will take to learning. They're anywhere; don't you think so, doc?"

"Surely," doc said.

"It's in the nature of missionary work," Miss Quimby said. "I understand it's very sparsely settled."

She made it sound very satisfactory to her, but Ibsen looked behind the pride, the same pride that touched doc, and could imagine the hidden consternation and dismay that must engulf her, if not now, at least later when she got a look at Faraway. He could imagine her more unwanted where she came from than wanted at the place where she was going. It was a retreat of the vanquished, a last desperate move made with as much pride as she could hold around her, but it was something she couldn't help any more than Deuce in his handcuffs could help his trip to Yuma.

"I'm sure they need you," Ibsen said, putting on a show of conviction.

"'Better build schoolrooms for the boy than cells and gibbets for the man'," doc quoted. "Eh, Deuce?"

"Could be," Deuce agreed.

"'There is one only good'," doc quoted again, "'namely, knowledge; and one only evil, namely, ignorance.'"

"Diogenes," Miss Quimby said with sudden sparkle.

Doc laughed. "The man with the lantern, and Eliza Cook. Ma'am, if you can find one youngster anywhere to teach something to, you are here on a better errand than any of us. Don't you agree, Ibsen?"

Buttering her up, too, Ibsen thought, but he nodded agreement. "At any rate, ma'am, we'll see that you get there, won't we, doc?"

Doc grinned. "She and the boy up there, the hope of the future."

The next time Tate Ibsen scanned the walls he saw what he was looking for, the glint of sun on a brown arm dangling over a rock. It drew back while he looked, like a snake into its den, and he couldn't find it again, but it was time to speak up. He let some time go past, as little and as much as he dared, then called up to the driver to stop. There was always an obvious reason for such occasions, and Boggs came to a stop.

He got down himself, giving the reins to the proud Mexican boy. Ibsen walked away, motioning him to follow. When they were out of earshot, he told the driver what he had seen.

Boggs wasn't impressed. "They never bother me," he said. "Besides, there ain't none hereabouts."

"I saw one," Ibsen insisted.

"Hell's bells!" Boggs exploded. "One Apache, good or bad, don't make an ambush."

"At any rate," Ibsen said, "I think the boy ought to get inside, and I'll get up there with you, at least till we get through the gorge."

The boy surrendered his place reluctantly, and Boggs promised him he could come back out later. "This gent needs a little air, is all."

He climbed up, and Ibsen took the other side. The gorge was roughly funnel-shaped. They were close to the narrowest section. The road was nearest the south wall. Ibsen, scanning the heights, saw another brown figure, and reached for his gun. Before he could use it, the whisper of an arrow went past his ear. It struck the driver and dug deep between his ribs near the armpit. He lurched off the seat before Ibsen could grab him, and toppled headfirst to the ground. Another arrow struck a lead mule and dropped it. The rest piled up in a snarl of harness. No more arrows were shot, no more brown men appeared.

Ibsen grabbed the shotgun that was up there and jumped down. He took Boggs' hand gun and put both weapons inside the coach.

"Don't anyone get out," he warned. "Keep away from the openings. If they come down, let 'em have it as fast as you know how."

In spite of his order, doc stepped out and took a look at Boggs, "I'm no good with a gun, but this is my line."

"I'm afraid not. It's past you." Ibsen moved forward, trying to quiet the mules.

The shot animal was dead. Ibsen cut the traces and hooked up the other lead mule, harness to harness with the dead brute, and got the road cleared. Then another arrow whistled down, and another mule dropped. The rest panicked. The two wheelers wound up facing the coach, one on its knees, the other with its legs over the whiffletree. Ibsen used his knife, cutting leather where it had to be cut, then got back into the coach.

The boy shoved over to the middle and sat between doc and Ibsen. Watts' hands were shaking. Ibsen studied him awhile and wrote him off as a dead loss. "Two of the mules are dead," he announced. "The rest are all snarled up, and the harness is torn to shreds. If we get out of here at all, it will have to be on foot, but for the time being we'll sit tight. It's good cover against arrows, and it seems as if that's all they have up there."

Miss Quimby opened her reticule and got out some smelling salts and held them to her nose. After one deep sniff, she offered them around.

"Later, maybe, ma'am," Ibsen said, and dared anyone to laugh. He studied the walls of the gorge and told the boy to look, thinking his young eyes might be sharper, but neither of them could see any life.

"Watts, won't you have a nip of this?" doc asked, carefully hiding the reason for his offer.

Watts did it, gratefully and long.

"Ye gods," doc breathed, "don't run me clear out."

The boy put his hands flat together between his legs as if he meant to sit it out that way. He was quiet and very attentive to everything that went on, but he didn't seem to be afraid. Miss Quimby, too, had made up her mind to be brave. This was death, and she meant to face it like a lady, smelling salts handy.

Ibsen pushed his hat back and scratched his head. "They'd come down if they were strong enough to risk it. There must be just a few of them on a spree. What they've done so far looks like plain teasing. Otherwise, they'd have shot me instead of that mule. They're having an afternoon's fun."

"We got to get outta here," Watts mumbled, gasping for breath. Deuce laughed in his face, and got another poke.

"You'll have to turn him loose, Watts," Ibsen said. "We may need him." He got out Boggs' big gun and tried to hand it to Deuce.

Watts struck it down. "Keep that gun away from him. What d'you think you're doing?"

"I'm trying to take a good look at what we're up against here," Ibsen said without losing patience. "I don't like to get bossy, but I can, and I will if I must."

"Not with me."

"What do you think, doc?"

Doc pursed his lips. "I want to ask a question. I have the impression that you're aboard here to help Deuce escape. That fuss about leg room didn't ring true to me somehow. It seems to me we ought to know what takes precedence here—our lives, or helping Deuce escape, if that's what you're at."

Ibsen hesitated with an answer, but he finally nodded. "That's what I'm here for. I have horses staked out at the end of the gorge, ready for a getaway. Deuce is a friend of mine. He's also the best shot I ever saw. That's why I want him turned loose. Right now, that's all that counts."

Watts didn't wait for doc's opinion. He raised his gun and told Ibsen to go.

Ibsen didn't move. "No, I won't get out," he stated, "but I'll guarantee this much. You turn Deuce loose, and when this is over you can handcuff him again and we'll start from scratch."

Watts wouldn't listen. "Get out. Head that way." He canted his head to the far wall. "There's nobody on that side."

Doc settled it with the bottle. As inconspicuously as possible he got a good grip on the neck and gave Watts a hard whack across the arm. The gun dropped, and Ibsen recovered it. "O.K., that's fine, doc," he said.

"I'm good with a bottle," doc admitted modestly. "To tell you the truth, I want to keep you around awhile. I shouldn't have asked the question. It was idle."

Ibsen unlocked the handcuffs. He gave Deuce the big gun and let

Watts have his own back. He wanted doc to take the shotgun, but doc shook his head and said the boy could do better.

"What's your name, anyway, son?"

The boy said it was Porfio, after a dead uncle.

"Can you handle a shotgun?"

"Si."

"All right. If they come down on us, blast away. But wait until they're close. That's the only way that weapon's any good."

"I know," Porfio said.

"Sorry about the fuss," Ibsen told Miss Quimby.

She gave him a speechless nod.

"Incidentally, there's nothing the matter with Deuce's leg," Ibsen went on. "He was shot, but it's all healed up. He was hanging onto it so Watts would think he couldn't move fast."

An arrow snapped against the coach to remind them of their troubles. Ibsen scanned the rim and the pockets of gloom in the walls. The mules moved farther away, their hoofs clattering. A wild taunting screech came down and Miss Quimby shuddered visibly and propped her wadded handkerchief against her mouth. Still another arrow came down, breaking through the roof.

Ibsen's conviction that the ambush was a flimsy one continued to grow. Still, there was a strong possibility the raiders would quit their fooling and close in for loot. They surely would after dark, he felt. He put no faith in the dubious saw that Apaches would not attack by night. "Those horses I mentioned are in a little box meadow at the end of the gorge," he explained. "There's a rope across the mouth. Porfio, can you catch a horse with a rope?"

"Si, señor."

"How about you, doc?"

"No. None of this is my dish, Ibsen, but don't bother about it. Concentrate on Miss Quimby and the boy. That school, you know."

Porfio lifted his eyes. "I would not like for anyone to worry himself about me because of how old I am," he announced gravely.

Doc grinned. "You see what I mean, Ibsen?" He turned to Miss Quimby. "Take that one by the hand, ma'am, and go your way."

Miss Quimby's eyes melted. The thin face took on a glow. "Doctor," she said, leaving all her fears behind for a moment, "sometimes I think they have more to keep than to learn, but I teach what I can."

This was spoken from the heart, with deep humility, and her

squeaky voice didn't spoil the words. Somewhere, deep down inside of her, was a dedicated purpose and the stanch bright hope that something must come of it as surely as day came out of night.

"Ma'am," doc said, "I wish I could be young again." He overlaid the words with his usual dry look, so it was hard to tell whether he meant them or not.

To Ibsen, this was more Diogenes-Eliza Cook talk, but he saw the point. Most men spoiled their lives before they used up their span; Watts with his fears, doc with his booze, Deuce with his temper, himself with his disdain, all with something they had found along the way. Especially, he thought, Watts with his sorry fears.

He shifted his position and searched the north wall again. "Nothing going on over there," he remarked. "I wonder. If there's nothing up there, we'd be in pretty good shape, once we got under that overhang."

"If we could get out of range from this side," doc commented.

"I think that's possible, but it wouldn't do much good if we ran head-on into more on the other side."

Watts leaned forward and took a look. He searched the far wall carefully from top to bottom and side to side. Ibsen stared at him with mild disdain, knowing what he had put into his head. Deuce gave Ibsen a puzzled look. Ibsen shook his head briefly, warning Deuce to mind his own business. Deuce looked at doc, and both their eyes went blank.

"No use everybody risking their necks," Watts stated finally, all his rancor gone. "I'll give it a try."

"I wouldn't ask you to," Ibsen said.

"That's not the point," Watts insisted. "Somebody's got to find out if it's clear over there."

It sounded generous, especially after the rumpus they had had, but the deputy couldn't quite hide the cunning look in his eyes, the avid look of a coward grabbing for his life at the expense of the others.

"Of course," Ibsen said, "there's always the chance there're some up there."

"Of course," Watts agreed, much too quickly to give the warning any thought. He obviously didn't believe it. "I'll take the risk."

Ibsen nodded. "All right then. We'll watch this wall and try to stop them from opening up on you from behind."

The deputy climbed down in the silence. He hesitated for some time in the protection of the coach, then started to run, zigzagging like a giddy snipe until he was out of range, when he slowed down.

"I hope you know he's running out on us," Deuce muttered.

"He's trying to, that's sure."

Watts didn't make the crossing. Ibsen saw the arrow come down and strike him in the chest. The deputy went down over a block of black lava and didn't move again.

"You knew it all the time, didn't you?" Deuce remarked.

Ibsen shook his head. "I didn't know."

"Any fool could guess."

"Guessing wasn't good enough. We know now, and we're stuck with it."

"Do you actually have horses out there?" doc inquired. "Or was that just bait for Watts?"

"The horses are there."

Doc sagged back in his seat and stared regretfully at the spilled whisky. "But it was still bait. I don't think I could do that, Ibsen. I'm not critical. I only mean to say I would rather go myself than send another."

"I didn't do it in fun, doc. I'm trying to figure out a way to get at least some of us out of here alive."

"Miss Quimby and the boy?"

"Maybe. You say they're the top items. In a pinch, Watts would have run out on them."

"I agree we could probably spare him better than anyone, including myself. We all saw what he was, I think, but still a man can be a coward under one circumstance and a brave man under another."

"We have only one circumstance here," Ibsen stated roughly.

"Why didn't you send me?"

"That may come, doc."

The words had a tired, regretful sound, but they had to be spoken, because they were the bitter fruit of hard, relentless thought. A man in mortal danger stripped himself down to bare essentials. He used what came to hand to save what he could, and let the rest go. He scouted for possible loopholes of escape, and if they were closed he turned to something else. Pick and choose.

But even without doc's Diogenes-Eliza Cook talk, Ibsen held the deepest conviction that he was charged with saving Miss Quimby and the boy beyond all others. The reasons were vague. A man could say the weak and helpless were wards of the strong, but any-one put to the test could quibble with such a statement. However, he couldn't quibble with his conviction, and now that he had learned the way out was blocked, he cast about for another possible move.

"I think the thing that bothers them up there," he thought aloud, "is that they don't know how many of us there are down here. To me that means there are fewer of them than could reasonably get into a coach like this."

"They want odds, and they don't know what they got," Deuce said.

Ibsen nodded. "There might be six—eight—ten up there."

"We could handle that many if they only came down and made a fight," Deuce claimed.

"Speaking of odds," Ibsen went on, "so far as they know, there's just one man and a boy in here. They saw the driver and the boy, and you and me, doc."

"And Watts," doc put in.

"Yes, but I'm assuming they wouldn't notice the difference between me and Watts, so they saw four, and two are dead. A man and a boy left. That ought to put the odds in their favor enough to tempt them down. We'll wait and see."

"S'pose it doesn't?" doc said.

"Then we ought to give them bigger odds."

They waited a long time. Doc picked up the empty bottle, took a long caressing look through the amber glass, then dropped it over the edge. It made a little explosion when it hit. Sweat stung Deuce's raw wrists, and he blew on them to keep them cool. Miss Quimby used her smelling salts again, and the sharp fumes engulfed them all. An arrow snapped against the coach.

"Hurry, hurry, hurry, the man says," doc commented.

"We're in a bigger hurry than they are," Ibsen stated, "but as soon as it gets dark they'll come down and pour it on. That makes it bad. They have bows and arrows, and you can't fight bows and arrows in the dark. They give you nothing to shoot at."

"If it's odds they want, I'll dig out," Deuce volunteered. "I could make a better job of it than Watts."

"No," Ibsen told him. "You're the best shot here. You stay to the last."

"You're aiming at me," doc said.

"I guess I am, doc."

"All right. Let's hear it."

"I'd like to make it look as if you and the boy are the last ones left in here. The two of you get into an argument about pulling out. You want to go, and he's afraid to make the try. You get out and haul him out with you. Make it a big argument. They'll be curious and apt to hold their fire till it's over. It's a risk for the boy, but if you make a big show, I think it will work. If I were up there watching, I believe I would come to the conclusion that you were the only man left. In the end, Porfio pulls free and gets back in here. You go on and make out the best you can."

"It all sounds very logical," doc finally spoke up without a quaver. "Surely, the boy ought to be the last to go. He was the last to come." His smile ranged toward Miss Quimby. "And he ought to have someone to take him by the hand. You see, ma'am, most of us have had our little say. If there was any good in it, you tell the boy. That's how things go on. It all makes good sense."

Miss Quimby swallowed several times, like a dry pump, before she could get out a word. "I—I don't know." Dismay engulfed her, as if here at last she had to look at what she was and what she ought to be. "I don't know," she breathed again. "What can one say that means enough?"

"By the time this is over, ma'am," doc said gently, "I should think you will know all there is to say."

"I better go," Deuce begged, looking at Ibsen.

Ibsen shook his head.

"I'm curious," doc said. "S'pose you had to give odds right down the line?"

"I've told you Deuce is the best shot. It's no game, doc."

"Hm'm'm," doc said. "Well, son." With a few grunts and groans, as though age were the worst of his troubles, he worked up steam and stepped outside, pulling Porfio along.

Ibsen wouldn't look. Miss Quimby clutched her embroidered reticule and the knob of her parasol until her knuckles turned white. Deuce watched the wall. Doc and Porfio bickered awhile, but Porfio finally broke away and climbed back into the safety of the coach. Doc, with an exasperated gesture that indicated he had done all he could, walked away alone.

Deuce spat out an oath and raised his gun. Ibsen batted it down. "Stay back out of sight," he ordered. "You know what the idea is."

"I see one. He's gettin' set to——"

Doc grunted suddenly. Ibsen heard him go down. Miss Quimby gasped and put her hand over her eyes.

"I could've stopped that," Deuce flared. "You——"

"No more talk," Ibsen ordered. "If there's anything to say, whisper it. Don't show yourself either."

Doc started moving again. Ibsen heard his boots dragging. He was probably traveling on all fours. Another swift whoosh and thump brought him to a halt. He called out something that got lost in his throat. Miss Quimby tried to get out, but Ibsen pushed her back. Doc wasn't heard from again.

Ibsen had a great capacity for calmness, and it stood him in good stead now. It was wait, wait, wait, and nothing else, while the sun moved away, and the shapes and shadows in the gorge changed. Deuce was boiling, and Miss Quimby nursed sharp resentments and antagonisms. A wild whoop bickered through the gorge, and Ibsen saw a stirring along the south wall. Deuce saw it too and whispered an oath.

Ibsen picked them out one by one, counting eight; three from the north wall and five from the south. For good measure, he added one from behind and one from ahead, but those he couldn't see. He assumed they would be there to make a tight ambush. He told Miss Quimby to get down to the floor between the seats, and he put Porfio on his knees behind her. "Lay the gun over her back," he instructed. "That'll steady it. Don't shoot till I say so. You've got to get two the first shot. Deuce, you keep your temper. It's got to be a big slaughter all at once."

Deuce flattened out on the seat, facing the north wall. Ibsen, on the other seat, faced the other way. With as much consideration as he could muster, Porfio placed the gun along the slant of Miss Quimby's back, the tip resting on the edge of the door.

The Apaches made no further attempt at concealment. They laughed and crowed as they came, but they halted before getting into range, and Ibsen thought he had failed in spite of all his precautions.

"On top," Deuce breathed. "There's one on top."

Ibsen looked up and saw the roof splinter. A stone blade showed through, then a steely eye. Ibsen fired straight up. A hair-raising shriek came back at him, then a clatter and thump, and the Apache slid over the edge and toppled to the ground.

The rest charged, and arrows hissed in through the openings. "Let 'em come, let 'em come," Ibsen told himself until they were all in point-blank range. Then he poked Porfio, and the scattergun roared. Deuce's gun joined in, and his own, and smoke simmered out through the openings, and arrows swept in.

One raider reached the door, and Ibsen shot him in the face before he could use his club or get the door open. Wails of anger and surprise and agony went up. The fight all went Ibsen's way, except that Deuce didn't keep his temper. Something happened on his side that brought it to a boil, and he lunged out the door before Ibsen could stop him. He couldn't look either. He was too busy on his own side.

The attack came and went like a roll of thunder in the sky. All at once, there were no more Apaches to shoot at. The wild fury died. Ibsen took a wary look and called Deuce, but he didn't get an answer. He got out and saw Deuce lying on the ground near Boggs and a dead Apache. Evidently, the Apache had tried to scalp Boggs. The sight had set Deuce on fire, and it had cost him his life.

Ibsen bent down and picked up the big gun that had belonged to Boggs and put it in his pants belt. "Doc'll think I welshed sure," Ibsen's lips moved around the words, but no sound came. "Tell him the facts, Deuce, if you two get together. I'd like to have him know."

He walked around and counted heads, and called Miss Quimby and Porfio. "No time to lose," he told them. "I made a count, and I think two got away. Let's travel, before they block us again."

The meadow where Ibsen had left his horses was a small enclosed place with a scattering of dry grass and a water seep. The walls were high, coming down to the floor in a series of rock terraces. He had stretched a rope across the mouth. The saddles were hidden nearby.

The horses came readily to hand, and Ibsen wasted no time getting Miss Quimby and the boy aboard, and on their way to the gate. He was desperately pinched for time. The two Apaches who had escaped were trailing them, and their obvious intention was to block the narrow opening to the meadow. Ibsen had no more deputies or doctors to dole out, only himself, if he meant to go that far.

It was far to go for anyone who had no desire to travel a glory road. But he did owe doc a forfeit, unless, of course, he wanted to say that doc, with his fast talk, was at the bottom of it all. It could be said. Doc had seen Ibsen go to work on Watts, baiting him out of the coach with smooth talk, and doc had taken hold of it and made it something of his own, throwing out bait that Ibsen thought was his own fine say until at last doc had his word to save the saints and let the sinners go. That much could be said without throwing reason to the winds, and it left Ibsen with a choice. A man had the right to draw back from cunning and trickery, and make his own way from where he stood when he discovered it. But it was getting late, too late. He stopped the horses short of the gate and pointed up. "There they are."

"Si, señor," Porfio said, his voice as quiet and steady as ever; "I see them."

"I'll climb up and try to get at them from behind. I'll yell when it's safe to move. When you hear me, clear out. Don't wait for me. Miss Quimby, can you hang onto that horse?"

"I shall try," Miss Quimby said.

Ibsen considered giving Porfio one of the guns, but decided against it. Boggs' big-calibered weapon had only one cartridge left, and Ibsen couldn't spare the other one where he was going. With a last word to wait for his signal, he walked away.

At first, the climb was easy. He made a wide circle to keep out of range, but he made no effort at concealment. Most of the time it took care of itself. Miss Quimby and Porfio were in plain view all the time, waiting patiently for his signal, waiting in their deep humility to inherit the earth.

His difficulties increased. Sheer walls faced him, and it was all he could do to claw his way up from terrace to terrace. Boggs' big peacemaker, stuck in his belt, was a nuisance. He holstered his own weapon so he could use both hands. He couldn't see the Apaches, but he had a fix on where they were, and when he thought he was high enough he moved their way. Before he got very far, however, the ledge he was on tapered to nothing, and he had to climb again, up a ten-foot wall.

Here, he lost his gun. Bad footing and hurry did it. Halfway to the top, a rock let go and threw him. He was lucky enough to catch himself on the narrow ledge, but his gun slid out of the holster and went on. Somewhere on its way the hammer hit rock, and a cartridge exploded.

The sound boomed and barked along the terraced walls and gave Miss Quimby's horse a fit. Porfio did what he could, but the animal got away and headed into the gap. Miss Quimby started to slide off. Porfio cut around in front and caught her mount by the head and brought it to a stop. Miss Quimby slid the rest of the way and hit the ground. An arrow swished down at her, but it fell short.

A little more pull and they'd make it, Ibsen thought. He climbed again. This time he made it and ran along the higher terrace, which brought him into the open two rows above the crouching Apaches.

They didn't hear him. One of them was watching the place where his gun had exploded, the other was stringing another arrow. Down below, Porfio held Miss Quimby's horse and tried to give her a boost into the saddle at the same time, but she was all skirts and couldn't throw her leg across. She couldn't even claw her way up. She made a ridiculous figure to a man who considered the back of a horse the only proper place for anyone to be, a flailing, inept scarecrow too exasperating to take seriously, regardless of doc's pretty words.

This, then, was the place for a man with only one load in his weapon to stop and think, or, better still, to move on out of reach, and content himself with what he had tried to do. It was still a possibility. The Apaches didn't know he stood behind them. The accidental gunshot had tricked them into thinking he was somewhere else. Miss Quimby and Porfio could try to run the gap on their own. A fast run might get them through. It was a risk, but it was an even chance.

Meanwhile, he could go on over the slant and probably catch a mule, or even go back for ammunition for the peacemaker. Boggs was bound to have some somewhere on the coach. This was reason, and the rest was folly, but he remembered the bright glow that had come to Miss Quimby's eyes when doc had told her to take Porfio by the hand, and the answer she had given him, like deep quiet water. He had seen and heard something there that was far beyond the cynic's tongue, and whether doc had outsmarted him or not had no bearing. He had to stand his ground, and, perhaps, go down when the last he had to offer was spent.

He stepped forward to the edge of the ledge and let out a yell.

The Apaches spun and stared up. Ibsen stared back. He held them so, under his gun, nailed in their tracks with surprise and dismay. The gun hung limp in his hand. He didn't threaten them with it, but he held them, and he saw Porfio give a final boost and get Miss Quimby aboard, and he saw them start forward.

So long, the two Apaches stood frozen, but the clatter of hoofs brought a stir. They didn't actually move, but Ibsen saw the swift ripple of muscle brought to bear on some intended move. Like wolves on a hunt, they had an intuition for teamwork, and Ibsen thought he saw what they meant to do. The ledge on which they stood was wide, so they were obliged to stay near the edge to look down into the gap. The next terrace down was narrow and deep, so a man could get an unobstructed view of the gap and keep his back protected at the same time. One of them meant to go over the edge to block the two riders, the other meant to jump forward for cover and hold Ibsen off.

Vague straws, mere shadows of thought and intention, warned Ibsen. He raised his gun, and the two Apaches took off, one forward, the other backward, giving Ibsen a last hard choice, whether to fend for himself or the safety of the riders below. He made it fast, and the Apache going over the edge got it. He crumpled like a shot bird, and, from the sound, bounced down clear to the bottom. An avalanche of scree poured after him.

The other crouched behind the wall. Only the tip of his bow showed. Hot fury poured off his lips, but he kept to cover. The last of the smoke, the very last, trickled off Ibsen's gun. The weapon was useless now, no better than a stick, but he put it in his holster. Porfio looked up, and Ibsen waved, but he didn't get an answer. Either Porfio didn't see him or he was too busy keeping Miss Quimby aboard.

"There they go, doc," Ibsen muttered, and with doc's words thrown around them, they made a sight worth looking at. A part of all that was gone, of Deuce and Boggs and that Diogenes and even Watts, and much of doc, and a little of himself, went with them. That beanpole woman had it in her keeping, like seed to plant, and it would make a harvest, as surely as day came out of night.

The Apache below moved. He showed himself, and automatically Ibsen's hand went for his gun. The Apache ducked. His bow tip moved along the ledge. It moved clear out of sight, and, much later, Ibsen saw the Apache circling around the far side of the meadow. He was on the run. Ibsen didn't mind, but he was surprised, until he let it soak in that a gun wasn't entirely empty until the one it was pointed at knew it.

FIDDLE-FOOTED
by Cliff Farrell

Eb Irons saw the wagon when it first came over the cap rock off the prairie, and he felt a trifle discouraged. A sunbonnet and a petticoat showed under the front bow, which meant they were aiming to settle.

The country, he reflected, was plowing in fast. Giving the devil his due, he was forced to admit that the Comanches had been of some benefit after all. They, at least, had scared folks into staying mostly where they belonged.

This was the third wagon in a month's time. It was a hoop-tilted Mitchell, with a plow team in harness, and two milk cows tied to the tail. A flea-trap hound flopped along under the reach, and the linchpin wheels screeched like the hinges of Gehenna.

The man allowed, with a self-effacing grin, that his name was Lute Rasmussen. They were from Missouri. Pike County folks, and they had wagoned it all the way, following the Austin military road. They had been six weeks on the trail and——

"Five weeks, five days, less three, four hours," his woman corrected from her vantage point on the wagon.

"Five weeks, five days, Ma," Lute agreed, and it was plain he was not the disputing kind. "You've got a right pert shack there, young feller."

"I'd have set it a mite nearer under the brow of the knoll," Ma declared, "and facin' more westerly to ketch the breeze."

Eb fetched a saddle of venison as an offering, which Ma sniffed and pronounced as having hung long enough.

"I'll drop a couple of turkeys for you directly," Eb promised. "I heard some gobblin' up in the plum a few minutes back. You folks headin' for the Nueces, I take it?"

Lute nodded. "We've been told there's good plow land to be

had." He had a habit of turning his mild, faded blue eyes to Ma for confirmation whenever he spoke.

"Your womenfolk away?" Ma demanded of Eb.

"I don't have me a woman."

If there was a touch of complacency in Eb's tone, it was perhaps justified. Eb had his memories. There had been that taffy-haired Arkansaw girl who had her cap set for him one winter in Kerrville. And a brown-eyed one who came within a case card of heeling him down in the Pedernales settlements. But Eb had been fiddle-footed. He had drifted down the country each time before things got too simmery.

Ma pushed her steel-rimmed specs up on her forehead. She possessed, Eb noticed, a firm underjaw.

"You batchin'?"

"I'm batchin'," Eb confirmed. He wasn't surprised by the battle glint that came into Ma's eye. Eb was a bass fisherman and he saw the resemblance in the way she rose. They were all alike. Seventeen or ninety, they all figured it was a challenge, and something ought to be done about it.

Ed winked at Lute and led the way to the back of the pole shack. He brought out a stone jug and a horn.

"Say when," he warned as he flipped the jug on an arm and let her gurgle. "I fetched 'er from Kerrville last month. Arkansaw-stilled."

Lute didn't say when until the horn was brimming. He took a quick look around the corner, then downed it at a jump. Fishing in a vest pocket, he produced an object, broke off a fragment and offered it to Eb.

"Sassafras bark," he cautioned. "Better chaw it, younker. Ma kin smell likker two miles upwind."

Both of them chewed.

"Batchin', hey?" Lute mused.

Eb had an uneasy hunch that, in addition to admiration and envy, there was a hint of prophetic warning in Lute's tone.

"I'm batchin'," Eb said firmly.

"I wasn't much past twenty when Ma married me," Lute stated. "I'm forty-three now, come January."

"I'm edgin' twenty-four," Eb pointed out. Again he couldn't keep the complacency out of his voice.

"Lute!" Ma's voice had considerable carry.

Eb just had time to shove the jug inside the door and drop a wolf pelt over it before she hove up. She was a broad-beamed woman, cushioned in all directions. Outmaneuvering Lute, she got to windward of him and sniffed. Then she gave Eb a look he wouldn't forget for a while. "It's high time," she told her husband, "thet we set camp."

"Too early, Ma," Lute protested. "It ain't fur past high noon. We'll peel off half a dozen more miles before sundown."

"I reckon," Ma said, "we'll settle here. You won't find land any better on the Nueces."

Eb had a sinking feeling. He waited for Lute to assert himself. Lute owed him something in return for that snort of Arkansaw-stilled.

Lute tried to meet his obligation. "We'd be safer on the Nueces," he said, but it was plain that he knew he was wasting words. "There's more settlers. The Injuns won't be as likely to bother."

"Injuns!" Ma sniffed disparagingly. "Wasn't we told in Kerrville that the Rangers had made 'em skedaddle for good? Gave 'em a larrupin' last fall they won't forget."

Eb was moved to speak up hopefully. "That's no sign they won't come back. Can't ever tell about Comanches. You're quite a spell from help here. Kerrville's the nearest settlement. Sixty miles."

"You're livin' here," Ma pointed out. "You're still wearin' your topknot."

"I'm a man," Eb said, as though that settled it. "I know how to take care o' myself."

"Fiddle-faddle," said Ma. "Batchin'. A strappin' feller like you. Wearin' skin clothes, with your hair down to your neck. You look like an Injun yourself. An' that shack looks like a pigsty. What you need is a woman to straighten you out."

She was, Eb comprehended, very opinionated. "There's better land down the crick," he argued earnestly. "Deep bottom soil. Clear too. Won't need much breakin'."

"How far?" Ma asked without interest.

"Five, maybe six miles."

As a matter of fact, it was ten or twelve. Eb felt he was justified in dallying with the truth in this case. Even that distance would be all too inadequate. The game would thin out in a hurry for a considerable radius. A presence like Ma's likely would spook even the bass and catfish.

"I like it better here," Ma said, and Eb understood the discussion was ended.

Lute had a hangdog look and wouldn't meet Eb's eye as they walked back to the wagon.

Eb paused in stride, looking at what stood by the Mitchell. Suddenly he got fiddle-footed again and wary as a creased buck. He began to understand that prophetic warning in Lute's voice a few minutes earlier.

The girl was eighteen or nineteen and done up in calico. Eb had to look down at her, for she wasn't much taller than a minute. Thick wavy hair and lively brown eyes. A pert nose and some freckles. She even had on button shoes, which proved that she had previously kept out of sight in the wagon, preening herself, so as to make a good appearance. That was always their way.

"We're settlin' here, Josie Belle," Ma said. "This here is Mr.——"

"Irons," Eb said distantly. "Eb Irons."

He gave Lute a look. And Lute accepted the indictment as justified.

Josie Belle curtsied. She patted the hound dog and looked Eb over, and looked the shack over—with a calculating eye, Eb thought.

"It'll be nice having a neighbor," Josie Belle said.

The worst of it was that she wasn't homely. But the lookers were always the worst. Sure of themselves. Figured a man would fall like a ripe plum.

"Eb is havin' supper with us as soon as we get the pot on," Ma said.

"I had calculated," Eb stated weakly, "on tryin' for a few hen turks up in the shinnery 'long toward sundown."

But he was licked, and he knew it. Common courtesy compelled him to offer to help Lute unload and pitch. From the way the wagon tilt bulged, they had an uncommon amount of possibles to handle. Which meant that he would be at it until dark.

He was correct in his estimate. He had to give up his plans for a hunt.

Ma picked a site a quarter of a mile south along the stream. Eb gloomily noticed that his own shack would be well under her visual thumb from that point.

Josie Belle took off her button shoes and stored away her calico in favor of homespun. Barefoot, she did her share of the work.

Ma gave her free hand with the cooking. Josie Belle, so Ma informed Eb, had been the best cook in Pike County. The way Ma told it, Lute had to use a swingletree to keep the dooryard clear of ardent swains every moonlight night.

Josie Belle herself had little to say. If she glanced his way, Eb didn't know it, for he took mighty good care to pay her no attention.

She could cook. Ma hadn't drawn the long bow in that respect at least. To demonstrate that he was a fair-minded man, Eb admitted as much, after partaking of the meal Josie Belle prepared.

"That hog jowel," he pronounced, ducking his head in Josie Belle's direction, "was more'n fair to middlin'. It was so. An' the potlikker didn't stick to my gullet either."

"Wait'll she really gits her hand in," Ma predicted.

However, Eb figured he could handle this. They weren't goin' to cook him before a preacher. He had considerable experience. The taffy-haired Arkansaw girl in Kerrville had been handy around a cook fire too. Her lye hominy, he judged, had been a mite smoother than Josie Belle's, if a man was inclined to split hairs, and she might have had a little more sabe as to how to baste a venison steak. The brown-eyed one on the Pedernales had shown a knack for it too. But he had got away from them, though it had been touch and go—'specially on the Pedernales.

Lute got a word with him alone as he said his good night. "I'd stache that jug out somewhere away from your shack, Eb," he counseled. "Ma's a white-ribboner."

A man's house, Eb pointed out, was his castle. He was entitled to keep his jug anywhere he danged pleased.

"I'm only a-warnin' you," Lute said gloomily.

The moon was up. Before turning in, Eb threw a halter on his Jack bay, and took a little *pasear* along the foot of the bluff and beyond the plum thickets upcreek. The turkeys were still roosting in the pecans along the stream, and he flushed a drowsing doe in the willow brakes.

Satisfied by these signs that there were no nocturnal prowlers in the vicinity, he returned to the shack. Recent rains had filled the *charcos*, or natural water holes, on the prairie. Full moon and full *charcos* sometimes brought the Comanches raiding down across the Staked Plains. However, there had been no reports of Indians south of the San Saba since the Rangers had taught them a lesson at Pipecreek the previous fall. Eb had helped in that fight. He had an orangewood bow and a few stone pipes scattered around his shack as relics of that episode.

Eb cleared out before daybreak. He carried his over-and-under gun —rifle barrel above and shotgun bore beneath. It was a muzzle-loader, and superior, in his opinion, in both balance and carry to any of the new breech guns he had tried.

Riding the Jack bay, he was over the cap rock before the first drift of smoke showed from the Rasmussen camp. He had mentioned the previous day that he aimed to plow in a forty to corn on this day, but he had decided, on second thought, that it was better for a man to prove his independence right at the start.

The world, he reflected, was full of cornfields, and the majority were planted by men who would rather have been giving their time to something more to their preference. Hunting antelope, for instance. Or bait fishing.

Lute Rasmussen, he imagined, would do a lot of plowing and planting on mornings when he would yearn for the solace of a gun in his hand and open miles ahead. Women had a way of making a man feel duty-bound to matters of providing. As far as Eb was concerned, there would be another day to plant corn.

He fetched an antelope along toward midmorning with as pretty a running neck shot as he had ever notched. At noon he clipped the head from a prime hen turkey in the mottled noon shade of a pecan grove. It was a neat trigger in that tricky light, and he paced off the distance. One hundred and twenty. It was, he assured himself, better than middlin', in view of conditions.

At late afternoon he jogged back to the shack, the Jack bay smothered to the withers in turkey fans and antelope quarters.

Eb knew there was something out of kilter with his shack before he was within gunshot. He dismounted and stood in the door, gazing. The puncheon floor had been swept and water-scrubbed. Its grainy dampness still exuded the tang of lye soap. The benches and table stood in military order in the exact center. There wasn't a speck of ash left in the fireplace, and his cooking outfit dazzled the eye. Someone had used considerable sand and elbowgrease on those pots. His spare clothing and gear had mostly vanished.

Lute Rasmussen appeared and joined him in surveying the damage. Lute had been plowing all day, hustling to get his seed in ahead of the advancing season.

"They found the jug too," Lute said with a sigh. "Ma smashed it on a rock. I warned you. I did that. Here's some cracklin' bread for you. Ma sent it. Told me to be sure an' let you know that Josie Belle made it with her own hands."

Afterward, Eb poked gingerly around the shack. He finally located the majority of his belongings, though some had been stowed away pretty deep. The shortage was still considerable, nevertheless.

However, the missing articles were lying on the table the next forenoon when he returned with a string of catfish from the creek. Socks and linsey shirts were neatly darned and washed to a frazzle. A Kiowa-made hunting shirt, which he had particularly prized, was stiff as a board and shrunk to child's size. Even a Missouri woman, Eb thought scornfully, ought to know better than to use lye soap and hot water on a hide shirt.

From his door he could see Josie Belle puttering around their cook fire. Oh, she was brazen enough about it. There was a pert swing to the hem of her petticoat as she worked. She was singing something about a lover who was dying with his sweetheart's name on his lips. Her voice wasn't bad. Eb had to admit that. But it was the way she carried herself. Plenty sure of herself.

Eb felt himself getting more fiddle-footed every minute. But he had his stubborn streak. It wasn't the inconvenience of drifting to new pastures that was holding him back. It was the principle of the thing. He would, he vowed, show even a looker like Josie Belle that he could hold out.

Anyway, the game hadn't left the country. He could afford to linger until the shooting thinned. He would then be justified in riding on over the hill.

Eb hung on. He helped Lute cut post-oak logs and set the walls of their house.

They sodded the roof, and added a fancy split-rail lean-to kitchen with a bear-grass top. Josie Belle's eyes were lovelier than ever as she helped thatch the kitchen. And the way she swung her petticoat as she hustled around was a sight to see.

Eb knew he was a fool moth batting around a candle flame, but he rather relished the gamble. It was almost as much fun as trailing Comanches—a sport in which a man also stood to win or lose considerable if he made a wrong move or was lured into an ambush.

He could see that he had Ma on the prod. Ma had figured he'd be brought to yoke long before this, he realized. His continued independence was both an affront and a goad to her.

As a field general, Ma lacked adroitness. Her system was akin to General Hood's, under whom Eb had fought in the recent Rebellion. Frontal attack and sledge-hammer blows.

Ma's chief maneuver was to place Josie Belle alone with Eb. But Eb was too shrewd for that. He always found a way to wriggle out.

They were a month getting the Rasmussens under roof. Eb found time to keep their larder filled. He even got his corn in, and a forty in beans as well, during one spell when the mood suited him.

He was beginning to believe he had underrated Josie Belle's culinary skill. Her lye hominy was as toothsome as any he had ever sampled, and she could turn a venison steak to a man's taste. No doubt about it.

When he realized the trend of his thoughts, he knew it was high time to ramble. He had, he understood, danced a trifle too close to the candle flame. He packed his war sack that night. He meant to be on his way before sunup.

But he had dallied too long. Ma beat him to the draw. He was rolling his bed tarp when the Rasmussen wagon squeaked into the dooryard.

It was Lute and Ma. "We're a-goin' to Kerrville," said Ma, "to do some buyin'. Hand me your store list an' we'll fetch it. Keep an eye on things for us. Josie Belle's stayin' to look after the milkin'."

Eb watched the wagon crawl up the bluff and over the cap rock onto the prairie. They'd be gone four, five days at best. A week, most likely.

He kicked his war sack across the shack. He couldn't just naturally pick up and pull out, leaving Josie Belle here alone. She'd likely be safe enough. But it was full moon again, and the *charcos* were brimming, for it was a summer of rains.

Chances were the Comanches had learned their lesson and would stay beyond the San Saba if they rode at all this year. There had been no Indian sign along the Frio all season. Still—— Eb kicked his war bag again.

He decided that he could manage it with a little planning. The main thing, he realized, was to keep her in her place. He got out his pole and hooks, and hit for the creek. Josie Belle must have spotted him, for he had hardly got settled down on his best catfish hole when she showed up with her pole and line.

"The two of us," she said, "ought to get a mess in a hurry for breakfast. Your hook, Eb, is too big, isn't it?"

"Seems about right to me," said Eb.

"You'll do better with a smaller one," she decided. "Here. I've got an extra one. Swing your line in."

It was about the same the next day. She overtook him after he thought he had got safely away on a turkey hunt. She had never, she told him, got a decent shot at a turkey.

Eb went to a lot of trouble getting her into position for an easy kill, and let her use his over-and-under. She missed it clean, and she blamed him, saying he had made her pull before she was set.

The lookers, Eb reflected, never make a mistake. He had a notion to tell her about that hunting shirt and her lye soap. But he refrained.

Eb counted the days. He kept his war bag ready, and secretly climbed to the cap rock often to peer eastward in the hope of seeing the linchpin wagon returning. It was his intention, once he was sure Lute and Ma were on their way, to be long gone before they arrived.

It was the sixth day and Josie Belle had given him both barrels that noon in the form of a dinner fit for a king. There had been suet-dumpling stew and plum pie with the juice rich and gummy on the brown crust. And potlikker like nectar from heaven.

It was midafternoon now, and Eb felt like sleeping it off, but she had him up in the plum brush picking fruit for preserving.

She gathered plums like she did everything else—with thoroughness and energy, and a swing to her petticoat. She was making two trips to Eb's one to the noggin tub that they were filling, and she had him shirking and sullen.

She came hurrying back to him through the brush, her eyes excited. "Visitors, Eb," she said, pleased by the prospect of a break in their solitude. "I saw two riders."

Eb came alive. The thought flashed in his mind that he had failed to bring his muzzle-loader. But he had his ball pistol, though it wasn't much in a brush fight.

"Where?" he demanded.

"I glimpsed them as they crossed the cap rock. Two of 'em. One seemed to be carrying a big round kettle lid on his arm. Or maybe I only imagined it. I didn't get much more than a peek at them."

Eb picked up the noggin tub. "We got enough plums," he said. "Maybe we better drift back home."

Not until he led the way through deep brush instead of staying in the open did she suspect. He heard her breath catch. After that she came close to him, so close her bare feet trod his heels. She clutched the slack of his shirt like a child who didn't want to be lost.

They moved forward at a crouch until they reached the fringe of the plum. There Eb paused, studying. A thousand feet of plowed fields lay between them and his pole shack, and the corn was up less than a foot.

The Jack bay stood hipshot in the feed meadow beyond the shack, and Eb decided to chance it. Here in the brush the odds would be too heavy. The shack offered better protection.

His fingers closed on Josie Belle's arm, and he felt the soft roundness of it as they started their race across the open fields. His long legs outmatched her, and at times her feet hardly touched the ground as he lifted her along with him.

Eb watched the bay horse, and he thought they were going to make it without argument. But the animal's ears suddenly cocked as he whirled to stare at something beyond Eb and the girl. Eb didn't take time to look back. He pushed Josie Belle in front of him, running in step with her, so as to shield her body.

They were half a dozen jumps from the shack when he heard the buzz-saw passage of an arrow and saw it stand trembling in the door frame. Next a bullet from a muzzle-loader had its say past their ears.

The door stood welcomingly only a stride or two away when something smote him on the back. The force of it drove him forward to his knees, and he tripped Josie Belle, so that she sprawled on her face.

She came to her feet. He saw that her eyes looked as big as tea-cups against the pallor of her cheeks. He tried to get off his hands and knees, but a queer inertia had palsied his mind and his brawn. The world was spinning, trying to toss him off into space, like it did when he drank too much pop-skull liquor. He wanted to dig his fingers into the earth to stay put.

Josie Belle's hands levered at his armpits, dragging him on to-ward the door. Her strength was surprising.

Together they fell through the door into the shack. She wriggled out from under him, and he caught a glimpse of the Comanches before she slammed and barred the door. There were half a dozen of them charging across the corn, all mounted. Some had buffalo-hide shields on their arms. These were the kettle lids Josie Belle had noticed.

Eb's mind cleared a little. He crawled to the wall beneath his muzzle-loader, which lay athwart the deerhorn bracket. He tried to get to his feet to reach it, but the effort was too great.

Josie Belle lifted the gun. He watched her poke the light from his front window and level the piece and fire.

He could hear the rifle slug screeing away into the distance, and he knew she had fired too high.

But he also heard the receding pad of unshod hoofs. The Comanches were retreating to the creek brush to palaver and plan their strategy. It wasn't the Indian way to charge a house in open daylight. Darkness would give them a better chance.

She lifted Eb partly to the bunk and bathed his face.

"Load the gun," he said in a faraway voice, for she had neglected that detail.

As she complied, Eb explored his wound.

It was an arrow, and the point of it was protruding at the front of his left shoulder.

He looked at Josie Belle. "Shove it clean through," he said, "an' break it off."

"Oh, Eb!"

"Do what I say, girl," he commanded, and got a hand grip on the frame of the bunk.

She finally went through with it, though she nearly keeled over before it was finished.

And Eb drifted completely out for a while. When he aroused again, he was weak as a wet kitten. He could barely lift his head. He discovered that Josie Belle had tied some kind of a bandage about his body.

To his horror, he learned that he had been divested of his shirt and breeches. He was tucked neatly in his bunk.

Swiftly he located his missing garments. Josie Belle was wearing them. The shirt and breeches were big enough to wrap more than half around her again. This she had done, and she had rolled up the arms and legs.

She had the muzzle-loader in her hands, and now she unbarred the door and stood boldly there for an instant while she emptied the rifle barrel in the general direction of the plum brush.

She ducked aside, closing the door quickly. An answering shot sounded. Eb spit and sputtered as the bullet hit the shack and shook chinking down in his face.

She looked at him, and had the grace at least to offer an explanation. "I reckoned it would be best to make them believe you were still able to fight," she declared. "They'll think twice if they know they're up against a man. That's why I took your clothes, Eb, an' gave 'em a glimpse of me at the door."

It was, Eb conceded, good generalship.

Things got a little fuzzy for him after that. He saw her pour powder into the muzzle-loader, ram a wad home and tamp down a bullet. Next she loaded the under barrel with a generous load of powder and buckshot.

She hefted the gun. Afterward Eb could have sworn that he saw her pouring more powder and wads and more buckshot into the under barrel. He guessed that his mind was only repeating itself.

But later on he saw her ramming something else into the fowling barrel. He vaguely identified it as a two-inch length of broken wagon bolt which had been lying around the shack for months.

"You're overloadin' her," he managed to comment.

But Josie Belle hefted the gun and looked satisfied. "I reckon I'll need to cut quite a swath if I have to use it," she stated.

You couldn't, Eb reflected, tell a woman anything. Not a looker, anyway. They were always sure of themselves.

He began to feel a little more chipper as the afternoon waned and sunset slanted through the window. He stayed in the bunk, husbanding his strength. He judged that if the Indians tried it, they'd come between first dark and moon-up. Then he'd be needed.

As twilight deepened, he got himself sitting up in the bunk. "I'll have my britches now," he said firmly.

Josie Belle started to refuse, but he gave her a look. Dutifully she retired into a corner while he turned his head. Presently, wearing her own homespun, she handed him his clothes.

Eb managed to get into his breeches. The shack danced around for a while after he got to his feet, but his head soon steadied a trifle.

He took the over-and-under gun from Josie Belle. "You use the ball pistol," he ordered. And as an afterthought, "Count your shots. When you've fired four, save the other one. No tellin' what you might need it for."

"I understand," Josie Belle said. "I won't let 'em take me alive, Eb."

Eb swallowed hard. He got to the window and braced himself there so he wouldn't fall easy, no matter what hit him.

A gray trace of daylight still lingered over the cap rock, but the creek brush was black and silent—too silent.

Josie Belle whispered a belief that the Comanches had pulled out. Eb didn't answer. He knew they hadn't gone. Not even a cricket was sounding off in the brush.

The last tinge of daylight drained away, leaving the creek bottom a black morass. Eb heard them then. The barest rustle in the corn.

"Look alive," he murmured to Josie Belle. "They're out there."

They came then. Not with screeching, but with a silent moccasined rush upon the shack, aiming to carry the door by surprise.

Eb pushed the over-and-under across the window sill, and waited until he could see two or three of them against the starlight almost at arm's length. A war club thudded against the door, and he pulled the back trigger, touching off the fowling barrel.

There was an earth-shaking jar and a sheet of flame. The concussion shook the last of the chinking out of the shack.

The kick knocked Eb flat on his back in the middle of the floor, and it was some little space of time before he remembered his prediction that Josie Belle had overloaded the gun.

A dying Indian was breathing haltingly and hard outside the door, and he heard crashing in the corn.

"They're skedaddling!" Josie Belle exclaimed. "Eb, you got some of 'em!"

Eb had taken about enough punishment for one day, but he managed to get to the window. His hand encountered the muzzle-loader as he crawled across the floor. He felt a twinge as though he had lost a friend. The over-and-under was done for. Half the barrel had been blown off.

"You loaded 'er too heavy," he said. "That wagon bolt was the last straw. I told you, didn't I?"

"You told me, Eb," she admitted. "You ruined your gun, didn't you?"

"I ruined it. I ruined it." His tone was scathing.

There were two painted braves lying before the door, and the one who had been breathing hard was silent, too, now, and quite dead.

The moon came up and lighted the creek thickets. After a time the crickets came to life down there, and the bullfrogs began booming.

"I calculate," Eb said, "they've shucked it for good."

That earth-shaker had done the work. He knew that, but he also knew it'd be a strategic blunder to admit it to Josie Belle.

"Soon as it comes daylight," he said, "we'll hook up the buckboard an' hit for Kerrville to warn the folks." And as an afterthought, he added, "Looks like you an' me better get married, Josie Belle. Us bein' alone here like this might be misunderstood."

"Oh, Eb!"

She kissed him. And he kissed her plenty. She was an armful, all right.

"We might ketch the circuit rider in Kerrville," he said, "if we're lucky. Last Sunday was his day there, but he might have got hung up."

"We'll catch him," Josie Belle said positively. "Ma allowed she'd hold him there a few days, till we showed up. She reckoned we'd be needin' him."

Eb thought it over. It was, he reflected, useless to try to outgeneral 'em. They had it all cut and dried from the start, and the Comanches had only helped out.

But there was the busted over-and-under to fall back on. He must, he realized, keep that shattered gun handy as an object lesson. Hadn't he told her she was overloading it? In that instance he had proved his superior knowledge at least. And then there was the lye-shrunk hunting shirt. He still had it stached away, and he'd bring it out someday when she got to flipping the hem of her petticoat around too gay. A man had to keep 'em in their place.

THE LADY FROM RED GULCH
by *Michael Fessier*

It was along about the end of calf-roping season when Don Rafael de Soto strutted into the Chinaman's Chance Saloon in Buffalo Bend and, with his silver spurs jingling and his pearl-handled six gun slapping at his thigh, walked up to the bar and downed a shot of redeye neat. He stood there a moment, an arrogant look on his handsome face; then walked over to the poker game and, without asking leave, sat down, threw a handful of gold pieces onto the table and demanded chips. Then, while Bud Conyears, Bart McCormack and some of the other rougher element of our citizenry watched him with considerable animosity, he proceeded to clean out the game, playing in an abstracted manner, as if his heart weren't in it.

"These game," he said, shoving his chair back, "was too tame." Then he grinned easily, almost affably, at the others. "Which one of you gentlemen desires the honor of fighting me first?" he inquired.

"Why should there be a fight?" asked Judge Gorman, who, as our justice of the peace, felt it incumbent upon him at least to pay lip service to the principle of law and order.

"Because," said Don Rafael, "some of these gentlemen seem to be under the impression that I cheated."

"I know doggone well you did," said Billy Feeney, our town troublemaker, whose favorite spectator sports were mayhem and murder, "all of which calls for you to sample the righteous wrath of outraged decency." Then he pointed. "And Bart McCormack here is just the guy that can do it," he announced and stepped aside as Bart made a rush at the slender Spaniard.

Then, while the rest of us watched incredulously, Don Rafael gave Bart the beating of his life. He swarmed all over the big man like a hiveful of hornets, stinging and slashing and circling until

Bart sank dizzily to the floor without having landed one solid blow.

"Which, if you ask me," said Bart, staring admiringly up at his late adversary, "I ain't changed my mind none whatever about you cheating. But," he went on, prying out a loose tooth and staring regretfully at it, "I hereby freely admit that I didn't see you do it when you done it."

Don Rafael grinned amiably, helped Bart to his feet, dusted him off and escorted him to the bar, where he bought drinks for the house. It was a convivial evening, and by final-drink time the general air of hostility that had greeted Don Rafael's arrival in our midst had thawed considerably.

The next day a swaggering Texan came into the Chinaman's Chance, beat up an inoffensive sheepherder; then recklessly offered to shoot it out with any three men we cared to put up against him. Don Rafael faced him coolly and insolently, waited until the visitor went for his gun, then shot him cleanly and neatly through the heart.

During the barbecue that always followed a wedding, a christening or a funeral in Buffalo Bend, Montana Martin, current owner of the Chinaman's Chance, delivered her considered opinion of Don Rafael. "He claims that he's a Castilian nobleman," she said, "but I claim he's a lowborn liar and a horse thief, and I wouldn't trust him any farther than I could throw a bull buffalo by the tail. However," she went on judiciously, "any man that can lick Bart McCormack and outdraw a tall Texan within the space of forty-eight hours is entitled to a few peccadilloes, such as pulling aces out of thin air."

"Until such time as he gets caught at it," said Judge Gorman.

With that pronouncement Don Rafael de Soto became a full-fledged and accepted member of our community. Although he was not unanimously admired, he was liked by some and respected by all and, outside of a few minor scuffles at the card table, he lived peacefully among us for a month. Then Tenney Grant hit town.

Tenney was about Don Rafael's age, with wide shoulders and a slim waist, and there was a look of long-suffering sorrow in his mild blue eyes as he entered the Chinaman's Chance along about fourth-drink time and stared about him as if he was looking for someone.

Don Rafael, who had been playing pinochle with Montana

Martin, dropped his cards, crossed the room and threw his arms around Tenney.

"Ah, my friend, my brother!" he cried exuberantly. "It has been so long a time!"

Tenney's eyes lighted up a moment and then they became somber. "It sure enough has been a long time," he said. "More than five years."

"But the pain of separation is always dissipated by reunion," said Don Rafael. "Come, my cousin, we shall drink to this happy occasion." They stepped up to the bar and downed a shot of redeye apiece.

Then Don Rafael grinned at Tenney and said, "What brings you to these town, my son?"

"Why, to kill you, of course, Rafael," said Tenney softly.

Don Rafael grinned easily. "I was afraid you had some such foolhardy notion in mind," he said. Then he shrugged. "Since I am to be the recipient of these great honor," he went on, "will you tell me when it is to be?" He stepped back and his eyes were alert, but his right hand made no move toward his hip.

"Why, that's up to you, Rafael," said Tenney. "Whenever you go for your gun."

"But I love you, my son," said Don Rafael. "What makes you think I would draw a weapon in anger against the best friend I ever had?"

"Because," said Tenney evenly, "you're plenty impatient, Rafael —impatient and nervous. In addition to which, you're curious. You've always wondered whether or not you could beat me to the draw."

"That is true. That is true," admitted Don Rafael. "But my curiosity has its limits. It does not extend to the point of killing you, my son."

"Don't worry about me, pal," said Tenney. "It'll be your funeral."

"After which there'll be a barbecue and athletic contests for one and all," said Billy Feeney, licking his lips. Then he stared from one man to another. "Say, what kind of a gun fight is this?" he demanded. "Why doesn't somebody shoot somebody?"

"Don't be impatient, little man," said Tenney. Then he looked Don Rafael in the eye. "I just want my friend here to take all the time he needs to consider what it feels like to be locked up in prison for five years," he said.

"I have often considered it," said Don Rafael sadly. "It makes me shudder."

"You mean," said Billy Feeney virtuously to Tenney, "that you're a ex-convict?"

Tenney looked up at the ceiling and spoke in a musing manner. "Once," he said, "I was in partnership on a mining claim down California way. The claim wasn't paying off much to speak of and my partner got impatient. He took and robbed the bank of Angels Camp of ten thousand dollars——"

"Eight thousand," said Don Rafael, who was listening attentively.

"Well, you know how these banks always exaggerate their losses," said Tenney. "Anyway, a posse got red-hot on the heels of my partner and he had to ditch his loot."

"What," asked Bart McCormack greedily, "did he do with it?"

"I planted it on my son, my cousin, my dear friend, Tenney," said Don Rafael disconsolately. "I shall never forgive myself."

"Neither will I," Tenney told him glumly.

"But you must admit that the circumstances were extenuating," said Don Rafael defensively. "You they only gave five years. Me they would have hanged. Remember, my son, that these jury which tried you and would have tried me was made up of a most narrow-minded group of married men, some of whom were possessed of unreasonable suspicions concerning their most delightfully adorable little wives."

"That I know," admitted Tenney, with the air of a man who wishes to be fair in all things. "But still and all, Rafael, I think that five years of my life was a whole heaping lot too much for me to pay on account of you never could detect a wedding ring in the dark."

Then he turned as the saloon doors flew open and a yellow-haired girl, who at first glance seemed to be no more than sixteen, came running in, closely followed by Jim Jessup, the stagecoach driver. Tenney's left arm shot out and pulled the girl protectively toward him, and the right hand was just a blur as it snaked down and came up holding a six gun pointed at Jim Jessup's brisket.

"What kind of a man are you to come achasing of a little girl into a dump like this?" he asked reproachfully.

"I'm not a little girl, and you let me be!" said the girl vehemently, and she kicked vigorously at Tenney's shins.

Finally she broke loose from Tenney, and the rest of us got a good look at her. She was as pretty as a mustang colt in a spring pasture and there was a look in her eyes that made some of us decide that she was a great deal more than sixteen. Probably eighteen.

"I know who you are," she told Montana Martin. "I've heard a lot about your place and I want to go to work for you."

"Which, with all due respect to you, Montana," said Jim Jessup, "it's the most sinful thing I ever hear of. This here's Corabelle Larkin, from Red Gulch. I knew her parents, which they're now both deceased, and she's led the kind of sheltered life which, again with apologies to you, Montana, don't qualify her to be found dead in your place. I was taking her to O'Leary's Lapse, where she was to catch a train and go live with her aunt in the East, but when I stop here for passengers, she tells me she's gonna be a dance-hall girl and she busts away from me."

"My aunt hates me," declared the girl. "All she wants me for is to be her cook and housemaid. . . . Please, Miss Montana, let me work for you."

"And what kind of work do you think you could do for me?" asked Montana.

"I want to live and know life," said Corabelle. "I'm tired of leading a sheltered existence. I crave excitement. I can sing real good, Miss Montana, and I can dance like anything. Look." Then she went into a splayfooted dance like a yearling calf chasing its mother, and out of her lovely lips came the most awful sound you ever heard. Soon, by our expressions, she realized she wasn't going over with any noticeable bang. She stopped singing and her shoulders sagged and she didn't seem to be a day over seventeen.

"Well, anyway," she said despondently, "I'm young and willing. Isn't there anything I can do?"

Don Rafael stepped forward and bowed to her. "There is, indeed, things you can do," he said. "You cannot dance, but your walk is as graceful as a willow in the wind. You cannot sing, but your speaking voice is as caressing as the conversation of a dove. So you shall walk among us and talk to us and touch our hearts with tender emotions. We shall make you our queen and we shall drink vast quantities of redeye in your honor."

Corabelle stared at him, dubiously at first, and then her eyes lighted up and her lips parted. There was something in his dark gaze that fascinated, almost hypnotized her. Even when he confidently placed his arm around her waist and lifted her face for a kiss, she uttered but a slight gasp and made only a half-hearted attempt to free herself. Then Tenney Grant caught Don Rafael by the collar, hauled him away and smashed him to the floor with one blow of his fist. It was obvious that the Spaniard wouldn't be able to rise within any reasonable length of time.

"That," Tenney told him, "is one thing you don't have to be curious about, Rafael. You always did know I could lick you."

"With your fists, yes," said Don Rafael. Then his cocky grin returned. "But if you want these girl for your own," he said, "you shall have to employ your gun as a persuader. I love you, my son, and I do not wish to hurt you, but I must remind you that you're a jailbird and no fit company for so tender a pigeon as Miss Larkin."

"Will you please," said Tenney, fighting for self-control, "go for your gun right now, Rafael?"

Montana moved in, pushed Tenney aside; then turned to the now-frightened Corabelle. "Do you still want to be a dance-hall girl?" she demanded. "Do you want to have men fighting over you like this?"

"No," said Corabelle miserably.

"Then maybe we can talk business," said Montana. "I own the Primrose Café and Restaurant across the street. Minnie Redwing, my cook, has resigned. Do you want that job?"

And then Corabelle's eyes went dead and her dreams of becoming the reigning siren of the Western saloon circuit turned to ashes. "Yes," she said, "rather than live with my aunt."

It developed that Corabelle Larkin couldn't cook either. She turned out steaks as hard and juiceless as flagstones, and her biscuits would have defied the digestion of a rock crusher. Still she grew steadily in beauty, and males from miles around flocked into the Primrose Café and Restaurant to bask in her presence.

As the quality of the food deteriorated and their weakerstomached rivals fell by the wayside, Don Rafael and Tenney, who seemed to possess alimentary tracts that were immune to shock or damage, began to forge far to the front in the race for Corabelle's affections. They ate three meals a day at the café and, each in his own fashion, courted Corabelle.

Whereas Tenney spoke soberly to the girl of his plans to buy a ranch, install her on it and raise cattle, horses and children, in the order named, Don Rafael crooned to her a siren song of travel and excitement, of fine clothes and bright lights. At such times Corabelle would lean over the counter and her eyes would glitter, and it seemed that her dreams of yesterday had risen from their ashes and were walking about, phoenixlike, in the smoke of an incinerated beefsteak.

This caused some of us to decide that Don Rafael had a slight edge in the contest, but Corabelle—on the surface, at least—treated them with strict impartiality. She knew about the trouble between them and appeared fearful of doing anything to contribute to what we all considered would be the inevitable shooting showdown.

There were times when it appeared that the showdown was at hand. Tenney and Don Rafael would meet in the Chinaman's Chance and there would be a gesture or a word, and a hot look of sudden death would come into their eyes and we could hear the rustle of black wings as their hands hovered near their guns. Then, after a long, suspenseful moment, they would shrug and walk away from each other. Such was their arrogance and self-confidence that each disdained to make the first move. Montana Martin considered them shining examples of self-control and courage, but Billy Feeney, who was beginning to despair of ever tasting barbecue again, disagreed.

"I could be brave, too," he said, "if I had an enemy which I knew he wouldn't ever pull a gun on me."

After several more weeks and several more near showdowns between the two men, Don Rafael vanished into thin air one day just a half hour before a United States marshal hit town with a warrant having to do with the stickup of a stagecoach carrying Government mail. As time passed with no word of his rival's whereabouts, Tenney Grant began to make unexpectedly rapid progress in his courtship of Corabelle. There was no longer a faraway, heedless look in her eyes as he discussed the land he was about to buy.

Instead she listened with interest and anticipation, and hers was the serene expression of a woman who had just about decided in favor of a soberly reliable rancher at hand against the dubious attractions of a long-gone road agent in the bush.

She did not, however, make her decision known to Tenney until that day when Chuckawalla Johnnie, a half-breed Comanche Indian hit town. Chuckawalla got himself full of tequila, mescal, redeye and a quart of hair tonic he stole from the general store, then went into the Primrose Café and Restaurant for lunch. After staring for some time at Corabelle out of beady black eyes, and deciding that she was far more appetizing than anything on the menu, he made what was for him an unprecedentedly generous gesture. He reached into the bosom of his dingy shirt and withdrew his most-prized possession—the dried scalp of a tribal enemy he had slain in battle—and, with the air of one bestowing priceless pearls, offered it to the girl as a token of his esteem.

Corabelle's resultant scream of horror and indignation unnerved the hitherto-well-intentioned redskin. That, plus the fact that he had partaken of a drop too much hair tonic, caused him to behave in a rash and impetuous manner. He seized Corabelle by the hair, dragged her over the counter, slung her across the back of his saddleless pony and bore her off for obscure and unstated purposes of his own.

Tenney Grant, who was riding into town from the opposite direction, wheeled his horse as they passed him in a screaming cloud of dust, and gave chase. He caught them a mile down the road, hauled Chuckawalla off the horse, disarmed him of three knives and a pistol, then beat him to within an inch of his life. Then he turned to look for Corabelle just as, with a glad cry, the girl flung herself into his arms.

While Chuckawalla writhed on the ground like a broken-backed rattler and uttered horribly obscene threats of vengeance against Tenney, Corabelle clung to her rescuer and muttered tender words of undying gratitude and affection. Then, all of a sudden, she pushed Tenney away from her and glanced beseechingly at him out of tear-filled eyes.

"Oh, Tenney!" she cried. "I do love you and I want to marry you, but first I've got a confession to make! I've betrayed you, darling! I'm a wicked woman!"

"Which, if you're a wicked woman, there's not a good one alive," said Tenney stanchly. "But nobody, not even you, will ever make me believe that you ever did anything that any angel wouldn't do in a big church before a large congregation at high noon on Easter Sunday. In the presence of a bishop," he added, by way of clinching the argument.

"No angel," said the overwrought girl tearfully, "ever kissed Don Rafael de Soto behind Pott Barr's livery stable at two o'clock in the morning, but I did."

"Which I agree with you," said Tenney unhappily. "I can't imagine an angel associating with Don Rafael anyplace at any time. But how come you didn't inform me of this state of affairs, Corabelle? It's bad enough that I gotta kill Rafael one of these days, without me standing here in the presence of Chuckawalla Johnnie akissing of his girl."

"But I'm not his girl!" insisted Corabelle.

"You mean you only kissed him once?" asked Tenney hopefully, apparently under the impression that initiation doesn't constitute lifetime membership in the lodge.

"Several times," confessed the girl, hanging her head. "At nights, when everybody was asleep and there wasn't anyone to see or hear, Rafael'd come to my window with a mandolin and serenade me. I'd close the window and put my fingers in my ears, but I couldn't shut out the sound and, before I knew it, I'd be walking with him in the moonlight. Then he'd talk like he oughtn't to and I'd listen like I shouldn't of, and then he'd put his arms around me and do what he had no right to, and I'd hate myself for letting him do it." She winced at the hurt look in Tenney's eyes. "But I didn't want to do it," she declared. "The reason I hated myself so much, darling, was that all the time I knew I was falling in love with you."

"You sure enough took a left-handed way of demonstrating your affection," said Tenney glumly. "I suppose when you were kissing me awhile back, you were hating yourself for doing it, on account of you're in love with Rafael."

"It isn't that way at all!" said Corabelle frantically. "I don't love Rafael and I never did. It's just that he excites me in spite of myself; he brings out everything that's bad in me and, oh, Tenney, darling, you'd be surprised how much bad there's in me when he's around."

"In which case," said Tenney after some reflection, "I guess there's only one thing to do. I'll just go find Rafael and kill him a little bit, and then he won't bother you any more."

"No! No!" said Corabelle, terrified. "'You can't kill what's bad in me by shooting Rafael!"

"You aren't," said Tenney, aghast, "suggesting that I shoot you, are you, Corabelle?"

"No, you stupid darling," she said, laughing and crying. "All you have to do is to marry me. Right now. Before it's too late."

"You mean," said Tenney joyfully, "that it ain't too late?"

Then she went into his arms again, and there was something so pristine in her maidenly kiss that all of Tenney's fears were put to rout. Leaving Chuckawalla Johnnie sitting on the ground, spitting out teeth, threats and curses, the two got on Tenney's horse, rode to O'Leary's Lapse and were married by a preacher.

Later on, Tenney showed up at the Chinaman's Chance, bought drinks for the house and then publicly granted amnesty to Don Rafael de Soto. "You can send word to him that I absolve him of the wrong he did me in Angels Camp five years ago," he announced, "and tell him that he need no longer live in fear of my vengeance. Unless," he added, "he ever comes skulking around my premises with a mandolin, in which case I'll kill him a whole heaping hatful."

Shortly after Corabelle and Tenney established themselves on a ranch at the edge of town, Don Rafael de Soto returned to Buffalo Bend. He came swaggering into the Chinaman's Chance, ordered a drink and stood at the bar as nonchalant as if he didn't have a worry in the world.

"Don't you know that they's a United States marshal looking for you?" Billy Feeney asked him.

"He found me," said Don Rafael, with a satisfied grin. Then he tossed onto the bar a gold badge that had been neatly perforated through the center by a bullet.

"In which case the United States Government is sure to be plenty petulant at you for killing one of its servants," said Montana.

"You'd better hit the trail, Don Rafael, before the cavalry gets here."

"All in good time," said Don Rafael composedly. "First I must felicitate my friend, Tenney, on his marriage to the adorable Corabelle."

"So you know about that, do you?" asked Montana.

"I rode by their place on the way in," said Don Rafael. "Unfortunately, Tenney was not there, but Corabelle told me with her own lovely lips. I must add," he went on arrogantly, "that there was a slight note of tender regret in her voice when she broke the news."

"And I know why," said Montana. "So, if there's one spark of decency in that carcass of yours, you'll shove off, Don Rafael."

"And if I do," said Don Rafael, shrugging, "will her feeling for me have been erased?"

"I don't know," sighed Montana. "There's something about you that's——" Then she glared at him. "Don Rafael," she demanded, "did you say or do anything to that child that someday, in a moment of weakness, might make her want to follow you?"

"Who knows?" said Don Rafael, grinning. Then he turned and his face lighted up. "Tenney, my cousin!" he cried.

Tenney had entered the saloon and was standing in a patch of sunshine coming through a window at his rear—a perfect target in the otherwise dimly lighted room.

Don Rafael advanced a few steps toward him and paused. "I wish to congratulate you on your so happy marriage," he announced.

"Thank you," said Tenney, "and I aim to keep it that way, Rafael. So please don't make me draw my gun on you. It'd sure enough upset Corabelle a whole heap."

"Corabelle," said Don Rafael, "has a heart of utmost tenderness and I love her. That is why I am so happy that you have decided not to make it necessary for me to kill you. I merely wish to shake hands with you, son, and then I shall depart."

He held out his hand, and Tenney grinned and stepped forward with his own hand extended. Then Don Rafael seemed to coil like a snake and his hand flashed down toward his gun and two shots rang out. It's still a matter of dispute as to who fired first, but it was Don Rafael who sank slowly to the floor and it was Tenney Grant who stood over him with a smoking gun in his fist.

"You always were curious, Rafael," said Tenney regretfully. "Now you know."

"Yes," said Don Rafael weakly, but still grinning, "now I know."

"I'm sure enough sorry," said Tenney.

"Don't worry, son," said Don Rafael. "It's my funeral."

Then Corabelle came running into the saloon and threw herself into Tenney's arms.

Afterward some of us decided that, although the majority of the tears she shed were from relief at Tenney's safety, at least a few of them were for the glittering, forbidden dream that died with Don Rafael de Soto.

Tenney led Corabelle away and Billy Feeney stared down at Don Rafael's body. "Which I never seen such a treacherous act in my life and it sure enough serves you right," he said unctuously. Then he smacked his lips in anticipation. "Well, I guess I'll go get things ready for the barbecue," he said and started away.

"You'd better make it a double-header," remarked Bud Conyears. "You'll find another corpse just outside that window, Billy."

Billy ran to the window and, sure enough, there was another body on the ground outside. It was Chuckawalla Johnnie, and there was a loaded shotgun at his side.

"Which, Don Rafael wasn't shooting at Tenney Grant none whatsoever," said Bud. "He saw that shotgun apoking through the window and his bullet was for Chuckawalla, which the unprincipled heathen was aiming to blow Tenney's head off behind his back."

Montana Martin leaned on the bar and wept gently for some time. Then she raised her tear-streaked face and said, "The drinks are on the house, boys—in honor of the finest Castilian gentleman that ever stuck up a stagecoach."

TEST BY TORTURE
by *Williams Forrest*

The American trapper, one of the tough, solitary mountain men, had come out of the foothills of the Sierra Madre in old Mexico onto the dun-gray plain. It was summer, 1839. He walked his brown horse, lounging in the saddle, his two pack horses nodding on their ropes. His face was clean-shaven and seemed old. His eyes were a clear frowning blue and were squinted. He seemed born to the saddle, and he showed no discomfort under the deep, unbroken heat. With a manner almost indolent, he headed his horse toward the hut of plaited wood and mud. The Mexican pastor, or sheepherder, and his Indian-boy helper were squatting beside the hut, preparing supper. The sheep, numbering over two thousand according to the calculation of the mountain man, were spread over the plain, the intelligent dogs caring for them.

The pastor stood up from his heels when the horseman drew close. The door of the jacal, a piece of skin, was pulled back over a peg, and just inside the hut was a ewe suckling a pup. The ewe came outside and toward the flock, the pup following hurriedly, already learning its trade. The Mexican peered out with great dark eyes from under his sombrero. His face was the gentle, brooding one of the pastor of sheep, and silence, mystery and poverty were smooth depths in the brown skin. The Apache boy stood straight and tense. His rank black hair was visible below his hat. He was short of leg, thick in the chest, like his people. He looked strong but oddly cowed.

"Good day, señor," said the pastor in Spanish.

Without answering, the mountain man dismounted, unsaddled and unpacked his horses, rubbed their backs where heat and pressure had made them itch; then he hobbled them to graze.

"Boy," he said to the Apache, "water my horses." He spoke in Apache.

The boy ran for water and a container. The mountain man sat cross-legged several feet from the fire.

The pastor looked at him. "I would be honored, señor, if you would have supper."

The mountain man laughed to himself; when he was asquatting here, everything was his that he wanted, and to offer it to him was a droll formality.

While he ate, the Apache boy watched in wonder. This man was like an Apache. He did not eat, he gorged. The Mexican stood close by, with the mien of a frightened servant. This great man ate as if food contained in a bowl formed by the desert horizons and the mountains would not be enough. There was something so fierce about the way he ate that it gave a man fears.

The mountain man was served tortillas, goat's milk, mutton and peppers. He ate and belched. Grease was on his chin. When he was finally finished, he spread the grease on his face and rubbed it in, easing the tight, sun-drenched skin. Then he demanded entertainment. His voice was so loud that the Mexican stepped back as if the wind of it was pushing him and the sound of it was breaking something thin in his ears. He shook his head over and over, the sombrero waggling. He was too intimidated to be able to entertain.

The mountain man roared, "Get your bijuela! Do you not know I am your guest?"

"Sí, sí," said the Mexican.

He scurried to the jacal. He returned with the giant jew's-harp that the mountain man knew that most pastors had. Night was coming. The sheep made a soft sound as if they walked and chewed on their own scraggly wool. A sudden current of air came from the mountains, broken as if by rocks and their heat. The Mexican began to play the soft music of the lonely pastor, the shepherds' songs that dwelt on plains high and low for those who followed the slow passage of the flocks.

The mountain man wept. Unashamedly, huge sobs clicked and snapped in his throat. The Apache boy stared at him incredulously. Apaches could not, would not cry. And yet, this man did not do it like a woman. There was something big, awesome about his lusty freedom to weep. Puzzled, the boy watched him, and wondered. Night capped the world. At last the songs stopped. . . .

In the morning, the mountain man asked. "What is your name, boy?"

"I am called Tuzimo."

The mountain man was looking out over the flock—the scrub sheep, lean, patient, enduring. "You are a slave, Tuzimo."

"*Sí.*" The boy's mouth grew tight. No Apache would be here otherwise.

"How long have you been in slavery, Tuzimo?"

"This I do not know, señor."

"Try to think about it," said the big man.

The dark, sharp eyes of the boy gazed at the mountains. Then he said, "I have been here four times."

The mountain man nodded. "And have you worked with the sheep all the time of your slavery?"

"*Sí.*"

"Then you have been a slave for four years. You have come here for the summer pasture four times."

"*Sí*"

In a softened voice, the mountain man said, "You are free. I will take you with me. An Apache must be free."

Tuzimo made no sign of gratitude, but he stepped eagerly closer, was offered a stirrup and mounted behind. The pastor rushed forward, so agitatedly that his hat fell into the dust. Words of protest were jumbled on his thick lips.

The mountain man laughed into the gaping face of the Mexican. "An Apache must be free!" cried the mountain man. "God made it that way! He put it in 'em! Waagh!" he cried suddenly, in the way of mountain men, who loved the fierce epithet of the bear. "Waagh!" And then he howled like a coyote, and the frightened sheep milled and poured outward from the shape they had been kept in by the pastor and his dogs. The pastor looked up at the big man and around over his shoulder at his charges. With a small cry, he got up and ran to mold his sheep again in the compliant wieldy form.

Hours later, the horses lifted their heads, whinnied. The mountains kept them down to a walk. Tuzimo, too, could smell water after a while. Near the spring the mountain man paused beside an anthill, and his laugh sounded like ripping skin. He let the horses go to water, but rationed them. When the horses were satisfied, he himself drank. Then he made a motion that permitted the boy to drink.

The mountain man scratched and cursed, speaking his first words for the afternoon. He made camp, then stripped. He laid his clothes over the anthill. He told Tuzimo to take off his clothes and throw them away. Then he led him to the anthill.

"Lie down on that anthill, Tuzimo," he said.

Without question, Tuzimo did as he was told. The mountain man stuffed bits of cloth into his ears. "Hold your nose," he said; "breathe through your teeth."

Tuzimo did as he was bidden; and, on his own, closed his eyes as tightly as he could. The agony started at once—slow, exquisite. He forced himself to lie still, ancient memories clothed his flesh with endurance. In his mind he saw a young man with a quiet face. Was it his older brother? And his leg had had to be cut off. He spoke of good hunting while it was done. And his face was calm.

The mountain man stood over the boy. "The ants will get all the lice," he said. "Right now they're taking millions of 'em from your hair."

Tuzimo did not permit himself to ask himself a question. When would the big man tell him he could stand up? Tribal memory was wrought in him, as if his teaching had never been interrupted. No tears came to his eyes, no sound from his lips. He remembered how it had been when he cried before he was captured by the Mexicans and made a slave by the patron who owned so many sheep; he remembered the taste of the animal skin that had muffled his cries and caught his tears. He had learned not to cry. It was better not to than to be suffocated. He had learned that an Apache boy who could not learn to be brave stood a good chance of dying in the folds of the skin held over his face.

"Get up, Tuzimo."

He did so, but he did not yelp and prance. Needles were in his body. His flesh screamed for him silently. Now, when he saw a man spread-eagled on an anthill, he would be able to enjoy that man's sensations. He smiled inside himself. He could see various Mexicans lying on anthills.

"Come here, Tuzimo." The mountain man rubbed him with whisky. The needles grew red hot. He tasted blood in his mouth, where he had bitten the tongue that wished to make an outcry. A hateful tongue, that would try to defy and dishonor him.

"See, Tuzimo, what I have made for you."

While he had stood still savoring his bravery, feeling the pain absorbed into a deep dark sense of well-being, the big man had been at work with knife and a strip of skin. And now Tuzimo had a clout, sewn in back on a strip of hide that circled his waist and could be tied; and then he drew the long oblong of skin under his crotch and looped it over the strip in front below his navel, and let it hang down.

They had supper of jerky, piki and coffee. Dark circled the stones and grew up over them. The mountains slipped away. The fire of mesquite wood burned slow. The mountain man tossed Tuzimo a blanket.

For several hours before they camped the next night, Tuzimo knew that the mountain man was reading sign. He was reading all the messages that animals or people left on the trail as they passed; messages that sometimes were so slight that only the most wise could find them; and certainly the sign of people had been read this time, otherwise the mountain man would not have seemed to care so much.

When they camped, no fire was built. But Tuzimo did not ask any questions, and no answers were plainly offered to him. They ate jerked beef and washed it down with a few swallows of water. They slept; the mountain man lightly, partly listening as he slept, and Tuzimo was listening with him, not knowing what for. The horses made scraping sounds nearby. The wind was dead. There was a musty smell of stones. The earth was glowing black and dusty, and the brush did not creak.

What had the mountain man seen? What made him restless? Tuzimo wondered and wished he himself could have read the knowledge that the land told to the mountain man. Tuzimo wished to be a great Apache, and to read sign was an important part of such a thing. There was more also, of course; there was fore-knowledge—to know what would happen. Visions, for example, were highly prized among the Apaches. People were expected to have them, but few did. And visions were easily believed in. Everyone wished to feel that they were true. And, remembering his Apache training, Tuzimo felt it was right so to wish. In the world there was much magic—anyone who was a nomad knew that; anyone who lived in the deserts and mountains, wild, free and under the stars. As a matter of fact, had it not been magic that the mountain man, a strange being, had come and rescued him, Tuzimo, from slavery? No one could deny that. Tuzimo nodded to himself on his bed of earth and blanket. Surely the great spirit had decided to do well for him.

Tuzimo considered and felt himself happy. After four years, a good and significant thing had happened. And, at length, in the dark stillness, he felt himself drifting away; and before night closed fully behind his lids, he wondered if the mountain man had read sign of Apaches who had passed. So wonderful this would be. His people nearby somewhere. What other people would have passed here, especially those that would make a great mountain man so careful that he did not make a supper fire?

Serene, Tuzimo slept, holding close his last thought, sleeping fearlessly, for, after all, he, too, was an Apache. He was a Coyotero Apache, of the people who believed in the coyote as a creature that could bring fine, pleasant messages. And he remembered, dimly, in a mist, in beginning sleep, that the mountain man had made the call of the coyote—and was this not a sign of its own, and an important one? The mountain man had done so as he carried Tuzimo away from the sheepherder. Yes, truly, it was a sign.

In his sleep, the boy found a coyote nearby. He heard the sound of its panting breath. He looked into its gleaming eyes and a vision came about.

His people were following the coyote, and he was among them. His people were hungry and were stumbling. Only he among them was strong. He ran beside the coyote and admonished him gently to wait for his people, who could not go so quickly. The coyote listened to him, which made the other Apaches murmur with approval and wonder. All through a dark night they followed

Tuzimo and the coyote. The eyes of the animal were the only light in the darkness. The eyes were like fires.

At dawn they were coming down from a hill and the coyote began to run. Tuzimo did not call to him now to slow down, because it was not necessary. The coyote was herding a flock of sheep toward the hill. Tuzimo thanked him. The coyote dragged down a lamb and began to devour it. With shouts of joy, the Apaches took out their knives and fell on the sheep. They had a mighty feast that lasted a long time. No one could tell how many days passed. And soon the plain had no more sheep. Even the blood was gone. And everybody was smiling. And they said Tuzimo was a leader and would be the chief of the band. And where the sheep had been killed, beautiful grass grew and a stream sprang from the ground. Great white and black horses came to graze and were captured. And then there were Mexican men to be killed, and women and children to take away as captives. The Apaches all knew that there would be other raids, and Tuzimo would lead them, always knowing where to go. His visions would make the band powerful and wealthy, and none of the Apaches would die.

In the morning, Tuzimo said steadfastly, "I had a vision. In this vision I was with my people."

"You had a true vision," said the mountain man. "Soon you will be with your people."

"You will take me to them?"

"In front of you there is a ridge. You will cross the ridge and walk to the west. It would be better if you ran, for the faster you go, the sooner you will be with your people."

Tuzimo looked long at the mountain man, and the big man recognized the heavy dark skin, the broad line of the chin, the rank jet hair, the big chest and the short, wiry thighs—Apache—and he understood the long look, without gratitude or friendliness, but touched with a certain admiration and even superstition—Apache.

Then the boy could not help but say, "I do not know why you have helped me."

The mountain man was surprised. An Apache would not have ordinarily asked. He looked closely at the boy. And he was embarrassed. "God believes this, this ol' hoss thinks: that men or children shouldn't be slaves. Do you know God?"

Solemnly, Tuzimo nodded. "I was sent to a mission school."

The mountain man smiled. "Good. It is good. There is a Christian word—compassion. It is to be kind and gentle, but bravely. In a man's way."

Tuzimo stiffened. He had despised the soft God of the Christians.

"Not only the Mexicans have slaves," said the mountain man; "we have also. Boy, remember compassion!"

Tuzimo did not know; he did not look at his benefactor.

"Go," said the mountain man.

The boy stood on the ridge, turned and waved. The big man waved back. The boy ran westward, disappearing over the ridge. And the mountain man began to work swiftly. He must obscure his trail, if possible.

Soon he was on his way. He did not regret his bravado in releasing the Apache from slavery and then sighting him toward the band that could not be many hours away across the ridge. Bravado was his second and toughest skin. It was better than whisky. It was the mark of the free man, who must exploit his very freedom in order to preserve his own sense of it. But he hurried. Once, a long time ago, he had trusted Apaches, but he no longer could. The reason was that they could no longer trust men like him; too many of their "friends" had massacred them; Apaches hated you if you stole from them—their territory or freedom—and they fought back with such cruelty that there was big bounty on their scalps.

So big—a hundred dollars for a man, fifty for a woman, and twenty-five for a child—that many men who had liked them now became greedy. He felt the justice of his present danger. And he hurried. He had no hope that Tuzimo would plead for him; nor had he dishonored himself by requesting secrecy. Nowadays, an Apache would even kill her who suckled him, if she was not Apache.

Tuzimo ran limberly, bent-kneed, almost crouching, yet with his thin, strong back straight. Because of his youth he had not been softened by the years of floating with the sheep, the misty, somber, steady grazing over the arid miles. His spirits were high, and, in fact, he felt that a spirit greater than himself was guiding him.

He had been observed for some time now without knowing it. He was moving through a canyon when a warrior stepped from behind a rock and fell in beside him. Tuzimo did not falter with surprise or fear, and the warrior made a sound of approval. On the western side of the canyon he was led north, and soon he came to the camp of his people. Word of his approach had preceded him. Curious women and children were standing in front of the tepees, watching him silently. Ahead of him, as he slowed to a walk, was a tall, haughty man with a long blade-like nose, a red rag around his head. As Tuzimo approached, men fell in around him, and he felt strangely lost in the pungent smell of his race that he had all but forgotten.

Tuzimo would never forget the next half hour. At first it was difficult for him; he was prodded and pushed when he could not fluently explain himself, where he had come from and why. He tried to tell his story in Apache and could not. The leader began to speak to him in Spanish, and seemed to look upon him kindly. The leader stood with his legs wide, his nearly knee-length moccasins curled over at the top. He wore a dirty white blouse and a dirty loincloth. Beside him stood a short, blunt-faced man wearing a tall black hat. There were red ribbons on the ends of his black braids. He was the shaman, or priest, of the band.

Tuzimo told about the mountain man, and then said that he had had a vision, that he would lead his people to much food. He was not laughed at and the hungry people crowded around him.

The men patted him on the shoulder as he spoke. Would there be horses, they asked, in this place where he would lead them? And although the herder he had left had not had a horse, Tuzimo replied that there would be horses. His vision had told him so. How many men would there be, he was asked. He said there would be a few men, not just one, and some would be old and some would be young. He said that the number of sheep would be enough to cover a large plain. He said there would be women and children.

They nodded and thought about this. He could tell that they were hungry and also that they wished war. He blazed with inner excitement, but did his best not to let them see it.

He said, almost unthinking, "I think it is the white man who has made this possible."

But they grumbled and prodded him, and the short man with the tall hat said, "He is an enemy, a white eye, and must be killed. Perhaps he will lead troops to us and they will kill us all."

Tuzimo shook his head. "He would not do that."

The short one exclaimed, "The Pinda Lick-O-Yi, the white eyes, will do anything." And somberly he spoke to the young one as he would to a man. It was required. Oftentimes the young ones had visions that were sacred, and people like the Apaches, who depended so much on providence, could not overlook such boons.

"The white eyes have forked tongues," said the short one. "We come from New Mexico. Our white and Mexican friends invited us to a feast. We ate and felt very good. And then they led us to a courtyard and told us to take all we wished of fine goods. And as we went to the pile of these goods, they fired a cannon into our midst. We died—our men, women and children. In the cannon were all manner of things. All manner of scraps and iron, and it exploded, and we died. And we are left, hungry and ready for revenge against all. For are not all against the Apaches?"

The short one said then, "We will follow Tuzimo. We will follow the white eye, too, and meet on the plain, with the sheep."

The tall leader said, "Wait. Tuzimo shall speak. It is his vision."

Tuzimo wanted to protest against the shaman, but something else covered it and he did not, and he said nothing. It could prove him more of an Apache, after four years with the Mexicans, if he could listen to the mountain man's cries under torture and not say anything. And it would prove him, too, as a judge of men, if his brave mountain man remained silent. He knew that among his people it was good to torture; it proved how weak were your enemies, and it showed you how high and bright could be the courage of man. There was no finer thing than to torture weaklings and feel contempt for them or torture the strong man and feel the wish to be as valiant as he.

"We go," said the leader.

There were thirty warriors in the band, and sixty women and children. Ten warriors stayed with the women and children, and a rendezvous was planned for a point farther south in the mountains, where a great number of sheep could be placed and grazed. The remainder of the warriors and Tuzimo set off for the camp where Tuzimo had spent the second night with the mountain man.

Traces of the morning fire were there, and the warriors searched for sign of the direction the mountain man had taken. The short one led a party of trackers after the mountain man. The others went on.

Tuzimo had a supreme confidence. Here he was leading brave armed warriors to food and a small war. Surely the vision would not be false, and all this taken from him and scorn put in its place. Logic told him that they would find the pastor and the flock, and nothing more. But logic mattered little in the face of a vision.

The day was late when, after a steady march, in the light and dark of two days, they came to the jacal. The warriors fanned out and looked around. They went on, following the flock. They came upon it in the dark, seeing the campfire. Around the fire they saw several shapes of men. They heard the nickering of a horse. Tuzimo was happy. He was allowed to wait beside the chief for the sacred hours of the dark to pass. The hours in which you could not attack because they belonged to the beloved dead. And when the sun rose, he ran forward with his Apaches and helped capture the pastor and others.

Tuzimo recognized the men: there was the vaquero, the rider, who was in charge of Tuzimo's pastor and several other pastors; there was another of the pastors who worked for the same patron; there was the caporal who was in charge of the range, and with him were his three armed guards. In the wagon, there were the caporal's two smallest children and the old woman who took care of them; and then there was the caporal's wife and his oldest daughter, who was thirteen. Undoubtedly, the caporal had been on his way to the hacienda of the patron, and was taking his family with him, as he had twice before in Tuzimo's memory.

All were captured without firing a shot, although one of the guards had been stabbed and was on the ground dying. Now the weapons were all in the hands of the Apaches, along with four horses, two oxen, three burros and two flocks of sheep numbering about four thousand. The captives were bound and left on the ground while the Apaches gorged themselves on mutton.

In the late afternoon, the short one and his men arrived, leading the mountain man with a rawhide cord about his neck; the short one was riding the brown horse. The mountain man was staked out with Tuzimo's pastor, stripped. Small slow fires were built near their heads. The other men who were still alive were bound to the wheels of the wagon, heads down, and fires were built under their heads. Soon they would be skinned alive, and as they fought the pain, they would scream and push their heads into the fire.

"Wait!" cried the mountain man. "Tuzimo, come here!"

Curiously, the boy stood above him. With contempt and shame, he waited for a plea of mercy or friendship.

But then the mountain man said, "You do know of God?"

"He is not my God."

"Then do you know this?" said the mountain man, and he tugged against his bonds and pushed himself against the fire, so that his hair flamed. Without rancor, without sign of pain, in the tradition of bravery of the Apache itself, the mountain man held his head as close to the fire as he could.

He said, "Tuzimo, I do this not for myself. But for the others. Waagh!" he cried, but grinned on the pain. "I have brought this on them. Tuzimo, if I am brave, will you try to release the others, as I did you? Waagh!" he cried, and laughed, as the torment was hot and brutal. "Waagh, are you enough, chile, to do that?"

Tuzimo watched the long hair of the mountain man burn. He saw the eyes, open and steady and unafraid. He felt the eyes on him. And a strange sympathetic fire burned in him.

And suddenly he cared about an enemy as well as about a member of his own race—and the white mountain man was said to be his enemy—and he kicked the fire away from the mountain man's head.

"Do not!" cried the short man. "Do not!" and tried to kick the fire back where it had been. And Tuzimo fought him.

Somber, the tall chief came. "Tuzimo. Tuzimo." The boy stood erect and steady. "You will speak," said the chief.

"I have a friend," said Tuzimo fiercely. "The white eye. It is my thought that all will be bad for us if he and the others die. I will fight for him," he said stanchly.

The chief looked on him long. He looked at the sheep and the other goods—the horses, the wagon, to which Tuzimo had led them—and these were magnificent things and Tuzimo must be respected.

He nodded at length. He said, "We have heard true words from you before; we will not say these are untrue. The prisoners will be released."

Night. The mountain man was gone, and the Mexicans. The Apaches were eating mutton around the fires. Tuzimo was lying, sleeping-awake, on the ground, in the face of the stars.

Hi-yah, he thought, and a happiness as deep and as wide as the sky filled him, and was mysterious. He had released enemies from torture, and yet he felt mighty. *I, Tuzimo,* he thought, *felt compassion, but brave—in the way of a man.* And now he knew it would always be so.

THE MARRIAGE OF MOON WIND
by Bill Gulick

It was their last night on the trail. Off to the northeast the jagged, snowcapped peaks of the Wind River Mountains loomed tall against the darkening sky and the chill, thin air of the uplands was spiced with the pungent smell of sage and pine. But Tad Marshall was not interested in sights or smells at the moment. A rangy, well-put-together young man of twenty with curly golden hair and sharp blue eyes, he leaned forward and spoke to the grizzled ex-trapper sitting on the far side of the fire.

"You'll fix it for me?"

"I'll try," Buck Owens said grudgingly. "But don't hold me to blame for nothin' that happens. Like I told you before, Slewfoot Samuels eats greenhorns raw."

"He takes a bite out of me, he'll come down with the worst case of colic he ever had."

"You're cocky enough, I will say that."

"Don't mean to be. It's just that I come west to be a beaver trapper, not a mule tender."

"With the knack you got fer handlin' mules, Captain Sublette won't want to lose you. He hears about this scheme you got to partner up with Slewfoot, he'll have a foamin' fit."

Tad shook his head. He liked Sublette and was real grateful for this chance to come west, but he wanted to see a chunk of the world with no dust-raising pack train clouding his view.

"Sublette can just have his fit. Me, I don't intend to go back to Missouri for a long spell."

"What're you runnin' away from—a mean pa?"

"Why, no. Pa treated me good."

"The law, maybe? You killed somebody back home?"

"Nothin' like that."

"Jest leaves one thing, then. Did you have woman trouble?"

Tad ran embarrassed fingers through his hair. "Guess you could call it that. There was three gals got the notion I was engaged to marry 'em. They all had brothers with itchy trigger fingers."

"Three gals wanted to marry you all to oncet?" Buck said in open admiration. "How'd that happen?"

"Darned if I know. Women have always pestered me, seems like. Now tell me some more about Slewfoot. You trapped with him for five years, you say?"

"Yeah. That's all I could stand him. Got a right queer sense of humor, Slewfoot has."

"A bit of joshin' never hurt nobody. I'll take the worst he can dish out, grin and come back for more."

"An' if you can't take it," Buck said, a gleam coming into his faded old eyes, "you'll stay with the mules like me'n' the captain wants you to do?"

"Sure."

"Fine! I'll introduce you to Slewfoot tomorrow."

The word got around. During the half day it took the fur brigade to reach rendezvous grounds in the lush, grass-rich valley of the Green River, the men gossiped and grinned amongst themselves, and their attitude riled Tad.

Greenhorn though he was, Tad had learned considerable during the trip out from St. Louis. There were several kinds of trappers, he'd discovered. Some worked for wages and some for commissions, but the elite of the trade were the free trappers—men who roamed where they pleased, sold their furs to the highest bidder and were beholden to nobody.

Usually such men worked in pairs, but Slewfoot, who'd been queer to begin with, and was getting queerer every year, did his trapping with no other company than a Shoshone squaw he'd bought some years back. Campfire talk had it that Indian war parties rode miles out of their way to avoid him; she grizzly bears scared their cubs into behaving by mentioning his name; and beavers, when they heard he was in the neighborhood, simply crawled up on the creek banks and died.

None of which scared Tad. But it did make him look forward

with considerable interest to meeting the man whose partner he hoped to be.

Shortly before noon they hit Green River and made camp. Already the valley was full of company men, free trappers and Indians from many tribes, come in from every corner of the West for a two-week carnival of trading, gambling, drinking, horse racing and fighting. Tad took it all in with keen, uncritical eyes. But other eyes in the party looked on with far less tolerance.

Traveling with the brigade that year was a minister named Thomas Rumford, a tall, hollow-cheeked, solemn-visaged man who was returning to a mission he had established some years earlier among the Nez Perce Indians, out Oregon way. Parson Rumford had made no bones of the fact that he disapproved of the language and personal habits of the mule tenders, and he liked even less the behavior of the celebrating trappers. While Tad was helping unload the mules, Parson Rumford came up, a reproachful look on his face.

"My boy, what's this I hear about your becoming a trapper?"

"Well, I was sort of figuring on it."

"Do you know what kind of man Slewfoot Samuels is?"

"Tell me he's some ornery. But I reckon I can put up with him."

Parson Rumford shook his head and stalked away. Feeling a shade uncomfortable, Tad finished unloading the mules. Then he saw Captain Sublette approaching, and the amused twinkle in Sublette's dark eyes made him forget the minister.

"Met your trapping partner yet?"

"No. Buck's takin' me over soon as we get through here."

"Well, the least I can do is wish you luck."

"Thank you kindly, captain."

"And remind you that your mule-tending job will be waiting, in case things don't work out."

Feeling more and more edgy, Tad joined Buck and they threaded their way toward the Shoshone section of camp.

"Lived with that squaw so long he's more Injun than white," Buck explained. "Even thinks like an Injun."

"I'd as soon you hadn't told everybody in camp what I was figuring to do. They're layin' bets, just like it was a dog fight."

"Well, you got my sympathy. Slewfoot's got a knack fer figgerin' out the one thing best calculated to rile a man. Goes fer a fella's weak spot, you might say. What's yourn?"

"Don't know that I got one."

"Mine's rattlesnakes. Slewfoot shore made my life miserable, once he found that out." Buck shivered. "Kind of gives a man a turn wakin' up from a peaceable nap to find a five-foot rattler lyin' on his chest—even if it is dead."

"Slewfoot done that to you?"

"Yeah, an' then near laughed himself to death."

They stopped in front of a tepee where a squat, red-headed trapper in greasy buckskins sat dozing in the shade, and Buck nodded his head. "Thar he is. Ain't he a specimen?"

Before Tad could make much of a visual appraisal, Slewfoot Samuels opened his eyes. Tad got something of a shock. One eye was green, the other black, and they were as badly crossed as a pair of eyes could be. Slewfoot glared up in Buck's general direction, took a swig out of the jug of whisky sheltered between his crossed legs and spat.

"Howdy, Buck. This is the greenhorn you're figgerin' on palmin' off on me?"

"This is him. Name's Tad Marshall."

"Sit," Slewfoot grunted.

They sat and Buck reached for the jug. Slewfoot extended his right hand to Tad. "Shake."

Tad gave Slewfoot his hand, which Slewfoot promptly tried to crush into jelly. Half expecting such a stunt and having a muscle or two of his own, Tad gave just about as good as he got, and they let go with the first engagement pretty much a draw. Slewfoot took the jug away from Buck.

"Drink, Tad? Or have you been weaned from milk yet?"

Tad raised the jug to his lips, held it there while his Adam's apple bobbed six times, then passed it back. "Been watered some, ain't it?"

"Have to cut it a mite, else it eats the bottom out'n the jug."

Slewfoot's squaw, a clean, sturdy-looking woman, came out and got an armload of firewood from the pile beside the tepee, and Slewfoot grunted something to her in the Shoshone tongue. She stared curiously at Tad for a moment, grunted a reply and disappeared inside.

Several dogs lay dozing in the shade. A half-grown, smooth-haired white pup wandered into the tepee, let out a pained yip and came scooting out with its tail tucked between its legs, followed by the squaw's angry scolding. The pup came over to Slewfoot for sympathy, got it in the form of a friendly pat or two, then trotted to Tad, climbed up into his lap and went to sleep.

Slewfoot grinned. "Seems to like you."

"Yeah. Dogs usually take to me."

"Mighty fine pup. I got plans fer him."

A dark-eyed, attractive young Indian girl appeared, started to go into the tepee; then, at a word from Slewfoot, stopped and stared in open-mouthed amazement at Tad. He colored in spite of all he could do. Suddenly she giggled, murmured something in Shoshone, then quickly ducked into the tepee.

"Who's that?" Buck asked.

"My squaw's sister. Name's Moon Wind."

"Tad is quite a man with the ladies," Buck said, gazing innocently off into space. "They was three gals at oncet after him, back home. Caused him some trouble."

"A woman can pester a man," Slewfoot said, "less'n he knows how to handle her. Have to lodgepole mine ever' once in a while."

"Lodgepole?" Tad said.

"Beat her."

"Can't say I hold with beating women."

Slewfoot grinned. "Well, you may have to beat Moon Wind to make her leave you alone. She sure admired that yaller hair of yourn." Slewfoot yawned. "I'm hungry. I'll git the women to stir up some vittles."

The squaw came to the tepee entrance. They talked for a spell, then Slewfoot looked ruefully at Tad. "She says we're plumb out of meat. Kind of hate to do this, but when a man's hungry he's got to eat. I'd be obliged, Tad, if you'd pass me that pup."

"This pup?"

"Shore. It's the fattest one we got."

"I ain't really hungry yet. Ate a big breakfast."

Slewfoot grabbed the pup by the scruff of the neck, handed it to his squaw and waved her inside, then turned to Buck and began a long-winded tale. Tad's mind wasn't on the story, but with Buck sliding a look his way every now and then, there was nothing for him to do but sit there and pretend to be enjoying the company. Would the squaw skin the thing, he wondered, or just toss it into the pot with the hair on? For the first time in his life, he felt a little sick to his stomach.

After a while the squaw brought out three wooden bowls of greasy, rank-smelling stew, and Tad, hoping his face didn't look as green as it felt, accepted his with a weak smile.

"Hungry now?" Slewfoot asked.

Glassy-eyed, Tad stared down at the mess in the bowl. If he didn't eat dog he'd have to eat crow, and, of the two, he reckoned tame meat was the easier to swallow. Grimly he dug in with his spoon.

"Why, yeah I am. Hungry enough to eat a horse. Shame you didn't have a fat one to spare."

When they headed back to their own part of camp a while later, Buck asked, "How'd you like that stew?"

"Fine, 'cept for it's being a shade greasy."

"Bear meat usually is."

"Bear? I thought it was dog."

"Shoshones ain't dog eaters. Slewfoot could of lodgepoled his woman till Doomsday an' she still wouldn't of cooked that pup for us. That was just his idea of a joke."

"Didn't think it was very funny myself."

"You said you could take his worst, grin an' come back for more."

"I can."

"Well, I'll hang around and watch the fun."

There were times during the next week or so when it wasn't easy for Tad to grin. The day Slewfoot near drowned him while pretending to teach him how to build a trout trap was one. The night Slewfoot put the physic in the whisky was another. But he came closest to losing his good nature the evening he got scalped by Moon Wind in sight of the whole camp.

Slewfoot arranged the thing, no doubt about that, even though it was rigged to look plumb accidental. The boys had got to finger wrestling around the campfire. Two trappers would pair off, face each other and interlace the fingers of both hands. At the word "go," they'd have at it, each one trying to force the other to his knees or break his back, according to how stubborn the fellow wanted to be.

Slewfoot threw all comers. Looking around for fresh meat, he allowed as how a certain young fellow from Missouri would chew good, so there was nothing for Tad to do but climb to his feet and give it a try.

Captain Sublette was watching. So were Buck Owens, Parson Rumford, the packtrain mule tenders and a whole mess of Indians. The bets flew thick and fast as Tad and Slewfoot squared off. Staring over Slewfoot's shoulder, Tad found himself looking right at Moon Wind, who was sitting on the ground with her deep black eyes glittering in the firelight and her soft red lips parted in excited anticipation. Kind of a purty little thing, Tad was thinking. A sight purtier than the girls back home. If only she wouldn't keep staring at him that way.

"Go!" Captain Sublette said.

Slewfoot grunted, heaved, and the next thing Tad knew, he was lying flat on his back on the ground. Dimly he heard the yelling of the crowd as he got to his feet.

Slewfoot gave him a cockeyed grin. "Want to try it again, partner?"

"Sure."

This time Tad kept his mind on the chore at hand. For some minutes they rocked this way and that, then Tad made his move. Slewfoot's knees buckled and he went down with a thud. The crowd roared even louder than before.

"Hurt you?" Tad asked solicitously.

"Once more," Slewfoot grunted, getting up.

They locked hands. Judging from the look on his face, Slewfoot really meant business this time. So did Tad. But the kind of business Slewfoot had in mind was a shade different from what Tad expected. Because they'd no more than got started good when Slewfoot dropped to his knees, heaved and threw Tad clean over his shoulders.

Tad did a complete somersault in the air, landing with his feet in the crowd and his head on the ground right close to Moon Wind's lap. Foolishly he grinned up at her. She gave him a shy smile. Then she whipped out a scalping knife, grabbed a handful of hair and lopped it off.

The crowd went crazy. So did Tad. He jumped up and made for Moon Wind, but she fled into the crowd. He whirled and went for Slewfoot, who was laughing fit to kill. Sublette, Buck Owens and half a dozen other men grabbed him and held him back.

"Easy, son; easy!" Sublette said between chuckles. "There aren't many men get scalped and live to brag about it!"

After a moment Tad quit struggling and they let him go. His face burning, he stalked off into the darkness.

Morosely Tad finished his breakfast and accepted the cup of coffee Buck poured for him. *Yellow-Hair-Scalped-By-a-Woman.* That was the name the Indians had given him. Buck eyed him sympathetically.

"I told you he was ornery. But you were so cocky——"

"He caught me off guard. It won't happen again."

"He's too cunning for you, boy. Why, I'll bet you right now he's windin' himself up to prank you agin."

"He gets wound up tight enough," Tad said grimly, "I'll give him one more twist and bust his mainspring."

"Better git ready to twist, then. Yonder he comes."

Uneasy despite his brag, Tad ran absent fingers over his cropped head as Slewfoot came shuffling up, looking as pleased with the world as a fresh-fed bear.

"Mornin', gents. Any coffee left in that pot?"

Buck poured him a cup. Slewfoot hunkered on his heels, his black eye studying Tad while his green one gazed at the mountains off in the distance. "That was a dirty trick we played on you last night, Tad. It's sort of laid heavy on my conscience. So I've decided to make it up to you."

"I can hear him tickin'," Buck muttered.

"Just how are you going to make it up to me?"

"I know you don't like yore new Injun name. So I had a talk with a Shoshone chief that happens to be a friend of mine. He says he'll fix it."

"How?"

"Why, he'll just adopt you into his tribe an' give you a new name. That'll cancel out the old one. It'll cost me a mite, but I figger I owe you somethin'."

"Adopt me?"

"Yeah. Injuns do that now an' then."

Buck eyed Slewfoot suspiciously. "Who is this chief?"

"Seven Bears."

"Why, ain't he the——"

"Yes, sir, he's top man of the whole tribe. No Injun'll dare laugh at an adopted son of hisn."

Tad thought it over. If there was a catch to it, he sure couldn't see it. He looked at Buck. "What do you think?"

"I ain't sayin' a word."

"Well," Tad said, "in that case——"

The ceremony in Chief Seven Bears' tepee took a couple of hours. A dozen or so of the most important men in the tribe were there, and one look at their solemn faces told Tad this was serious business with them. Slewfoot must have been dead serious, too, because before the palaver began he gave Seven Bears a couple of horses, half a dozen red blankets, a used musket, several pounds of powder and lead, and a lot of other trinkets in exchange for his services.

When the ceremony was finally over, they left the tepee and Slewfoot walked to the edge of the Shoshone section of camp with him. His grin seemed genuine.

"How does it feel to be an Injun?"

"Fine. What was that new name he gave me?"

"White Mule. It's a good name."

"Reckon I'm obliged to you."

"Don't mention it. Well, I'll see you later."

Buck was taking a nap when Tad got back to his tent, but at the sound of his step the old trapper's eyes jerked open. "What'd they do to you?"

"It was all real friendly. Name's White Mule now."

"So he did do it! What'd it cost him?"

"Well, he gave Seven Bears some blankets, a couple of horses——"

"Hosses? Fer two hosses he could of bought you a——" Buck

suddenly broke off and stared at something behind Tad. He shook his head. "He did too. Look around, boy."

Tad turned around. Moon Wind was standing there, smiling shyly. Behind her were four horses, two of which he recognized as the ones Slewfoot had given Seven Bears a while ago, and all four were laden down with Indian housekeeping gear. As Tad stared at her with stricken eyes, Moon Wind gestured at him and at herself, then made a circling motion with both hands.

"She wants to know where she'd ought to pitch your tepee."

"My tepee?"

"Yourn and hern."

"She's—she's mine now?"

"Reckon she is. Slewfoot bought her for you."

"But Seven Bears——"

"Is her pa. Also happens to be Slewfoot's squaw's pa."

"Tell her I don't want her! Tell her to go home!"

Buck laid a restraining hand on Tad's forearm. "This may be just a prank where you an' Slewfoot're concerned, but I don't reckon it's one Moon Wind and her pa would laugh at much. She must of liked you. An' Seven Bears must have thought a lot of her, else he wouldn't of outfitted her so fancy an' given you back them two hosses of Slewfoot's as a special weddin' present."

"Well, I sure can't keep her!"

"Easy. They's a way out of this, maybe, but it'll take some tall thinkin'. Let her set up her tepee. You an' me are goin' to have a talk with Captain Sublette."

Captain Sublette was not in the habit of losing his temper, but when they told him what had happened he was fit to be tied. So was Parson Rumford. When Tad declared that what he had a mind to do was grab a club and beat Slewfoot half to death, then make him take Moon Wind back to her father and explain the whole thing, the parson gave the idea his hearty approval. But Sublette shook his head.

"You can't send her back. No matter how much explaining Slewfoot did—assuming we could make him do any—the whole Shoshone tribe would be so angry they'd be down on our necks in a minute. You've got to accept her and pretend to live with her until rendezvous breaks up."

"I won't hear to such a thing!" Parson Rumford exclaimed.

"I said 'pretend,' sir. . . . When the brigade goes back to St. Louis, you'll go with it, Tad. I'll tell Moon Wind that you're coming back next summer to stay. That will save her pride and our necks."

"But I won't come back? Is that the idea?"

"Yes."

Tad gazed off at the mountain peaks rimming the valley. "Seems kind of a dirty trick to play on her. Lettin' her wait for a man that won't never be comin' back to her. It's downright deceitful."

"Better a little deceit than a full-scale Indian war. She won't wait for you long, I'll wager. Next year I'll cook up some story about your having died of smallpox or something, and she'll be free to pick herself another man."

Reluctantly Tad nodded, but the deceit of it still weighed on his mind. "She's an innocent little thing and not to blame for this. I'd kind of like to give her something to remember me by—for a while, anyhow. Could I draw some of my wages and buy her a trinket or two?"

Sublette smiled understandingly. "Of course."

Pausing with the clerk in charge of the trade goods to pick out a few items he thought might appeal to her, Tad walked back to the spot where his tent had been pitched. But the tent was gone. In its place stood a roomy, comfortable skin tepee around which a dozen or two Shoshone women bustled, chattering happily as they helped Moon Wind set her household in order.

Seeing Tad, the women smiled, exchanged knowing looks amongst themselves, then quickly wound up their tasks and drifted away. When the last one had gone, he went to Moon Wind, who was on her knees building a fire.

"Moon Wind, I got something for you."

Her eyes lifted. Black eyes, they were, black and soft and deep. He got the sudden notion that she didn't know whether he was going to beat her for what she had done to him last night or caress her because she was now his woman. He took her hand and pulled her to her feet.

"These here trinkets are for you."

He dumped them into her hands. One by one, she examined them. First the glittering silver-backed mirror. Then the long double strand of imitation pearls. Then the small gold ring, which by some accident just managed to fit the third finger of her left hand. For a long moment she stared down at them. Then without a word she whirled away from him and ran toward the Shoshone section of camp.

She was gone so long that Tad, weary of trying to figure out what had got into her, went into the tepee and took himself a nap. Except for an unpleasant dream or two about Slewfoot, he slept fine. Presently he was awakened by angry voices arguing violently in the Shoshone tongue outside the tepee. He got up and went out to see what the ruckus was all about.

There, toe to toe, stood Slewfoot Samuels and his woman, jawing at each other like a pair of magpies. Off to one side and admiring her new trinkets stood Moon Wind.

Suddenly Slewfoot saw Tad and spun around. "What in the name of all unholy tarnation do you think you're doin'?"

"Me?" Tad said. "Why, I was just takin' a nap."

"That ain't what I'm talkin' about!"

"What are you talking about?"

"Them things!" Slewfoot roared, pointing a trembling hand at the ornaments Moon Wind was admiring. "That foofaraw she's wearin'! You got any idea how much that stuff costs?"

"Sure. I bought it. What business is that of yours?"

"My squaw wants the same fool trinkets!"

"Well, buy 'em for her."

"Waste a big chunk of my year's wages for junk like that?"

"Then don't buy 'em."

"If I don't, she'll pester the life out of me."

"Lodgepole her. That'll make her quit."

Slewfoot shot his woman a sidelong glance and shook his head. "Don't hardly dare to right now. She'd raise such a racket I'd have all her relatives on my neck." Slewfoot sidled closer, a pleading look in his eyes. "Look, boy, the joke's gone far enough. Now you take that foofaraw away from Moon Wind an' cuff her a time or two. Then my woman won't be jealous of her no more."

Tad looked at Slewfoot's squaw, who had gone over to Moon Wind and was gabbling with her over the beads, mirror and ring. Sure was queer how some men would spend any amount for their own pleasure, but wouldn't put out a dime for their women. He grinned and shook his head.

"Why, I don't have to cuff 'em to make 'em behave. Treat 'em kind, I say, if you want the best out of 'em. Buy 'em presents, help 'em with the chores, give 'em the respect they're due and crave— that's the way I treat my women."

Slewfoot stared at him. "You're goin' to keep her?"

"Sure am. Going to marry her, in fact, soon as I can get Parson Rumford to tie the knot. Come to think about it, I'll make a real shindig of it. Invite her pa and ma and all her relatives. Invite the whole camp. After the wedding I'll throw a big feed with food and drinks for all."

"That'll cost you a year's wages!"

"What if it does? Man like me only gets married once."

"But when my woman sees it," Slewfoot said hoarsely, "she'll squawl to high heaven fer the same treatment. First thing you know, I won't dare lay a hand on her. She'll keep me broke buyin' her foofaraw. She'll have me totin' wood an' takin' care of the hosses an' wipin' my feet 'fore I come into the tepee—why, she'll have me actin' jest like a regular husband!"

"I wouldn't be at all surprised," Tad said, and stolled off in search of Parson Rumford.

It was quite an affair, that double wedding, and the party afterward was real good fun for all concerned. Except Slewfoot Samuels, who didn't seem to enjoy it much. He'd lost his sense of humor, somehow. Maybe he'd get it back after they'd spent a few months in the mountains trapping beaver. Tad sure hoped so, anyhow. Worst thing you could have as a partner was a man that couldn't take a joke, grin and come back for more.

A WIDOW OF
THE SANTA ANA VALLEY
by Bret Harte

The Widow Wade was standing at her bedroom window, staring out in that vague instinct which compels humanity in moments of doubt and perplexity to seek this change of observation for superior illumination. Not that Mrs. Wade's disturbance was of a serious character. She had passed the acute stage of widowhood by at least two years, and the slight redness of her soft eyelids as well as the droop of her pretty mouth were merely the recognized outward and visible signs of the grievously minded religious community in which she lived. The mourning she still wore was also partly in conformity with the sad-colored garments of her neighbors and the necessities of the rainy season. She was in comfortable circumstances, the mistress of a large ranch in the valley, which had lately become more valuable by the extension of a wagon road through its centre. She was simply worrying whether she should go to a "sociable," ending with a "dance"—a daring innovation of some strangers—at the new hotel, or continue to eschew such follies that were, according to local belief, unsuited to "a vale of tears."

Indeed, at this moment the prospect she gazed abstractedly upon seemed to justify that lugubrious description. The Santa Ana Valley —a long, monotonous level—was dimly visible through moving curtains of rain or veils of mist to the black mourning edge of the horizon, and had looked like that for months. The valley—in some remote epoch an arm of the San Francisco Bay—every rainy season seemed to be trying to revert to its original condition, and long after the early spring had laid on its liberal color in strips, bands and patches of blue and yellow, the blossoms of mustard and lupin glistened like wet paint. Nevertheless, on that rich alluvial soil Nature's tears seemed only to fatten the widow's acres and increase her crops. Her neighbors, too, were equally prosperous. Yet for six months of the year the recognized expression of Santa Ana was one of sadness, and for the other six months—of resignation. Mrs. Wade had yielded early to this influence, as she had to others, in the weakness of her gentle nature, and partly as it was more becoming to the singular tragedy that had made her a widow.

For the late Mr. Wade had been found dead with a bullet through his head in a secluded part of the road over Heavy Tree Hill, in Sonora County. Near him lay two other bodies, one afterward identified as John Stubbs—a resident of the hill, and probably a traveling companion of Wade's—and the other a noted desperado and highwayman, still masked, as at the moment of the attack. Wade and his companion had probably sold their lives dearly and against odds, for another mask was found on the ground, indicating that the attack was not single-handed, and as Wade's body had not yet been rifled, it was evident that the remaining highwayman had fled in haste. The hue and cry had been given by apparently the only one of the travelers who escaped, but, as he was hastening to take the overland coach to the East at the time, his testimony could not be submitted to the Coroner's deliberation. The facts, however, were sufficiently plain for a verdict of willful murder against the highwayman, although it was believed that the absent witness had basely deserted his companion and left him to his fate, or, as it was suggested by others, that he might even have been an accomplice. It was this circumstance which protracted comment on the incident and the sufferings of the widow far beyond that rapid obliteration which usually overtook such affairs in the feverish haste of the early days. It caused her to remove to Santa Ana, where her old father had feebly ranched "a quarter-section" in the valley. He survived her husband only a few months, leaving her the property and once more in mourning. Perhaps this continuity of woe endeared her to a neighborhood where distinctive ravages of diphtheria or scarlet fever gave a kind of social preëminence to any household, and she was assisted so sympathetically by her neighbors in the management of the ranch that, from an unkempt and wasteful wilderness, it became paying property. The slim, willowy figure, soft, red-lidded eyes and deep crêpe of "Sister Wade" at church or prayer-meeting were grateful to the soul of these gloomy worshipers, and in time she herself found that the arm of these dyspeptics of mind and body was nevertheless strong and sustaining. Small wonder that she should hesitate to-night about plunging into inconsistent, even though trifling, frivolities.

But apart from this superficial reason there was another instinctive one deep down in the recesses of Mrs. Wade's timid heart which she had secretly kept to herself, and, indeed, would have tearfully resented had it been offered by another. The late Mr. Wade had been, in fact, a singular example of an idle, frivolous existence carried to a manlike excess. Besides being a patron of amusements, Mr. Wade gambled, raced and drank. He was often home late, and sometimes not at all. Not that this conduct was exceptional in the "roaring days" of Heavy Tree Hill, but it had given Mrs. Wade, perhaps, an undue preference for a less uncertain, if even a more serious life. His tragic death was of course a kind of martyrdom which exalted him in the feminine mind to a saintly memory, yet Mrs. Wade was not without a certain relief in that. It was voiced, perhaps crudely, by the widow of Abner Drake in a visit of condolence to the tearful Mrs. Wade a few days after Wade's death. "It's a vale o' sorrow, Mrs. Wade," said the sympathizer, "but it has its ups and downs, and I reckon ye'll be feelin' soon pretty much as I did about Abner when *he* was took. It was mighty soothin' and comfortin' to feel that whatever might happen now I always knew jist whar Abner was passin' his nights." Poor slim Mrs. Wade had no disquieting sense of humor to interfere with her reception of this large truth, and she accepted it with a burst of reminiscent tears.

A long volleying shower had just passed down the level landscape and was followed by a rolling mist from the warm, saturated soil like the smoke of the discharge. Through it she could see a faint lightening of the hidden sun, again darkening through a sudden onset of rain, and changing, as with her conflicting doubts and resolutions. Thus gazing, she was vaguely conscious of an addition to the landscape in the shape of a man who was passing down the road with a pack on his back like the tramping "prospectors" she had often seen at Heavy Tree Hill. That memory apparently settled her vacillating mind; she determined she would not go to the dance. But as she was turning away from the window, a second figure, a horseman, appeared in another direction by a cross road, a shorter cut through her domain. This she had no difficulty in recognizing as one of the strangers who were getting up the dance. She had noticed him at church on the previous Sunday. As he passed the house he appeared to be gazing at it so earnestly that she drew back from the window lest she should be seen. And then, for no reason whatever, she changed her mind once more and resolved to go to the dance. Gravely announcing this fact to the wife of her superintendent, who kept house with her in her loneliness, she thought nothing more about it. She would go in her mourning, with perhaps the addition of a white collar and frill.

It was evident, however, that Santa Ana thought a good deal more than she did of this new idea, which seemed a part of the innovation already begun by the building of the new hotel. It was argued by some that as the new church and new schoolhouse had been opened with prayer, it was only natural that a lighter festivity should inaugurate the opening of the hotel. "I reckon that dancin' is about the next thing to travelin' for gettin' up an appetite for refreshments, and that's what the landlord is kalkilatin' to sarve," was the remark of a gloomy but practical citizen on the veranda of The Valley Emporium. "That's so," rejoined a bystander, "and I notice on that last box o' pills I got for chills, the directions say that a little 'agreeable exercise'—not too violent—is a great assistance to the working o' the pills."

"I reckon that Mr. Brooks, who's down here lookin' arter mill property, got up the dance. He's been 'round town canvassin' all the women folks and drummin' up likely gels for it. They say he actually sent an invite to the Widder Wade," remarked another lounger. "Gosh! he's got cheek!"

"Well, gentlemen," said the proprietor judicially, "while we don't intend to hev any minin' camp fandangos or 'Frisco falals 'round Santa Any (Santa Ana was proud of its simple agricultural virtues), I ain't so hard-shelled as not to give new things a fair trial. And, after all, it's the women folk that has the say about it. Why, there's old Miss Ford sez she hasn't kicked a feet since she left Mizoori, but wouldn't mind tryin' it ag'in. Ez to Brooks takin' that trouble —well, I suppose it's along o' his bein' *healthy!*" He heaved a deep, dyspeptic sigh which was faintly echoed by the others. "Why, look at him now, ridin' 'round on that black hoss o' his, in the wet since daylight, and not carin' for blind chills or rheumatiz!"

He was looking at a serape-draped horseman, the one the widow had seen on the previous night, who was now cantering slowly up the street. Seeing the group on the veranda, he rode up, threw himself lightly from his saddle, and joined them. He was an alert, determined, good-looking fellow of about thirty-five, whose smooth, smiling face hardly commended itself to Santa Ana, though his eyes were distinctly sympathetic. He glanced at the depressed group around him and became ominously serious.

"When did it happen?" he asked gravely.

"What happen?" said the nearest bystander.

"The Funeral, Flood, Fight or Fire. Which of the four F's was it?"

"What are ye talkin' about?" said the proprietor stiffly, scenting some dangerous humor.

"You," said Brooks promptly. "You're all standing here croaking like crows this fine morning. I passed *your* farm, Johnson, not an hour ago, the wheat just climbing out of the black adobe mud as thick as rows of pins on paper; what have *you* to grumble at? I saw *your* stock, Briggs, over on Two Mile Bottom, waddling along, fat as the adobe they were sticking in, their coats shining like fresh paint; what's the matter with *you*? And," turning to the proprietor, "there's *your* shed, Saunders, over on the creek, just bursting with last year's grain that you know has gone up two hundred per cent, since you bought it at a bargain; what are *you* growling at? It's enough to provoke a Fire or a Famine to hear you all groaning— and take care it don't some day, as a lesson to you."

All this was so perfectly true of the prosperous burghers that they could not for a moment reply. But Briggs had recourse to what he believed to be a retaliatory taunt. "I heard you've been askin' Widow Wade to come to your dance," he said with a wink at the others. "Of course she said 'Yes!'"

"Of course she did," returned Brooks coolly. "I've just got her note."

"What!" ejaculated the three men together, "Mrs. Wade comin'!"

"Certainly. Why shouldn't she? And it would do *you* good to come, too, and shake the limp dampness out of you," returned Brooks as he quietly remounted his horse and cantered away.

"Darned ef I don't think he's got his eye on the Widder," said Johnson faintly.

"Or the quarter-section," added Briggs gloomily.

For all that, the eventful evening came, with many lights in the staring, undraped windows of the hotel, coldly bright bunting on the still damp walls of the long dining-room, and a gentle downpour from the hidden skies above. A close carryall was especially selected to bring Mrs. Wade and her housekeeper. The widow arrived, looking a little slimmer than usual in her closely buttoned black dress, white collar and cuffs, very glistening in eye and in hair—whose glossy black ringlets were perhaps more elaborately arranged than was her custom—and with a faint coming and going of color, due, perhaps, to her agitation at this tentative reëntering into worldly life, which was nevertheless quite virginal in effect. A vague solemnity pervaded the introductory proceedings, and a singular want of sociability was visible in the "sociable" part of the entertainment. People talked in whispers or with that grave precision which indicates good manners in rural communities; conversed painfully with other people whom they did not want to talk to, rather than appear to be alone, or rushed aimlessly together like water drops, and then floated in broken, adherent masses over the floor. The widow became a hopeless religious centre of deacons and Sunday-school teachers, which Brooks, untiring yet fruitless in his attempt to produce gayety, tried in vain to break. To this gloom the untried dangers of the impending dance duly prefigured by a lonely cottage piano and two violins in a desert of expanse added a nervous chill. When at last the music struck up—somewhat hesitatingly and protestingly, from the circumstance that the player was the church organist and fumbled mechanically for his stops— the attempt to make up a cotillon set was left to the heroic Brooks. Yet he barely escaped disaster when, in posing the couples, he incautiously begged them to look a little less as if they were waiting for the coffin to be borne down the aisle between them, and was rewarded by a burst of tears from Mrs. Johnson, who had lost a child two years before, and who had to be led away, while her place in the set was taken by another. Yet the cotillon passed off; a Spanish dance succeeding "Money Musk" with the Virginia reel put a slight intoxicating vibration into the air, and healthy youth at last asserted itself in a score of freckled but buxom girls in white muslin, with romping figures and laughter at the lower end of the room. Still a rigid decorum reigned among the older dancers, and the figures were called out in grave formality, as if, to Brooks' fancy, they were hymns given from the pulpit, until at the close of the set in half real, half mock despair he turned desperately to Mrs. Wade, his partner:

"Do you waltz?"

Mrs. Wade hesitated. She had, before marriage, and was a good waltzer.

"I do," she said timidly, "but do you think they——"

But before the poor widow could formulate her fears as to the reception of "round dances," Brooks had darted to the piano, and the next moment she heard with a "fearful joy" the opening bars of a waltz. It was an old Julien waltz, fresh still in the fifties, daring, provocative to foot, swamping to intellect, arresting to judgment, irresistible, supreme! Before Mrs. Wade could protest Brooks' arm had gathered up her slim figure, and with one quick, backward sweep and swirl they were off! The floor was cleared for them in a sudden bewilderment of alarm—a suspense of burning curiosity. The widow's little feet tripped quickly, her long black skirt swung out; as she turned the corner there was not only a sudden revelation of her pretty ankles, but, what was more startling, a dazzling flash of frilled and laced petticoat which at once convinced every woman in the room that the act had been premeditated for days! Yet even that criticism was presently forgotten in the pervading intoxication of the music and the movement. The younger people fell into it with wild rompings, whirlings, and claspings of hands and waists. And, stranger than all, a corybantic enthusiasm seized upon the more emotional among their elders, and those priests and priestesses of Cybele who were famous for their frenzy and passion in camp-meetings seemed to find an equal expression that night in the waltz. And when, flushed and panting, Mrs. Wade at last halted on the arm of her partner, they were nearly knocked over by the revolving Johnson and Mrs. Stubbs in a whirl of gloomy exaltation! They all waltzed together until the long room shook, and the very bunting on the walls waved and fluttered with the gyrations of these revolving dervishes. Nobody knew, nobody cared, how long this frenzy lasted—it ceased only with the collapse of the musicians. Then with much vague bewilderment, inward trepidation, awkward and incoherent partings, everybody went dazedly home; there was no other dancing after that—the waltz was the one event of the festival and of the history of Santa Ana. And later that night, when the timid Mrs. Wade, in the seclusion of her own room and the disrobing of her slim figure, glanced at her spotless, frilled and laced petticoat lying on a chair, a faint smile—the first of her widowhood—curved the corners of her pretty mouth.

A week of ominous silence regarding the festival succeeded in Santa Ana. The local paper gave the fullest particulars of the opening of the hotel, but contented itself with saying, "The entertainment concluded with a dance." Mr. Brooks, who felt himself compelled to call upon his late charming partner twice during the week, characteristically soothed her anxieties as to the result.

"The fact of it is, Mrs. Wade, there's really nobody in particular to blame, and that's what gets them! They're all mixed up in it; and when old Johnson tried to be nasty the other evening and hoped you hadn't suffered from your exertions that night, I told him you hadn't quite recovered yet from the physical shock of having been run into by him and Mrs. Stubbs, but that you being a lady, you didn't tell just how you felt at the exhibition he and she made of themselves. That shut him up."

"But you shouldn't have said that," said Mrs. Wade with a frightened little smile.

"No matter," returned Brooks cheerfully, "I'll take the blame of it with the others. You see, they'll have to have a scapegoat, and I'm just the man, for I got up the dance! And as I'm going away I suppose I shall bear off the sin with me in the wilderness."

"You're going away," repeated Mrs. Wade in more genuine concern.

"Not for long," returned Brooks laughingly. "I came here to look up a mill site and I've found it. Meantime I think I've opened their eyes."

"You have opened mine," said the widow with timid frankness.

They were soft, pretty eyes when opened, in spite of their heavy red lids, and Mr. Brooks thought that Santa Ana would be no worse if they remained open. Possibly he looked it, for Mrs. Wade said hurriedly: "I mean—that is—I've been thinking that life needn't *always* be as gloomy as we make it here. And even *here*, you know, Mr. Brooks, we have six months sunshine—though we always forget it in the rainy season."

"That's so," said Brooks cheerfully; "I once lost a heap of money through my own foolishness and I've managed to forget it, and I even reckon to get it back again out of Santa Ana if my mill speculation holds good. So good-by, Mrs. Wade—but not for long." He shook her hand and departed, leaving the widow conscious of a certain sympathetic confidence, and a little grateful for—she knew not what.

This feeling remained with her most of the afternoon and even imparted a certain gayety to her spirits, to the extent of causing her to hum softly to herself, the air being, oddly enough, the Julien waltz. And when, later in the day, as the shadows were closing in with the rain, word was brought to her that a stranger wished to see her in the sitting-room, she carried a less mournful mind to this function of her existence. For Mrs. Wade was accustomed to give audience to traveling agents, tradesmen, working-hands and servants as châtelaine of her ranch, and the occasion was not novel. Yet on entering the room, which she used partly as an office, she found some difficulty in classifying the stranger, who at the first glance reminded her of the tramping miner she had seen that night from her window. He was rather incongruously dressed, some articles of his apparel being finer than others; he wore a diamond pin in a scarf folded over a rough "hickory" shirt; his light trousers were tucked in common mining boots that bore stains of travel, and a suggestion that he had slept in his clothes. What she could see of his unshaven face in that uncertain light expressed a kind of dogged concentration, overlaid by an assumption of ease. He got up as she came in, and with a slight "How do, ma'am," shut the door behind her and glanced furtively around the room.

"What I've got to say to ye, Mrs. Wade—as I reckon you be—is strictly private and confidential! Why, ye'll see afore I get through. But I thought I might just as well caution ye ag'in our being disturbed."

Overcoming a slight instinct of repulsion, Mrs. Wade returned: "You can speak to me here; no one will interrupt you—unless I call them," she added with feminine caution.

"And I reckon ye won't do that," he said with a grim smile. "You are the widow o' Pulaski Wade, late o' Heavy Tree Hill, I reckon?"

"I am," said Mrs. Wade.

"And your husband's berried up thar in the graveyard with a monument over him setting forth his virtues ez a Christian and a square man, and a high-minded citizen! And that he was foully murdered by highwaymen?"

"Yes," said Mrs. Wade, "that is the inscription."

"Well, ma'am, a bigger pack o' lies never was cut on stone!"

Mrs. Wade arose, half in indignation, half in vague terror.

"Keep your sittin'," said the stranger with a warning wave of his hand. "Wait till I'm through and then you can call in the hull State o' Californy—ef ye want."

The stranger's manner was so doggedly confident that Mrs. Wade sank back tremblingly in her chair. The man put his slouch hat on his knee, twirled it around once or twice, and then said with the same stubborn deliberation: "The highwayman in that business was *your husband*—Pulaski Wade and his gang—and he was killed by one o' the men he was robbin'. Ye see, ma'am, it used to be your husband's little game to rope in three or four strangers in a poker deal at Spanish Jim's saloon—I see you've heard o' the place," he interpolated as Mrs. Wade drew back suddenly—"and when he couldn't clean 'em out in that way, or they showed a little more money than they played, he'd lay for 'em in a lone part o' the trail and go through them like any road agent. That's what he did that night—and that's how he got killed."

"How do you know this?" said Mrs. Wade with quivering lips.

"I was one o' the men he went through before he was killed. And I'd hev got my money back, but the rest o' the gang came up, and I got away jest in time to save my life and nothin' else. Ye might remember thar was one man got away and give the alarm, but he was goin' on to the States by the overland coach that night, and couldn't stay to be a witness. I was that man. I had paid my passage through and I couldn't lose *that*, too, with my other money, so I went."

Mrs. Wade sat stunned. She remembered the missing witness and how she had longed to see the man who was last with her husband; she remembered Spanish Jim's saloon—his well-known haunt; his frequent and unaccountable absences; the sudden influx of money which he always said he had won at cards; the diamond ring he had given her as the result of "a bet"; the forgotten recurrences of other robberies by a secret masked gang; a hundred other things that had worried her, instinctively, vaguely. She knew now, too, the meaning of the unrest that had driven her from Heavy

Tree Hill—the strange unformulated fears that had haunted her even here. Yet with all this she felt, too, her present weakness—knew that this man had taken her at a disadvantage, that she ought to assert herself indignantly, deny everything—demand proof—and brand him a slanderer!

"How did—you—know it was my husband?" she stammered.

"His mask fell off in the fight; you know another mask was found; it was his. I saw him as plain as I see him there!" He pointed to a daguerreotype of her husband which stood upon her desk.

Mrs. Wade could only stare, vacantly, hopelessly. After a pause the man continued in a less aggressive manner and more confidential tone, which, however, only increased her terror: "I ain't sayin' that *you* knowed anything about this, ma'am, and whatever other folks might say when they know of it, I'll allers say that you didn't."

"What, then, do you come here for?" said the widow desperately.

"What do I come here for?" repeated the man grimly, looking around the room; "what did I come to this yer comfortable home —this yer big ranch and a rich woman like yourself for? Well, Mrs. Wade, I come to get the $600 your husband robbed me of, that's all! I ain't askin' more! I ain't askin' interest! I ain't askin' compensation for havin' to run for my life, and"—again looking grimly around the walls—"I ain't askin' more than you will give."

"But this house never was his—it was my father's," gasped Mrs. Wade; "you have no right——"

"Mebbe 'yes' and mebbe 'no,' Mrs. Wade," interrupted the man with a wave of his hat, "but how about them two drafts to bearer for two hundred dollars each, found among your husband's effects and collected by your lawyer for you—*my drafts*, Mrs. Wade!"

A wave of dreadful recollection overwhelmed her. She remembered the drafts found upon her husband's body, known only to her and her lawyer, and believed to be gambling gains, and collected at once under his legal advice.

"But you shall have to prove it—before witnesses."

"Do you *want* me to prove it before witnesses?" said the man, coming nearer. "Do you want to take my word and keep it between ourselves, or do you want to call in your superintendent and his men, and all Santa Ana, to hear me prove your husband was a highwayman, thief and murderer? Do you want to knock over that monument on Heavy Tree Hill, and upset your standing here among the deacons and elders? Do you want to do all this, and be forced, even by your neighbors, to pay me in the end as you will? Ef you do, call in your witnesses now and let's have it over."

He made a step toward the door, but she stopped him.

"No! No! Wait! It's a large sum—I haven't it with me," she stammered, thoroughly beaten.

"Ye kin get it."

"Give me time!" she implored. "Look! I'll give you a hundred down now—all I have here—the rest another time!" She nervously opened a drawer of her desk, and taking out a buckskin bag of gold thrust it in his hand. "There! Go away now!" She lifted her thin hand despairingly to her head. "Go! Do!"

The man seemed struck by her manner. "I don't want to be hard on a woman," he said slowly. "I'll go now and come back again at nine to-night. You can git the money—or what's as good, a check to bearer—by then. And ef ye'll take my advice you won't ask no advice from others, ef you want to keep your secret. Jest now it's safe with me; I'm a square man—ef I seem to be a hard one." He made a gesture as if to take her hand, but, as she drew shrinkingly away, he changed it to an awkward bow, and the next moment he was gone.

She started to her feet, but the unwonted strain upon her nerves and frail body had been greater than she knew. She made a step forward, felt the room whirl around her and then seem to collapse beneath her feet, and, clutching at her chair, sank back into it, fainting.

How long she lay there she never knew. She was at last conscious of some one bending over her, and a voice—the voice of Mr. Brooks—in her ear, saying: "I beg your pardon—you seem ill. Shall I call some one?"

"No!" she gasped, quickly recovering herself with an effort. "Where is—when did you come in?"

"Only this moment. I was leaving to-night, sooner than I expected, and thought I'd say good-by. They told me that you had been engaged with a stranger. I beg your pardon—I see you are ill. I won't detain you any longer."

"No! No! Don't go! I am better—better," she said feverishly. As she glanced at his strong and sympathetic face a wild idea seized her. He was a stranger here, an alien to these people, like herself.

The advice that she dared not seek from others, from her half-estranged religious friends, from even her superintendent and his wife, dare she ask from him? Perhaps he saw this frightened doubt, this imploring appeal, in her eyes, for he said gently: "Is it anything I can do for you?"

"Yes," she said with the sudden desperation of weakness, "I want you to keep a secret!"

"Yours—yes!" he said promptly.

Whereat poor Mrs. Wade instantly burst into tears. Then amidst her sobs she told him of the stranger's visit, of his terrible accusations, of his demands—his expected return and her own utter helplessness. To her terror, as she went on she saw a singular change in his kind face; he was following her with hard, eager intensity. She had half hoped, even through her fateful instincts, that he might have laughed, manlike, at her fears. But he did not.

"You say he positively recognized your husband?"

"Yes, yes!" sobbed the widow, "and knew that photograph!" She pointed to the desk. Brooks turned quickly in that direction. Luckily his back was toward her, and she could not see his face nor the quick, startled look that came into his eyes. But when they again met hers it was gone, and even their eager intensity had changed to a gentle commiseration. "You have only his word for it, Mrs. Wade," he said gently, "and in telling your secret to another you have shorn the rascal of half his power over you, and he knew it. Now, dismiss the matter from your mind and leave it all to me. I will be here a few minutes before nine—*and alone in this room*. Let your visitor be shown in here—and don't let us be disturbed."

It lacked a few minutes of nine when Mr. Brooks was ushered into the sitting-room. As soon as he was alone he quietly examined the door and the windows and, having satisfied himself, took his seat in a chair casually placed behind the door. Presently he heard the sound of voices and a heavy footstep in the passage. He lightly felt his waistcoat pocket—it contained a pretty little weapon of power and precision, with a barrel scarcely two inches long.

The door opened and the person outside entered the room. In an instant Brooks had shut the door and locked it behind him. The man turned fiercely, but was faced by Brooks quietly—with one finger carelessly hooked in his waistcoat pocket. The man slightly recoiled from him, not so much from fear as from some vague stupefaction. "What's that for? What's your little game?" he said half contemptuously.

"No game at all," returned Brooks coolly. "You came here to sell a secret. I don't propose to have it given away first, to any listener."

"*You* don't—who are *you*?"

"That's a queer question to ask of the man you are trying to personate—but I don't wonder. You're doing it badly!"

"Personate—*you*?" said the stranger with staring eyes.

"Yes, *me*," said Brooks quietly. "I am the only man who escaped from the robbery that night at Heavy Tree Hill and who went home by the overland coach."

The stranger stared, but recovered himself with a coarse laugh. "Oh, well, we're on the same lay, it appears! Both after the widow —afore we show up her husband."

"Not exactly," said Brooks with his eyes fixed intently on the stranger. "You are here to denounce a highwayman who is dead and escaped justice. I am here to denounce one who is *living*! Stop! drop your hand, it's no use—you thought you had to deal only with a woman to-night and your revolver isn't quite handy enough. There! down! down! So! That'll do."

"You can't prove it," said the man hoarsely.

"Fool! In your story to that woman you have given yourself away. There were but two travelers attacked by the highwaymen. One was killed—I am the other. Where do *you* come in? What witness can you be except as the highwayman that you were? Who is left to identify Wade but you, his accomplice?"

The man's suddenly whitened face made his unshaven beard seem to bristle over his face like some wild animal's. "Well, ef you kalkilate to blow me, you've got to blow Wade and his widder, too," he said whiningly.

"I've thought of that," said Brooks coolly, "and I calculate that to prevent it is worth about that hundred dollars you got from that poor woman—and no more! Now sit down at that table and write as I dictate."

The man looked at him in wonder, but obeyed.

"Write," said Brooks, "I hereby certify that my accusations against the late Pulaski Wade, of Heavy Tree Hill, are erroneous and groundless, and the result of mistaken identity, especially in regard to any complicity of his in the robbery of John Stubbs, deceased, and Henry Brooks, at Heavy Tree Hill on the night of the thirteenth of August, 1854."

The man looked up with a repulsive smile. "Who's the fool now? What's become of your hold on the widder now?"

"Write!" said Brooks fiercely.

The sound of a pen hurriedly scratching paper followed this first outburst of the quiet Brooks. "Sign it," said Brooks. The man signed it.

"Now go," said Brooks, unlocking the door, "but remember, if you should ever be inclined to revisit Santa Ana you will find *me* living here also."

The man slunk out of the door and into the passage like a wild animal returning to the night and darkness. Brooks took up the paper, rejoined Mrs. Wade in the parlor and laid it before her.

"But," said the widow, trembling even in her joy, "do you—do you think he was *really* mistaken?"

"Positive," said Brooks coolly. "It's true it's a mistake that has cost you a hundred dollars—but there are some mistakes that are worth that to be kept quiet."

They were married a year later, but there is no record that in after years of conjugal relations with a weak, charming woman, Henry Brooks was ever tempted to tell her the whole truth of the robbery of Heavy Tree Hill.

DEAD-MAN TRAIL

by Ernest Haycox

Johnny Potter had only squatted himself in the cabin's doorway for a smoke when he heard Plez Neal's footsteps rattling along the stony trail in a rapid return from town. Plez came across the sooty shadows of the yard and made a mysterious motion at Johnny. He said, "Come inside."

Johnny followed Plez into the cabin and closed the door. A third partner, Thad Jessup, lay on a bunk, stripped to socks, trousers and iron-stained undershirt. He had been half asleep, but his eyes opened and were instantly alert.

"Buck Miller's in town again," said Plez Neal. "He's huddled up with that saddle-faced barkeep in the Blue Bucket. They were talking about me—I could tell." He went over to a soapbox to fill his pipe from a red tobacco can.

"Add those three other fellows that drifted in yesterday," said Thad. "There's your crowd. They smell honey."

"They smell us," said Plez. "Now we're sittin' ducks, not knowin' which way we'll be flushed."

"How'd you suppose they know we're worth a holdup?" asked Thad.

"Talk of the camp. I wish we hadn't let that damned dust pile up so long."

Johnny Potter sat hunched over on the edge of a box, arms across his knees. He spread out his fingers and stared at them while he listened to the talk of his partners. Both Plez and Thad were middle-aged men from the Willamette who had left their families behind them to come here and grub out gold enough to go back and buy valley farms. He was the youngster who had a good many more years to throw away than they had; he didn't dread the loss of the dust as they did, but he understood how they felt about it. He riffled his fingers through his hair, and once he looked toward the fireplace, beneath whose stones lay twenty thousand dollars in lard cans. His eyes were a flashing blue against the mahogany burn of his skin; he was a slender young man and his face had a listening silence on it. In the little crevices around his features, boyishness and rough knowledge lay uneasily together.

"We've made our stake," said Thad. "We could pack and pull out."

"Won't do. We've got some protection in camp. On the trail we'd be easy marks."

"But," said Thad, "if we stay here we'll get knocked over. It's a Mexican standoff. If they want us they'll get us. Just a question of how and when."

There was a silence, during which time Johnny Potter decided that his partners had no answer to the problem. He straightened on the box and made a small flat gesture with both hands against his legs.

"The three of us would travel too slow, but one of us could travel light and fast," he said. "I'll take my horse and your horse, Plez. Tonight. With a head start, I can outrun that crowd and get into The Dalles with the dust in four days or less."

"Why two horses?" asked Plez.

Johnny nodded toward the fireplace. "That stuff weighs around ninety pounds. I'll change horses as I go."

Plez said, "We'll cook up some bacon and you can take bread. You can make cold camps."

"I got to have coffee," said Johnny. "Pack the dust in the two sets of saddlebags."

Thad said, "If they're watchin' us, they'll notice you're gone in the morning."

"While you're packing," said Johnny, "I'll drop in at the Blue Bucket and play sick. Tomorrow you tack a smallpox sign on the cabin. They'll think I'm in bed."

Plez thought about it, sucking at his pipe. "Johnny, it's a long way to The Dalles. If they pick up your tracks you're a gone chicken."

"Fall of the dice," said Johnny, and opened the door and stepped into a full mountain darkness. Cabin lights and campfires glimmered through the trees and along the gulch below him, and men's voices drifted in the windless air. He took the trail to the creek bottom, threaded his way past tents and gravel piles thrown back from bedrock, and came upon Canyon City's shanties wedged at the bottom of the ravine. The sound of the saloons reached out to him. He turned into the Blue Bucket, stumbling slightly; he saw a few friends at the poker tables and nodded to them in a drawn and gloomy manner, and he made a place for himself at the bar beside Pete Hewitt. The saddle-faced barkeep was at the far end of the counter, talking to a man whose face Johnny couldn't see at the moment. The barkeep broke off the talk long enough to bring Johnny a bottle and glass, and went back to his talk. Johnny took his cheer straight and poured another. The saddle-faced barkeep was at the edge of his vision; he noted the man's eyes roll toward him.

Pete Hewitt said, "What's the matter with you, Johnny?"

"I ache. I'm hot, I'm cold, I feel terrible."

"Ague. Get good and drunk."

Johnny eased his weight on the footrail, swinging to have a look at the man with the barkeep. It was Buck Miller, no question—big nose, face the color of an old gray boulder, a set of rough and raking eyes.

Johnny called the barkeep back to pay for his drinks. He said to Hewitt, "I'm goin' to bed, and I'm not getting up for a week."

As he left the bar, he felt Buck Miller's eyes upon him. Outside, he remembered a chore and dropped into the Mercantile to buy caps for his revolver; when he came from the store he again noticed Buck Miller in the doorway of the Blue Bucket, staring directly at him. Short gusts of sensation wavered up and down the back of Johnny's neck as he traveled the stony gulch back to the cabin. *No question about it*, he thought. *He's got his mind made up for that dust.*

Plez met him in the yard's darkness and murmured restlessly, "Come on."

He followed Plez along the creek to a corral which boxed in a bit of the hillside, and found the horses packed to go. He tried his cinches and patted the saddlebags. There were two sets of bags, one behind his saddle and one hooked to a light rig thrown over the spare horse. Plez said, "Bacon and bread's in your blanket roll. Coffee, too, but get along without it, Johnny. A fire means trouble."

"Got to have coffee, trouble or no trouble."

"Tobacco and matches there. It's Thad's rifle in the boot. Shoots better than yours."

Johnny Potter stepped to his saddle, taking hold of the lead rope. Thad whispered, "Listen," and the three of them were stone-still, dredging the night with their senses. A few stray sounds drifted up the slope; a shape passed across the beam of a campfire. "Somebody around the cabin," whispered Thad. "Get out of here, Johnny."

Plez said in his kind and troubled voice, "Don't hold no foolish notions. If you get in a vise, dump the damned dust and run."

Johnny turned up the ravine, reached the first bench of the hill, and paralleled the gulch as it ran northward toward the wider meadows of the John Day, two miles distant. He was tight with the first strain of this affair; he listened for the sound of a gun behind him; he made quick searches of himself for things done right or done wrong, and presently he fell down the hill into the John Day and saw the dull glittering of the creek's ford ahead of him.

He held back a moment. There were lights along the valley, from other diggings and other cabins, and the trail was well traveled by men going to and coming from Canyon City. At this moment he neither saw nor heard anybody, and left the shadows of the hill and soon crossed the creek. The racket of his horses in the water was a signal soon answered, for, looking behind him, Johnny saw a shape slide out of the canyon shadows and come to the ford. Johnny swung from the trail at once and put himself into the willows beside the river.

He waited, hearing the rider cross the water and pass down the trail perhaps two hundred feet and there stop and remain motionless for a full three minutes. Suddenly Johnny understood he had made a mistake; he had tipped his hand when he had gone into the store to buy the caps. It wasn't a thing a sick man would do.

The rider wheeled and walked his horse toward the ford. His shadow came abreast of Johnny and faded, but at the creek he swung again and came back, clearly hunting and clearly dissatisfied. It was time, Johnny guessed, to use a little pressure; drawing his gun, he cocked the hammer and sent that lean dry little sound plainly into the night. The rider whipped about immediately, racing over the ford and running full tilt toward Canyon City. He would be going back for the rest of Miller's bunch.

Johnny came out of the brush and went down the trail at a hard run, passing cabins and campfires, and sometimes hearing men hail him. He followed the windings of this rough-beaten highway as it matched the windings of the river; he watched the shadows before him; he listened for the rumor of running horses behind him, and once—the better to catch the tomtoms of pursuit—he stopped to give the horses a blow and to check the saddlebags. The lights of the diggings at last faded, and near midnight he reached another cluster of cabins, all dark and sleeping, and turned from the valley into the hills. Before him lay something less than two hundred miles of country—timber, rough mountain creases, open grass plains and rivers lying deep in straight-walled canyons.

He slowed the horses to a walk and wound through the black alleys of these hills while the night wore on and the silence deepened. In the first paling dawn he stopped at a creek for a drink and a smoke, and went on steadily thereafter until noon found him on the edge of timber overlooking a meadowed corridor through these hills. Out there lay the main trail, which he watched for a few minutes; then he staked the horses, cooked his coffee and curled on the needle-spongy soil to rest.

It was less than real sleep. He heard the horses moving; he came wide awake at a woodpecker's drumming, and drifted away again, and moved back and forth across the border of consciousness, straining into the silence, mistrusting the silence.

He woke before sunset, tired. He threw on the gear and moved the horses to the creek and let them browse in the bottom grasses while he boiled up another pot of coffee. Afterward, he returned to the edge of the timber and, as long as light lasted, he watched the trail, which was a wriggling pale line across the tawny meadows below. He had to take that trail for the speed it offered him, but when he took it he also exposed himself. Thus far, he had been pretty secure in the breadth of country behind him—a pin point lost within a thousand square miles of hills and crisscross gullies. Ahead of him, though, the trail squeezed itself narrowly through a bottleneck of very rough land. Buck Miller knew about that, and might be waiting there.

Under darkness he moved over the flats to the trail and ran its miles down. He stopped to water at a creek, and later, well beyond the creek, he paused to listen, and thought he heard the scudding of other horses, though the sounds were so abraded by distance that he could not locate them. Riding west, he saw the ragged rising of hills through the silver gloom. The trail went downgrade, struck the graveled bottom of a dry wash and fell gradually into a pocket at the base of the hills. His horse, seeing some odd thing, whipped aside, going entirely off the trail. A moment later it plunged both forefeet into a washout, dropped to its knees and flung Johnny Potter from the saddle.

He turned in the air, he struck, he felt pain slice him through; the odor of blood was in his nostrils and his senses ran out like a fast tide, leaving him dumb on the ground. His left leg burned from hip to ankle and he kicked it out straight with a rough wish to know the worst. Nothing wrong there. He tried his right leg, he moved his arms, he stood up. He was all right.

He crouched in the washout and ran his hands along the down horse's front legs and discovered the break. He wanted a smoke, risk or no risk, and he filled his pipe and lighted it close to the ground. Then he brought in the lead horse, which had strayed out toward grass, and transferred the gear to it from the down horse.

When he was ready to travel again, he put a bullet into the head of the down horse, that report shouting and rumbling and rocketing away in all directions. It appeared to follow him and point him out when he rode forward.

In the first streaky moments of dawn he found himself in the bottom grasses and the willow clumps of Bridge Creek near its junction with the John Day. The ridges rose to either side of him, and he sat a moment motionless in the saddle and felt naked under such exposure; it would be a better thing to get out of this meadow land and to lose himself in the rough and treeless stringers of earth which made a hundred hidden pockets as they marched higher and higher over the mountains toward Central Oregon. But that was the slow way, and he had not enough knowledge of the country to leave the trail, and thus, his restless nerves pricking him into action, he went down the creek bottom at the best gallop he could kick out of his horse and reached the still more open bottoms of the John Day.

It was a wonderful thing at last to see the trail rise up from the river through a notch and go directly into the broken land. As soon as the ridge permitted him, he went up its side and got into another draw; he pressed on, climbing and turning and searching the land until he felt his horse lag. Thereupon he changed his course until he reached a ridge from which he saw the trail visible in the ravine below. He fed the horse and put it on picket in a gulley and lay down to rest.

Through his curtain of sleep, broken as it was by strain and weariness, he heard the clear running sound of horses below. He reached for his rifle, rolled and crawled to the rim of the ridge all in a motion, and saw four men swinging along the trail below him; the lead man's head was bent, carefully reading signs, and in a moment this man signaled for a halt and swung his horse around, bringing his face into view—that dark skin and big-boned nose sharp in the sunlight. The four made a close group on the trail while they talked. Their words lifted toward Johnny.

"No," said Buck Miller, "we've gone too far this way. The kid left the trail back there where the ridge began. He went the other side. We'll go back and pick up his tracks."

"He's tryin' to fool us," said another man. "He may be settin' behind a rock waitin' for us to walk right into his shot."

"He's just a kid," said Buck Miller. "He'll run; he won't stand and fight. All he wants to do is keep ahead of us and get to The Dalles."

The other man wasn't convinced. He said, "You go back and pick up his tracks while I ride this way a couple miles. If I don't see anything, I'll cut over the ridge and find you."

"No," said Buck Miller. "If I see anything moving ahead of me, I'll shoot it, and it might turn out to be you. We'll stick together. When we locate the kid we can box him in. He ain't far ahead. He's got two horses, and the dust weighs enough to slow him down."

The other man said, "He's got the advantage and I don't like it much. He can watch us come and he's above us."

Miller shook his head. "If it was a hard customer we were trailin', I'd say you were right. But he's never shot a man. That makes a difference, Jeff. It's a hard thing to pull the trigger if you ain't done it before—and while he's makin' up his mind about it, we'll get around him. I figure we can bring him to a stop. Then one of us can slip behind and get above him. I can hit him with the first bullet, anywhere up to four hundred yards."

Johnny Potter drew his rifle forward and laid its stock against his cheek. He had Buck Miller framed in the sights, with no doubt left in his mind; it was a matter of kill or be killed—it was that plain. Yet he was astonished that Buck Miller knew him so well; for he had trouble making his finger squeeze the slack from the trigger. It was a hard thing to kill, and that was something he hadn't known. *Well*, he thought, *I've got to do it*, and had persuaded himself to fire when the group whirled suddenly and ran back along the trail. He had missed his chance.

It would take them a couple hours, he guessed. With Miller behind him, he had a chance for a clear run on the trail, and maybe he could set a trap. He figured it out in his mind as he rode directly down the ridge's side into the trail and galloped westward. They were careless in the way they boomed along; they had no particular fear of him—which made the trap possible, maybe.

He came to a creek and turned the horse into it; he dismounted and dropped belly-flat in the water at the feet of the horse, and he drank in great, strangling, greedy gusts. Somewhere ahead of him the canyon would run out and the trail would then move directly up the face of the hills. When he took that, he was an open target. Meanwhile the creek, coming closer to its source, fed a thicker and thicker stand of willows, and presently he left the trail and put the horse well back into the willows. He walked a few yards away from the horse, parted the willows and made himself a covert. He took a few trial sights with the rifle down the trail, and sat back to wait. He closed his eyes, gently groaning. Canyon City was maybe a hundred miles behind him, and The Dalles a like distance ahead.

It was well into the afternoon when he heard the small vibrations of their coming. He turned on his stomach and brought the gun through the willows and took another trial sight, and had the muzzle swung against the bend when they came around it, riding single file and riding carelessly. They had convinced themselves he wouldn't stop to fight. They came on, loosely scattered, the lead man watching the trail and Buck Miller bringing up the rear.

Miller was the man he wanted, and he had terrible moments of indecision, swinging and lifting the gun to bring it on Miller, but the others made a screen for Miller, and at last Johnny took a sure aim on the lead man, now fifty feet away, and killed him with a shot through the chest.

He dropped the rifle and brought up his revolver as he watched the lead man fall and the riderless horse charge directly up the trail. The others wheeled and ran for the shelter of the bend. Two of them made it, but Johnny's snap shot caught the third man's horse, and it dropped and threw its rider into the gravel. The man cried as he struck, and his arm swung behind him in an unnatural way; he got to his knees and turned his face—bleeding and staring and shocked—toward Johnny. He tried to get to his feet, he shouted, he fell on his chest and began to crawl for the bend on one arm.

Johnny retreated into the willows, got his horse and came into the trail at a charging run. The fallen man made no move; the two others were sheltered behind the point of the ravine. Rushing along the trail, away from them, Johnny overtook the riderless horse, seized its reins as he passed by, and towed it on. He was, presently, around another turn of the trail and thus for a moment well sheltered, but in the course of a half mile the trail reached a dead end, with the bald rough hills rising in a long hard slant, and up this stiff-tilted way the trail climbed by one short switchback upon another.

He took to the switchbacks, coming immediately out of the canyon. Within five minutes he was exposed to them against the hillside, and waited for a long-reaching rifle bullet to strike. He looked into the canyon, not yet seeing them. He shoved his horse on with a steady heel gouging. He rode tense, the sharp cold sensations rippling through him; he jumped when the first shot broke the windless, heated air. The bullet, falling short, made its small "thut" in the ground below him. He kept climbing, exposed and at their mercy, and having no shelter anywhere.

He kept climbing, his horse grinding wind heavily in and out. He tried a chance shot with his revolver and watched both men jump aside, though he knew the bullet came nowhere near. They were both aiming, and they fired together. It was the foreshortened distance of the hillside which deceived them and left their bullets below him again. By that time he had reached a short bench and ran across it, temporarily out of their sight; then the hill began again and the trail once more began its climbing turns, exposing him. At this higher level he was beyond decent shooting, and he noted that the two had abandoned their rifles and were bending over the man lying on the trail. An hour later he reached the top of the hill and faced a broken country before him, bald sagebrush slopes folding one into another and hollow rocky ravines searching through them.

He dismounted and gave the horses a rest while he sat down on the edge of the hill and kept watch on the two dark shapes now far below. They hadn't come on. From his position he now had them on his hip unless they backtracked through this slashed-up country and took another ridge to ride around him. As long as he stood here they couldn't climb the open slope. He stretched out, supporting his head with a hand. He closed his lids and felt gritty particles scraping across his eyeballs, and suddenly he felt a sharp stinging on his cheek and jumped to his feet. He put a hand to his cheek and drew a short bit of sagebrush from his skin. He had fallen asleep and had rolled against the sagebrush.

The two men were at the creek, resting in the shade of the willows, no doubt waiting night. He rose to the saddle of the borrowed horse and started along the ravine which circled around a bald butte. Near sundown the ravine came out to the breakoff of this string of hills, and he saw the slope roll far down into a basin about a mile wide, on the far side of which lay a dark rim. Beyond the rim the high desert ran away to the west and the north; through the haze, far to the west, he saw the vaguest silhouette of snow peaks in the Cascades. He descended the slope as sunset came on in flame and violence.

Darkness found him beside a seepage of water in a pocket of the high rolling sagebrush land. He fed the horses half the remaining oats, ate his bacon and bread and built a fire to cook his coffee. He killed the fire and made himself a little spell of comfort with his pipe. Haze covered the sky, creating a solid blackness; the horses stirred around the scanty grasses. He rose and retreated twenty yards from where his fire had been and sat against a juniper. He got to thinking of the two men; they knew he was somewhere in this area, and they no doubt guessed he'd camp near water. If he were in their boots, he decided, he wouldn't try to find a man in this lonesomeness of rolling earth; he'd lie out on some ridge and wait for the man to come into view. The trail—the main trail to The Dalles—was a couple miles west of him.

He seemed to be strangling in water; he flung out a hand, striking his knuckles on the coarse-pebbled soil, and then he sprang up and rammed his head against the juniper. He had been sleeping again. He walked to the seepage and flattened on his stomach, alternately drinking and dousing his head until coldness cleared his mind; then he led the horses to water and let them fill, and resumed his ride, following little creases he could scarcely see, toward a shallow summit. An hour later he came upon the main trail and turned north with it. Having been once over this route, he knew the deep canyon of the Deschutes was in front of him, with a wooden toll bridge, but of its exact distance from his present location he had no idea. Around midnight he identified the blurred outline of a house ahead of him—a single wayside station sitting out in the emptiness—and he left the trail to circle the station at a good distance. By daylight he found himself in a rutty little defile passing up through a flinty ridge, and here, at a summit strewn with fractured rocks, he camped his horses in a pit and crawled back to the edge of the trail, making himself a trench in the loose rubble. The defile was visible all the way to its foot; the plain beyond was in full view. Two riders were coming on across the plain toward the ridge.

He settled his gun on the rocks and, while he waited, he slowly squirmed his body against the flinty soil, like an animal gathering tension for a leap. They were still beyond his reach when they came to the foot of the defile and stopped; and then, in tremendous disappointment, he saw that they would not walk into the same trap twice. They talked a moment, with Buck Miller making his gestures around the ridge. Afterward Miller left the trail and traveled eastward along the foot of the ridge, away from Johnny, for a half mile or so before he turned into the slope and began to climb. The other man also left the trail, passing along the foot of the ridge below Johnny.

Johnny crawled back into the rocks and scrambled in and out of the rough pits and boulder chunks, paralleling the man below him. He went a quarter mile before he flattened and put his head over the rim, and saw the rider angling upward. Johnny retreated and ran another short distance, gauging where he'd meet the man head on, and returned to the rim. He squeezed himself between two rocks, with the aperture giving him a view of the rider so slowly winding his way forward. He looked to his left to keep Buck Miller in sight, and saw Miller slanting still farther away as he climbed. He returned his attention to the man below him, and pulled his rifle into position; he watched the man grow wider and taller as he got nearer, he saw the man's eyes sweep the rim. Suddenly, with a fair shot open to him, Johnny stood up from the rocks—not knowing why he gave the man that much grace—and aimed on a shape suddenly in violent motion. The man discovered him and tried to turn the horse as he drew. Johnny's bullet tore its hole through the man's chest, from side to side.

The pitching horse threw the man from the saddle and plunged away. Johnny gave him no more thought, immediately running back toward his own horses. Miller, having reached the crest of the ridge half a mile distant, paused a moment there to hear the shot, to orient it, and to see Johnny. Then Miller ran down the slope, toward the toll bridge, toward The Dalles. Johnny reached his animals and filled his pipe and smoked it while he watched Miller fade out of sight in the swells of land to the north. Now he had trouble in front of him instead of behind him, for there was no way to reach The Dalles except by the toll bridge. But the odds were better—it was one and one now. When he had finished his pipe he started forward, plodding a dusty five miles an hour along a downhill land under a sky filling with sunlight. The trail reached a breakoff, the river running through a lava gorge far below. He took the narrow trail, winding from point to point.

Rounding a last bend and dropping down a last bench, he found the bridge before him—a row of planks nailed on two logs thrown over waters boiling violently between narrow walls. There was a pack string on the far side and four men sitting in the dust. Coming to the bridge, he had a look at the men over the way, and the shed beyond the house, and the crooked grade reaching up the hill behind the bridge. He went across and met the tollkeeper as the latter came out of the house.

"Two dollars," said the tollkeeper.

"Can you fill that nose bag with oats?"

"All right."

Johnny Potter pushed the horses toward a trough and let them drink. He waited for the man to furnish the oats and went to a water barrel with a cup hanging to it. He drank five cups of water straight down. When the man brought the oats, Johnny scattered a good feed on the ground for the horses. He paid his bill, watching the packers, watching the shed, watching all the blind corners of this place.

"Man pass here little while ago?"

The tollkeeper nodded and pointed toward the north. Johnny looked at the hill before him, the long gray folds tumbled together and the trail looping from point to point and disappearing and reappearing again. The sight of it thickened the weariness in his bones. "How long into The Dalles?"

"Ten, twelve hours."

Johnny said, "You know that fellow ahead?"

The tollkeeper said most briefly, "I know him." Then he added, "And he knows me." But this was still not enough, for he again spoke, "You know him?"

"Yes."

"Well, then," said the tollkeeper, and felt he had said everything necessary.

That made it clear, Johnny thought. Since Miller knew that the tollkeeper knew him, he probably wouldn't risk a murder so near witnesses. It was his guess he could climb the canyon without too much risk of ambush; it was only a guess, but he had to go ahead on it.

A hopeful thought occurred to him. "That pack outfit going my way?"

"No. South."

Johnny mounted and turned to the trail. Half an hour of steady riding brought him to a series of blind, short turns above which the gray parapets of land rose one after another, and the sense of nakedness was upon him once more. His muscles ached with the tension of waiting for trouble, and his nerves were jumpy. When he reached the summit, long afterward, he faced a country broken into ridges with deep canyons between.

In the middle of the burning afternoon he reached the beginnings of a great hollow which worked its way downward between rising ridge walls. The road went this way, threading the bottom of the hollow and curving out of sight as the hollow turned obediently to the crookedness of the ridges. He followed the road with his growing doubt, meanwhile watching the ridges lift above him, and studying the rocks and the occasional clusters of brush. Three miles of such traveling took him around half a dozen sharp bends and dropped him five hundred feet. He thought, *This is a hell of a place to be in*, and thought of backing out of the hollow. But his caution could not overcome his weariness; the notion of extra riding was too much, and so he continued forward, half listening for the crack of a gun to roll out of some hidden niche in the hills above him. The road curved again, and the curve brought him against a gray log hut a hundred yards onward, its roof shakes broken through in places, its door closed and its window staring at him—not a window with its sash, but an open space where a window once had been.

He halted. He drew his gun and he felt the wrongness of the place at once. Why, with the cabin showing the wear and tear of passing travelers, should the door be closed? He kept his eyes on the window square, realizing he could not turn and put his back to it; a rifle bullet would knock him out of the saddle long before he reached the protection of the curve. Neither could he climb the steep ridge and circle the cabin, for on that slope he would be a frozen target.

He got down from the horse and walked forward, the gun lifted and loosely sighted on the window square. The chinking between the logs, he noticed, had begun to fall away, but the logs, from this distance, didn't appear to have spaces between them large enough to shoot through. At two hundred feet he began to listen, knowing that if Miller was in the place he'd have his horse with him. He heard nothing. He pushed his feet forward and began to fight the entire weight of that cabin. It shoved him back, it made him use up his strength, it was like walking against a heavy wind.

The sun had dropped behind the western ridge and quick shadows were collecting in the hollow; he felt smaller and smaller underneath the high rims of the ridges, and the empty window square got to be like an eye staring directly at him. His stomach fluttered and grew hollow. He called out, "Hello! Anybody in there?"

His voice rolled around the emptiness. He stooped, never taking his eyes from the window square, and seized a handful of gravel from the road—walnut-sized chunks ground out of the roadbed by the passing freight teams. A hundred feet from the cabin he heaved the rocks at the window square. He missed the opening, but he heard the rocks slap the log wall, and suddenly he heard something else—the quick dancing of a disturbed horse inside the cabin. He jumped aside at once, and he straightened his aim on the squared window. A shadow moved inside the cabin and disappeared. Johnny broke into a run, rushing forward and springing aside again. He had thought there could be no moisture left within him after this brutal day, but he began to sweat, and his heart slugged him in the ribs. Energy rushed up from somewhere to jolt his muscles into quickness. A gun's report smashed around the inside of the cabin and its bullet scutted on the road behind Johnny. He saw the shadow moving forward toward the window. He saw Buck Miller stand there, Miller's face half concealed by his risen arm and his slowly aiming gun.

Johnny whipped his shot at the window, jumped and dodged, and fired again. Buck Miller's chest and shoulders swayed; the man's gun pulled off and the bullet went wide. Johnny stopped in his tracks. He laid two shots on that swinging torso and saw his target wheel aside. He ran on again and got to the corner of the house, hearing Miller's horse threshing about the cramped enclosure. Johnny got to the door, lifted the latch and flung it open; he was still in quick motion and ducked back from the door to wait out the shot. None came.

He held himself still for ten or fifteen seconds, or until a great fright made him back away from this side of the house and whirl about, half expecting to find that Buck Miller had got through the window and had come around behind him. He kept backing until he caught the two sides of the cabin. He stepped to the right to get a broader view of the cabin through the doorway, and presently he saw a shape, crouched or fallen, in the far corner. He walked toward the doorway, too exhausted to be cautious. The figure didn't move, and when he reached the doorway he found Buck Miller on his knees, head and shoulders jammed into the corner. He looked dead.

Johnny caught the horse's cheek strap as it got near the doorway; he pulled it outside and gave it a slap on the rump, then stepped into the cabin and went over to Miller. He moved Miller around by the shoulders and watched him fall over. Miller's hat fell off, and he rolled until he lay on his side. This was the fellow who figured that he, Johnny Potter, would run rather than stand up and kill a man. He thought, *How'd he know that much about me? He was right, but how'd he know?* He was sick and he was exhausted; he turned back through the doorway and leaned against the casing a moment to run a hand over his face and to rub away the dry salt and caked dust. His horses were three hundred feet up the road. His knees shook as he walked the distance, his wind gave out on him and he stopped a little while; then he went on and pulled himself into the saddle and started on through the growing twilight.

Even now, knowing he was safe, he found himself watching the shadows and the road with the same tension. It wouldn't break; it had been with him too long; and he reached the hill and rode down a last grade into The Dalles near ten o'clock at night with his ordeal behind him and the watchfulness screwing him tight. Wells Fargo was closed. He had to get the agent's address and go find him and bring him down to the office; he leaned against the desk while the dust was weighed out, and took his receipt. He found a stable for the horses, and from there went to the Umatilla House and got a room. He walked into the bar, went over to the steam table and ate a meal. Then he went to his room, took off his boots and laid his gun under the pillow. He flattened on the bed with nothing over him.

He thought, *Well, it's done, and they can buy their damned ranches*. He lay still, and felt stiffness crawl along his muscles like paralysis, and his eyelids, when he closed them, tortured him with their fiery stinging. The racket of the town came through the window, and a small wind shifted the curtain at the window. He opened his eyes, alert to a foreign thing somewhere in the room and searching for it. Finally, he saw what troubled him—a small glow of street light passing through the window and touching the room's wall. The curtain, moved by the wind, shifted its shadow back and forth on the wall. Saddle motion still rocked him and, soothed by this rocking, he fell asleep. It was not a good sleep; it was still the tense and fitful sleep of the trail, with his senses struggling to stay on guard, and quite suddenly the strongest warning struck him and he flung himself out of bed, straight out of his sleep, seized the revolver from beneath the pillow, and fired at the wall.

The roar of the gun woke him completely, and he discovered he had put a bullet through the curtain's shadow which wavered along the wall. He stared at it a moment, reasoning out his action, and he listened for somebody to come up the stairway on the heels of the shot. But nobody came; apparently this hotel was accustomed to the strange actions of people out of the wild country. He put the gun on the dresser and rolled back under the quilt and fell so deeply and peacefully asleep that a clap of thunder could not have stirred him.

DAKOTAHS COMING!
by MacKinlay Kantor

On a barren undulation which men called the Backbone, the three fugitives let their horses rest. They sat in their sweat, but with breath blowing white, as they examined the gray-and-brown prairie sloping into the south and east behind them.

A rising breeze came from the northwest; the high gray clouds of an April afternoon moved with it. Even in the wind's raw breath there was a shivering mention of spring. But the few ragged black butterflies which had strayed from hibernation when last week's sun showed its kindness, had long since made their lame way back into tree trunks or hollow boles.

Jo Phister said to Ansel Chambers, "Let me take the spyglass."

Silently, Chambers dug within the folds of his blanket and brought out a brass telescope. With great deliberation, Phister adjusted the instrument and pressed the lens against his eye.

The third member of the party, Samuel Rague, leaned forward to wipe his horse's muzzle. "I could take my ramrod," he said, "and sight a spot against the prairie, and see just as much."

Ansel Chambers grinned down at the plump little man beside him. "I've seen strange stars with my spyglass. That's more than you can see along your ramrod."

Rague asked, "Where'd you ever pick up that contraption, Anse?"

The tall young man took off his ragged fur cap and ran bony fingers through his hair. "It was three years ago, in fifty-four, over in the Cedar River country. The main thing that attracted me was its shininess. I thought it was gold. It belonged to a Methodist preacher, and I don't think he had any real need of it."

Jo Phister rapped the glass against his saddle and returned it to Anse.

"Well, Bright-eyes?" Rague demanded.

"I seen a jack rabbit," said Jo.

The others laughed. "Was he going at a trot or a canter?"

Phister squeezed his red beard. "He was traveling square south toward Swedes' Grove," he said in his Missouri whine.

Rague grunted contentedly and began to fill his pipe. Ansel Chambers closed his holster flaps; he spread the folds of his blanket to cover them. "Then we've shook a posse again."

"Yes," said Phister, "though I do conclude we'd better not visit Larkin City in the near future."

Rague wound an old blue tippet around his fat neck. "It's funny they never traced the horses' tracks into the Box-trap neighborhood. There was more snow on the ground than I thought there'd be; why, I was betting we'd lose all four horses. And we spent a good ten days accumulating them."

"You forgot the Bull River stage," Chambers reminded him.

"That's so. We did spend a day on that."

"And a night," added Phister. "We burnt powder, and lost some hide, and got scairt nigh to death." He spread the slash in the left sleeve of his coat and explored a bandage beneath with cautious fingers.

Rague grumbled, "But we only got thirty-eight dollars and a satchel of peddler's jewelry, for all our trouble. I still say that we spent ten days on them four horses alone. I'd make an easier living if I took up a claim, and broke the prairie, and planted a crop."

"I can just see you losing fat at the hind end of a plow, Sammy." Chambers squinted at the prairie again, and then turned his little blue horse into the wind. "All right, boys. The citizens have gone back to Larkin City and we can take it easy. Where do you want to make for tonight?"

Phister said, "We might as well turn back to Boxtrap Grove. Bonner has got the horses hid by this time; and we'll make him cut down a hog ham, and have the old lady cook us some biscuits. I do admire her gravy. She always has it plumb full of cracklings."

Ansel Chambers shook his furry head. "The last gravy she cooked was only fair-to-middling. She's not running true to form, since the Spirit Lake massacree. The very idea of Indians has got her scairt defenseless."

"It's the same with everybody else in Ioway," said Phister. "Just aching to be scairt! But I still do believe she's an A-1 cook, Indians or no Indians. If you don't want to go back there, Anse, I reckon we could put up for the night at Limpy Corbin's, over here on Vanishing Creek."

Sammy Rague objected, "Putting up at Limpy Corbin's will cost us five dollars hush money. I sometimes think it would be better to clout him on the head with a gun butt."

"Hold on," said Anse quietly.

His companions followed the direction of his motionless finger. After a few minutes Phister unlashed the buckskin case containing his rifle, and drew out the ramrod. He held it level with his eye, and covered with the tubular tip a single dark speck in the solemn expanse of brown grass and ice-rimmed sloughs. The empty prairie rolled beyond, all the way to a gray line that marked the Bull River timber.

"It's moving," Jo said at last. "Anse, how come you ever believed I had better eyes than yours?"

Chambers passed him the telescope. Phister watched a lone rider, who was skirting the nearer border of a slough.

As the men sat waiting, the northwest wind grew keener, and shook sleet out of the matted reeds. It forgot the spring, and spoke only of imagined Novembers and the false onrush of winter. Chambers and Rague drew their blankets over their shoulders; their horses swung tails in the wind, waiting patiently, subdued, with bowed heads.

Phister gave the telescope back to its owner. He was laughing. "It's old Teke Howell. I'd know that little spotted pony of his anywhere."

"We'd better get off the ridge," said Rague, in some alarm. "I know Tecumseh Howell, and he's a mean man with a gun. He's one of the Larkin City Border Scouts."

Anse ordered: "Stay where you are, Sammy. He can't make anything out of us, so long as we're not moving. We've got the ridge at our backs, and there's burnt patches hereabouts."

"I know old Teke Howell well enough," declared Phister. "I used to dance with his daughter whenever they had a doings down at Homer. I never knew him when he didn't travel with a flask of forty-rod. And my innards are mighty chilly."

Chambers frowned. "Teke Howell is one of the Larkin City Scouts."

"That don't make difference," said Phister, quickly. "He's looking for Dakotahs, not for gentlemen of the road such as we be. I don't mind admitting that I've slept more than one night in Teke Howell's stable. That was when the vigilantes were looking for me, too. No, he isn't interested in how many people lose their horses down in the south end of the county."

Chambers gripped his reins. "Let's go after him, then. We haven't bit food in fifteen hours. I could do with a swallow of forty-rod myself."

They brought their horses out of a chilly huddle, and started into the southwest. As the steep hummock gave into a more gradual slope, Ansel Chambers began to lope; the others came behind. There was a trail, worn by wandering buffalo in earlier years, and still the avenue of elk or other hoofed creatures that retreated into northern wildernesses, where most of the Indians had gone.

The brown dot became an insect with feet and heads; it stood motionless, as if the scout turned to watch the riders. Jo Phister whooped and flapped the skirts of his blanket. The toy rider by the slough's edge shifted his position. Before the distant figure had separated into component parts of horse and man, he moved rapidly forward.

"He's coming to meet us!" Sammy Rague yelled. "I hope he's got the liquor with him!"

Anse pulled in his horse so quickly that the others were ahead before they, too, came to a standstill. "Look," said Anse, "he's only riding around that little arm of the slough, nearest our side. Now he's going away, hell for leather."

The solitary scout's maneuver had brought him into closer view; they could see the white and chestnut patches of the pony he rode, and Jo Phister swore that he could see Teke Howell's long hair flying in the wind.

"Hell," said Anse, "he's afraid of us."

"Thinks we're Indians," Jo Phister agreed, and he began to yelp in the Dakotah fashion.

Sam Rague was rolling in his saddle with laughter. "Look at that old goat make tracks!"

"I reckon we're scaring him senseless," said Jo.

Together they galloped on Teke Howell's trail; Rague joined in the war whoop, and their outcry sent a covey of half-frozen quail buzzing from the bent grass. Anse yelled angrily, but his warning went unheeded, drowned by the gobbling chorus.

They stopped to rest near the margin of the slough. Old Teke Howell was only a dusty blur of steam and hoarfrost, a safe mile ahead of them. The grassy slough lay dark and muddy between; the northwest wind sent flat waves like venturing fleets, from under the splintered ice on the slough's edge.

But Anse was thinking hard as he came forward to join his companions. They were sober by this time, and Jo was chagrined to realize that his prank had surely cost them a warming refreshment.

"He's pointing straight for Morton's sugar bush. I reckon we can't catch him, and I did want a smell of that red-eye."

Anse ordered, "Hush your mouth, Missouri. I've got a wonderful notion," and the others rode close to hear him.

"It's near time to sugar off, isn't it?" asked Anse.

"Squirrel-ear leaves," said Rague, nodding. "I noticed the maples this morning, but I reckon they'll be froze solid in this weather."

Anse said, "Nevertheless, I saw fires burning all last night, where other people were sugaring. It was warm for ten days, and there's a good run of sap this year. There won't be much to flow, even if it warms up tomorrow, so the Mortons will be finishing off, and there'll be several men in the bush."

The others nodded in some perplexity.

"Teke Howell will come raring in. He'll claim he saw Dakotahs out here on the prairie, and probably that's what we looked like to his eyes. Now, what will those men in the sugar bush do about it?"

Phister slapped his leg. "They'll make for home, and they'll tell every living soul on the way."

"True enough," said Anse. "They'll make the fastest tracks they can towards Larkin City and I reckon they'll spread out to notify all the settlers. There's twenty cabins in the next twelve miles, some on the prairie and some along the timber, and what do you suppose those twenty families will do?"

Phister whispered, in admiration, "They'll lay on gad. They won't stop to draw breath. They'll fling their womenfolks and younguns aboard the wagons; I reckon the citizens of Larkin City will be building barricades around the Palmer Hotel by the time it's dead dark."

Sam Rague's fat face was shining with excitement. "Twenty

cabins, and not a soul left in them! But the trouble is, they'll take any money or important valuables they've got, even though they leave in haste."

"Sure enough," said Anse. "But there are plenty of things they won't have time to take, and won't think to take. They'll drive their teams, but there may be a colt or two left behind. There'll be hogs, and side meat and all manner of odd belongings that we can sell if we act quick. We'll have Frank Bonner freight the stuff eastward —a whole wagonload—and sell it in Waterloo or Iowa City. We don't need to clean anybody out, but we can get enough."

Phister licked his lips under his beard. "We'll just take the crack-lings out of the gravy, so to speak."

"Are you dead sure it will work out that way?" asked Sam.

Chambers snorted. "Come along to the Corbin house, if you don't believe me. That's the first place they'll make for when they leave the sugar grove. We've just got time to hide in the brush alongside."

Half an hour later, the three men crept through a brake of hazel that bordered the hollow above Limpy Corbin's house. It was a comfortless pastime, in this sudden duplicity of April; the men shivered in their blankets.

Neither Corbin nor any member of his family was in sight. A dog huddled disconsolately on the puncheon step; there were two pigs in the rail pen adjoining the little log barn. After a few minutes Anse hissed softly, and the men watched a flock of crows rising out of the woods in a hill toward the west. Presently the dog stood up and began to bay and bark, in alternate fright and challenge.

Three horsemen broke from the gray shadows of the western woods and rode rapidly between the stumps of the hillside. Limpy Corbin came out on the step with a rifle in his hand.

"Dakotahs!" yelled a voice. "Dakotahs coming!"

Jo Phister swore under his breath, and his hand jerked to the revolver that lay against his flank.

"Mind now," said Anse angrily.

"That's young Millard Morton," whispered Jo in a rage. "He led folks after us twice, and he's deviled the life out of me a dozen times. I'd like to accumulate his scalp."

Chambers patted Jo's elbow. "If you shot him now, you'd spoil the batch for us. Anyway, I never shot a man from ambush, and I don't think you ever wanted to before."

"No," grunted Phister, "but I do dislike a man who's so mean and smug and righteous."

Chambers nudged him into silence. They watched the house below them. The three men from the sugar camp were grouped before the doorstep; Chambers could not identify two of them, though their faces were familiar to him. But the figure of young Millard Morton was unmistakable. He was a huge man with round, smooth-shaven cheeks, and he sat his horse as if he had a rifle barrel for a spine.

"Teke Howell saw their scouts," Morton was telling old Limpy Corbin. "They chased him clear down to our sugar bush. Then Teke swam his horse across the river, and he's spreading the news on the other side."

One of the other men laughed grimly. "Morton was heartbroken," he said, "because he didn't have strychnine to put into the sirup. He thought the Indians might come and pizen themselves."

"By mighty," said Millard Morton, "I would have done it, too, if I'd had the poison. Come on; we've got to get to the Hempstead place."

Limpy Corbin shrieked to his son inside the cabin: "Hoist yourself out of that, Algy, and get some leather around the team! We won't stay here to be chawed." He said to the riders, "Take the top, boys. I'll drive the river road, and leave word at the Fishers' and the O'Connors' as I go."

He popped back into his cabin, and the men from the sugar camp loped across the cleared land, forded a little creek, and climbed the hill where the three outlaws lay hidden. They passed perilously close to the hazel brush; Jo Phister bared his teeth as the round, pink face of Millard Morton crossed his vision.

"I never could abide a skunk like that," he said, after the last hoofbeat had died away. "They say that Ezra Hempstead's gal is promised to him, and that's a fool choice for her. I heard him talk rude and ornery to his mother in the streets of Larkin City. Any man that will speak that way to a nice old lady deserves to have his hair lifted."

"Don't you worry," Anse told him. "There's plenty of people

would like to shave you to the bone, too. You don't talk mean to nice old ladies—you just take their silver spoons whenever you get a chance."

"Anyways," said Phister, reluctantly, "I always speak to them gentlemanly and polite. Now where are we bound?"

Chambers said, "Over to Hempstead's."

"They'll get there first."

"No, they won't," said Sam Rague. "We know the short cut across Mormon Hollow, and I reckon nobody else does."

They ran to their horses, untied the rude muzzles with which the animals were kept from nickering, and raced along the crest which hemmed the ravine.

"We'll strike the Hempstead place," said Anse Chambers, "from the southwest. Morton will come in from the north, and I wager we beat him by ten minutes."

Chambers would have lost his wager. Vanishing Creek ran high and frothy in its lower reaches, still swollen by the snows which had melted before this sudden freeze spread over the land; they had difficulty crossing into Mormon Hollow, and when they halted opposite the Hempstead house, they knew that there were only moments to spare.

A waste of dry leaves and rusty sunflower stalks lay north of the river timber, and the men halted behind this screen, confident that they were well hidden.

"Has Hempstead got a smart dog?" asked Chambers.

Rague said, "I remember hearing him tell, in Larkin City, that his dog froze to death in the February blizzard. We won't be smelt out of here."

"I'm going close," said Anse. "I want to hear the talk."

He wormed his way through the reedy tangle. A low barn built of poles and prairie sod lay between him and the Hempstead house, and he ran quickly the length of the vegetable garden, where stumps thrust up like hard little islands in the stiff, silver-crusted mud. There was an aperture in the south wall of the stable, and he could see the head of a cow inside. He spoke gently to the animal, scratched its astonished nose, and crawled through the window.

He exclaimed in surprise. There was a horse crowded into this stable, and even Chambers, a comparative newcomer in the neighborhood, knew that Ezra Hempstead owned neither horses nor oxen. Hempstead's land was cultivated with the aid of an ox team belonging to his son-in-law, who lived two miles distant on the prairie.

This stranger horse, wrapped with a ragged comforter, lifted its head to neigh at his coming. He cajoled the animal into silence, and then plunged beneath a pile of marsh hay, hurriedly raking it over his body. There were plenty of cracks before his eyes; he could have counted the wooden buttons on Millard Morton's deerskin jacket as the three messengers rode into the yard.

They had begun to cry, "Hello the house!" before they were out of the timber, and Iowa Hempstead was on the step when they dismounted from their horses.

Chambers had never seen Ezra Hempstead's daughter before. She was red-haired and very slender, and it excited him to realize that she did not twist her hair into a tight knot, like other women of the region. It fell thick and glimmering, in a short mane that brushed her narrow shoulders, and Anse fancied that he could see the marks of the wide-toothed retting comb with which she had performed a hurried toilet.

"Don't make so much noise, Mill," she said to Morton.

The pink-faced man did not dismount. "Iowa," he said, "go in and get your pa. You've got to light out. The Dakotahs are coming!"

The girl put her hands against her mouth.

"Hurry up, miss," cried one of the other men. "You daren't waste any time."

She said, "We can't go. I tell you we can't go!"

"Look here, honey," exclaimed her lover. He bent down stiffly and patted her shoulder. "I know you ain't got any team to run away with. But hurry and get on your duds, and rout out the old man. Two of us can carry double until we get to Guthrie's; then you can ride in their wagon."

Iowa shook her head, and her hair made a warm light in the dull afternoon. "We can't go," she said. "Dru's in there in the big bed, and Granny Norton is tending her. Pap went to fetch Granny this morning, but she says it won't happen for another hour or two."

Morton's face was flaming. "Drusilla! What in damnation is she doing here? Why can't your sister have her young'un in her own cabin?"

"Pete had to go to Larkin City. He brought her here yesterday."

"Well," said Morton's companion who had spoken before, "I'd never leave my wife on a childbed."

The girl cried, angrily, "Pete Carson had to go, I tell you! They were out of meal and out of pork, and he figured also that he could bring Doctor Lester to look after Drusilla. She was feeling poorly and——"

Morton dismounted stiffly, and stood with clenched hands on his hips. "Damn it, I've got to get you out of this! The Dakotahs will gobble up the whole lot of you."

The girl swallowed. "No, Mill," she said, "I reckon they won't. Maybe they won't even know our house is here. You can't see it from the prairie."

"That big, pock-faced Wahpakootah knows!" cried Morton. "If it's any of his tribe that's coming, he knows well enough. He begged his way up and down Bull River for the last three years, before he ran wild."

One of the other men said, "Inkpahdutah. He's a mean one."

As if she had heard a sound within the cabin, the girl turned and entered quickly, closing the door behind her.

"Mill," said the men, "we've got to make tracks."

"I know it."

Anse Chambers had risen out of his enshrouding hay. His first impulse had been to rush from the barn and laugh enormously, and say that it was all a mistake. But he was unarmed—both his revolvers and his rifle were attached to his pony saddle, and now he wished that he wore a weapon at his belt, like Jo Phister. Unarmed, it was certain that these men would shoot him down; all of them carried rifles. Millard Morton would shoot the quickest, and would take satisfaction in doing it.

Iowa Hempstead came out of the cabin again. "She's having the pains," she said. "I can't leave my sister behind, and we can't move her."

"Then I'll stay," said Morton, slowly.

The others cried, "No, you won't, Mill Morton! We've got to

spread out and warn everybody between here and Larkin City. There may be twenty-five lives hanging on your hands."

Morton considered for a moment; his sweetheart watched him silently, and Anse Chambers felt his own lip curling with disgust. He thought, *If that was my girl, I wouldn't care if there were a thousand lives hanging on my hands.*

She lifted her head calmly. "Go along, Mill."

Morton climbed quickly upon his horse. "I've just thought," he said. "I can wet-ford the river at Guthrie's, while Luke and Patrick bear to the east and south. I'll send one of the Taggarts on to do the message-bearing, and then I'll come back with the rest of the Taggart boys."

"You'll need more than Taggarts," said his companions, grimly.

The men rode out of the yard and splashed across Little Bull Creek. Morton turned and bellowed from the opposite bank, to Iowa, who still stood motionless on the doorstep: "Barricade the doors, honey, and have your pa get out his gun! I'll be back before dark."

Chambers slipped back to his friends and told them what had happened in the dooryard.

Rague began to laugh, but Phister was coldly indignant.

"I told you Morton was a weasel, for all his good size," he said. "I reckon he ain't even that! I reckon not even a weasel would run off and leave its mate, without showing fight."

"I'm going to go up and tell them not to worry," said Anse. He turned toward the house.

Rague said, "Keep your shirt on, Ansel Chambers. If you show your face now, it's a sure way to get it stretched. If this country once learns that we made out to be Dakotahs and scairt everybody liverless, people will track us down if they have to follow us to Wisconsin."

"There's more than one word of truth in that, Anse," agreed Jo Phister.

Chambers sighed. "All right, boys. But I do hate to wherrit a girl like that."

"She's a cute trick," said Rague, slyly. "Did you ever see such poison-orange hair in your life?"

"You shut your gab," said Anse. They rode away in silence, though the older men exchanged winks behind Chambers' back.

Laboriously they picked their way through scrawny timberland to the ridge which curled like a lizard along the western border of Hempstead's little valley. Their horses' hoofs had torn great rents in the clammy clay as they came down, and the ascent was difficult. They climbed into a level oak forest; the gloom lightened at its northern boundary, where the prairie begrudged all forests the liberty to grow.

"We're up," said Rague. "We're high and dry, and the whole county's moving to Missouri, and where do we go first?"

Anse Chambers leaned down and patted his tired little horse. "I wish somebody would leave some saddle horses in these parts. Ours are going to be tuckered before they're through."

"We could start with Limpy Corbin," urged Rague. "It would kind of square us up for all the money he's extorted from us."

"Pshaw," said Anse, "that don't seem decent!"

Phister scowled at his fat friend. "You do have the meanest ideas, Sammy. That wouldn't be fair play, no way."

"We'll ride the prairie to the Guthrie place," said Anse. "They'll all have skun out by the time we get there, and we'll help ourselves. Peter Guthrie has got a fine beaver hat that would look good on Jo there, and I calculate he'll forget to take it with him."

Jo Phister grinned amiably. "He'll remember to take his gold watch, though—that's the sore point. Anse, you do have the most remarkable ideas; your head isn't filled with wickedness like Sammy's."

They pushed forward. The cold oak woods grew paler ahead; the wads of dry, clinging leaves caught a reflected light from the prairie's blankness, and the freebooters could find no melancholy in any breeze that came to meet them.

They circled speedily among the trunks and crushed the hazel brush. It was as if they passed through a door from the region of somber branches and sleeping squirrels, to a ragged veranda fifty miles wide with only dun clouds to shadow it.

Neck deep in the bushes, they saw the frosty grass, woven by wind and winter, rolling into northern miles against Backbone Ridge. The prairie sloughs glimmered, spilled out like pools of lead amidst it.

But this formless precinct was being reclaimed by those people to whom destiny had so long allotted it; they chanted and yipped as they came. There was a long file of them, and they were half a mile away. Straight toward the tip of the valley timber they rode, at measured intervals—a file of mottled blankets and wild-maned ponies.

The white men dropped from their horses, and Jo Phister cut his cheek on a broken branch of hazel. With hands against their horses' mouths, they strained back among the sheltering oaks.

"Pottawottomies?" asked Sammy Rague in a dry voice.

"Hell," said Anse Chambers, "didn't you ever see Dakotahs before?"

Jo Phister brushed the blood from his chin. Chambers examined his revolvers; his hand jerked to his cartridge pouch. "How many rounds have you boys got?"

They counted with quivering fingers. Between them they had forty-nine rounds of revolver ammunition, but more than that for their rifles.

Phister opened his rifle holster. "If I were religious-minded," he whispered, "I'd say that Jehovah had done this on purpose to punish us."

"Maybe so," said Anse, "but we've got to see to it that He doesn't punish those womenfolks too. We'll make Hempstead's house before the Dakotahs do. Maybe we can hold them off a spell."

They had ridden on other desperate flights; never before, not even when angry men bawled within their hearing, had they penetrated a forest with such reckless speed. The branches tore at their blankets, and Chambers' horse slipped as they descended the last incline, throwing him heavily.

The little blue got up, painted with clay, whinnying. The others reined in momentarily, but Anse waved them on. He limped after his horse and mounted again, to come up with his comrades as they raced among the stumps of Ezra Hempstead's vegetable patch.

"Think they'll shoot?" gasped Jo. "Maybe we better give them a yell."

"No yell," Anse Chambers said. He dropped off his horse before the doorstep.

Inside the cabin, they heard a frightened murmur of voices and the straining sound of heavy furniture being moved.

Anse stepped up and pounded on the plank door. "Ezra Hempstead," he said, "open up!"

He heard the girl say, unbelievingly, "Why, pap, it's white men!" and then an old man's voice trembled as it asked who was outside.

"You know us by name," cried Chambers. The blood pounded at his temples. "But we don't mean harm. This is Anse Chambers; and Jo Phister and Sammy Rague are with me. There's a whole gang of Dakotahs up above on the prairie, and they'll be here in two shakes!"

There was silence inside—too long a silence, it seemed—and Chambers drove his nails into his palms. Then once more came the squeak of a moved trunk, and the door opened three inches. Iowa Hempstead stood inside, with her face close by the opening. She had her toe against the door, and she held a little pistol. Her face was very pale, but she looked at Anse with a certain proud contempt.

"You don't appear so mean," she said. "I've never seen you before, but I know the other two. Are you telling us the honest truth?"

Chambers sobbed, "Good God, miss, indeed I am! We were at the edge of the timber! We saw them coming!"

"How do you know they mean trouble?"

"Don't be a little fool," he said roughly. "You know what happened at Spirit Lake. The volunteers and the soldiers from Fort Ridgely have been chasing Dakotahs all over kingdom-come. They've got no good business in these parts, and they'll swill this house in a minute."

Jo Phister got out his tobacco and took a serious bite. "Not if we can help it, they won't, lady."

Iowa brushed her hair back from her eyes; the door opened a little wider. "I've heard such awful stories about you folks," she said. "I reckon you're all pretty ornery."

"Beside those murdering Wahpakootahs," said Rague, "we're just like three preachers."

The girl flung the door wide and let the pistol fall to her side. "My sister," she said, "Peter Carson's wife. She's—she's almost——"

"I know," Anse nodded, and the girl looked at him, wide-eyed. Chambers turned and put his reins in Sammy Rague's hand.

"Get off, Jo, and let Sam take your horse. . . . Put all three critters in that patch of cottonwood up the creek, Sammy; there's a chance that the Indians will miss them there."

Iowa cried to him, "Granny Norton rode over here on a horse!"

"I know," replied Anse again. "It's out in the stable. . . . Sam, you better take the Norton horse too."

"No, I won't," Rague declared in amazement. "What ails you, Anse? That horse don't know ours, and they'd kick and make a lot of fuss. We don't dare."

Phister climbed out of his saddle and came to the step, rifle in hand. The girl stepped back, still stern and terrified; she motioned nervously for the men to enter.

The room was dim and already chilly; Iowa had tried to put out the fire after Millard Morton left. Her father, Ezra Hempstead, was seated on a bunk which was built into the corner with a single leg to support it. He had an old smooth-bore musket which he was trying to load, but as he worked with a large book spread open on his knees, he was spilling the powder right and left.

Anse looked at the father and smiled. He had heard of Hempstead and his eccentricity. The man had been a schoolmaster in Dubuque before he had moved farther west; he had married one of his pupils, and Chambers could not forget his amazement at the beautiful fruit which had grown on this wintry bough.

Ezra Hempstead was very thin. His shoulder blades stood out like bony plates on his bent back; his eyes slept behind thick spectacles, and every movement he made was the motion of a man in a dream. He looked up at the two strangers and nodded vaguely.

"It's strange," he said, "to figure that birth and violence of this nature should happen so close together."

His daughter cried, "Pap, don't you understand who these men are? They're Phister and Anse Chambers, and the other one will be here in a minute! You've heard about them. They're——"

The old man blinked. "Yes," he said, "I've heard. You know what Montaigne says——" and his hand went fumbling toward the volume on his knees. He quoted: " 'The worst estate of man, is where he loseth the knowledge and government of himself.' "

Anse said, "Miss, I'm sorry, but I forgot to bring my shooting irons from the saddle."

Phister scampered outside and then came back. "Sam's bringing them along with him. Anse, I never reckoned you could be so wool-brained."

Rague entered, breathing hard. He slammed the weapons into Chambers' hands. "We ought to feed you to the Dakotahs for that, Anse."

"Anyway," said Chambers, "I'll try to use them well. What bothers me is—— I mean, in the next room and——"

The old man stood up, with wasted powder trickling from his trouser folds. "Speaking of childbirth, gentlemen," he said, "I cannot understand how so wise a man as Montaigne should be so set against children. I mean by that, the companionship with little folks and young people. Why, I taught forty scholars day in and day out, for——"

Iowa Hempstead had gone into the bedroom, but now she came back.

"Is your sister resting easy, miss?" asked Chambers.

"I guess it's never comfortable," said the girl. "I guess it hurts a lot, but it's bad coming like this. We got things ready as best we could, before I put out the fire."

Phister muttered, "Somebody will have to take that side of the house," and the men shuffled their feet.

Iowa said, shrilly, "My father can do that. Pap can! There's a window on the west, and we've got an old chest set against it. He can watch carefully, can't you, pap?"

The old man nodded. "I can get on with my reading between times."

Chambers ground his teeth. He went over and looked at Hempstead's musket. Then, with a rod, he dug out the clumsy wad and reloaded it more securely.

"If you see anything that looks like an Indian, mister," he ordered, "you blaze away. Can we depend upon you?"

"Yes," said Ezra Hempstead. "Oh, yes, indeed. We don't want them in here," and he chuckled at the idea.

The girl retreated with her father into the bedroom, and the three men looked at each other helplessly.

Sammy Rague shrugged. "I hope they don't come from the west; then some more of us will have to move into that room."

"Jo," said Anse, "take the north. Sam, you keep watch at the east. I'll take this south side."

As efficiently as was possible in such unfamiliar surroundings, the three made their preparations. The impending ordeal of the bedroom, the transition from careless brigandry to furious defense, left them silent and uncertain.

They had faith in themselves, but they knew that Ezra Hempstead would be useless when it came to the fight. They stared into the world of forests and half-frozen mud—the realm of crudeness and discomfort in which they had lived with a kind of savage satisfaction, until now. They felt themselves betrayed, and wished to riddle the very face of Nature for having deceived them.

There were no crows to give warning. There was no dog to act as sentry; the men waited at their stations, tense and silent. They could hear the young wife moaning in the adjoining room, and presently Iowa came out and closed the door. She sat on the one-legged bed opposite the chimney corner and tried to smile at Jo Phister.

Anse was at the south window. He had shoved a pork barrel underneath, and piled wood on top. There were glass panes, but he was ready to break them the moment hostilities began. There were four inches between the top log of his pile and the top of the window. He decided that would be enough.

He turned and looked at the girl in the corner. Her hair was like a lantern in the gloom; it gave more light than the few visible coals of the squelched fire, which still sighed amid its steam and ashes. Anse put his face back at the window. He wished that when he saw the Indians he would see Millard Morton among them, leading on with treacherous energy, like Simon Girty in the old stories.

Phister had punched out the chinking at two places in the north wall, and Rague had made a hole in the east side. He had objected to taking that post, for the hill rose abruptly beyond, and he was eager to fire the first shot. It would be a telling shot, Chambers knew. There was the metal of certainty and experience in Sammy Rague's trigger finger and in his washed-out eyes. Sometimes he displayed a badge which he had won for sharpshooting, long before he deserted the Army at Fort Leavenworth.

Iowa spoke softly. "I hate to see the chinking pushed out that way. I remember how pap was hard put to get it in. It was cold weather like this, and the clay froze his fingers apart. They were just like stiff claws."

"Can he work?" marveled Rague.

She laughed nervously. "Of course. He just gets spells when he won't do anything but sit around with a book. That's whenever he gets a new book. A mover gave him Montaigne in January, and he's scarce taken his nose out of it since."

"Do you see anything, Jo or Sammy?" asked Chambers.

They gave negative grunts. The bedroom door swung open and Ezra Hempstead appeared. For one moment the men heard the preliminary agony of labor, as if the awful miracle were occurring at an arm's length; then the thick door closed out the sound.

Hempstead's face was shining.

"Did you see anything in there, mister?"

"Certainly, certainly," said the old man. "I'm rereading, you know, and I found some good advice for you on Page Eighteen." He held the book close before his eyes and began to read: "'To deceive may serve for the instant, but he only is judged to be overcome, that knows he was not vanquished by craft or deceit, nor by fortune nor chance, but by mere valor, between troop and troop, in an overt and just war.'"

Phister held his eye against the cranny in the wall. "Old man," he said, without turning, "if you want to save your hide and that of your daughters, don't you desert your place again."

Chambers bawled, "Hempstead, are you crazy? Get back in the other room!"

"All right," said the householder, with sorrow. "But don't try to deceive those Indians. You meet them fair and honest, face to face. You can't win decently, otherwise." He tiptoed into the bedroom.

Iowa said sharply, "I'll go and keep watch there, no matter what he says."

"Do," said Anse, "for God's sake! He's reading that book, not watching the woods."

The girl went away, and Rague announced that he had seen two cottontails come bounding down the eastern slope. The men tightened their gaze on the outside world; every scrap of leaf or weed that rolled in the wind was a harbinger of foreboding and hostility.

Anse heard underbrush crackling in the distance. Twice more he counted the paper cartridges laid on the barrel top beside him;

then a discord of prairie-wolf howls and shrill laughter came from the lower creek; horses were splashing the water. Silently, Phister left his position and came over to peek out of the window. On that instant the Dakotahs moved into view below the stump-studded vegetable garden.

Anse smashed out the windowpanes.

"Circled clear around," muttered Phister, "and came in from the south. That's the way they do it."

Twenty or twenty-five Sioux rode in the party; they could not be counted properly, for they took shelter behind sunflower stalks and dried reeds which had screened the horse thieves only an hour before.

There was a yell, and lower-pitched hubbub.

"Found our tracks," said Anse.

"Maybe they'll follow them," whispered Rague from the wall, "and pass this place by."

It was a forlorn hope and an impossible one; he knew it even as he spoke. He went over and tapped on the bedroom door, and the red-haired girl peered out at him.

"They're moving in from the south," he said. "Tell your old man to get his gun, and be sure the bureau is shoved against the window. If you got anything else to move there, do that too. Make sure the drawers are tight filled; they'll help to stop the lead."

"And you," cried Anse over his shoulder, "get under a bed!"

The girl looked at him with scorn. "Dru can't get under the bed. I reckon I'll stay beside her and let her clutch to my hands." She closed the door.

Four of the Dakotahs left their shelter and began to wade rapidly toward the stable. They sank deep into the mud as they came, and they were shouting Hempstead's name, or trying to. "Hep-sed," they called, over and over, "Hep-sed." Coming from a point farther east than that where the white fugitives had hidden, they were not in the shelter of the barn; they made an easy target.

"Come here, Sam," said Anse. "You take the tall one ahead, and, Jo, you take the next, and I'll get the little one on the end."

Phister growled, "You're plumb uncertain in your head. Don't pick them off now. Maybe we can still talk them out of it."

"Like the devil," said Chambers, but he held his fire.

One of the Dakotahs wore a black slouch hat and a filthy, whiteman's overcoat. His legs were bare, and he had moccasins on his feet. The tallest man, who seemed to be a leader, held a green-and-red trader's blanket around him; he wore jeans breeches torn to rags between knee and ankle. All carried rifles or muskets, except the smallest Indian. He was drunk. He staggered in his tracks, and he was taken up with contemplation of a small saw which he waved in one hand.

"They've raided a cabin or two before this," said Anse, "sure as shooting."

The Indians stopped for a moment at the stable corner and surveyed the house. They seemed to find its closed silence not to their liking, and they moved more cautiously. One of them kept calling shrilly on Hempstead; the drunk man made a few dancing steps and waved his glimmering saw.

"Better give them a dose," said Chambers.

"No," insisted Jo, "they're funny. I still hanker to debate them out of it, for I've known of it being done. If we shoot only one, it's a fight."

Anse said, "Debate, for the love of God."

Phister yelled, "What do you want?"

The Sioux retreated to the corner of the stable and stood close against its wall, so that a shot could not reach them.

A voice asked, in Dakotah, "Who is in that house besides the man with four eyes whose name is Hempstead?"

"Ten men," Phister replied. "We have many guns, and we will kill you all if you make trouble. But if you promise to go away, we will make you a present. We will give you a horse."

There was mumbled discussion. The men could hear the shrill, spasmodic advice and opinion of other Indians in the thickets south of the garden.

Red-and-green showed at the stable corner. A voice demanded, "Where is the horse?"

"In the stable."

A silence followed. Fearful that unseen Dakotahs were creeping upon the cabin from other angles, Rague went back to the north wall, and Anse told Iowa Hempstead, through the closed door, to keep careful watch on the west.

The Indians must have entered the stable through the south window, for presently one of them appeared in the shadows of the low doorway. "It is an old horse and its teeth are bad. We do not want it. We want sugar and whisky, and a butcher knife that shoots."

Phister translated in a low voice, and said, "He means a pistol. Do you reckon we better dicker any longer?"

"No," said Chambers.

"Well, it means time. It'll be a long time before any white folks reach here. It'll be dead dark."

Anse said, "If we can hold them off for an hour, I don't think they'll stay past dusk. They know there's too many houses near by, and somebody would hear the shots."

From the stable sounded a commotion, and then a frightened bellow, cut short by the report of a shotgun. "They've killed the cow," said Anse. "I never knew an Indian that could let a tenderloin go by him. Usually that's all they butcher off, too. Do you see anything over there?"

"Not a wiggle," Sammy Rague replied.

Anse said, "Come here, then. We'll start shooting as soon as we see anybody."

The small Indian with the saw in his hand staggered heedlessly away from the sheltering stable, and Anse fired. The Indian spun on one foot and sprawled flat; the saw flew wide.

Inside the stable, the Indians yowled; and more hullabaloo came from the woods beyond. "Aren't you mean, Anse?" said Jo dryly. "You took the least one."

"It's fair," said Chambers, reloading his rifle. "That saw's got blood on it. Didn't you see? I reckon he's carved somebody's gizzard before this."

The Sioux in the stable began firing through the cracks. Their bullets chinked harmlessly against the logs and thick door planks. Iowa Hempstead peered out of the bedroom, and Chambers moved toward her, ramrod in one hand and rifle in the other. He thought that he might find the girl quivering in abject misery, but her face was merely cold and stern.

"The baby's being born," she said. "Pete Carson and Dru will have another mouth to feed."

Anse grinned through the gloom. "I hadn't thought of it until now, but we wouldn't mind feeding our own."

The girl's mouth tried to twist in a smile to match that of Anse Chambers. Her hands were muffled in white rags.

"You've got a level head, Miss Iowa."

She looked into his eyes. "Your head's level enough. It's hard to believe all the evil I've heard told about you. . . . I'd better go and help Granny. If you get a chance, there's pickled meat in the big barrel, and a pot of hominy and pork there on the hearth. I did have some barley coffee in the pot, but likely it's cold now." She closed the door.

Rague and Phister had not fired a shot. They stood close behind the barricade at the south window, with guns ready, watching intently, and now Phister yielded his place to Anse.

Chambers told him about the food, and the Missourian lifted his eyebrows. "I'll peek in the other directions," he said, "and then dig out some victuals for us. Damn that stable! I never thought about it before, but it gives them mighty fine shelter; they can shoot, and not be seen no way."

A bullet came through the window aperture; it broke a pitcher on an opposite shelf. Rague stepped back and blinked his eyes. A dozen Wahpakootahs rose in one motion, out of the brush at the south end of the garden. They started across the muddy ground toward the stable. Sam Rague leaned beside the window with the gun against his shoulder. "Give me your rifle," he said. "Get Jo's too."

He fired, and dropped his weapon into Chambers' ready hand, seizing his friend's gun in the same gesture. One Indian was on his knees in the mud and trying to crawl behind a stump, as the others came baying forward. Rague fired again, but missed; and his third shot, from Phister's rifle, caught one laggard Wahpakootah in the belly just as the mob reached shelter. The Indian doubled up, squealing; then he was pulled from view.

Iowa Hempstead opened the bedroom door and stood with her hands wound in her apron. She managed to say, "It's a girl. Drusilla's got a little girl."

"I hope she grows up as pretty as you," said Anse. He wondered why she should be terrified now, when she had been calm past human endurance before.

"Don't make a joke of my red hair," she whispered.

"Miss," said Chambers, "I do love red hair!"

Iowa pressed her thin hands against her mouth, as she had done so long before, when she stood on the doorstep. The hands sprang loose from her face, wrenched by a spasm of pure terror.

"Don't you understand?" she cried softly. "It's Drusilla. She——"

Chambers heard Phister whispering solemnly, "Sammy, I'm afeard the woman is dead."

"No, no!" sobbed Iowa Hempstead. "But she's—— The baby's born. It's all right. But Dru is growing weaker and weaker, and Granny Norton can't seem to bring her round. If Doctor Lester was here——"

Anse said sharply, "How far from here to Larkin City, the shortest way?"

"Nigh onto thirteen mile," muttered Phister, behind him.

Another bullet came through the window aperture, to splash its lead against the chimney stones.

The girl's face was tight and drawn. "You might meet Pete Carson coming back with Doctor Lester, out on the prairie. He intended to fetch him as soon as he could. Dru hadn't been well, and—— I guess the ride over here in the wagon, and the Dakotahs coming, and——"

Chambers turned and gazed at his companions. Sammy Rague took up a fold of his woolen tippet and mopped his face; it seemed not at all strange that there was no moisture for him to wipe away.

"They haven't spotted our ponies," said Anse. "They're in the cottonwoods, due north of this house."

"How would a man get out?" demanded Phister.

The girl whispered, "There's a north window in the bedroom. We could move away the other bureau."

"My God, lady," Phister muttered, "all this time you didn't tell us there was a north window."

Chambers said, "Let me look." He pushed open the heavy puncheon door. He did not look at the bed or the mass of suffering therein, nor at the old woman who fumbled at the bedside, nor at the dreaming man with his musket and his Montaigne. The north window was small, but he could estimate its size even with a battered chest of drawers drawn close. It would be simple for a man to scramble through.

"There's no time to waste," he heard himself saying. "Jo, you'd better take my rifle. I won't need it." He closed the door.

Iowa stood motionless. "Suppose they catch you?"

"They won't catch him," said Jo Phister, and swore heartily. "They'll catch me."

Rague stared at him, and then at Chambers, and merely grinned. He leaned down; working slowly and deliberately, he spread the already-frayed dry splinters of a rush-bottomed chair.

"The longest sliver goes," he said, "and goes quick." Still holding his rifle in his right hand, with his left he picked up the chair and held it toward Phister. "Peel away, John Phister, my Jo!"

Not seeming to breathe, Phister closed his bony fingers on a strip of the brown rush and tore it loose. It snapped short at a four-inch length.

"Anse," said Sammy, and Chambers came forward. He wrenched away; he held aloft a wisp an inch longer than Phister's.

Rague said, "You boys ain't light-fingered enough. Here's the way to do it." He placed the chair upon the table and carefully selected a ragged edge. Then, with one hand against the chair bottom, he worried the brown strip. It separated, grew narrower and narrower, but when he brought it out, it was as long as an eagle feather.

"Now I guess that chair is utterly ruined," he said. "It won't even hold your old man, miss, when he sets down to read that big book."

Anse could say nothing. Phister swallowed. "You better take a pistol at least, Sammy."

"One," said Rague. "You'll need the others here." He drew out a single heavy revolver and placed it beside the chair, which stood atop the table like a grotesque and deserted throne. He pulled his second revolver from its holster, looked at the caps, and then dropped it back again.

"You'll stick in that window!" cried Anse. "You're too heavy and fat! You——"

"No, I won't," said Rague. "You always said I was like a chunk of grease, and I'll go through there like a chunk of grease too." He slapped Phister on his lean rump and jammed his elbow against Chambers' side. "Now you got to shoot for three, gentlemen," he said. . . . "Miss Carrottop, will you please to open that door?"

Still with their backs to the bed and the sighing, whispering girl who lay in it, they moved the chest of drawers aside. They heard the old man murmuring in his scholarly dream: "'I utterly condemn all manner of violence, in the education of a young spirit.'" And outside, the world held more than a suggestion of dusk. In their frenzy, the men had been unaware of steady gloom occupying all space beyond the clouds, thickening until the distant cottonwoods were gray as ghosts.

A scatter of shots struck the house, and something smashed and fell in the outer room. "Go back to the front, boys," Rague grunted, twisting through the window. "Let them know you're handy, or they'll be down on you."

Phister and Anse pushed into the other room, closing the door behind them; Chambers' knees were trembling. Then he was at the window. Two Indians crouched in the barn door, and another was creeping forward, halfway across the dooryard. Chambers fired, and the crawling Indian rolled on his back.

Behind Anse, Phister made a whistling sound; then he had thundered across the room and was wrenching an old hair trunk away from the outside door.

Chambers heard Sammy Rague's voice. It seemed to come from a great distance, and all the venom of a thousand Irish warriors was in it.

"Get away," Rague was saying, "you damn niggers!"

Phister swung the chest aside, but Chambers tripped him, and he fell.

"For God's sake," said Jo, "they've got him! Some crawled around there. The old man never saw them."

"I'm going," said Anse. The wooden bar of the door defied him; splinters were stabbing his palms.

Phister said, "Think of her, Anse. You've got to look after these women!"

They gripped together in a struggling desperation which they could not understand, but Chambers was the stronger.

He stood on the open step with his two revolvers. The Dakotahs ran toward him from the barn and from its corners. Later, he knew that there were only six or eight, but then the world was patterned with bobbing black heads, with vermilion-splotched faces and ragged hats. He emptied his guns. Several of the Dakotahs were down and coughing, but others sprinted forward, and one caught Anse around the waist. They wrestled clear of the step. A steel knife flashed, but it only scraped the side of Chambers' head. Anse drew back his knee and drove his boot into the Indian's belly, and the Indian screamed to high heaven.

Chambers struck the ground, with two more Wahpakootahs on top of him. He thought that he would be suffocated with the smell of old grease and vermin that coated them; he thought, *Maybe I shouldn't have opened the door at all*, and he hooked his thumb into an eye socket, and felt the pulp of the eye squeeze out.

Someone was yelling. It wasn't Phister or the Indians, but a vociferous and angry challenge that pierced the wooded slopes far above Chambers' head, as if the trees themselves were moving to take part in the battle. The yell went on. It was sprinkled with shots now, and the splashing of horses that tore through water; so Anse knew that the trees were mounted; there was nothing fantastic in the idea of forests galloping to aid him. An enraged voice yelled something in the Dakotah language, and was answered. Anse had his hands around a throat that quivered and bulged, and slowly stiffened as his hands turned to stone.

The pressure upon his body was lifted suddenly. When he sat up, he could see figures flapping away toward the underbrush where the Indian ponies were hidden. He heard Millard Morton's voice, and was sorry to hear it. Iowa Hempstead left the cabin door and was floating toward him; she held a pistol that dangled aimlessly, with smoke trailing away from it. "Like that color hair," Anse said to himself. He went away from the world.

He saw the Taggart boys and knew them. They kept telling him, over and over again, how they, like the Mortons, had been making maple sugar. Old Mr. Dummer had cut his foot half off, while chopping wood the evening before; neighbors were at the Taggart house, and Doctor Lester, too, when the drenched Millard Morton came panting in upon them.

"But," Anse kept saying, "where's Sammy Rague? I've got to see Sammy," though they tried to persuade him otherwise. He would not rest until they had taken him into the weeds north of the cabin, and let him look at Sammy's feet sticking out stubbornly from under an old comforter.

They had covered Sammy at once, because the Dakotahs had

taken off his hair and hadn't made a neat job of it. He had company, too. There was another man lying ten feet away, with paint and charcoal unaltered on his face. Iowa had fired from the north window, and that was why the Indian stayed beside Sammy, and why Iowa's pistol was smoking when she came to meet the men.

In all, there were eleven Dakotahs who stayed at the Hempstead place, although one was long about his dying. He lay in the mud beside the stable, and remarked clearly again and again: "*Ho, wah sech che neepo Dakotah.*"

The Taggarts and other neighbors stood around in the yard, drawn into a group that watched Anse and Jo Phister sitting on the step. The darkness grew thicker and thicker all the time.

Phister could speak very few words. His jaw was swollen and purple; his ear was like a fat pancake where a rifle barrel had struck him as he came out of the house. When Iowa's brother-in-law shook his hand and Anse's, and kept crying, Phister did try to say something. But the first movement of his jaws made his eyes water.

The other men talked, and once Mill Morton's voice went high: "Why do I have to keep reminding the whole mess of you that you said it would be hanging, as soon as you laid hands on them?" There was a scuffle, then, and more was said. Big Winn Taggart dragged Morton away from the group and talked to him angrily.

They had built up the fire in the house. Light framed the door as Doctor Lester came out, looking very slight and uncertain, but speaking with reassuring conviction that made the men fall silent.

"I never did know a midwife who could handle a matter like that," Lester said curtly. "It's lucky I was at the Taggart place, and didn't have to ride all the way from Larkin City."

"Yes," they all said, "lucky enough."

And then Iowa Hempstead came out, and Anse stood up. His bandage stuck to his scalp and hurt him.

"Miss," he said, "will you see to it that Sam gets Christian burial?" She nodded without speaking.

"He'll have a board coffin," sobbed Pete Carson, "if I have to freight planks all the way from the Lick-skillet Mill. If I have to dig his grave myself——"

The doctor said, "You won't. Not in this community," and went in to see if the kettles were boiling.

"We've got to ride along," said Anse. Phister mumbled in painful agreement. "They brought our horses from the cottonwoods, a while ago."

Somebody asked, "How about those other horses, Anse? One of them belongs to my sister's folks."

"I might as well tell you," said Chambers. "They're over at Box-trap Grove, and Frank Bonner has got them hid for us. But you've got to swear you won't manhandle him, nor call in Judge Lynch."

Winn Taggart said, "Chambers, you've got our word for it. Maybe Bonner had better move out, now that we know about him. But he won't have to move out on no rail—no matter what Mill Morton's got to say, or anybody else."

Chambers looked down at the girl. He muttered, "Has Mill Morton still got anything to say about you?"

"Not a word, Anse," she sobbed. "Not a living, breathing word."

"Are you the kind of a girl who could give a man the mitten?"

She whispered, in one hot breath, "Not your kind, I couldn't! I couldn't hand you the mitten."

"Then I'll be back."

She said warningly, "But not to steal things! You daren't do that any more!"

"Well," he said, "I use to be apprenticed to a harness maker, but that's an awfully tiresome trade. I don't think I could make a go of it."

"Pap wanted me to give you this." She put the big book into his hands. "He's mighty grateful to you, and so are all of us. But he keeps quoting from this Montaigne book and saying, 'The worst estate of man, is where he loseth the knowledge and government of himself.' . . . Just when do you think you might be back?"

"As soon as I can," Chambers promised. He gripped the book tightly. "I'm not much on reading, but I'll take this along because you wish it. Might I ask you for some victuals?"

She cried, "There's a big sackful tied on to your saddle, or one of the saddles." She went with him and Phister into the darkness where their tired horses waited. Phister, fumbling as if he were drunk, unfastened the girth of Sammy Rague's saddle and dropped it to the ground. He put the bridle rein into Iowa's hand.

"Keep this horse here, miss," he said, his words distorted by the stiffness of swollen jaws, "until Anse Chambers comes back."

The door of the house was orange. Little light found its way into the cold fastnesses. They knew that Millard Morton and the other men watched without seeing them.

"Now," said Iowa sharply, "mind you don't steal any more horses or things!"

"Let me touch that hair of yours," whispered Anse. "I want to see if it's real."

The girl's kiss was printed against his mouth. She clung to him convulsively for a moment before he broke away and climbed into his saddle.

HOW MR. HICKOK
CAME TO CHEYENNE
by Alfred Henry Lewis

Within two days after his arrival Mr. Hickok was established in the best society of Cheyenne. This, when one reflects upon the iron-bound exclusiveness of Cheyenne first circles, should talk loudly in Mr. Hickok's favor. It was something whereof any gentleman might be proud. The Inter-Ocean, being that hostelry which he honored with his custom, was as his home; and he stood good for a dozen stacks of blues at any faro table in the camp. And this, mind you, in days when Cheyenne confidence came forward slowly, and the Cheyenne hand was not outstretched to every paltry individual who got off the stage.

Two weeks prior to these exaltations, Mr. Hickok, then of Kansas City, might have been seen walking in that portion of Main Street known as Battle Row. For one of his optimism Mr. Hickok's mood showed blue and dull. One might tell it by a brooding eye and the droop which invested his mustache with a gravity not properly its own. Moreover, there was further evidence to prove the low spirits of Mr. Hickok. His hair, long as the hair of a woman, and which in lighter moments fell in a blond cataract about his yard-wide shoulders, was knotted away beneath his hat.

For myself, I do not praise long hair in the case of any man. But Mr. Hickok had much in his defense. He had let his hair grow in years when the transaction of his destinies gave him a deal to do with Indians. The American savage possesses theories that yield neither to evidence nor argument. He believes that every paleface who cuts short his hair does so in craven denial of a scalp to what enemy should rise victorious over him. Such harehearts be contemns. On the guileless other hand, he holds that the long-haired man is a warrior bold, flaunting defiance with every toss of his mane. That long-haired one may rob and cheat and swindle and cuff and kick your savage: the latter will neither murmur nor lift hand against him. For is not he who robs and cheats and swindles and cuffs and kicks a chief, and is not his flowing hair a franchise so to do? There lurks a dividend in hair for any who traffics with your savage. Wherefore, in an hour of aboriginal commerce Mr. Hickok encouraged a hirsute luxuriance in the name of trade. Later, he continued it for the sake of habit and old days. That much for Mr. Hickok's hair—as plentiful and as coarse as a pony's. Let me repeat, that to find it furled from view was notice that his soul was sad.

What should be it to prey upon the sensibilities of Mr. Hickok? Kansas City was a town of mud and dust and hill and hollow that quenched all happiness and drove the male inhabitants to drink. Was it that to bear him down? No; if it were mere environment Mr. Hickok would have made his escape to regions where the sun was shining.

Not to run the trail too far, Mr. Hickok was ruminating the loss of his final dollar, which had fled across a faro layout in the Marble Hall Saloon. As he strolled dejectedly in Battle Row he couldn't have told where his next week's board was coming from, not counting his next week's drinks. It was the dismal present, promising a dismal future, which exhaled those mists to take the curl from Mr. Hickok's mustache and teach his hair to hide beneath his hat. A short-haired man may be penniless and still command respect; a long-haired man without a dollar is a creature to be laughed at.

Having nothing to engage him but his gloom, Mr. Hickok glanced upward and across the street where, over the fourth story windows, an Odd Fellows' sign was bolted. The sign was painted black upon white. The "O" that stood as initial of "Odd" showed wood-color inside the black.

It was years before when, to please a bevy of tender tourists and by permission of Mr. Speers, then chief of police, Mr. Hickok emptied his six-shooters into the centre of that "O." It was a finished piece of shooting; the tourists told of it about their clubs when safe in the East again. The "O," where the original white had been splintered into wood-color by those dozen bullets it had stopped, showed plain as print.

Mr. Hickok sighed as he considered his handiwork.

Mr. Hickok did not sigh because of any former accuracy with

pistols; but he recalled how on that fine occasion—in contrast to present bankruptcy—he harbored $1400 in his clothes. He had beaten the bank at Old Number Three, and was rich and gay in consequence.

"I think I shoot better when I've got a roll."

Thus murmured Mr. Hickok as he meditated on that miracle of the guns, done seven years before. Mr. Hickok might have extended his surmise: a man does all things better when he has a roll.

The panorama of life had been moving swiftly for Mr. Hickok. Two years before, he was marshal of Hays and had shot his way into general confidence. In an evil hour a trio of soldiers came over from the fort, led by one Lanigan, and took drunken umbrage at Mr. Hickok's hair. This rudeness touched Mr. Hickok tenderly, and in reproof thereof he snuffed out those three as gallery Frenchmen snuff candles at ten paces.

Since there arose carpers to say that Mr. Hickok went too far in those homicides, he laid down his trust and removed to Abilene. Mr. Hickok was welcomed with spread arms by Abilene. Its marshal had just been gathered home through the efforts of a cowboy with a genius for firearms. Abilene offered the vacant place to Mr. Hickok, and to encourage acceptance showed him where it had hanged the cowboy. Mr. Hickok accepted, drew on the public purse for five hundred rounds of ammunition, and entered upon his duties.

Mr. Hickok reigned as marshal eight months, and kept Abilene like a church. Then he put a bullet through the head of Mr. Coe, a gentleman whose pleasure it had been to go upon tri-weekly sprees and leave everything on both sides of the street.

As on that day in Hays, there were local narrowists to fling reproach upon Mr. Hickok. They said the affair might have been sufficiently managed by the simple process of bending a gun over Mr. Coe's head; the dead gentleman had yielded to such treatment on former occasions. They declared that the intemperate haste of Mr. Hickok had eliminated from Abilene one who spent his money with both hands; the taking off of Mr. Coe might conduce to communal peace; it was none the less a blow at Abilene prosperity.

Mr. Hickok, made heartsore by such mean strictures and weary with complaints which found sordid footing in a lust for gain, gave up his marshalship of Abilene as he had given up the post in Hays, and again wandered abroad in search of better fortune.

About the time he shook the Abilene dust from his moccasins there came to Mr. Hickok's hand a proposal from Mr. Cody to join that gentleman in the production of a spirited drama. It was to be a drama descriptive of the Arcadian West; one wherein stages were robbed, maidens rescued, and Indians put to death. Mr. Hickok in real life had for long been familiar with every fraction of the stage business; the lines he could learn in a night. Mr. Cody was confident that Mr. Hickok would take instant part in that drama and do it without rehearsal. If Mr. Hickok accepted, the financial side should be framed and phrased to meet his views. His social life, so Mr. Cody explained, should be one of splendor and Eastern luxury.

Mr. Hickok, pausing only to ruin himself at faro-bank, took up the proffer of Mr. Cody. He journeyed East, and found that excellent personage sojourning at the Brevoort House in New York.

"Where's your trunk?" asked Mr. Cody, as he grasped Mr. Hickok's hand.

"Haven't any," returned Mr. Hickok, whose trunk had been left to keep a boarding-house in countenance. "But I've brought my guns." This last hopefully.

"That's right," observed Mr. Cody, whom nothing was ever known to daunt. "While a gentleman may be without a change of linen, he should never let his wardrobe sink so low that it leaves him without a change of guns."

Mr. Hickok was not a permanency in the theatres. His was a serious nature, and there abode much behind the footlights to irk the soul of him. For one stifling matter, he was allowed nothing lethal wherewith to feed his six-shooters. Blanks by the hundreds he might have; but no bullets.

Now this, in a blind sort of way, told upon Mr. Hickok as something irreligious. A Colt's .45 was not a joke; its mechanism had not been connived in any spirit of facetiousness. It was hardware for life and death; it owned a mission; and to make of it a bauble and a tinsel thing smote upon Mr. Hickok as sacrilege.

And, then, to shoot over the heads of folk shook his faith in himself. It was as though he mocked the heavens! In good truth, Mr. Hickok never did this last. It was his wont to empty his weapons right and left at the legs of Indian-seeming supers.

The practice was not lacking in elements of certain excellence. The powder burned the supers and brought yells which were real from those adjuncts of the drama. In that way was the public gratified and the integrity of the stage upheld.

But the supers objected, and refused to go on with Mr. Hickok. They might love their art, but not to that exent. It was the rock on which they split. Mr. Hickok would not aim high, and the burned ones would take no part in the presentation unless he did. The situation became strained. As a finale, after bitter words had been spoken on both sides, Mr. Hickok quit the mimic world and returned to a life that, though it numbered its drawbacks, might make the boast that it was real. It was then he came to Kansas City, there to experience many ebbing, flowing nights at faro-bank, with that final ebb adverted to, and which left him dollar-stranded, as described.

We left Mr. Hickok in Battle Row thinking on the strangeness of things. Let us get back to him with speed; I warrant him one to notice a too long neglect and desperately resent it.

Mr. Hickok, having sufficiently surveyed his bullet-work of another day as set forth by the Odd Fellows' emblem, was about to resume his walk, when a telegraph boy rushed up. His rush over, the urchin gazed upon Mr. Hickok with the utmost satisfaction for the space of thirty seconds. Then he took a message from his book.

"Be you Mr. Hickok?" he asked.

"Yes, my boy," replied Mr. Hickok blandly. Mr. Hickok was tolerant of youth.

"Mr. Wild Bill Hickok?"

Mr. Hickok frowned; he disliked the ferocious prefix. It had been granted him, by certain romanticists with a bent to be fantastic, for deeds of erratic daring done long before. It was a step in titles the more strange, perhaps, since Mr. Hickok was not baptized William but James.

But "Wild Bill" they made it, and "Wild Bill" it remained; albeit, in deference to Mr. Hickok's known wishes—he once made them plain by shooting a glass of whisky from the hand of a gentleman who had called him Wild Bill, to that gentleman's disturbance and a loss to him besides of one drink—he was never so named except behind his back. When folk referred to him they called him

Wild Bill; when they addressed him they did so as Mr. Hickok. The moment that the world and Mr. Hickok understood each other on this touchy point of titles every sign of friction ceased. The compromise won tacit adoption; and everybody went satisfied, since everybody went not without his partial way.

Mr. Hickok tore open the message, while the boy who had brought it admired him to the hilts. The message was long, from which Mr. Hickok sagaciously deduced it to be important. Mr. Hickok was not over-quick with written English; he had been called in the theatres a "slow study." To expedite affairs, Mr. Hickok went at once to the signature. This was intelligent enough. Any man as a rule could give you every word of any eight-page letter he receives by merely glancing at the signature. This will prove peculiarly the case when the signature is a lady's.

However, this time the rule failed. Mr. Hickok, though he knew the name, was driven to wade through the communication before he could come by even a glint of its purport. This he did slowly and painfully, feeling his way from word to word as though fording a strange and turbid stream. At last, when he made it out, Mr. Hickok's face came brightly forth from the shadows like the sun from out a cloud. Evidently the news was good.

Mr. Hickok glanced again at the name. It was that of a generous man whose life he had saved. Lest you gather unjustly some red and dripping picture of Mr. Hickok as one to whom the slaughter of his fellows was as the air he breathed, it should be shown that he had saved many lives. The record of this truth would gratify Mr. Hickok were he here to read it, for he often remembered it in conversation.

"If I've took life," Mr. Hickok would remark defensively, "I've frequent saved life. Likewise, I've saved a heap more than I've took. That's straight; the world's ahead by me. If you'll foot up the figgers you'll see I've got lives comin' to me right now."

What the saved one who was grateful said was this: He had staked out a claim in the Deadwood district; the assay showed it full of yellow promise. Mr. Hickok was to be half owner. Mr. Hickok was to meet the grateful one in Cheyenne. Incidentally, the grateful one had notified the American National to cash Mr. Hickok's draft for two hundred dollars, so that poverty, should such have Mr.

Hickok in its coils—which it had—might not deter him from proceeding to Cheyenne at once.

Nothing could have better dovetailed with the worn destinies of Mr. Hickok for their rehabilitation. Within thirty minutes he had drawn those two hundred dollars; in forty he had sent three messages. The first was to the grateful one, promising instant appearance in Cheyenne. The others were of grimmer purpose, and went respectively to Abilene and Hays. These latter were meant to clear the honor of Mr. Hickok.

When Mr. Hickok went into the drama there broke out in Hays and Abilene a deal of invidious comment. There were folk of bilious fancy and unguarded lip who went saying that Mr. Hickok had fled to the footlights as a refuge. He had made enemies, as one who goes shooting up and down our Western streets is prone to do; certain clots and coteries of these made Hays and Abilene their home camps. It was because he feared these foes, and shrunk from the consequences of their feuds, that he called himself an actor, and was shouting and charging and shooting blank cartridges at imitation Indians throughout an anaemic East. Such childish employment kept Mr. Hickok beyond the talons of his enemies: that was the reason of it; and the reason was the reason of a dog. Thus spake Mr. Hickok's detractors; and none arose to deny, since Mr. Hickok's honor was his honor, and the West does business by the aphorism: "Let every man skin his own eel."

Mr. Hickok had not gone in ignorance of these slanders; he had heard them when as far away from Abilene and Hays as Boston Common. Now, he would refute them; he would give all who desired it an opportunity to burn condemnatory powder in his case. He would pass through Hays and Abilene on his slow way to Cheyenne. These hamlets should be notified. Those who objected to Mr. Hickok's career in any of its incidents might come down to the train and evince their disapproval with their guns. With this fair thought, Mr. Hickok addressed as follows the editors of Abilene and Hays:

"I shall go through at such and such an hour, on such and such a day. I wear my hair as long as ever."

The press is a great and potent engine; and who has public interest more at heart than has your editor? Those of Abilene and Hays posted with all diligence the messages of Mr. Hickok on their bulletin-boards, and then made preparation to tell fullest stories of the homicides.

Mr. Hickok cleaned and oiled his guns, and took the train. He looked forward cheerfully to Hays and Abilene. Experience had taught him that the odds were as fifty are to one that not a warlike soul would interrupt his progress. Humanity talks fifty times where once it shoots, and Mr. Hickok was not ignorant of the race in its verbal ferocities. Indeed, being a philosopher, he explained them.

"A man," observed Mr. Hickok, "nacherally does a heap more shootin' with his mouth than with his gun. An' for two reasons, to wit"—here Mr. Hickok would raise invoking finger—"he's a shorer, quicker shot with his mouth; and it costs less for ammunition. A gent can load and fire his mouth off forty times with a ten-cent drink of licker."

To be sure, some vigorous person, whether at Abilene or Hays, might appear in the path of Mr. Hickok on battle bent. Wherefore, as aforesaid, he loaded his Colt's .45's.

"Because," as Mr. Hickok stated it, "I wouldn't want to be caught four-flushin' if some party called my bluff."

It will seem strange that Mr. Hickok was willing thus to invite hostilities. But there were reasons. The perilous case of his honor has already been set forth. Beyond that Mr. Hickok was indifferent. He proposed no attack; he arranged only for defense, and Mr. Hickok knew just enough of the land he lived in to be aware that his right of defense was perfect under the Constitution. The personal danger he thus courted never once addressed the thoughts of Mr. Hickok.

Mr. Hickok was, like most of those who put in their lives upon the dreary, shadowless, outstretched deserts of the utter West, a fatalist. He would live his days; until his time arrived he was safe from halter, knife and gun. If one had asked Mr. Hickok why was he born he couldn't have told. But he would have explained that he didn't care. Mr. Hickok had all unconsciously become a fashion of white Indian, and based existence on a fearlessness that never wavered, added to an indifference that never asked a question. He was what he was; he would be what he would. Men were merest arrows in the air, shot by some sightless archery of nature, one to have a higher and one a lower flight, and each to come clattering back to earth and bury itself in the grave. That was the thought of

Mr. Hickok, or rather Mr. Hickok's instinct; for he never shaped it to an idea nor piled it up in words.

It was as Mr. Hickok surmised: there were scores to greet him at Hays and Abilene, but none in hostile guise. While the train paused Mr. Hickok swung down from the platform and stood with his back against the car. There he received his friends and searched the throng for enemies. He was careful, but invincible, and his hair floated bravely as for a challenge.

As the bell rang Mr. Hickok backed smilingly and watchfully aboard. He had no notion of exposing himself to any with military talent enough to manage an attack in flank. But the peace of those visits to former scenes of smoky effort passed unbroken; and Mr. Hickok's honor was repaired. Mr. Hickok was not above a sedate joy concerning his healed honor, for though he might not own a creed he had a pride.

Now that Hays and Abilene had become parcel of the things that were, Mr. Hickok sat himself down to a contemplation of Cheyenne. This would be his earliest visit to that metropolis. Nor had he in days gone made the acquaintance of any who gave Cheyenne as his home. For which reasons Mr. Hickok decided on a modest entrance.

"Which if thar's one thing that's always made me tired," observed Mr. Hickok, as he talked the subject over with himself, "it's a strange party jumpin' into camp an' domineerin' 'round as though he owned the yearth an' was thar to let it out on shares."

Mr. Hickok planned an unobtrusive descent upon Cheyenne. He would appear in its midst without announcement. He would uncover his merits one by one and permit Cheyenne to learn his identity only when events should point the day and way. He would claim no privileges beyond the privileges of common men.

Such was the simple plan of Mr. Hickok, and he arrayed himself to be in harmony therewith. The corn-colored mane that had flaunted at Hays and Abilene was made prisoner—as in Kansas City —beneath a small-rimmed, soft felt hat which would kindle rage in no man. Because the whiteness of the sun on the parched pampas hurt his eyes, worn as they were with much scanning of midnight decks, Mr. Hickok donned dark goggles. His coat was black and long—to cover his artillery—and almost clerical. To put a finish on a *tout ensemble* that spoke of lambs'-wool peace, Mr. Hickok, limping with a shade of rheumatism, the harvest of many nights on rain-soaked prairies, carried a cane. This latter implement was a resplendent creature, being the butt end of a rosewood billiard-cue, and as heavy, withal, as a Sioux war-club. Thus did Mr. Hickok appear when he made his Cheyenne début. Had any observed him as he went halting up the street he would have been held for one of those evangelists common of the West, present with a purpose to hold services.

Mr. Hickok's Deadwood friend had not arrived. There was word waiting at the Inter-Ocean Hotel that he would not come for a week. Mr. Hickok, at that, decided for recreation.

It was ten of the clock on the first evening, and Mr. Hickok concluded to creep about on his billiard-cue and take a friendly view of Cheyenne. It was well to go abroad with what decent speed he might and acquire a high regard for Cheyenne people; it would be a best, quick method of teaching them to entertain a high regard for him.

"But no trouble!" exclaimed Mr. Hickok with a decisive shake of the head. He was, according to his custom, advising with himself. "No trouble! Thar's nothin' in it. Besides, the first thing I know I'll get bumped off. The pitcher that goes often to the well gets busted at last." And Mr. Hickok sighed sagaciously. Then, as one who registers a good resolve: "From now on I keep out of every row. The next sport who gets a rise out o' me will have to back me into a corner an' prove concloosive that he's out to skelp me. Then, of course, I'll take my usual measures. Thar's nothin' in a row; I never won a white chip in one. Besides, thar's two ends to a row, same as thar's two ends to a faro layout. An' no gent's cunnin' enough to see the finish. While he's tryin' to win a bet in the 'pot' he may lose one in the 'big square'; an' thar you be!"

Such were the cogitations of Mr. Hickok when he turned into the Gold Room Saloon.

"What'll you have, Sport?" asked the barkeeper.

"Licker," said Mr. Hickok, leaning on the bar.

The barkeeper tossed up glass and bottle in a manner of scorn. He had called Mr. Hickok "Sport" not for compliment, as one might think, but in derision, and because Mr. Hickok looked like an agriculturist who had strayed from the fold.

"Got a potato ranch some'ers?" remarked the barkeeper. "Or mebby is it hay?"

Mr. Hickok made no retort as he paid the double price which the astute barman charged him. He knew he was derided, and he knew he was robbed; but, full of peace, he bore it in a spirit of wordless humility.

"Now, if that barkeep," he reflected, "knowed who I was he'd about hit three or four high places and be miles away."

Mr. Hickok inched toward a faro game which was raging in the rear. Though he had but one hundred dollars he bet the half on the "high card." The turn came, king-trey; Mr. Hickok's fifty were swept into the bank. Nothing discouraged, Mr. Hickok wagered the other fifty on the "high card." The turn came, deuce-eight. The dealer counted down twenty-five dollars.

"How's that?" asked Mr. Hickok.

"The limit's twenty-five," spake the dealer, and the lookout echoed: "Limit's twenty-five!"

"But you took fifty when I lost," observed Mr. Hickok.

"Oh! fifty goes if you lose," retorted the dealer insolently, and the lookout with echoing insolence repeated: "It goes if you lose!"

Then did Mr. Hickok rejoice because of a provident rheumatism that furnished him his excellent billiard-cue.

Biff! bang!

Mr. Hickok tapped the dealer and lookout. They fell from their respective perches like apples when one shakes November's bough. Having cleared a path to the feet of justice, Mr. Hickok reached across and helped himself to a roll of money which, to quote the scandalized barkeeper who beheld the rapine from afar, was "a roll big enough to choke a cow!"

Having repaired his money wrongs, as that portion of the Cheyenne public then and there present fell upon him, he recurred to his billiard-cue. A dozen heads suffered. He fought his way to the wall.

"Now, everybody fill his hand!" shouted Mr. Hickok. With that his eight-inch six-shooters came to the fore.

Mr. Hickok's goggles had fallen to the floor; his loosened yellow mane was flying like a war banner. Altogether, when thus backed against the wall, and behind a brace of Colt's best pistols, flowing locks, and eyes like gray fire, Mr. Hickok made a striking figure and one to live long in Cheyenne memory. Then one, sophisticated, yelled:

"It's Wild Bill!"

There was no dispute over Mr. Hickok's identity. The public at once conceded it, and began going through doors and windows in blocks of five. Mr. Hickok, thus deserted, limped slowly toward the front door. As he passed the bar its once supercilious custodian raised his head above its sloppy levels and asked in meekness: "Mr. Hickok, will you have a drink? It's on the house."

It was the next afternoon; the Cheyenne marshal, accompanied by Mr. Bowlby, proprietor of the Gold Room Saloon, paid a courtly visit to Mr. Hickok. The marshal was aggrieved.

"You ought not to come ambuscagin' into camp that a-way," he remonstrated, speaking of Mr. Hickok's modest advent into town. "It might have got a passel of Cheyenne people killed—some of our best people, too. It wa'n't right, Mr. Hickok. Only it's you I'd think it bordered on the treacherous."

"It ain't that I'm askin' it back, Mr. Hickok," observed Mr. Bowlby diffidently, "but I want to check up my game. Sech bein' my motive, would you-all mind informin' me how big a wad you got outen that drawer?"

"Which I shore couldn't say, Mr. Bowlby," returned Mr. Hickok languidly. "You see, I ain't counted it none as yet." Then, as one who arouses himself to deeds of friendly generosity: "But, Mr. Bowlby, I don't reckon now I oughter keep all that money. I'd feel easier if you'd let me split it with you."

"No 'bjections in the least," replied Mr. Bowlby politely.

"Which I should shorely say as much!" exclaimed the marshal, in enthusiastic admiration of Mr. Hickok's liberality. "Thar's an offer good enough for a dog! An' now, gents," concluded the marshal, linking arms with Mr. Hickok and Mr. Bowlby, "let's go some'ers an' licker."

THE HASTY HANGING
by Morgan Lewis

The coffeepot spouted steam from its snout, finally forcing its way
through Chris Holden's painful musing. He set it back to draw and
was again still, standing hip-shot beside the stove, a tall and rangy
youngster just past twenty with a shock of wild black hair. His wide-
spaced gray eyes wandered over the room with all its closely familiar
things; the battered old dresser, the table and chairs made in slack
winters, the magazine pictures tacked to the wall and, in the next
room, his stripped bunk, the bedding rolled for travel.

He had been on his own since he was fourteen, and the fight
to survive and amount to something had stamped its marks in the
tough angles of his brown young face. He had schooled himself
to be hard and efficient, like big Jim Dunkle, who owned the vast
Box D ranch down on the flats, but a glint of misery showed in his
eyes; getting this last meal on his ranch was a sad thing. The arctic
cold and obliterating snows of the winter had wiped him out. Now,
in the springtime, the bodies of his cattle rotted where they had
died. And there was no chance for a fresh start; panic had the country by the throat, prices were below costs and money was scarce as
water in the desert.

A hail from outside startled him and took him out onto the shallow porch.

Jim Dunkle sat his bay horse five feet from the house, a solidly
built man with a face flat as a spade, his coat buttoned against the
fresh spring breeze. Behind him the broken foothills fell away to
the lush, level plateau that was his.

He slapped his hard thigh with a gloved hand. "Grab your horse,
Chris, and come along! We've got the buzzards that've been
stealin' stock! Ed Fuller and Stumpy are holdin' 'em over on
Pawnee Flats." Anger was a vibration in his voice.

From habit Chris nodded and turned away. Dunkle had employed him for three years, had helped him to get a start, and he felt a certain obligation. He took two steps, turned back.

"I don't reckon I'll go along, Mr. Dunkle." The big rancher liked to have a handle put to his name. "I'm finished here. I was aimin' to pull out."

Thick tufts of reddish hair above Dunkle's ears and a trick of widening his amber eyes gave him an owlish look. "Last winter was a snorter, but I didn't know it cleaned you." His voice was grave. "I don't like to see you leave—I like to have one man around here I can depend on." There was a touch of the feudal overlord in his manner. "Maybe we can work out a way to get you started again." Impatience came into his voice. "Anyway, get your horse and come along. We'll talk about it later."

Chris felt a tremendous admiration for this successful rancher. Jim Dunkle had drive and force, a single-track mind and a relentless determination to get what he wanted, qualities which had carried him to the top. And Chris wanted to be at the top.

"All right, Mr. Dunkle," he said, and ducked back into the house for his gun belt. Jim Dunkle never went back on his word; if he said he would help a man, he would do it.

Dunkle was already moving out when Chris joined him. He said, "These gents are the ones killed Sam Helfinger over to Sentinel the other day."

"Did they own up to it?"

"Hardly! But they've got his stock, no bill-of-sale, and Sam is dead. That draws a picture."

Chris nodded. It would seem so. "How many of 'em?"

Dunkle hesitated for the flicker of an eyelash. "Three." He turned in the saddle and put his heavy-lidded gaze upon Chris. "A lynchin' always raises a stink when just one outfit does it." His voice was utterly calm. "That's why I want you along. You can see things are done fair and square." A glint of humor showed in his eyes.

Chris scrubbed the flat side of his jaw. "You're not takin' them into Sentinel for trial?"

"It don't pay. We tried it with a couple last year and they went scot-free. Townspeople don't feel the way we do—they ain't bein' hit."

"They'd swing for killin' Sam Helfinger."

"If we could prove it. But no one saw them do it." He shook his heavy head. "We'll take care of this ourselves and then we'll know it's done."

They came down the timbered flank of a ridge and onto Pawnee Flats. The line shack was centered in a pine clearing and, as they rode in, Ed Fuller hoisted himself from the doorstep, a lanky man, black of hair and of eyes.

Dunkle swung down, letting fall the reins to ground-hitch his horse. "Any trouble?"

"Nope. They ain't been out." Fuller gave Chris a careless nod. "Come along for the fun?"

Chris tilted an eyebrow. "Is that what you call it?"

Fuller grunted and dug the makings from his shirt pocket, a man who never smiled or showed any emotion at all.

As Chris stepped from the saddle, Stumpy came into the clearing, lugging a pail of water. Dunkle crooked a finger and Stumpy set the pail before him, a short, bowlegged puncher with a freckled red face that was never done peeling. He gave Chris a brief grin, and Dunkle lifted the dipper, drank deeply and dropped it back into the pail.

"Nothin' like water when a man's dry." Dunkle wiped his lips on his sleeve.

Stumpy looked at the shack, and quickly looked away. "Whisky is better for some jobs."

"All you need is a little sand," Dunkle said brusquely.

No air stirred in this clearing ringed with virgin pine, and sun's heat fell straight down with full force. Chris tied his horse off in shade and tramped back.

"Where's the stock?"

Ed Fuller put his black-eyed stare upon him. "Over yonder in a pocket. You got to see everything?"

"Why not?" Chris's voice was sharp.

And then Dunkle interrupted. "Take him over, Stumpy. I want him to see."

They went down a moderate slope and Stumpy pointed upward. "Plenty of straight limbs around here." His voice was wry. It was plain the coming hanging weighed on the little puncher's mind.

The cattle were bunched in a pocket through which a stream swiftly ran. They were mostly she stuff, wearing different brands.

In addition, each had been recently branded with a Lazy S. Mixed in with them were some ten head of Dunkle's Box D stock, the only animals without the Lazy S brand.

As they started back Chris said, "I reckon that Lazy S is a road brand. Looks like part of a trail herd, except for Dunkle's stuff."

"That wasn't smart." Stumpy waggled his head. "They might've got by if they hadn't grabbed his stock. The rest of the brands ain't from around here."

Dunkle swung around as they came back into the clearing. "Satisfied?"

Chris nodded. "Looks like a trail herd. How does Sam Helfinger figure in this?"

"The gent trailin' this herd was about broke when he reached Sentinel. Sam bought some of his stuff dirt cheap. These gents in here"—Dunkle jerked his thumb at the shack—"killed him and ran off his stock."

"How do you know this?"

"I was in Sentinel yesterday." Dunkle turned to Ed Fuller. "Bring 'em out."

Fuller kicked open the door. "Come on!"

They filed out: a tall, gaunt old man with white hair; a considerably younger man with a strained, starved look on his lean face, and taffy-colored hair that straggled over his eyes and hung low on the collar of his blue shirt; and—Chris felt a deep shock run through him—the third was a girl.

She came out into the sunlight to stand beside the two men and he saw that she was almost as tall as the younger man. And she was young, about eighteen, he judged. Her hair rippled back in waves the dark gold of wild honey, and was held by a ribbon at her neck. Her eyes were a startling blue, but with a wildly troubled look.

Now her eyes flashed terribly at Dunkle. "You have no right to hold us! We have done nothing wrong!" Her voice was hot and wild, and the younger man put his hand on her arm, saying, "Hush, Lissa," in a low voice.

Chris drew Dunkle aside. "You didn't tell me there was a girl mixed up in this. Hadn't we best take them into Sentinel?"

"That's the main reason I won't." Dunkle's tone was forceful. "A woman can always swing a jury." He tapped Chris on the chest.

"I'm not askin' you for advice. You're here to witness that things are done fair an' square."

He walked back to confront the three, and Chris shrugged and followed. She was probably the younger man's wife and Dunkle was right in believing a jury would think twice before handing in a conviction. Anyway, this was Dunkle's show.

The big rancher planted himself before them. "We'll give you a chance to clear yourselves. Now, who are you?"

"Randolph Fickett." The younger man pointed to the tall old man. "My uncle, Jake Fickett, and this is my sister, Melissa."

"All right, Fickett." Dunkle nodded. "We find you with cattle wearin' five or six different brands—what have you got to say?"

"I told your foreman. They're from a trail herd that was headin' for market. The owner was shot of cash. We're lookin' for summer range. I hear there's some up in the Owls."

Dunkle pulled his sharp, curving nose. "How about the ten head of my stock over there with them?"

The man spread wide his hands. "I reckon this is your range with your stock runnin' it. They must've drifted in during the night."

"And they'd drift out again—with you!" Dunkle snapped. "But we'll let that slide. Where's your bill of sale?"

Some of the certainty went out of Randolph Fickett. He turned troubled blue eyes to the old man, who stared vacantly at the surrounding pines. "I don't know. Uncle Jake took it, but he can't recollect what he did with it."

Chris knew now that the man was lying. Here was the old pattern, the familiar cry of thieves caught with stolen goods: They had lost their receipt—it had mysteriously disappeared.

Dunkle looked at the blank-faced old man. "What's the matter with him? Is he half-witted?"

"He is not!" The girl Lissa came forward. "It's just"—she lowered her voice—"he was kicked by a horse. Look at his forehead. When he gets excited his mind turns—well, sort of cloudy. He doesn't know——"

"You expect me to believe a tale like that?" Dunkle interrupted. "Who'd let an idiot handle their business?"

Color came into the girl's thin face. "He was all right when he got the receipt."

Dunkle stretched wide his eyes. "So? Who signed it?"

She hesitated, and turned back to her brother. "What was his name, Randy?"

"I——" He paused and his brown forehead furrowed. "I just can't seem to speak it."

"Was it by any chance Sam Helfinger?"

Randolph Fickett's eyes conferred with his sister. "I believe it was. I believe it was him gave it to us. But Uncle Jake handled——"

And now Dunkle's voice became silky smooth. "Was it before or after you shot him?"

They stared numbly, then it hit the girl and she went back a step, hands trembling to her throat while the blue eyes became too large for her face. "Is—is he d-dead?"

For a moment Chris' hard skepticism was shaken; it was possible she did not know what her brother had done. Then he dismissed the thought; they were too closely tied.

Randolph Fickett shoved back his tangle of taffy-colored hair with a hand that would not hold steady. He licked his lips. "When was he shot?"

"The night you stole his cattle," Dunkle said grimly.

"We didn't! I tell you we didn't!" Fickett's voice rose high, shrill with angry desperation. "We bought them. He was all right when we left."

"You can't even keep your story straight." There was open contempt in Dunkle's face. "First you said you got them from a trail herd; now you admit it was from Helfinger." He swung around to Ed Fuller. "No sense in stringin' this out. Get your rope!"

The girl's face whitened with fear as Fuller started for his horse, and her eyes darkened to purple. "Wait! You can't do this! These cattle were part of a trail herd, but Mr. Hel—Helfinger bought them and sold them to us. I—I guess he made a little money." She turned to her brother and put her hands on his arms. "Can't you think where Uncle Jake put the paper?"

He stared at her, a wildness in his eyes. "I don't know. Helfinger gave him the paper; then he was talkin' to me; we were lookin' at the stock. I didn't see what Uncle Jake did with it." He raised his eyes to Dunkle. "But I know he got it. I saw him take it right in his hand."

"Did you try his pockets?" Dunkle spoke with the Godlike patience of a man whose mind is made up.

"We have, but I'll try again." He went up to the old man and took him by the shoulders. He shook him. "Where's the paper, Uncle Jake? What did you do with it?"

Something shadowy moved in the depths of those gray eyes. The old man put his hands to his hat and settled it more firmly on his head, and now Chris saw the white crescent in the brown forehead just above the eyebrows, the horns pointing at the hairline.

"He can't remember!" Fickett shook his head in a helpless way and began a swift rummaging of pockets, emptying out their contents, turning the pockets inside out until the old man was a white-patched scarecrow. He ran his fingers inside the waistband, he ripped the coat lining and felt inside.

"Try his boots," Dunkle suggested in the voice of last justice.

"I never thought of that!"

Fickett made the old man sit down, and with nervous, eager fingers pulled off the boots. He held them up and he shook them. He rammed his hand deep into them. He pulled off the socks and turned them inside out while Uncle Jake stared at his bare toes.

Fickett slowly dropped the last sock and shook his head. "It might have been in his pocket and come out when he pulled out his tobacco and he not noticed." Despair was in his voice.

"Sure he didn't give it to you?" Dunkle's voice was properly grave, but it came to Chris that he was playing with Fickett, sure that there was no paper and never had been.

Fickett shook his head. "No-o-o-o, I'm sure." But he started through his own pockets. He dropped to his knees and made a little pile of his belongings; a pocket knife, a bandanna, some loose change, the odds and ends that a man collects. He looked up at Dunkle. "It's no use. We haven't got it!"

"How about your boots?"

Fickett stared. A flush came into his face and his lips tightened. "So, you're havin' your fun!" He swept up the things and stood up.

Chris put a hand to his face and, surprisingly, found it damp. It was one thing to hang a man and quite another to string it out like this. And the girl being here made it tough.

Dunkle turned to Fuller, who was standing by, the rope coiled on his arm. "We'll take the old one first."

Fuller pulled Uncle Jake to his feet and Lissa gave a queer, muffled cry and flung herself upon the gaunt old form.

"You can't! He hasn't done anything! He——" Her voice broke on a sob.

Fickett came up to Dunkle. "At least give us a jury trial." His voice was hoarse, as though he had been shouting. "Give us a chance." Sweat ran in bright worms down his face. "If you kill us, what'll my sister do? Where will she go? If you'll just give us a chance——"

For the first time, Dunkle showed anger. He put the rough edge of his stare upon the man. "There's nothin' on God's green earth I hate like a killer; a man that will murder another for no good reason. Sam Helfinger was found with two bullets in his back. We'll give you the same chance you gave him!" He slapped his thigh with his rolled gloves. "I've seen your kind before; sneaking through the country, stealin' everything they could lay hands on. You're just no damn good!"

He brushed past him, put his hands on the girl's shoulders and tore her loose from the old man. "Take him away, Ed!"

The girl screamed. She twisted in his grasp, and Fickett gave a low moaning cry and went for him. Dunkle lashed out with his fist, caught him alongside the head and knocked him off his feet. "Stumpy!" His voice was harsh. "Put your gun on him! If he moves, shoot!"

Fickett got up unsteadily, his face red where the fist had landed, and Stumpy pulled his gun and stepped behind him. Dunkle released the girl and went over to where Fuller was getting the old man onto a horse from which the saddle had been stripped.

Lissa took her brother's face between her hands, holding it so for a moment. Then she came straight to Chris.

"Please——" Her voice shook. She closed her eyes, face inches from his, and bright drops squeezed from beneath the lids and lay upon her cheeks. "Please, can't you—won't you—stop this?" Her voice broke and her hands writhed together. "Have you no pity?"

Her voice plucked nerves deep in his body. Heat flowed through him, flooding into his neck and causing its pressure. He flicked a glance across the clearing and met Dunkle's skeptical gaze. Chris looked back to the girl, his face hardening. "As much pity as they showed Sam Helfinger."

"They didn't do it!" Her eyes opened wide, showing their inward fire. "They didn't do it! Won't you believe me?"

This beating she was giving his emotions stirred anger within him. "There's nothing can be done," he said roughly. "You'd best go inside; this ain't somethin' you want to see."

"I won't go in!" Her voice rose, husky, panting, as though torn from her throat. "I'll watch! I'll remember! And then I'll see that Dunkle is hanged!"

Her blue eyes seared him with their fierce burning. She whirled and marched back to her brother, shoulders stiff. But then they started to shake and she threw herself forward upon his chest with a sob that was half groan. Randolph Fickett gazed over her at Chris with a terrible violence in his eyes.

Chris turned and moved to the side of the clearing where Fuller and Dunkle were working. Most of his life had been spent on the rough edge of things; he had seen men swing, he had witnessed various forms of violent death, and he had hardened himself and fought his way up in a bitter world. Dunkle's way was the successful way, but his palms grew damp, and for a moment he had his black doubts. Then he encountered the calm certainty of Dunkle's glance and felt assurance come back to him.

Uncle Jake was on the horse, the noose about his neck, his bare feet stuck out stiffly at either side, with the toes turned up instead of hanging, Indian fashion. Fuller led the horse beneath a sweeping limb, threw the rope over it and snubbed the free end, while the old man gazed stupidly ahead, untouched by these portents.

The only sound now, in the heated air of this bright clearing, was Lissa's dry sobbing. It grated on Chris; it filled him with a hurrying, an urgency to get this over and done with. He threw a glance backward and saw that her face was still buried in Fickett's chest. Behind them was Stumpy with drawn gun, his eyes immovably fixed upon the old man beneath the tree. He kept licking his lips.

A pulse pounded in Chris' head as Fuller cut a withy branch and methodically began to strip it for a whip.

As Dunkle watched, a muscle began to jump in his cheek and, with a grunt of impatience, he grabbed the branch from Fuller. "Stand back!" He whirled it above his head, and momentarily it poised high in air. Dunkle's lips pinched together; with full-arm swing he slashed down across the horse's rump.

The startled brute bolted forward, the rope jerked the old man backwards, his legs flew up as he went off the horse, and he fell straight down. There was a jerk and the rope twanged. He kicked twice, his hands clawed upward and dropped. He was still, slowly spinning, his shadow stretching out long and black.

The breath went out of Chris with a sighing sound. He dully noticed that the sobbing had stopped and he made a half-turn.

Lissa was on her knees, hands balled beneath her chin and her lips were silently moving while Fickett stood awkwardly stiff behind her, staring as though inward pressure would force his blue eyes from their sockets. There was no sign of Stumpy, and then there came a retching sound from behind the shack.

Chris tramped after the horse, which had stopped just beyond the edge of trees. The sun was losing its brightness, and looking up he saw it beginning its nightly descent behind the Owls. Day was short here under their high-flung pinnacles, and the chill, advancing breath of night brought the feeling that he had seen his last day of full brightness. But having started they must go on. They could no more turn back than they could halt the black flow of shadow from the peaks.

He returned with the horse as Fuller released the rope, letting the old man slump to the ground.

Dunkle bent and removed the noose. "All right, let's get this finished." His voice was brisk.

Uncle Jake's hat rolled off, and his white head lay upon the brown, dead pine needles. It seemed indecent to leave him there, bare toes pointing starkly at the sky. Chris picked up the hat, mechanically straightening it, putting his hand into the crown and pushing out the dents. It was warm from the old man's head, and the sweatband was damp under his fingers.

He looked over at the man and girl in front of the shack. Lissa was standing now and the horror, the fierce loathing in her eyes, came across the fifty feet of space and hit him a blow.

Stumpy came uncertainly from the shack, his freckles black against the sickly hue of his face, and took his place behind them. It was strange Fickett had not run while unguarded, Chris dully thought, and then he knew; Lissa held him more effectively than any armed guard, and by that he sensed the greater fear that must be in the man's mind.

His jaw muscles clamped and his fingers strongly gripped the hat.

Then a tightness froze his muscles. He stared into the crown at this paper that had not been there before. It had slipped from under the sweatband. Slowly he put out his hand and as he took it an awareness of tragedy seeped into him through his finger tips. He let fall the hat and in the act of opening this paper knew what it would be. He raised his eyes to Dunkle.

The big rancher had paused and was watching with a sudden strained attention. Now he came to Chris and read over his arm.

Chris held open the paper for a full minute, aware of the change in Dunkle's breathing, before slowly refolding it. And this paper seemed to have grown insupportably heavy, so that its weight ran into his arms and numbed them.

He said, heavily, "We've made a bad mistake."

His eyes went around the edge of the clearing, saw the horse standing under the big limb, the old man lying so still in the sunlight, and Fuller, with the rope coiled in his hand, watching, as though he suspected, and were amused at, this turn of events. And now Stumpy, sensing trouble, came over to Fuller with his rolling walk.

Chris saw Dunkle's face lose its assurance. "We've made a bad mistake," he said again.

Dunkle turned his big body, he stared at Lissa and Fickett, he turned back again, looked at the body of Uncle Jake, raised his eyes to Chris; doing all this slowly, giving himself time to think. When he spoke it was with the deliberation of a man who has done his reckoning and come to his answer.

"Maybe we're wrong—and maybe we ain't. Sam Helfinger is dead. It's my bet these are the men did it; nothin' to prove they ain't. And they've got ten head of my stock."

There was a confused heaviness in Chris' head. "Maybe you're right, Mr. Dunkle," he said uncertainly. "But maybe somebody killed him for the purchase money. We'll just have to wait and see. And if you're wrong, we—we'll have to face the music."

"Wait?" Some of the color left Dunkle's heavy face. "Do you know what will happen if they get loose? They'll ride straight for the sheriff!"

Chris nodded. "I reckon they will. Wouldn't you?"

A fine beading of sweat appeared on Dunkle's forehead. He put his face close to Chris. "If you hadn't found that paper we'd have strung up the second man and that would've ended the business." His eyes stretched wide. "What's to stop you touchin' a match to it?"

Shock, like a cold blade, hit Chris in the belly. He stared at the rancher. "And then what?"

Dunkle's eyes were hot, dogged. "We go on like we hadn't found it. The girl's got no proof. She can't make trouble. We'll ship her out of the country."

Cold spread through Chris from his stomach, deadening his muscles, freezing him in its icy grip. He licked his lips. "Do you know what you're sayin', Mr. Dunkle? A while back you told how you hated a murderer."

Red came into the rancher's big face. He took out his bandanna and wiped his forehead. "Chris," he said solemnly, "I'm talkin' as much for you as for me. That bill-of-sale don't prove they didn't kill Sam. We've got to look out for ourselves. You just leave things to me and we'll come out all right."

He put his hand on Chris' shoulder. "I said I'd help you and I will. What would you say if I gave you enough stock for a fresh start? And how'd you like a chunk of that level land next to yours?"

Chris had seen men die for far less than this bribe that was being offered him. And maybe Dunkle was right. He shoved his hand into his pocket and the fingers clamped hard on the paper. Here was the big ranch he had always wanted, and some of Dunkle's fine heavy stock. Dunkle had got to be big and powerful by driving straight for what he wanted without thought or care for anyone else. That was the pattern to follow. He would not have to leave his ranch and go back to the weary grind of punching other men's cattle.

His eyes fell upon the body of Uncle Jake lying beneath the big limb, and an invisible something stirred in the shadowed air and took him by the throat. He could have his big ranch, but it would be darkened by the shadows of two hanged men. And the memory of the girl would be a torture that would shrivel his soul until it became a dead thing like—like Dunkle's.

He looked at him with a new appraisal, seeing the essential ruthlessness, the blind selfishness that would sacrifice anyone to its own ends; and he knew he could not force himself into Dunkle's mold. He said slowly, "I don't want it that bad, Mr. Dunkle."

The friendliness, the persuasiveness faded from Dunkle's face, leaving it strained. He went back a step, studying, gauging, and Chris saw fear start in his mind, saw it grow and spread, saw it crowd into his eyes; and he saw the signs of breakage as the man's inner fiber went to pieces under the force of its hammering. In these still moments he witnessed the death of much that had been fine and good in the man. And now Dunkle threw a swift glance at Ed Fuller and went back, step by step.

Chris saw the sudden alertness on Fuller's dark face and beside him, Stumpy, gun in hand, his face still green—and danger sharpened him and turned the air cold in his nose.

"Chris!" Dunkle's voice was harsh. He stopped moving and his eyes strained wickedly wide. "I will not let you turn them loose. Give me that paper!" His lips drew back, giving him the look of a fighting stallion, the flesh sucked tight to the skull.

Seeing that look, Chris got a full, dismal awareness of what was coming. Nothing could change Dunkle; nothing could stop him. There could be but one end to this. His face went bonehard. He said, "I will not give it up!" and waited, muscles bowstring-tight.

For a moment there was a wild hope that Dunkle would back down, and then that hope died as Dunkle's hand started for his hip. Chris whipped up his gun and fired.

The bullet shook Dunkle and rocked him back on his heels. He teetered while red stained his shirt front and the blazing light in his eyes dulled. The gun slid from his hand and he pitched forward to strike on his face. Off to the side, Fuller was frozen in the act of drawing; Stumpy's gun was rammed into his ribs, and Stumpy said in a voice that was a miserable croak, "There's been enough killin'. Let go your gun, Ed!"

The stench of burned powder was strong in the air. Chris said, "Thanks, Stumpy. You still want to use that gun, Ed?"

Fuller's hand left his gun. He stared down at Dunkle and he shook his head. "I work for money. Who'd pay me now if I shot you?" He was still for a long minute staring down at the body. Then he shrugged, tramped to his horse and stepped into the saddle. He gathered the reins and looked over at Stumpy. "I'm pullin' out. If you've got good sense you'll do the same."

"Can't be too fast for me," Stumpy said fervently. "I'm right with you." He hustled to his horse, flung himself up, lifted his hand to Chris and followed Fuller into the pines.

As the muffled beat of hoofs died away, a barren loneliness came to Chris, and a sense of loss. He had just had to kill the man upon whom his life had been patterned, and with him all his old standards. He was shaken and adrift.

In the shadows filling the clearing the still face of old Jake Fickett mutely accused him and he saw with a fearful clarity how far he had gone along Dunkle's path.

He started as a hand gripped his arm. "I was watchin'. You found it?" Randolph Fickett's blue eyes were blazing. He flopped back the taffy-colored hair.

Chris handed over the bill of sale. "In his sweatband."

Fickett's eyes raised to Lissa as she came beside him. They dropped back to the paper and his face tightened, showing his thought; it had come just too late for Uncle Jake.

"Dunkle still wanted to hang Randy, even after he knew?"

Chris felt the horror in Lissa's voice. He saw the fairness and honesty in her, the good human feeling, and now he knew a black disgust at himself. Had he not been blinded by his own chance to gain he would have seen that these people could not have shot Sam Helfinger.

Without waiting for an answer she turned and walked slowly to Uncle Jake. She knelt and in silence looked down upon the still face. Her fingers closed the gray eyes and smoothed back the white hair, lingering on it. She arose and got the socks and returned to pull them on the bare feet.

As he watched, a sense of guilt grew in Chris and became an oppressive torment. He went over and hunkered down across from her. "I'm sorry——" He stopped, his voice rough in his throat. Nothing he could say would change things. The deed was done; that was the hard and bitter truth.

Melissa's head came up, showing damp blue eyes. "I know." Her voice was softly brooding. "I know how you feel. This is a rough, wild country without much law. Sometimes men have to take things into their own hands; but if it had not been for you, Randy would have died." A gentle expression came into her face. "You must not blame yourself; we owe you too much."

Chris had expected hate and he found forgiveness. It stirred him, it made him feel worse. He had an overwhelming desire to help her. "Look," he said in a strained voice, "you don't have to go lookin' for grass. I've got a place over the ridge a piece. You move your stock there." The words rushed out, without thought or heed.

Her eyes opened wide, startled. Warmth lighted them and she reached out and put her hand on his arm. "You are generous, but we couldn't use your range, we couldn't crowd you."

"You don't owe us a thing," Fickett said beside him. "You wiped the slate clean when you threw down on Dunkle."

The girl's hand fell away as they stood up, but Chris could still feel its warm, disturbing pressure on his arm.

His eyes came upon Dunkle's body, shadowy in the glassy twilight. He said, "I'll have to pack him in to Sentinel and report to the sheriff."

"We'll go with you," Randolph Fickett said in a firm voice, "and see you don't run into trouble. You had to shoot in self-defense, but it won't do any harm to have witnesses along."

"We certainly will!" Melissa said quickly. "And you have no guilt about Uncle Jake. It was Dunkle! Why, when you found there'd been a mistake you risked your life to save Randy! No jury would convict you!"

Chris stared off into the darkening pines. They were generous, even in their grief. They would help him from their overflow of human compassion, their fairness. It made him feel humble; it roughed him up inside.

He swung around to Fickett. "I meant what I said about usin' my place. You won't crowd me. Last winter killed off my stock. I was leavin' anyway."

Fickett shook his head, his face pinching with the understanding of a man who has endured his own share of troubles. He turned to his sister and for a long moment they wordlessly conferred.

"We're in a bad way," he said at length. "Short-handed, no grass and no place to stay." He hesitated. "If you're shy of stock we might work a deal. It would sure help us, and you wouldn't have to leave. It might work out well for all of us."

Seeing the sudden hope in the girl's face, a warm tide moved in Chris. He had never known people like this. Theirs was a different pattern from the one he had followed, but he knew deeply and with certainty that it was the better one. It made him feel warm, it made him feel fine. Out of evil would come something good. Otherwise they might have met and passed, each unaware and heedless of the other's need.

He put out his hand to Randy Fickett. "I reckon it will work out. I reckon it will work out fine."

THE FOOL'S HEART
by Eugene Manlove Rhodes

Charley Ellis did not know where he was; he did not know where he was going; he was not even cheered by any hope of damnation. His worldly goods were the clothes he wore, the sixshooter on his thigh, the horse between his legs, and his saddle, bridle and spurs. He had no money; no friend closer than five hundred miles. Therefore, he whistled and sang; he sat jauntily; his wide hat took on the cant joyous; he cocked a bright eye appreciatively at a pleasant world—a lonesome world just now, but great fun.

By years, few-and-twenty; by size, of the great upper-middle class; blond, tanned, down-cheeked. Add a shock of tow-colored hair, a pug nose of engaging impudence—and you have the inventory.

All day he had ridden slowly across a dreary land of rolling hills, northward and ever northward; a steepest, interminable gray ridge of limestone on his right, knife-sharp, bleak and bare; the vast black bulk of San Mateo on the west; and all the long day the rider had seen no house, or road, or any man.

One thing troubled him a little: his big roan horse was road-weary and had lost his aforetime pleasing plumpness. He had also lost a shoe to-day and was intending to be very tender-footed at once.

Charley was pleased, then, topping a hill, to observe that some-body had chopped a deep notch into the stubborn limestone ridge; and to see, framed in that tremendous notch, a low square of ranch buildings on a high tableland beyond. A dark and crooked chasm lay between—Ellis could see only the upper walls of it, but the steep angle of the sides gave the depth.

A deep and broad basin fell away before his feet. Westward it broke into misty branches between ridges blue-black with pine. Plainly the waters of these many valleys drained away through the deep-notched chasm.

It was late. The valley was dark with shadow. Beyond, the lonely ranch loomed high and mysterious in a blaze of the dying sunlight. Ellis felt his blood stir and thrill to watch it higher and higher above him as he followed down a plunging ridge. Higher and higher it rose; another downward step and it was gone.

Ellis led his horse now, to favor the unshod foot on the stony way. He came to a road in the valley; the road took him to a swift and noisy stream, brawling, foaming-white and narrow.

They drank; they splashed across.

A juniper stood beside the road. To it was nailed a signboard, with the rudely painted direction:

BOX O RANCH, FIVE MILES

Below was a penciled injunction:

DON'T TRY THE BOX CANON. IT'S FENCED.
TOO ROUGH ANYWAY. KEEP TO THE ROAD.

"Vinegaroan, you old skeesicks," said Charley, "I'm goin' to leave you here and hoof it in. Good grass here and you're right tired. Besides, that foot of yours'll be ruined with a little more of these rocks. I'll rustle a shoe and tack it on in the morning." He hung the saddle high in the juniper—for range cattle prefer a good sixty-dollar saddle to other feed. Tents and bedding are nutritious but dry. A line of washing has its points for delicate appetites; boots make dainty titbits; harness is excellent—harness is the good old stand-by—harness is worthy of high praise, though buckle-y; but for all-round merit, wholesome, substantial, piquant, the saddle has no equal. Bridle and blankets are the customary relishes for the saddle, but the best cattle often omit them.

Charley hobbled old Vinegaroan and set out smartly, hobbling himself in his high-heeled boots. As the dim road wound into the falling dusk he regaled himself with the immortal saga of Sam Bass:

> "Sam Bass he came from Indiana—it was his native state;
> He came out here to Texas, and here he met his fate.
> Sam always drank good liquor and spent his money free,
> And a kinder-hearted fellow you'd seldom ever see!"

The Box O Ranch stands on a bone-dry mesa, two miles from living water. It is a hollow square of adobe; within is a mighty cistern, large enough to store the filtered rain water from all the roofs. The site was chosen for shelter in Indian times; there is neither hill nor ridge within gunshot. One lonely cedar fronts the house, and no other tree is in sight; for that one tree the ranch was built there and not in another place. A mile away you come to the brink of Nogales Cañon, narrow and deep and dark; a thousand feet below the sunless waters carve their way to the far-off river. The ranch buildings and corrals now mark one corner of a fenced pasture, three miles square; the farther cliffs of Nogales Cañon make the southern fence.

The great mesas pyramid against the west, step on step; on that heaven-high pedestal San Mateo Peak basks in the sun, a sleeping lion. But the wonder and beauty of San Mateo are unprized. San Mateo is in America.

Two men came to the Box O in the glare of afternoon—a tall man, great of bone and coarse of face, hawk-nosed; a shorter man and younger, dark, thin-lipped, with little restless eyes, gray and shifting. He had broad eyebrows and a sharp, thin nose.

A heavy revolver swung at the tall man's thigh—the short man had an automatic; each had a rifle under his knee. They were weary and thirst-parched; the horses stumbled as they walked—they were streaked and splashed with the white salt of sweat, caked with a mire of dust and lather, dried now by the last slow miles, so that no man might know their color.

The unlocked house lay silent and empty; the stove was cold; the dust of days lay on the table. "Good enough!" croaked the shorter man. "Luck's with us."

He led the way to the cistern. They drank eagerly, prudently; they sluiced the stinging dust from face and neck and hair.

"Ain't it good?" said the short man.

"Huh! That wasn't such a much. Wait till you're good and dry once—till your lips crack to the quick and your tongue swells black."

"Never for mine! I'm for getting out of this. I'm hunting the rainiest country I can find; and I stay there."

"If we get away! What if we don't find fresh horses in the pasture? There's none in sight."

"Reed's always got horses in the pasture. They're down in the cañon, where the sun hasn't dried up the grass. Oh, we'll get away, all right!"

"They've got to track us, Laxon—and we've left a mighty crooked trail. They can't follow our trail at night and the Angel Gabriel couldn't guess where we are headed for."

"You don't allow much for chance? Or for—anything else? We sure don't deserve to get away," said Laxon.

He led his horse in, took off the bridle and pumped up a bucket of water. The poor beast drank greedily and his eyes begged for more.

"Not now, Bill. Another in ten minutes," he said in answer to a feeble nickering. He unsaddled; he sighed at the scalded back. "I'll douse a few bucketfuls on you quick as your pard gets his."

He turned his head. The younger man leaned sullenly against the wall. He had not moved. Laxon's face hardened. It was an ugly and brutal face at best—the uglier that he was slightly cross-eyed. Now it was the face of a devil.

"You worthless cur, get your horse! I thought you was yellow when you killed poor Mims last night—and now I know it! No need of it—not a bit. We could 'a' got his gun and his box of money without. Sink me to hell if I've not half a mind to give you up! If I was sure they'd hang you first I'd do it!"

"Don't let's quarrel, Jess. I'll get the horse, of course," said Moss wearily. "I'm just about all in—that's all. I could sleep a week!"

"Guess your horse ain't tired, you swine! I ought to kick you through the gate! Quarrel? You! Wish you'd try it. Wish you'd just raise your voice at me! Sleep, says he! Sleep, when somebody may drop in on us any time! All the sleep you get is the next hour. We ride to-night and sleep all day to-morrow in some hollow of the deep hills, over beyond the Divide. No more daylight for us till we strike the Gila."

Moss made no answer. Laxon hobbled stiffly into the house and brought back canned tomatoes, corned beef and a butcher knife. They wolfed their food in silence.

"Sleep now, baby!" said Laxon. "I'll stand watch."

He spread the heavy saddle blankets in the sun; he gave the horses water, a little at a time, until they had their fill; with a gunny sack and pail he washed them carefully. Their sides were raw with spurring; there were ridges and welts where a doubled rope had lashed.

A cruel day to the northward two other horses lay stark and cold by Bluewater Corral; a cruel night beyond Bluewater the paymaster of the Harqua Hala Mine lay by the broken box of his trust, with a bullet in his heart.

Laxon found a can of baking powder and sprinkled it on the scalded backs.

"Pretty hard lines, Bill," he said, with a pat for the drooping neck. "All that heft of coin heaped up behind the cantle—that made it bad. Never mind! You'll come out all right—both of you."

His thoughts went back to those other horses at Bluewater. He had shot them at sunrise. He could not turn them loose to drink the icy water and die in agony; he could not stay; he could not shut them in the corral to endure the agony of thirst until the pursuit came up—a pursuit that so easily might lose the trail in the rock country and never come to Bluewater. It had been a bitter choice.

He built a fire and investigated the chuck room; he put on the coffeepot, took a careful look across the mesa and came back to Moss. The hour was up.

Moss slept heavily; his arms sprawled wide, his fingers jerking; he moaned and muttered in his sleep; his eyes were sunken and on his cheek the skin was stretched skull-tight. The watcher was in less evil case; his reserves of stored-up vitality were scarcely touched as yet. Conscious of this, his anger for the outworn man gave way to rough compassion; the hour had stretched to nearly two before he shook the sleeper's shoulder.

"Come, Moss! You're rested a little and so's your horse. I've got some good hot coffee ready for you. Get a cup of that into your belly and you'll be as good as new. Then you go drive all the horses up out of the pasture—just about time before dark. While you're gone I'll cook a hot supper, bake up a few pones of bread for us to take along, and pack up enough other truck to do us. I'd go, but you're fifty pounds lighter'n me. Besides, you know the pasture."

"Oh, I'll go," said Moss as he drank his coffee. "There's a little corral down in the bottom. Guess I can ease a bunch in there and get me a new mount. The rest'll be easy."

"We'll pick out the likeliest, turn the others out and throw a scare into 'em," said Laxon. "We don't want to leave any fresh horses for them fellows, if they come. And, of course, they'll come."

"Yes, and they'll have a time finding out which is our tracks. I'll just leave this money here, and the rifle," said Moss, in the corral. "That'll be so much weight off, anyway." He untied a slicker from behind the saddle. Unrolling it he took out an ore sack and tossed it over beside Laxon's saddle; it fell with a heavy clink of coins. "Say, Jess! Look over my doin' the baby act a while ago, will you? I should have taken care of my horse, of course—poor devil; but I was all in—so tired I hardly knew what I was about." He hesitated. "And—honest, Jess—I thought Mim was going after his gun."

"Guess I didn't sense how tired you was," said Jess, and there was relief in his voice. "Let it all slide. We're in bad and we got to stick together—us two."

At sundown Moss drove back twelve head of saddle stock. He had caught a big rangy sorrel at the horse pen in the cañon.

"This one'll do for me," he announced as he swung down.

"I'll take the big black," said Laxon. "Trot along now and eat your supper. I'll be ready by the time you're done. I've got our stuff all packed—and two canteens. Say, Moss, I've got two bed blankets. I'm goin' to carry my share of grub behind my saddle. My sack of money I'll wad up in my blanket and sling it across in front of me, see? We don't want any more sore-backed horses. You'd better do the same."

"All right!" said Moss. "You fix it up while I eat."

Laxon roped and saddled the black, and tied one of the grub sacks behind the cantle; he made a neat roll of his own sack of money and the blanket and tied it across behind the horn. Then he fixed his partner's money sack and grub sack the same way and thrust the rifle into the scabbard. He opened the outer gate of the corral and let the loose horses out on the eastern mesa.

"Hike, you! We'll fall in behind you in a pair of minutes and make you burn the breeze! . . . Now for Bill, the very tired horse, and we'll be all ready to hit the trail."

Bill was lying down in a corner. Laxon stirred him up and led him by the foretop out through the pasture gate. The saddle-house door opened noiselessly; Moss steadied his automatic against the doorframe and waited.

"You go hunt up your pardner, old Bill. You and him orter be good pals from now on. So long! Good luck!" said Laxon. He closed the gate.

Moss shot him between the shoulder blades. Laxon whirled and fell on his face; the swift automatic cracked. Laxon rose to his elbow, riddled and torn; bullet after bullet crashed through his body. He shot the sorrel horse between the eyes; the black reared up and broke his rope. As he fell backward a ball from Laxon's forty-five pierced his breast; falling, another shot broke his neck. Then Laxon laughed—and died.

White, frantic, cursing, the trapped murderer staggered out from his ambush. Shaking horribly he made sure that Laxon was dead.

"The squint-eyed devil!" he screamed.

He ran to the outer gate. The band of freed horses was close by and unalarmed, but twilight was deepening fast. What was to be done must be done quickly.

He set the outer gate open. He bridled old Bill and leaped on, bareback; with infinite caution he made a wide circle beyond the little bunch of horses and worked them slowly toward the gate.

They came readily enough and, at first, it seemed that there would be no trouble; but at the gate they stopped, sniffed, saw those dim, mysterious forms stretched out at the farther side, huddled, recoiled and broke away in a little, slow trot.

Moss could not stop them. Poor old Bill could only shuffle. The trot became a walk; they nibbled at the young grass.

Once he turned them back, but before they reached the gate they edged away uneasily. Twilight was done. Twice he turned them back. All the stars were out and blazing clear; a cool night breeze sprang up. Nearing the gate the horses sniffed the air; they snorted, wheeled and broke away; the trot became a gallop, the gallop a run.

Moss slipped the bridle off and walked back to the corral. His whole body was shaking in a passion of rage and fear.

He drank deeply at the cistern; he reloaded the automatic; he went to the dead horses. Whatever came, he would not abandon that money. After all, there was a chance. He would keep the notes with him; he would hide the gold somewhere in the rocky cliffs of the cañon; he would climb out over the cliffs, where he would leave no tracks to follow; he would keep in the impassable hills, hiding by day; he would carry food and water; he would take the rifle and the first time he saw a horseman alone he would have a horse.

Eagerly he untied the two treasure sacks and emptied one into the other. He started for the house. Then his heart stopped beating. It was a voice, faint and far away:

"Rabbit! Rabbit! Tail mighty white!
    Yes, good Lord—he'll take it out o' sight!
    Take it out o' sight!"

In a frenzy of fear the murderer dropped his treasure and snatched up the rifle. He ran to the gate and crouched in the shadow. His hair stood up; his heart pounded at his ribs; his knees knocked together.

"Rabbit! Rabbit! Ears mighty long!
    Yes, good Lord—you set 'em on wrong!
    Set 'em on wrong!"

It was a gay young voice, coming from the westward, nearer and nearer. Slinking in the shadows, Moss came to the corner. In the starlight he saw a man very near now, coming down the road afoot, singing as he came:

"Sam Bass he came from Indiana—it was his native state."

From the west? His pursuers would be coming from the north along his track—they would not be singing, and there would be more than one. Why was this man afoot? With a desperate effort of the will Moss pulled himself together. He slipped back into the kitchen and lit the lamp. He threw dry sticks on the glowing coals

—they broke into a crackling flame; the pleasant tingling incense of cedar filled the room. He dabbed at his burning face with a wet towel; he smoothed his hair hastily. Drawn, pale and haggard, the face in the glass gave him his cue—he was an invalid.

Would the man never come? He felt the mounting impulse to struggle no longer—to shriek out all the ghastly truth; to give up—anything, so he might sleep and die and rest. But he had no choice; he must fight on. Someway he must use this newcomer for his need. But why afoot? Why could not the man have a horse? Then his way would have been so easy. His throat and mouth were dust-dry—he drank deep of the cool water and felt new life steal along his veins.

Then—because he must busy himself to bridge the dreadful interval—he forced his hands to steadiness; he filled and lit a pipe.

"Hello, the house!"

Moss threw open the door; the dancing light leaped out against the dark. Along that golden pathway a man came, smiling.

"Hello yourself, and see how you like it! You're late. Turn your horse in the corral while I warm up supper for you."

"I left my horse back up the road. I just love to walk," said Charley. At the door he held up a warning hand. "Before I come in, let's have a clear understanding. No canned corn goes with me. I don't want anybody even to mention canned corn."

"Never heard of it," said Moss. "Sit ye down. How'd fried spuds, with onions and bacon, suit you?"

"Fine and dandy! Anything but ensilage." Ellis limped to a box by the fire and painfully removed a boot. "Cracky! Some blisters!"

Moss bent over the fire.

"You're not from round these parts, are you?" he asked. He raked out coals for the coffeepot and put the potatoes to warm.

"Nope. From Arizona—lookin' for work. What's the show to hook up with this outfit?"

"None. Everybody gone to the round-up. Oh, I don't live here myself. I'm just a-stayin' round for my health." . . . If I could only get to this man's horse—if I could leave this man in the trap! The pursuit must be here by to-morrow. Steady! I must feel my way. . . . "Horse played out?"

"No; but he's right tired and he lost the shoe off his nigh fore-foot to-day. Stake me to a new shoe, of course?"

"Sure!" . . . But this man will tell his story. I can never get away on a tired horse—they will overtake me; they will be here tomorrow. Shall I make it seem that Laxon and this man have killed each other? No; there will still be his tracks where he came—mine where I leave. How then? . . . "Sorry I can't let you have a horse to get yours. Just set myself afoot about sunset. Had all the saddle horses in the corral—saw a coyote—ran out to shoot at him —did you hear me, mister? I didn't get your name. Mine's Moss."

"Ellis—Charley Ellis. No; I was 'way over behind that hill at sundown. You're sure looking peaked and pale, Mr. Moss."

"It's nothing—weak heart," said Moss. The heavy brows made a black bar across his white face. . . . How then? I will stay here. I will be the dupe, the scapegoat—this man shall take my place, shall escape, shall be killed resisting arrest. . . . "Just a little twinge. I'm used to it. Where was I? Oh, yes—the horses. Well, I didn't shut the gate good. It blew open and away went my horses to the wild bunch. Idiotic, wasn't it? And I was planning to make a start to-night, ten mile or so, on a little hunting trip. That reminds me— I got a lot of bread baked up and it's out in my pack. You wash up and I'll go get it. There's the pan." . . . This man Ellis was the murderer! I left my horse. Ellis stole away while I was asleep. He tried to escape on my horse. He can't get far; the horse is about played out. When I woke and missed Ellis I found the dead man in the corral!

The black thought shaped and grew. He hugged it to his heart as he took bread from the pack sacks; he bettered it as he hid the sack of money. He struck a match and picked out a sheaf of five-dollar bills; he tore them part-way across, near one corner, perhaps an inch. Then he took one bill from the torn package, crumpled it up and wadded it in his pocket, putting the others back in the sack.

Next, he found the empty ore sack, the one that had carried Laxon's half of the plunder. With a corner of it he pressed lightly over the dead man's back, so that a tiny smear of drying blood showed on the sack.

Then he took the bread and hurried to the house, dropping the

ore sack outside the door. It was swiftly done. Ellis was just comb-
ing his hair when his host returned.

"There! Coffee's hot and potatoes will be in a jiffy. Sit up.
Where'd you say you left your horse?"

"Where the wagon road crosses the creek west of the Box Cañon
—where there's a sign nailed to a tree."

"Which sign? There's several—different places."

" 'Five miles to the Box O Ranch,' it says."

"Hobbled your horse, I reckon?"

"Yep. Wasn't really no need of hobbling, either—he won't go
far. Some gaunted up, he is. He'll be glad when I get a job. And
I'll say this for old Vinegaroan—he's a son-of-a-gun to pitch; but
he don't put on. When he shows tired he's tired for fair. Only for
his wild fool ways, he'd be the best horse I ever owned. But, then,
if it hadn't been for them wild fool ways the V R wouldn't never
'a' let me got my clutches on him. They never raised a better horse,
but he was spoiled in breaking. He thinks you want him to buck.
Don't mean no harm by it."

"I see! Roan horse, branded 'V R' and some devilish; you might
say he named himself."

"That's it."

"What is he—red roan?"

"Naw—blue roan. Mighty fine looker when he's fat—the old
scoundrel!"

"Old horse? Or is that just a love name?"

Charley laughed.

"Just a love name. He's seven years old."

Moss poured the coffee and dished up the potatoes.

"There! She's ready—pitch in! I'll take a cup of coffee with you.
Big horse?"

"Fifteen hands. Say, this slumgullion tastes mighty ample after
—you know—fodder. Last night I stayed in a little log shack south
of the peak."

Moss interrupted.

"How many rooms? So I can know whose house it was."

"Two rooms—'H G' burned on the door. 'Chas. J. Graham,
Cañada Alamosa,' stenciled on the boxes. No one at home but
canned corn and flour and coffee. Night before at the Anchor X
Ranch. No one at home. Note sayin' they'd gone to ship steers at

Magdalena. Didn't say nothing about goin' after chuck—but I know. There wasn't one cussed thing to eat except canned corn—not even coffee. Blest if I've seen a man for three days. Before that I laid up a couple of days with an old Mexican, right on the tip-top of the Black Range—hunting, and resting up my horse."

"I knowed a V R brand once, up North," said Moss reflectively. "On the hip for mares, it was; thigh for geldings; side for cattle."

"That one's on the Gila—Old Man Hearn—shoulder for horses; hip for cattle."

"Let me fill your cup," said Moss. "Now I'll tell you what—I wish you could lay up with me. I'd be glad to have you. But if you want work bad, and your horse can make eighteen or twenty miles by noon to-morrow, I think you can catch onto a job. They're meetin' at Rosedale to-morrow to start for the north round-up. This country here has done been worked. They'll light out after dinner and make camp about twenty-five miles north. You follow back the road you came here for about a mile. When the road bends to come here, at the head of the draw, you bear off to the left across the mesa, northwest-like. In six or eight miles you'll hit a plain road from the river, running west, up into the mountains. That'll take you straight to Rosedale."

"Well! I'll have to be up and doin', then, and catch 'em before they move. Much obliged to you! Think I'm pretty sure of a job?"

"It's a cinch. Them V cross T cattle are a snaky lot, and they never have enough men."

"Look here! Stake me to a number-one shoe and some nails, will you? Loan me a rasp and a hammer? I'll stick the tools up in the tree where the sign is. Clap a shoe on at daylight and shack along while it's cool. I'll make it by ten o'clock or later."

"But you'll stay all night?"

"No—we might oversleep. I'll chin with you a while and then hike along back and sleep on my saddle blankets. Then I'll be stirrin' soon in the mawnin'."

"Well, I'm sorry to see you go; but you know your own business. No more? Smoke up, then?" He tossed papers and tobacco across. "Say, I want you to send a Mex. boy down here with a horse, so I can drive my runaways in off the flat. Don't forget!"

"I'll not. May I have a bucket and wash up these blistered feet of mine before I hike?"

"Sure you can! Sit still; I'll get the water. I'll rustle round and see if some of the boys ain't left some clean socks too; and I'll wrap you up a parcel of breakfast."

"Well, this is luck!" declared Charley a little later, soaking his feet luxuriantly and blowing smoke rings while his host busied himself packing a lunch. "A job, horseshoe, socks, supper and breakfast—and no canned corn! I'll do somebody else a good turn sometime—see if I don't! I wasn't looking for much like this a spell back, either. About an hour by sun, I was countin' on maybe makin' supper on a cigarette and a few verses of The Boston Burglar—unless I could shoot me a cottontail at sundown—most always you can find a rabbit at sundown. Then I sighted this dizzy old ranch peekin' through the gap at me. Bing! Just look at me now! Nobody's got nothin' on me! Right quaint, ain't it? What a difference a few hours'll make—the things that's waiting for a fellow and him not knowin' about it!"

Moss laughed.

"Well, I got to be steppin'," said Charley.

"Hold on! I'm not done with you yet. That's a good pair of boots you've got there—but they'll be just hell on those blistered feet. How'd you like to swap for my old ones? Sevens, mine are."

"So's mine. Why, I'll swap with you. Yours'll be a sight easier on me. I'm no great shakes on walking, me."

"Why, man, did you think I meant to swap even? Your boots are worth ten dollars—almost new—and mine just hang together. I wouldn't take a mean advantage of you like that. Come! I'll make you an offer: Give me your boots and your forty-five, with the belt and scabbard, for my automatic, with its rigging and five dollars, and I'll throw in my boots."

"Shucks! You're cheating yourself! Trade boots and guns even—that'll be fair enough." Charley unbuckled his spurs.

"Don't be silly! Take the money. It's a long time till pay day. I've been all along that long road, my boy. If you're broke—I'm just guessing that, because I've been broke myself—why, you don't want to ask for an advance the first thing."

"I'll tell you what, then—swap spurs too. That'll make about an even break."

"Nonsense! Keep your spurs. You don't want these old petmakers of mine. They'd be a hoodoo to a cowboy. Take the money, son. I wish it was more. I've got plenty enough, but not here. If you feel that way about it, call it a loan and pay it back when you're flush. Better still, pass it on to somebody else that needs it."

Charley surrendered.

"I'll take it, then—that way. You're all right, Mr. Moss! Try on your new boots and see how they fit."

"Fine as silk! Couldn't be better if they was made to order," said Moss. "Good boots. That's always the way with you young fellows. Every cent goes for a fancy outfit. Bet you've got a fire-new saddle—and you without a copper cent in your pocket."

"Well, purty nigh it," admitted Charley, grinning. "Set me back fifty-four pesos less'n a year ago. But she's a daisy."

"Swell fork?"

Charley snorted.

"Swell fork nothin'! No, sir; I don't need no roll. I ride 'em slick—take off my spurs and grease my heels! I been throwed, of course—everybody has—but I never clawed leather yet and I don't need no swell fork!"

Moss smiled indulgently.

"Well, I must rig you out for horseshoein'. You stay here and rest up. Number one shoe, I think you said?"

He came back with the horseshoe and tools, bringing also the discarded ore sack, now bulging with a liberal feed of corn.

"For Vinegaroan, with my love!" he said, laughing, and clapping Ellis on the shoulder.

A lump came into Charley's throat.

"I reckon you're a real-for-certain white man, Mr. Moss. If old Vinegaroan could talk he'd sure thank you. I'm going now and let you go to bed. You don't look so clean beat out as you did, but you look right tired. *Adiós!* And I hope to meet up with you again."

"Oh, you'll see me again! Good-by!"

They shook hands. Charley shouldered his pack and limped sturdily along the starlit road, turning once for a shouted "Good-by!" Moss waved a hand from the lighted doorway; a gay song floated back to him:

"*Ada! Ada! Open that do',*
Ada!

> Ada! Ada! Open that do'
>   This mawnin'.
> Ada! Ada! Open that do'
> Or I'll open it with a fohty-fo'
>   This mawnin'!"

"Oh, yes! you'll see me again!" said Moss, smiling evilly. Then he closed the door. "Tired?" he said. "Tired? I've got to sleep if I swing for it!"

Box O Ranch, August fifth.
Statement of Elmer Moss

My name is Elmer Moss. I left Florence, Arizona, three weeks ago, looking for work. I did not find a place and drifted on to this ranch. I stayed here a week or two, six years ago, when George Sligh worked here.

Last night my horse was pretty well give out and had lost a shoe; so I left him at the crossing of Nogales Creek, west of the pasture fence, and walked in.

I got in soon after dark and found a man who said his name was Charley Ellis, and that he was working here. He was a young fellow, with rather a pleasant face. He was about my size, with light hair and blue eyes and a pug nose. He made me welcome. Said he couldn't say about the work, but for me to stay here till the boss came back. We talked quite late.

I woke up early in the morning. Ellis was not in his bed. I supposed he had gone to wrangle horses out of the pasture and I went back to sleep, for I was very tired from riding a slow horse. I woke again after a while and got up. Ellis was not back yet. I went out into the corral. And there I found a dead man. He was shot all to pieces—I don't know how many times. There were two dead horses, both shot and both saddled.

I found the boot tracks where Ellis had gone back the way I came. He is trying to get away on my horse and leave me with a murdered man on my hands to explain.

I was so scared I didn't know what to do. I went out in the pasture to the rim, where I could see all over the cañon. If I could have got a horse I would have run away. There wasn't a horse in sight except one. That one was close up under the rim-rock. He had been ridden almost to death. He wouldn't have carried me five miles. After I came back I found another one, in worse shape than the first, outside the corral gates. I let him in and gave him water and hay. There were horse-tracks of all sizes round the corral.

I don't know what to do. I don't know what has happened here. It may be a week before anybody comes. If anyone comes to-day, or while the tracks are fresh that I made coming and that Ellis made going away, I'm all right. The story is all there, plain as print. My boots are new and his was all worn out. There's no chance for mistake. And my horse has lost a shoe from his left forefoot; so he will be easy tracked. And he's badly jaded—he can't go fast. If anybody comes to-day they can trail him up and catch him easy. If no one comes to-day I'm a goner.

I just now went and spread a tarp over the dead man. He was laughing when he died. He's laughing yet—and his eyes are wide open. It's horrible! Left everything else just as it was. Am writing this now, and taking my time at it, to get everything straight while there's no one to get me rattled and all mixed up. And in case I go out of my head. Or get hold of a horse somehow and try to get away. No, I won't try to run away. If I did it would be just the same as confessing that I was the murderer. If they caught me I'd hang sure.

Nothing can save me except the straight truth. And that won't help me none unless somebody comes along to-day. This man Ellis was about my size—but I told you that before. He wore blue over-alls, pretty badly faded, and a gray flannel shirt. I didn't notice his hat; he didn't have it on much. I saw a revolver belt under his pillow and it's gone now; but I didn't see the gun.

That made me think. I went back and looked round everywhere to see where Ellis had reloaded his gun. I found fresh shells—nine of them, thirty-twos, automatic shells, smokeless, rimless—scattered over the floor of the saddle room just as an automatic would throw them. He killed his man from ambush. I went back and looked at the dead man. He was shot in the back—twice anyway. Hit six times in all, as near as I could see. I couldn't bear to touch him. He looked too terrible, laughing that way—and I'm about to break down. There was a hole in his neck about the size a thirty-two would make.

There was a sixshooter in the sand near his hand with three empty shells in it. Them shells was what killed the horses—after the dead man was first shot, I reckon. I covered him up again. I see now that I shouldn't have gone near him. I see now—too late—that I never should have made one single foot-track in that corral. If I had only known—if I had only thought in time—the tracks in there would have cleared me. All I had to do was to stay out. But how could I think of that?

Later: There is a tree in front of the house and I have started a grave there. If no one comes by sundown I'll bury the poor fellow. I will rig up some sort of a sled and put the body on it and make the give-out pony drag it out to the grave.

The work of digging has done me good and steadied my nerves. I am half done and now I am able to set a little. I will go back and finish it now.

Later—ten o'clock: Thank God! When the grave was done and I climbed out I saw a big dust off in the north coming this way. I am saved! They are closer now and coming very fast—ten or twelve men on horseback. I have looked over this statement carefully and don't think I have forgotten anything. This is the truth and nothing but the truth, so help me God.

I want to make one thing straight: Moss is not my right name. I have used that name for nine years. I was of good family and had my chance in life; but I was wild. Whatever happens I will bring no more disgrace to the name. I shall stick to Elmer Moss. If it had rained and washed the tracks out—if the wind had covered them with sand—what a shape I would be in now! They are quite close. I am leaving my gun on these sheets of paper. I am going out to meet them.

"That's all," said Tom Hall.

No one answered. Every man drew a long, deep breath—almost a sigh. There was a shuffling of feet.

The dark looks that had been bent on Moss, where he sat leaning heavily on the table, were turned long since to pity and rough friendliness. A dozen stern-faced men were crowded in the kitchen —a little white and sick, some of them, from what they had seen in the corral.

Each man looked at the others. Young Broyles let his hand rest lightly on Moss' shoulder. Then Old Man Teagardner frowned into his beard and spoke:

"Your story sounds like the truth, Mr. Moss," he said. "The boot-tracks going away from here are the same tracks we found in Blue-water Pens, and these two played-out horses came from Bluewater. If you're telling the truth you've been up against it hard. Still, you must be held as a prisoner—for the present, at least, till we find your man. And we'll want you to answer a few questions. What kind of a horse did you have?"

"A blue roan, V R brand, thin, fifteen hands high, no shoe on left forefoot, seven or eight years old. Saddle nearly new," answered Moss dully.

Then he raised his head and his voice swelled to sudden anger:

"You can ask me questions any time—you got me. Why don't you go after Ellis? That's your business! He's gettin' farther away every minute. Of course you'll keep me prisoner. What do you take me for—a fool? S'pose I'd think you'd find a man in the shape I'm in an' let him go foot-loose as soon as he said: 'Please, mister, I didn't do it? Send some of your gang after Ellis and I'll answer all the fool questions you can think up."

"Son," said Teagardner evenly, "your party won't get away. We've sent men or messages all over the country and everybody's forwarded it on. Every man not accounted for will be held on suspicion. Some of the boys will go in a little while; but, ten to one, your man Ellis is caught now—or killed. Say, boys, let's get out where we can get a breath of air."

"He won't fight, I tell you!" urged Moss as he followed his questioner outdoors. "He'll be as innocent as a lamb. If he don't ooze away without bein' seen his play is to saw it off onto me."

"All the more reason, then, why you should answer our questions."

"Questions!" cried Moss bitterly. "I wish somebody'd answer me a few. Who was that dead man? What did Ellis kill him for? Who was your gang lookin' for?"

"We don't know the dead man's name. None of us ever seen him before," said Cook. "We've followed them for two days. Robbery and murder. Now one has killed the other for his share of the stolen money."

"Then you didn't know the man you was after? But," said Moss, "this man may have got killed himself for reasons of his own. He may have nothing to do with your bank robbers. There was all sorts of shod horse-tracks leading away from the gate—I saw 'em this morning. Maybe that was the outfit you're after."

Teagardner stroked his long white beard and motioned the others to silence. Said he:

"Some of us'll follow 'em up, to be sure—but them was only saddle horses that they turned out, I judge—so us fellows couldn't get 'em. As I figure it out, that's how come your Ellis man to be in the fix he was. He shot his pardner and his pardner set him afoot before he died. So, when you come, Ellis left you to hold the sack. . . . Well! Cal, you and Hall pick out two other men to suit yourselves, and follow Ellis up. Watch close for any sign of him hiding out the money. He dassent keep it with him. We'll look for it here. Made your choice?"

"These two sticks'll do us, Uncle Ben."

"All right, then; get a mouthful to eat first and take something with you. I'll see you before you start. Broyles, you and Dick take the trail of that bunch of saddle horses after dinner. Bring 'em back—or see where they went to. It's just barely possible that there's been two separate gangs on the warpath here; but I judge not. I judge them's just saddle horses. Sam, you and Spike cook dinner. You other chaps make some sort of a coffin. Keep Moss with you. After while we'll all turn to and see if Ellis hid the money here."

In the kitchen Teagardner spoke aside to the four who were to follow Ellis.

"Now, whatever happens, you fellows get that man alive—*sabe*? No shooting. I ain't quite satisfied. Moss, he tells a straight-enough story and everything seems to back him up so far; but this man

Ellis—where does he get off? If he comes along peaceful and un-suspicious—why, he's guilty and playin' foxy, layin' it all onto Moss. If he's scared it hangs hims; if he keeps his upper lip right he's brazening it out, and we hang him for that. If he fights you he's guilty; if he hides out that proves he's guilty. If he gets clean away that's absolute proof. Any game where a man hasn't got one chance to win don't look just right."

Young Broyles burst into the room.

"See what I found! It was out in the corral, in the sand. I kicked at that ore sack layin' there by the dead horses—and I kicked up this! Nineteen five-dollar bills, done up like a pack of envelopes."

"They're all torn—see? And they're usually put up in hundred-dollar bunches, aren't they?" said Hall. "There's one gone—maybe."

"Yes," said Cal eagerly; "and that ore sack—there was two of 'em likely, and after the murder Ellis put all the stuff into one and dropped this bundle doin' it! Say! We ought to call Moss."

"I'll tell him," said Teagardner.

"But how'd them bills get torn? And where's the other one?" demanded Cal.

Hall shrugged his shoulders. "How'd I know? Come on, fellows —let's hike!"

Dinner was eaten; Broyles and Dick departed on their search; the coffin was made; and the dead man was laid in it.

"Shall you bury him now?" asked Moss.

"I hope so!" said Spike with a shudder.

"Me, too," echoed Sam. "I can't stand that awful laugh on his face. Let's get him out of sight, Uncle Ben."

"No. We want Ellis to see him, for one thing. Then again the sheriff may come and he may want to take charge. Besides, I think maybe we'll bury the murderer here and take this one to San Marcial."

Moss licked his lips.

"Put them both in one grave—why not? It's deep enough," sug-gested Cook. "They killed old Mims—let them talk it over together."

"Only one man shot Mims," said Teagardner. "This poor fellow may not have been the one. The man that killed him—his own pardner—the man that shot him in the back from behind a 'dobe wall, and then left an innocent man to stand for it—that's the man killed Mims. I don't think we've any right to force such company on this dead man. Come on! Let's get to work."

They dragged the dead horses far out on the plain; they piled sand where the blood pools had been; roof and wall and floor, they ransacked the house, the outbuildings and the stables for the stolen money.

"You're forgetting one thing," said Moss. "As I am still your prisoner I am naturally still under some suspicion. I may be the murderer after all and Ellis may be the victim—as, of course, he'll claim to be. Somebody ought to follow my track where I walked out to the rim this morning."

Teagardner eyed him, with mild reproach.

"Set your mind at rest, Mr. Moss. We're taking all bets. We did exactly that while you were resting just before dinner. You didn't take a step that isn't accounted for. You didn't ride one of the give-out horses down in the cañon and hide it there, either. And it will be the same with Ellis. That money will be found. We need it—as evidence."

"Well, if you've done looking I'd like to rest—go to sleep if I can. I'm done!"

"Yes—you look fagged out. No wonder—you've been under a strain. It's blistering hot—we'll all go out to the grave, under that tree. It's the only cool place round here. Bring some water, you boys."

"Nice pleasant place for a sleep," suggested Sam, with a nervous giggle, at the grave side. "What's the matter with the shady side of the house?"

"No air," said Moss. "This suits me."

Teagardner sat on a stone and gazed long into the grave, smoking placidly. He was a very old man—tough and sturdy and straight and tall for all that. Long and long ago, Teagardner had been an old-timer here. Half a lifetime since—at an age when most are content to become spectators—he had fared forth to new ventures; after a quarter century in Australia and the Far East—Hong-Kong last—he had come back to the land of his youth—to die.

If Napoleon, at eighty, had come back from St. Helena, some such position might have been his as was Uncle Ben's. Legend and myth had grown about his name, wild tales of the wild old days

—the days when he had not been the Old Man, or everybody's Uncle Ben, but strong among the strongest. The chase had passed his way that morning and he had taken horse, despite his seven-and-seventy years, with none to say him nay.

"It is a deep grave—and the soil is tough," he said, raising his eyes at last. "You have been a miner, Mr. Moss?"

"After a fashion—yes."

"You must have worked hard digging this."

"I did. It seemed to do me good. I was nervous and excited. Shucks! I was scared—that's the kind of nervous I was."

"You say you rode across from Arizona. Where did you stay night before last?"

"In a two-room log house under San Mateo Peak, to the south; H. G. Ranch—or it has been once, for them letters are branded on the door. No one was there."

Spike nodded. "Charley Graham's. Charley, he's at the round-up."

"Well, I'm right sorry he wasn't there, as things turned out; but if you'll send a man over to-morrow he'll find the corn cans I opened—and some flour and coffee, and nothing else—only my horse's tracks and the shoe he lost somewhere on the road. That'll prove my alibi, all right—at least, as far as your bank robbery's concerned. The greenbacks you found seem to hook these two other gentlemen up with that."

"We'll send a man there, all right, if needed. And it wasn't a bank that was robbed—it was a mine—a paymaster," said Uncle Ben.

"Well, you didn't tell me."

"No; I didn't tell you. And the night before that?"

"I stayed at the Anchor X Ranch. No one there, either. If your man goes that far he'll get canned corn straight—not even coffee to go with it. And he'll find a note to the effect that the outfit has gone to ship a bunch of steers at Magdalena."

Again Teagardner's quiet eye went round the circle and again the prisoner's story was confirmed.

"That's right. They load up to-day. Aw, let the man sleep, Uncle Ben. He's giving it to you straight."

But Uncle Ben persisted.

"And before that? You must have seen some man, somewhere, sometime."

Moss shook his head impatiently.

"For nearly a week before that I camped with an old Mexican hunter, on the divide south of Chloride, letting my horse rest up and hunting deer. Leastwise he hunted and I went along for company. I didn't have any rifle and he wouldn't lend me his. His name was Delfin Something-or-Other, and he lived in Springerville, he said. Say, old man, you make me tired! Am I to blame because no one lives in this accursed country? By George! If I could have taken a long look ahead I'd have hired me a witness and carried him with me."

"If we could take a long look ahead—or a short one—we'd be greatly surprised, some of us," Teagardner answered, without heat. "There—go to sleep, all of you. I slept last night. I'll call you when it's time."

He changed his seat to a softer one on the fresh mound of earth; he twisted his long gray beard and looked down into the grave. Moss watched him through narrowed lids. Then fatigue claimed him, stronger than horror or hate or fear, and he fell asleep.

"You chuckle-headed idiots!" gasped Charley Ellis.

"Oh, that's all right too," said Tom Hall. "Some folks is too smart for their own good. You keep still."

Three men held Charley, one by each arm and one by the collar. His eyes were flashing; he was red with anger and considerably the worse for wear, having just made a sincere and conscientious attempt to break the neck of Mr. Moss—an almost successful attempt. It had taken more than three men to pull him off. Moss, white and smiling, mopped his bruised face beyond the coffin and the open grave; the sun setting between the clouds threw a red, angry light over all.

"Quiet having been resumed," observed Teagardner patiently, "let us pass on to unfinished business. Tom, we've been so all-fired busy explainin' the situation to Mr. Ellis that we haven't got your report yet. Spit it out!"

"Uncle Ben, this Ellis is the man we want," said Tom Hall. "We found where he'd tacked a shoe on the horse—of course Moss couldn't know that. We tracked him a ways toward Rosedale and then we met these three Rosedale men coming back with him.

They told him they was holdin' everybody and gathered him in. He made no objection—handed over his gun without a word. It was an automatic thirty-two. Horse and saddle just as Moss described 'em, all right—and this ore sack tied on the saddle besides."

Uncle Ben shook his head.

"It won't do, Tom. Everything is as Moss told it—but everything is just as Ellis tells it, too. So far as I can see they've got only one horse, one saddle and one interestin' past between them."

"You blithering, blistering, gibbering, fat-headed fools!" said Charley pleasantly. "If you'd told me about what Moss said I would 'a' told you to leave my horse and let Moss try his hand at describin' him. He's got one white hoof; he's been cut with barbed wire; and my saddle's been sewed up with buckskin where the linin' ripped. Moss couldn't have told you that. Did you give me a fair chance for my life? No, sir; you come blunderin' in and let Moss look 'em all over—pertendin' to be petting old Vinegaroan. I wasn't mistrustin' anything like this. They said there'd been trouble and they was makin' all strangers account for themselves. That seemed reasonable enough and I wasn't worrying."

"We've got only your word for that," sneered Sam. "I reckon Moss could have told us all about it if we had asked him."

"And maybe again he couldn't—Ellis is right," said Hall soberly. "He didn't get an even break. I'm sorry."

"What about the ore sack?"

"Boys," said Uncle Ben, "you're going at this all wrong. Mr. Ellis says he took feed in that sack—that's reasonable. And that he kept the sack by him counts in his favor, I think."

"So do I," said Cal. "And I'll swear that if he had any money in it he must 'a' eat the bills and flung the coins away, one piece at a time. He never hid it after he left this house—that's sure. I know every inch of ground he's been over and my eyes is pretty near out from reading sign. I even went on, to make sure, after we met the Rosedale men, clear to where he met them and loped all the way back to catch up with 'em."

"How about this then?" cried Spike triumphantly. He was one of those who held Ellis. "I just took it out of his pocket."

It was a new five-dollar bill, and it was torn. Teagardner produced the package of bills. The tears matched exactly.

A horrible snarl burst from a dozen throats. They crowded and jostled, Moss with the rest; hands reached out to clutch at the prisoner.

"Hang him! Hang him!"

"Stand back! Stand back, you blind fools! I'll shoot the next man that touches him!" shouted Teagardner. "Stand back."

"You'll hang nobody, you howling dogs!" said Ellis coolly. "We stand just where we did before—my word against Moss'."

"Exactly!" said Uncle Ben. "Have a little sense, can't ye? Cook, if you was this man, and guilty, how would you say you got this bill?"

"I'd say Moss gave it to me, of course."

"And you, Spike, if you knew positively that Ellis was innocent —then how did he get this bill?"

"He must have got it from Moss," said Spike reluctantly.

Charley laughed. "Well, that's where I got it—when we traded boots and guns, like I was tellin' you."

"You're a damned liar!"

No one was holding Charley's foot. It now caught Moss squarely in the breast and hurled him over the mound of earth and almost into the grave.

"Old gentleman—Uncle Ben, as they call you"—said Charley then, "you seem to have charge here, and you're old enough to have a real idea once in a while. There's just as much against Moss as against me, and no more—isn't there?"

"Precisely—up to date."

"Well, then, why aren't we treated the same? Why am I held this way while he goes free?"

"That's right!" said Cal.

"Hold Moss, a couple of you," said Uncle Ben. "Now, Mr. Ellis, look here!" He pushed aside the unnailed coffin lid to show the dead man's face. "Do you know this man?"

"Hell, he's laughing! No; I never saw him before. What's he laughing at? What's the joke?"

"He is laughing at his murderer."

"Well, I know who that is," said Charley. "And that's more than the rest of you do."

Teagardner replaced the lid.

"All we know—yet—is that he is either laughing at you or laughing at Moss. Your stories exactly offset each other. What are we going to do next? Understand me—there'll be nobody hanged till he's proved guilty."

"Keep us!" said Charley. "Watch us night and day! Chain us together with every chain on the ranch. One of us is a liar. Send some of your men along the back track till you find where the liar's story don't fit with the certain truth. I can describe every little trifling thing at the ranches where I stayed; I can tell what my old Mexican hunter looks like, if you can find him. Can Moss?"

"Son," said Teagardner, "you've got the right idea, and your plan would work—if we had to do it; but we don't have to do it. You've overlooked one thing. There's two ends to every lie—and one end of this lie is on this side of the murder. If we find the money where you hid it after you left here—you swing, Ellis. If we find it here at the ranch—why, either of you may have hid it. Everything that's happened at the ranch may have been done by either of you two men—everything but one."

He turned a slow eye on Moss, who stood by the coffin, white and trembling, with a man at each arm. His voice rang—measured, stern and hard.

"Everything but one," he repeated. "Ellis had nothing to do with one thing. . . . Moss dug the grave. And the grave is too deep. I always thought the grave was too deep. Jump into the grave, Sam, and see why Moss made it so deep!"

Moss dropped to his knees; his guards held him up; they forced him forward to the edge of the grave. A shudder ran through the crowd; they swayed forward; the last ray of the sun fell on them in a golden shaft. Sam leaped into the grave.

"Moss dug his grave too deep—because he was afraid somebody might want to make it a little deeper," said Teagardner. "Ground solid there? Try the other end."

Sam found loose earth at the other end. He shoveled furiously; he came to a package wrapped in slickers. He threw it up. They slashed the cords; they unrolled the slickers; at the grave's edge they poured the blood-bought money at the murderer's feet.

TOP HAND
by *Luke Short*

Gus Irby was out on the boardwalk in front of the Elite, giving his swamper hell for staving in an empty beer barrel, when the kid passed on his way to the feed stable. His horse was a good one and it was tired, Gus saw, and the kid had a little hump in his back from the cold of a mountain October morning. In spite of the ample layer of flesh that Gus wore carefully like an uncomfortable shroud, he shivered in his shirt sleeves and turned into the saloon, thinking without much interest *Another fiddle-footed dry-country kid that's been paid off after round-up.*

Later, while he was taking out the cash for the day and opening up some fresh cigars, Gus saw the kid go into the Pride Café for breakfast, and afterward come out, toothpick in mouth, and cruise both sides of Wagon Mound's main street in aimless curiosity.

After that, Gus wasn't surprised when he looked around at the sound of the door opening, and saw the kid coming toward the bar. He was in a clean and faded shirt and looked as if he'd been cold for a good many hours. Gus said good morning and took down his best whisky and a glass and put them in front of the kid.

"First customer in the morning gets a drink on the house," Gus announced.

"Now I know why I rode all night," the kid said, and he grinned at Gus. He was a pleasant-faced kid with pale eyes that weren't shy or sullen or bold, and maybe because of this he didn't fit readily into any of Gus' handy character pigeonholes. Gus had seen them young and fiddle-footed before, but they were the tough kids, and for a man with no truculence in him, like Gus, talking with them was like trying to pet a tiger.

Gus leaned against the back bar and watched the kid take his whisky and wipe his mouth on his sleeve, and Gus found himself getting curious. Half a lifetime of asking skillful questions that didn't seem like questions at all, prompted Gus to observe now, "If you're goin' on through you better pick up a coat. This high country's cold now."

"I figure this is far enough," the kid said.

"Oh, well, if somebody sent for you, that's different." Gus reached around lazily for a cigar.

The kid pulled out a silver dollar from his pocket and put it on the bar top, and then poured himself another whisky, which Gus was sure he didn't want, but which courtesy dictated he should buy. "Nobody sent for me, either," the kid observed. "I ain't got any money."

Gus picked up the dollar and got change from the cash drawer and put it in front of the kid, afterward lighting his cigar. This was when the announcement came.

"I'm a top hand," the kid said quietly, looking levelly at Gus. "Who's lookin' for one?"

Gus was glad he was still lighting his cigar, else he might have smiled. If there had been a third man here, Gus would have winked at him surreptitiously; but since there wasn't, Gus kept his face expressionless, drew on his cigar a moment, and then observed gently, "You look pretty young for a top hand."

"The best cow pony I ever saw was four years old," the kid answered pointedly.

Gus smiled faintly and shook his head. "You picked a bad time. Round-up's over."

The kid nodded, and drank down his second whisky quickly, waited for his breath to come normally. Then he said, "Much obliged. I'll see you again," and turned toward the door.

A mild cussedness stirred within Gus, and after a moment's hesitation he called out, "Wait a minute."

The kid hauled up and came back to the bar. He moved with an easy grace that suggested quickness and work-hardened muscle, and for a moment Gus, a careful man, was undecided. But the kid's face, so young and without caution, reassured him, and he folded his heavy arms on the bar top and pulled his nose thoughtfully. "You figure to hit all the outfits, one by one, don't you?"

The kid nodded, and Gus frowned and was silent a moment, and then he murmured, almost to himself, "I had a notion—oh, hell, I don't know."

"Go ahead," the kid said, and then his swift grin came again. "I'll try anything once."

"Look," Gus said, as if his mind were made up. "We got a newspaper here—the Wickford County Free Press. Comes out every Thursday, that's today." He looked soberly at the kid. "Whyn't you put a piece in there and say 'Top hand wants a job at forty dollars a month'? Tell 'em what you can do and tell 'em to come see you here if they want a hand. They'll all get it in a couple days. That way you'll save yourself a hundred miles of ridin'. Won't cost much either."

The kid thought awhile and then asked, without smiling, "Where's this newspaper at?"

Gus told him and the kid went out. Gus put the bottle away and doused the glass in water, and he was smiling slyly at his thoughts. Wait till the boys read that in the Free Press. They were going to have some fun with that kid, Gus reflected.

Johnny McSorley stepped out into the chill thin sunshine. The last silver dollar in his pants pocket was a solid weight against his leg, and he was aware that he'd probably spend it in the next few minutes on the newspaper piece. He wondered about that, and figured shrewdly it had an off chance of working.

Four riders dismounted at a tie rail ahead and paused a moment, talking. Johnny looked them over and picked out their leader, a tall, heavy, scowling man in his middle thirties who was wearing a mackinaw unbuttoned.

Johnny stopped and said, "You know anybody lookin' for a top hand?" and grinned pleasantly at the big man.

For a second Johnny thought he was going to smile. He didn't think he'd have liked the smile, once he saw it, but the man's face settled into the scowl again. "I never saw a top hand that couldn't vote," he said.

Johnny looked at him carefully, not smiling, and said, "Look at one now, then," and went on, and by the time he'd taken two steps he thought, *Voted, huh? A man must grow pretty slow in this high country.*

He crossed the street and paused before a window marked WICK-FORD COUNTY FREE PRESS. JOB PRINTING. D. MELAVEN, ED. AND

PROP. He went inside, then. A girl was seated at a cluttered desk, staring at the street, tapping a pencil against her teeth. Johnny tramped over to her, noting the infernal racket made by one of two men at a small press under the lamp behind the railed-off office space.

Johnny said "Hello," and the girl turned tiredly and said, "Hello, bub." She had on a plain blue dress with a high bodice and a narrow lace collar, and she was a very pretty girl, but tired, Johnny noticed. Her long yellow hair was worn in braids that crossed almost atop her head, and she looked, Johnny thought, like a small kid who has pinned her hair up out of the way for her Saturday night bath. He thought all this and then remembered her greeting, and he reflected without rancor, *Damn, that's twice*, and he said, "I got a piece for the paper, sis."

"Don't call me sis," the girl said. "Anybody's name I don't know, I call him bub. No offense. I got that from pa, I guess."

That's likely, Johnny thought, and he said amiably, "Any girl's name I don't know, I call her sis. I got that from ma."

The cheerful effrontery of the remark widened the girl's eyes. She held out her hand now and said with dignity, "Give it to me. I'll see it gets in next week."

"That's too late," Johnny said. "I got to get it in this week."

"Why?"

"I ain't got money enough to hang around another week."

The girl stared carefully at him. "What is it?"

"I want to put a piece in about myself. I'm a top hand, and I'm lookin' for work. The fella over there at the saloon says why don't I put a piece in the paper about wantin' work, instead of ridin' out lookin' for it."

The girl was silent a full five seconds and then said, "You don't look that simple. Gus was having fun with you."

"I figured that," Johnny agreed. "Still, it might work. If you're caught short-handed, you take anything."

The girl shook her head. "It's too late. The paper's made up." Her voice was meant to hold a note of finality, but Johnny regarded her curiously, with a maddening placidity.

"You D. Melaven?" he asked.

"No. That's pa."

"Where's he?"

"Back there. Busy."

Johnny saw the gate in the rail that separated the office from the shop and he headed toward it. He heard the girl's chair scrape on the floor and her urgent command, "Don't go back there. It's not allowed."

Johnny looked over his shoulder and grinned and said, "I'll try anything once," and went on through the gate, hearing the girl's swift steps behind him. He halted alongside a square-built and solid man with a thatch of stiff hair more gray than black, and said, "You D. Melaven?"

"Dan Melaven, bub. What can I do for you?"

That's three times, Johnny thought, and he regarded Melaven's square face without anger. He liked the face; it was homely and stubborn and intelligent, and the eyes were both sharp and kindly. Hearing the girl stop beside him, Johnny said, "I got a piece for the paper today."

The girl put in quickly, "I told him it was too late, pa. Now you tell him, and maybe he'll get out."

"Cassie," Melaven said in surprised protest.

"I don't care. We can't unlock the forms for every out-at-the-pants puncher that asks us. Besides, I think he's one of Alec Barr's bunch." She spoke vehemently, angrily, and Johnny listened to her with growing amazement.

"Alec who?" he asked.

"I saw you talking to him, and then you came straight over here from him," Cassie said hotly.

"I hit him for work."

"I don't believe it."

"Cassie," Melaven said grimly, "come back here a minute." He took her by the arm and led her toward the back of the shop, where they halted and engaged in quiet, earnest conversation.

Johnny shook his head in bewilderment, and then looked around him. The biggest press, he observed, was idle. And on a stone-topped table where Melaven had been working was a metal form almost filled with lines of type and gray metal pieces of assorted sizes and shapes. Now, Johnny McSorley did not know any more than the average person about the workings of a newspaper, but his common sense told him that Cassie had lied to him when she said it was too late to accept his advertisement. Why, there was space and to spare in that form for the few lines of type his message would need. Turning this over in his mind, he wondered what was behind her refusal.

Presently, the argument settled, Melaven and Cassie came back to him, and Johnny observed that Cassie, while chastened, was still mad.

"All right, what do you want printed, bub?" Melaven asked.

Johnny told him and Melaven nodded when he was finished, said, "Pay her," and went over to the type case.

Cassie went back to the desk and Johnny followed her, and when she was seated he said, "What do I owe you?"

Cassie looked speculatively at him, her face still flushed with anger. "How much money have you got?"

"A dollar some."

"It'll be two dollars," Cassie said.

Johnny pulled out his lone silver dollar and put it on the desk. "You print it just the same; I'll be back with the rest later."

Cassie said with open malice, "You'd have it now, bub, if you hadn't been drinking before ten o'clock."

Johnny didn't do anything for a moment, and then he put both hands on the desk and leaned close to her. "How old are you?" he asked quietly.

"Seventeen."

"I'm older'n you," Johnny murmured. "So the next time you call me 'bub' I'm goin' to take down your pigtails and pull 'em. I'll try anything once."

Once he was in the sunlight, crossing toward the Elite, he felt better. He smiled—partly at himself but mostly at Cassie. She was a real spitfire, kind of pretty and kind of nice, and he wished he knew what her father said to her that made her so mad, and why she'd been mad in the first place.

Gus was breaking out a new case of whisky and stacking bottles against the back mirror as Johnny came in and went up to the bar. Neither of them spoke while Gus finished, and Johnny gazed absently at the poker game at one of the tables and now yawned sleepily.

Gus said finally, "You get it in all right?"

Johnny nodded thoughtfully and said, "She mad like that at everybody?"

"Who? Cassie?"

"First she didn't want to take the piece, but her old man made her. Then she charges me more for it than I got in my pocket. Then she combs me over like I got my head stuck in the cookie crock for drinkin' in the morning. She calls me bub, to boot."

"She calls everybody bub."

"Not me no more," Johnny said firmly, and yawned again.

Gus grinned and sauntered over to the cash box. When he came back he put ten silver dollars on the bar top and said, "Pay me back when you get your job. And I got rooms upstairs if you want to sleep."

Johnny grinned. "Sleep, hunh? I'll try anything once." He took the money, said "Much obliged" and started away from the bar and then paused. "Say, who's this Alec Barr?"

Johnny saw Gus's eyes shift swiftly to the poker game and then shuttle back to him. Gus didn't say anything.

"See you later," Johnny said.

He climbed the stairs whose entrance was at the end of the bar, wondering why Gus was so careful about Alec Barr.

A gunshot somewhere out in the street woke him. The sun was gone from the room, so it must be afternoon, he thought. He pulled on his boots, slopped some water into the washbowl and washed up, pulled hand across his cheek and decided he should shave, and went downstairs. There wasn't anybody in the saloon, not even behind the bar. On the tables and on the bar top, however, were several newspapers, all fresh. He was reminded at once that he was in debt to the Wickford County Free Press for the sum of one dollar. He pulled one of the newspapers toward him and turned to the page where all the advertisements were.

When, after some minutes, he finished, he saw that his advertisement was not there. A slow wrath grew in him as he thought of the girl and her father taking his money, and when it had come to full flower, he went out of the Elite and cut across toward the newspaper office. He saw, without really noticing it, the group of men clustered in front of the store across from the newspaper office. He swung under the tie rail and reached the opposite boardwalk just this side of the newspaper office and a man who was lounging against the building. He was a puncher and when he saw Johnny heading up the walk he said, "Don't go across there."

Johnny said grimly, "You stop me," and went on, and he heard the puncher say, "All right, getcher head blown off."

His boots crunched broken glass in front of the office and he came to a gingerly halt, looking down at his feet. His glance raised to the window, and he saw where there was a big jag of glass out of the window, neatly wiping out the Wickford except for the W on the sign and ribboning cracks to all four corners of the frame. His surprise held him motionless for a moment, and then he heard a voice calling from across the street, "Clear out of there, son."

That makes four times, Johnny thought resignedly, and he glanced across the street and saw Alec Barr, several men clotted around him, looking his way.

Johnny went on and turned into the newspaper office and it was like walking into a dark cave. The lamp was extinguished.

And then he saw the dim forms of Cassie Melaven and her father back of the railing beside the job press, and the reason for his errand came back to him with a rush. Walking through the gate, he began firmly, "I got a dollar owed——" and ceased talking and halted abruptly. There was a six-shooter in Dan Melaven's hand hanging at his side. Johnny looked at it, and then raised his glance to Melaven's face and found the man watching him with a bitter amusement in his eyes. His glance shuttled to Cassie, and she was looking at him as if she didn't see him, and her face seemed very pale in that gloom. He half gestured toward the gun and said, "What's that for?"

"A little trouble, bub," Melaven said mildly. "Come back for your money?"

"Yeah," Johnny said slowly.

Suddenly it came to him, and he wheeled and looked out through the broken window and saw Alec Barr across the street in conversation with two men, his own hands, Johnny supposed. That explained the shot that wakened him. A little trouble.

He looked back at Melaven now in time to hear him say to Cassie, "Give him his money."

Cassie came past him to the desk and pulled open a drawer and opened the cash box. While she was doing it, Johnny strolled soberly over to the desk. She gave him the dollar and he took it, and their glances met. *She's been crying,* he thought, with a strange distress.

"That's what I tried to tell you," Cassie said. "We didn't want to take your money, but you wouldn't have it. That's why I was so mean."

"What's it all about?" Johnny asked soberly.

"Didn't you read the paper?"

Johnny shook his head in negation, and Cassie said dully, "It's right there on page one. There's a big chunk of Government land out on Artillery Creek coming up for sale. Alec Barr wanted it, but he didn't want anybody bidding against him. He knew pa would have to publish a notice of sale. He tried to get pa to hold off publication of the date of sale until it would be too late for other bidders to make it. Pa was to get a piece of the land in return for the favor, or money. I guess we needed it all right, but pa told him no."

Johnny looked over at Melaven, who had come up to the rail now and was listening. Melaven said, "I knew Barr'd be in today with his bunch, and they'd want a look at a pull sheet before the press got busy, just to make sure the notice wasn't there. Well, Cassie and Dad Hopper worked with me all last night to turn out the real paper, with the notice of sale and a front-page editorial about Barr's proposition to me, to boot."

"We got it printed and hid it out in the shed early this morning," Cassie explained.

Melaven grinned faintly at Cassie, and there was a kind of open admiration for the job in the way he smiled. He said to Johnny now, "So what you saw in the forms this mornin' was a fake, bub. That's why Cassie didn't want your money. The paper was already printed." He smiled again, that rather proud smile. "After you'd gone, Barr came in. He wanted a pull sheet and we gave it to him, and he had a man out front watching us most of the morning. But he pulled him off later. We got the real paper out of the shed onto the Willow Valley stage, and we got it delivered all over town before Barr saw it."

Johnny was silent a moment, thinking this over. Then he nodded toward the window. "Barr do that?"

"I did," Melaven said quietly. "I reckon I can keep him out until someone in this town gets the guts to run him off."

Johnny looked down at the dollar in his hand and stared at it a moment and put it in his pocket. When he looked up at Cassie, he surprised her watching him, and she smiled a little, as if to ask forgiveness.

Johnny said, "Want any help?" to Melaven, and the man looked at him thoughtfully and then nodded. "Yes. You can take Cassie home."

"Oh, no," Cassie said. She backed away from the desk and put her back against the wall, looking from one to the other. "I don't go. As long as I'm here, he'll stay there."

"Sooner or later, he'll come in," Melaven said grimly. "I don't want you hurt."

"Let him come," Cassie said stubbornly. "I can swing a wrench better than some of his crew can shoot."

"Please go with him."

Cassie shook her head. "No, pa. There's some men left in this town. They'll turn up."

Melaven said "Hell," quietly, angrily, and went back into the shop. Johnny and the girl looked at each other for a long moment, and Johnny saw the fear in her eyes. She was fighting it, but she didn't have it licked, and he couldn't blame her. He said, "If I'd had a gun on me, I don't reckon they'd of let me in here, would they?"

"Don't try it again," Cassie said. "Don't try the back either. They're out there."

Johnny said, "Sure you won't come with me?"

"I'm sure."

"Good," Johnny said quietly. He stepped outside and turned up-street, glancing over at Barr and the three men with him, who were watching him wordlessly. The man leaning against the building straightened up and asked, "She comin' out?"

"She's thinkin' it over," Johnny said.

The man called across the street to Barr, "She's thinkin' it over," and Johnny headed obliquely across the wide street toward the Elite. *What kind of a town is this, where they'd let this happen?* he thought angrily, and then he caught sight of Gus Irby standing under the wooden awning in front of the Elite, watching the show. Everybody else was doing the same thing. A man behind Johnny yelled, "Send her out, Melaven," and Johnny vaulted up onto the boardwalk and halted in front of Gus.

"What do you aim to do?" he asked Gus.

"Mind my own business, same as you," Gus growled, but he couldn't hold Johnny's gaze.

There was shame in his face, and when Johnny saw it his mind was made up. He shouldered past him and went into the Elite and saw it was empty. He stepped behind the bar now and, bent over so he could look under it, slowly traveled down it. Right beside the beer taps he found what he was looking for. It was a sawed-off shotgun and he lifted it up and broke it and saw that both barrels were loaded. Standing motionless, he thought about this now, and presently he moved on toward the back and went out the rear door. It opened onto an alley, and he turned left and went up it, thinking, *It was brick, and the one next to it was painted brown, at least in front*. And then he saw it up ahead, a low brick store with a big loading platform running across its rear.

He went up to it, and looked down the narrow passageway he'd remembered was between this building and the brown one beside it. There was a small areaway here, this end cluttered with weeds and bottles and tin cans. Looking through it he could see a man's elbow and segment of leg at the boardwalk, and he stepped as noiselessly as he could over the trash and worked forward to the boardwalk.

At the end of the areaway, he hauled up and looked out and saw Alec Barr some ten feet to his right and teetering on the edge of the high boardwalk, gun in hand. He was engaged in low conversation with three other men on either side of him. There was a supreme insolence in the way he exposed himself, as if he knew Melaven would not shoot at him and could not hit him if he did.

Johnny raised the shotgun hip high and stepped out and said quietly, "Barr, you goin' to throw away that gun and get on your horse or am I goin' to burn you down?"

The four men turned slowly, not moving anything except their heads. It was Barr whom Johnny watched, and he saw the man's bold baleful eyes gauge his chances and decline the risk, and Johnny smiled. The three other men were watching Barr for a clue to their moves.

Johnny said "Now," and on the heel of it he heard the faint clatter of a kicked tin can in the areaway behind him. He lunged out of the areaway just as a pistol shot erupted with a savage roar between the two buildings.

Barr half turned now with the swiftness with which he lifted his gun across his front, and Johnny, watching him, didn't even raise the shotgun in his haste; he let go from the hip. He saw Barr rammed off the high boardwalk into the tie rail, and heard it crack and splinter and break with the big man's weight, and then Barr fell in the street out of sight.

The three other men scattered into the street, running blindly for the opposite sidewalk. And at the same time, the men who had been standing in front of the buildings watching this now ran toward Barr, and Gus Irby was in the van. Johnny poked the shotgun into the areaway and without even taking sight he pulled the trigger and listened to the bellow of the explosion and the rattling raking of the buckshot as it caromed between the two buildings. Afterward, he turned down street and let Gus and the others run past him, and he went into the Elite.

It was empty, and he put the shotgun on the bar and got himself a glass of water and stood there drinking it, thinking, *I feel some different, but not much.*

He was still drinking water when Gus came in later. Gus looked at him long and hard, as he poured himself a stout glass of whisky and downed it. Finally, Gus said, "There ain't a right thing about it, but they won't pay you a bounty for him. They should."

Johnny didn't say anything, only rinsed out his glass.

"Melaven wants to see you," Gus said then.

"All right." Johnny walked past him and Gus let him get past him ten feet, and then said, "Kid, look."

Johnny halted and turned around and Gus, looking sheepish, said, "About that there newspaper piece. That was meant to be a rawhide, but damned if it didn't backfire on me."

Johnny just waited, and Gus went on. "You remember the man that was standing this side of Barr? He works for me, runs some cows for me. Did, I mean, because he stood there all afternoon sickin' Barr on Melaven. You want his job? Forty a month, top hand."

"Sure," Johnny said promptly.

Gus smiled expansively and said, "Let's have a drink on it."

"Tomorrow," Johnny said. "I don't aim to get a reputation for drinkin' all day long."

Gus looked puzzled, and then laughed. "Reputation? Who with? Who knows——" His talk faded off, and then he said quietly, "Oh."

Johnny waited long enough to see if Gus would smile, and when Gus didn't, he went out. Gus didn't smile after he'd gone either.

GUEST'S GOLD

by Stewart Edward White

Nifty Barnes was an orphan. He was nineteen years old. He had lived most of them by his wits. They had been spent along the wharves and back streets of Boston. He had run errands, done odd jobs, sold papers. Because he had had, always, to fight in order to keep anything he got, he had early developed the scrapper's belligerence and skill. Once or twice he had capitalized this skill in the ring, but he did not care for prize fighting. There were in that profession too many chances for double-crossing; not so much by one's opponent as by all the managers and promoters and gambling men with whom one must do business. Nifty preferred the lone hand. He not only did not trust any of his fellow humans but he was certain that those of them with whom he came in contact were definitely against him. Why shouldn't they be? For this reason, Nifty had not joined a gang. He was like a cornered, snarling animal, except that he had in himself an arrogant self-confidence. That co-operation is sometimes essential, even if only in self-interest, was borne in on him after he had whaled the daylights out of Bugs McCoy. Bugs was the head of one of Boston's gangs.

In other words, Nifty Barnes was a tough baby, and he was on a hot spot, and if he didn't wish to be bumped off, it was up to him to take it on the lam. That this was about a hundred years ago, and that Nifty would have used different words, did not alter the situation itself.

The spot on which Nifty found himself was so hot that he signed before the mast aboard the brig Mercury, California bound; Ezekiel Stanton, master; Michael Dolan, mate. He did so with no enthusiasm, for he possessed no knowledge of ships; from the theory and practice of hard work he withheld his approval, and to the idea of discipline he was antipathetic. Still, anything was better than facing the organized vengeance of Bugs McCoy's gang.

The case of those aboard the Mercury was little better or worse than the average for those days. The food was, of course, bad. Stanton was a good skipper who took a pride in his ship and would tolerate no sloppy work. The work itself was sailor's work in any language, which the Roaring Forties and Cape Stiff emphasized to hardship at times. Mike Dolan was an efficient mate who got things done. He had no genuine animosities, but, on the other hand, he knew no mercies, no compunctions, and certainly no faintest sentiment of human fellowships forward of the break in the quarter-deck. He knocked 'em about with his fists or a belaying pin when they were obstinate or slow or even stupid, but it would have surprised him—or indeed any of the old shellbacks under him —had he ever heard anybody describe him as a "bucko," or had he realized that he was an object of enmity; except, of course, the natural hatred of any crew for its first officer. If a man did not do his work, he got after him. The work must be done, mustn't it?

Nevertheless, Nifty Barnes reached the coast of California with his natural asocial tendencies defined into three simplicities: (a) He had been a fool; better to have taken a chance than to have got himself into this mess. (b) The world was cruel, unjust and against him; you can trust nobody; everybody was out to do you dirt. He had known this before. (c) Mike Dolan personified, for the moment, that cruelty and injustice. What he was going to do about it was not yet clear. His helplessness in the matter curdled his bitterness, in which was an element of cynical contempt that indicated his spirit was not yet broken. His ambitions focused on getting even with Mike Dolan.

The Mercury, under shortened sail, moved slowly up the coast. The sun was dropping into the Pacific. Already its disk, touching the horizon, was strangely refracted, flattened at the top, exaggerated in size, reddened, so that it hung for a moment, before making its final plunge, like a weird fire temple to which led the broad molten carpet of the gilded sea.

To eastward, the waters gnawed at the feet of naked mountains, golden velvet in the light of evening.

These beauties were lost on Nifty Barnes. He was clasping and unclasping his fingers, stiffened by the cords that had bound his wrists. A sailor was lowering the grating against which he had been spread-eagled. His back burned. Another sailor slushed a bucket of sea water over his shoulders. It dripped from him, faintly pink. His eyes were fixed sullenly on the deck. He did not look up, but he was perfectly aware, as though he saw them, of the crew standing silently forward, and of the bos'n coiling the ninetails around the stock, and of Captain Stanton back there on the quarter-deck, looking down, and of Dolan, his legs apart, his head on one side, near his elbow.

"You've been asking for this all the way from Cape Stiff," the mate was saying dispassionately.

Nifty did not look up or make reply. Someone handed him his shirt. He jerked it over his head. The rough cloth scraped his back, but he did not wince. He started forward.

"Avast, Barnes," the mate's voice stopped him. "Stand by to man the shore boat. You can try out that back of yours pulling an oar."

Nifty turned aside. He leaned sullenly against the rail. He saw nothing. His face was set and grim.

Somebody sidled alongside of him. He paid no attention. A soft voice spoke to him. This was Marco. Damn Portugee! It was inconceivable to Nifty that he could be an object of compassion; that such a thing as compassion existed. Why was Marco always sucking around? He wanted something. Nifty was unable to imagine what it could be. These foreigners were sly. Well, he wouldn't get it.

"Too bad," the soft voice murmured. "What for you act so? You too cocky. No good. Makes for you nothing. Don't do heem no more."

Nifty Barnes disdained reply. He stared at the shore.

The golden velvet had darkened to purple. Night hid the base of the mountains; was creeping out over the lustrous sea.

"This California," Marco was telling him, unrebuffed by his silence. "I been here many time—the Red Wing, the Flying Spray, now the Mercury. Once he belong Spain; now Mexico." Marco laughed, showing white teeth, but the boy did not look toward him. "Mexico ver' bad for California. She tell California that she shall buy onlee from her, and then she forget to send things to buy! That's funnee!" He laughed again. "But these peoples mus' have things. They cannot grow them on the trees. So we bring them, and to hell with Mexico. Onlee we mus' not let Mexico catch us! She's against the law. It's bad to go against the law," continued Marco in comfortable argument, "but the good *padres*, they come buy. Pret' soon, when she come night, you see a fire on the beach. They light heem. Then we go in wid the boat." Nifty jerked aside impatiently from the pleading insistence of the Portugee's voice.

"What the hell's it to me?" he growled.

Marco faded away.

The ship drew slowly toward the shore, now a band of black between the green lucence of the sky and the gun-metal lucence of the water. Abruptly, against this band, a tiny flame sprang into being. From it a needle of reflected light pointed straight at the ship.

"Lower away!" came the hoarse order from the mate.

Nifty Barnes and three of his mates rowed slowly toward the shore. The Mercury had already stopped at San Diego, San Pedro, San Buenaventura, Santa Barbara, and the port for San Luis Obispo. Nevertheless, Nifty had not set foot on soil now for nearly eight months. Dolan knew better than to give the stubborn and pugnacious youngster a chance of escaping where there were missions and people. So, reflected Nifty sourly, but logically, undoubtedly this part of the coast would prove uninhabited. However, that did not completely spoil his satisfaction. It would be good to feel earth under his feet.

The signal fire on the beach had gone out or been extinguished. The immediate world was crouched, muffled, cherishing its darkness like a cloak whose comfort shortly it must cast aside to honor the triumphant emergence of the moon. Sea and land were indistinguishable, unseen. Nifty felt the oar in his palms and the resistance of the water against its stroke. He felt beneath him the gentle strength of the rollers as they lifted and eased down the structure in which he sat. He heard the click and dip of the oars, and the roar of waves breaking, and the sucking, short, breathless hush that followed. But for a time he could see nothing.

Then suddenly a reef broke at his right hand, startling as the burst of a shell. Over his shoulder Nifty saw other patches of broken water, surf over other reefs and rocks and ledges, like white hands snatching from the deep and withdrawn in balked emptiness, and his ears were filled with the roar of their discomfiture. They seemed to rise up all around him, as though they had been lying in wait. For an instant he lost his stroke. Dolan swore at him.

Dolan seemed to know what he was about; seemed able to feel his way. Shortly an intensification of the blackness on their right marked a headland. The boat slipped into the quieter waters of a cove and grounded on the steep shelf of a beach.

They disembarked and pulled out the boat. Dolan growled an order. Nifty's three mates sat down against the side of the boat. "You come with me, so I can keep an eye on you," growled Dolan to Nifty.

He had to follow as best he might. It was even blacker here ashore than it had been on the sea, if that were possible. After the sand of the beach was a beaten earthen trail. Nifty could feel its packed surface beneath his feet. He tried to follow accurately Dolan's dim figure, for when he failed to do so, he stumbled badly, all but fell.

They climbed briefly, and matters improved. The firmament was full of stars, but they seemed to have crowded back toward the western part of the heavens, where they clustered thick, like an audience in expectancy. To the east, the rim of mountains had sharpened against the sky, which now glowed with a waiting glory. It was the waxing reflection of this which was making visible to Nifty surrounding dim phantoms of things. He could follow Dolan with greater confidence.

Three men materialized out of the blackness of a tree to confront them. With Dolan one of them carried on a low-voiced conversation in Spanish, which Nifty could not understand. He had nothing to do but chew over his thoughts. What did Dolan expect, that he had to "keep an eye" on him? The man was a fool, which Nifty was not. What would Nifty do in a country like this, even if he did run away? No, Nifty knew better than that! He'd have to stick it out, but once he got back to Boston—Nifty lost himself in the satisfactions of imagination—what he'd do to Dolan. He glanced with hatred at the mate's broad back.

At what moment the light from the growing effulgence in the heavens had bestowed the boon of visibility, Nifty had not noticed. But he found he could see. The man with whom the mate conferred he perceived to be a priest. The two others were Indians.

They were not much, in the way of Indians, as the mountain men of the day knew them, but upon the urban Nifty their personification of the wild legends of the wilder West was startlingly complete. He stared, fascinated, and drew a little away from them and a little closer to Dolan, who, for that moment, also became a personification—that of the known and the familiar and the safe. The savages stared at him stolidly, with eyes that did not seem to blink. Nifty experienced a feeling like the lifting of a repression when finally the conference ended and the sailors turned to retrace their steps toward the sea.

Apparently the discussion he had had with the priest had not been satisfactory to Dolan. At least he was in bad temper. He cursed Nifty savagely for not keeping up, and when, in his haste, Nifty stumbled against him in the darkness, he turned to strike Nifty heavily in the face, and followed this up with a hearty kick of his sea boots in the young man's shins. And Nifty struck back.

The blow seemed to release in Nifty the snarling beasts of long repressions. He was no longer a thinking animal. For the first time he was alone with Dolan. Dolan was without his usual backings of traditional discipline or weapon. It was man to man. And Nifty was young and fit; he was as big; what with his stormy youth and his prize-ring adventures, he was as experienced. His rage gave him a great advantage in sheer dynamics. In a short and furious interchange he beat the mate to his knees. "I'll kill you!" he half sobbed.

"Wait till I get you aboard!" Dolan mumbled, lunging sideways to regain his feet.

Those half dozen words were like a dash of cold water to Nifty Barnes. His naturally keen endowment of wits had been sharpened by his orphaned boyhood in the Boston streets. The situation he had brought upon himself was defined to him instantaneously and clearly. He knew by now only too well what could happen to him aboard ship. He stooped, smashed Dolan once in the face, and ran. At this moment, unheeding of these small fevers of earth, the austere and tranquil ceremonial of the heavens came to its climax. The moon rose.

When Nifty Barnes awakened, the sun was high. He opened his

eyes. Above a ledge of rock he saw leaves. He lay for a few moments recalling.

He had run for a while; then he had pushed on at a slower pace. He had had no idea, except to get as far as possible from the beach, and that he must not be captured and returned to the ship. He had broken through low hills and come to a wide valley in which was a river. He knew that water flows to the sea, so he had followed up the valley. For hours. He had lost himself in thick brush. He had there encountered several large animals that had snorted at him. These might have been bears, which were then abundant, but were more likely range cattle—rather more dangerous to a man on foot. Gradually, Nifty's bewilderment and terror gained on him. He had plenty of courage, but he was a city boy. This sort of thing was wholly unknown to him. Even courageous men are afraid of the unknown. All the instinctive dread of the wilderness that the sight of the Indians had inspired in him returned. Finally, pretty well exhausted and thoroughly scared, a remnant of common sense prompted him to hunt out a sheltered place beneath a rock.

He rolled over to become aware of three men on horseback. They were queer dark men, dressed in very fancy costumes. Nifty eyed them narrowly and suspiciously. He did not like their looks; they were much too queer, much too fancy. One said something to the others, and they laughed, showing white teeth. The first man spoke to Nifty. Nifty could not understand him, but the man motioned suggestively in the direction of the sea, and laughed again, so Nifty, on instinct, leaped to his feet and tried to dive into the thick brush. Something whistled through the air and slapped stingingly about his shoulders. He was jerked up short, and found that he had been circled by a rawhide rope. This he attempted to throw off, but his arms were instantly pinned to his sides by another rope. He struggled, but he was helpless.

The men turned their horses and rode slowly away. As Nifty's legs were free, he had to follow. They led him down the valley like an animal on the end of a chain. Whenever he lagged or balked or tried to throw off his bonds, one of his captors spurred his horse slightly. After a time, when he had ceased objecting, they threw off the loops and re-coiled the *reatas*. It was useless to think of escape. Nifty trudged along.

By and by they stopped and dismounted near a large tree. They loosened the *cinchas* and slipped off the bridles of the horses. The animals grazed, dragging the lengths of the rawhide *reatas* along the ground.

The three men squatted down. They had bread and cheese, which they cut in great hunks with knives which they had carried in their garters. They offered some of the bread and cheese to Nifty. They were gay and friendly, without ill feeling. Nifty could not understand this. They spoke to him repeatedly, smilingly; he could not understand that. But he knew they were taking him back toward the sea. He accepted the bread and the cheese because he was very hungry, but at first he was sullen to their advances. Then he had a second thought. Apparently he was making an effort to respond, and he mustered a half dozen Portuguese phrases he had picked up from Marco. This interested them because they could almost comprehend the words of the language so closely allied to their own. When Nifty had sufficiently withdrawn them from the grasp of their knives—which remained thrust in the loaves of bread and of cheese—he knocked one of them down. This maneuver, needless to say, was not the result of any considered plan, for the simple reason that no considered plan was possible. Nifty had some vague idea of getting hold of the horses or—or something! At any rate, he was desperate. Of one thing only he was certain—these men were taking him back to the ship for the reward paid for runaway sailors. Anything was better than the ship and the calculated terrible two-year stretch of torture that Dolan could mete out to him.

Nifty drove his fist as hard as he could, and in the split-second paralysis of sheer astonishment, he butted the second man so hard in the midriff that he, too, went down. But the third was ready for him.

Californians of that day were wholly unaccustomed to the use of their fists. In all probability, the experienced Nifty would have been quite competent to handle him. But, though unskilled, the *vaquero* was strong and agile. Before Nifty could stow him away, the two others had recovered.

Three to one is prohibitive odds, no matter what the relative experience, or lack of it. Nevertheless, the ensuing battle was a notable one. Nifty knew all the tricks of the Anglo-Saxon manner. These men did not know a right cross from a cross-buttock, and they had no defense. But they were strong. Nifty could hit them, but at the same time he must not permit himself to be seized. If they really got hold of him, it would be all off. He could not set himself for his punches. It was a lively occasion. Nifty charged now at one, now at another. He twisted and turned, elbowed and kneed, butted and kicked. He was as elusive as an eel. Some of his blows told heavily. A man went down. But he was up again. And Nifty himself took plenty. Once he was tripped and went down, and two piled atop of him, but he managed somehow to heave himself to his feet and fight them off.

The pace was much too fast to last. Ensued one of those curious pauses that occur in close contests when both sides, as though by mutual consent, draw apart to breathe. Nifty stood alone, bleeding, his clothes torn, panting heavily. He was not yet licked; but he was badly winded and a little damaged, and he knew he soon must be licked, especially as, now that the first heat of encounter was over, his captors must recollect their knives or their rawhide ropes. However, he hadn't quit yet!

For the first time he became aware of the presence of two more men. They sat on horseback, a little apart. They must have ridden up unseen during the combat. Nifty stared at them resentfully. This was a little too much!

The newcomers were of a different type from Nifty's captors. They were younger. They were dressed in bright and gay costumes with many silver buttons, and white frilled linen, and yes, by gosh, ribbons—like women! One of them carried a guitar slung across his back! They had fine-featured, pretty faces—like women! They had silly little mustaches, like eyebrows. They sat horses that glinted like silk and held proud heads and tails; and that should have caught Nifty's admiration, had he known anything whatever about horses. The silvered and embroidered and carved richness of their saddles and bridles he did notice, but with the swift sneer of contempt his harsh upbringing had bred in him for all elegancies. They were laughing. The one with the guitar clapped his hands together. "Bravo! bravo!" he cried. A pair of sissified macaronis! But they both carried slender rapiers slung at their sides. And now Nifty saw, holding themselves discreetly in the background, yet two other men, also on horseback, or the type of his three antagonists.

"Hell!" he said disgustedly. "I give up! I can't lick all California!"

To his surprise, the young man with the guitar answered in English. "*Hola!* I think so mebbe you can!" said he. He spurred his horse forward and leaned from his saddle. Nifty tightened to a defensive attitude. But the young man merely clapped him on the shoulder. He seemed enthusiastic, "Never have I seen a so-great fight!" he cried. He turned and said something very rapidly, and with a certain faint flavor of haughtiness, to the three Californians on foot. At the conclusion of his speech, he thrust his hand into the pouch at his saddle bow. To each of the three he spun a coin. The coins flashed in the sun, so that Nifty perceived them to be of gold. "*Si, señor,*" they said submissively, and at once set about gathering their belongings. The young man watched them for a moment; then returned to Nifty.

"I am," said he, "Ramon Rivera. And thees is my *amigo,* Don Justo de la Cuesta. He do not speak the Engleesh. I visit heem at the rancho of his peoples"—he waved his hand up the valley. "You will come with us, no? He will be honor by so brave a fighter to be his *huésped*—what you call?—his guest. *No es, amigo?*" he turned to his companion. The latter nodded. "*Si, si, Ramon!*" he agreed.

Ramon uttered a command. The two men in the background approached. One of them dismounted. The young man made a courteous gesture. "Climb up," said he. "We go."

Nifty hesitated; then obeyed. What else was there to do? And anyway, this rancho he talked about was evidently up the valley, away from the sea. The *vaquero* held the justifiedly skeptical horse until Nifty had managed to clamber awkwardly to the saddle. Then he himself mounted behind the other *vaquero.*

"*Adelante!*" cried Ramon.

The animals leaped forward at a bound into their swiftest gait. Nifty promptly fell off. He had never been a-saddle before in his life. He was not hurt. They caught the horse and brought it back. At a soberer pace they then proceeded up the valley of the Carmel to the *Rancho de la Cuesta.*

Nifty examined everything from the shelter of a tight wariness. He did not know what it was all about, and he did not believe in any of it. This Ramon Rivera had bought him off from being returned for the reward as a deserter. That was all right, but what did Ramon Rivera want of him? Of course, he wanted something. Nifty could not figure what it could be. Unless he wanted him to fight. The gentry did these things. And Rivera apparently liked to show him off. He was always calling Nifty in for that purpose, clapping him on the shoulder, explaining him in a torrent of language Nifty could not understand.

"I tell them," Ramon explained aside, "how that you mak' the great fight with three estrong men and leeck them."

Some of these people before whom he was exhibited also clapped him on the shoulder, and felt of his muscles, and smiled at him in what seemed to be a friendly fashion. Nifty knew better than to believe in any of that, of course. He stared at them from beneath surly brows. He wondered how soon they'd come to what they expected of him. Well, he could lick any man this crowd could dig up, and he'd as soon! He flexed his biceps. But hold on! Perhaps it wouldn't be a man; perhaps it would be a bull, or a wild beast! He had heard of such things. That would not be so good. The more he thought of it the more likely that seemed to be. They fed him; they gave him a lot of good clothes; they gave him a separate small room in which to sleep. Everybody he met grinned at him as though relishing in advance what was coming to him. That was how Nifty interpreted this people's smiling, careless friendliness. His suspicions were confirmed when he came face to face with the three *vaqueros* with whom he had had the fight down the valley. His body tightened, but they greeted him warmly, and as far as he could understand their gestures, they, too, like Ramon Rivera, tried to express admiration. Nifty resented this. They were mocking him, of course, from their vantage point. They, too, knew what was going to become of him, and they were satisfied that whatever it was, it would avenge them. Ramon, who stood by, explained it differently.

"They do not weesh you the bad; they are not the enemy," said he. "So long the ship is here, they try tak' you back for the reward. But so soon the ship she is sail, then they help you all they can. They like to be friends of so brave a man." He shot a volley of speech at the three men, repeating the same thing in Spanish. They nodded emphatically, flashing white teeth. "*Si, si, si!*" they cried. Nifty took their proffered hands guardedly; not because he believed for a minute, but because he must play along until something turned up.

In the fashion above described, he met—or was exhibited to—a number of people. For all of these but one he entertained a profound and secret contempt. They were foreigners; Nifty despised all foreigners on principle. They were exquisitely mannered —and to Nifty all manners were affectations to be resented. They were gaily dressed—and Nifty came from Boston. In short, they stood for all the class differences, accentuated, that Nifty resented. He resented being brought before them and shown off by Ramon's enthusiasm. There was in them a certain hidden, faint amusement. He sensed it, but he could not know that the amusement was not at himself, but at Ramon's enthusiasm, nor that it was kindly. There was the old boy, Don Cristoval, with the white side whiskers, who looked like a puffed-out old turkey cock; and the fat old woman, his wife, who sat there as if she expected all the others to fall on their faces; and three or four dandified, supercilious young whippersnappers, brothers of this Don Justo. Nifty despised the lot, and he stood there because he must. The only one he could not at first quite manage to resent was the girl; Conchita, they called her. She was good looking enough, but it was not that. It was the way she looked at him. But Nifty ended by resenting even that, for the simple reason that he recoiled from anything that threatened his hard compactness.

He saw, shrewdly enough, that this Ramon was sweet on this Conchita. Obscurely, without reason, this added to his resentment.

The house in which these people lived was low and wide, with thick walls and polished wooden floors. Nifty saw of it only the small passageway and the spacious *sala* to its left, and the enclosed patio to which it opened straight ahead. His own room was in a separate small building. In spite of Ramon's first enthusiastic invitation, the Californian was well enough conscious of Nifty's station in life, and the latter was a guest only in a sense. Nifty caught glimpses of other apartments opening into the patio. On his second summons he stood near the door of one of them. A servant, an Indian, was sweeping in it. Nifty saw a great bed with four posts supporting a canopy, two heavily built chairs, a crucifix on the wall, and next the door a polished table on which stood a ewer and basin, and beneath it, as though forgotten, a squat earthen pot heaped to the top with metal disks. The disks were powdered thickly with dust. The Indian stared at the American. He continued mechanically at his task, but so absorbed was he in his curiosity that his broom collided violently against the earthen pot. The pot teetered for a moment, overturned with a crash. The metal disks were scattered in all directions.

The Indian servant cried out in dismay. Don Justo and Don Cristoval laughed. Ramon laughed, too, but his amusement was at the expression on the sailor's face.

"It is the money for the guest of the house," said he. "An old custom," Ramon explained carelessly; "one that in these days is dying out. But a few of the old hidalgos—like Don Cristoval, like Don Sylvestro, my own *papá*—still keep it up. For the traveler who might find himself in need of gold. Though for what," said Ramon in parenthesis, "can one need gold in traveling? There is always a horse and food and a bed for the asking. As you see, this gold has been there for long; the dust has all but buried it."

"You mean," Nifty was startled into question, "that anybody could take what he wants of that?"

"And for why not?" asked Ramon carelessly.

"Is—is it real?"

Ramon picked up one of the coins and flicked it at the sailor. It was a duller yellow than the American coins known to Nifty, but unmistakably gold, a doubloon. He turned it over with awe, handed it back. Ramon tossed it to the Indian, who had righted the pot and was busily scooping up its scattered contents.

Nifty waited some days, to be sure that the Mercury had left the coast as had been planned. Then it was absurdly easy. No one seemed to keep any sort of guard or lookout, and they slept soundly, though it was well after midnight before the last was abed. Nifty loaded up with as much of the gold as he could reasonably carry. He was no such fool as to overburden himself, and he was careful to substitute pebbles in the pot beneath the top layer of doubloons. Then he set off on the road down the valley. He had managed to find out that this led to Monterey, and was five-something long, but whether they meant miles, or leagues, or hours, he had not been able to guess. Once in Monterey with his gold pieces, Nifty would know well enough what to do. He had heard, aboard ship, of Portugee Joe. Joe would take care of him, for a price, until another vessel came along on which he could ship, or take passage.

He set off down this road—which was little more than a trail—as rapidly as possible in the dark. He must reach Monterey before his absence was discovered. That should be as easy as the theft of the gold, even assuming that the "five" meant five hours. Even at that rate he should make it by soon after daylight.

But, unfortunately, daylight found him in a maze of hills. He had followed the path faithfully, as he thought; but largely, of course, by the feel of its packed earth. Now, too late, he realized that this countryside was seamed with trails beaten hard by generations of cattle. Sometime in the night he had got off on one of these cattle trails. This was annoying. But Nifty knew that the sea was to the west, and Monterey was on the sea. He could not lose himself for long. He turned to follow cross country the shadows from the morning sun. Glancing back, he noticed a small lazy cloud of dust. After a few moments he determined that this arose from horsemen, and after another few moments he realized that the horsemen were following, slowly, the tracks made by himself.

At first he was startled, then reassurance came. It would take them some time, at this rate, to catch up. Nifty occupied himself in blinding his trail. Finally he bestowed himself in the crotch of a white oak. To his delight, he found that the bend of the crotch had rotted into a hollow so deep that he was able to withdraw himself completely. From this concealment he could identify his pursuers. They were four—Ramon Rivera, his friend Justo, a *vaquero*, and that girl Ramon was sweet on, the one with the slow, puzzling smile, Conchita de la Cuesta. Why should she be along? And how, Nifty wondered resentfully, did it happen they were out so early? The *vaquero* led a spare horse. "To take me back on," reflected Nifty. "Well, let 'em find me!" He felt secure; he flattered himself he had done a very clever job. His lips curled when they halted where his traces ended.

The three men stood up in their stirrups and looked all about them. They conferred. Then the *vaquero* handed the led horse to

Don Justo and began very slowly to ride in expanding circles, look-ing for traces. Well, he wouldn't find any! Nifty bit his self-congratulation short. The two young men and the girl lifted their bridle hands and rode directly and unhesitatingly toward the white oak in which Nifty perched.

Beneath the tree they drew rein.

"Come down," said Ramon; but Nifty's sharpened wits caught something of an experimental quality in the command. Swiftly it came to him that this was a shot in the dark; that the three were, almost idly, exploring possibilities while the *vaquero* searched for something tangible. He withdrew himself like a turtle. His spirits revived. Let them find him! Then he saw the young man swoop down gracefully from his saddle to pluck some object from the ground. He held up the object and laughed.

"Come down, my frien'," he repeated; this time with confidence. "You are discover'!"

The object was one of the gold pieces, fallen from Nifty's pocket when he had climbed the tree.

He stood facing them sullenly, awaiting their pleasure. They all looked at him. After a moment, Ramon shook his head at him.

"You mus' not go like this on foot. The cow is very bad for the man on foot. He kill you if he find you. Do not you know that? You mus' always go on the horse." His manner was curiously re-proachful, but in it was no anger. "And," Ramon continued in the same vein, "you see, you get lost. Over there is Monterey. If you wish to go to Monterey, why you no tell? And for why do you not come say *adiós*? Is it that someone has not treat you well? Is it that someone has not please you? You should tell that to me, to Don Justo."

The girl interposed in swift Spanish. Her head was back; her eyes expressed scorn. Ramon replied in apparent deprecation. She struck her hand on her knee. The young man turned to Nifty again. His face was faintly flushed.

"The Señorita de la Cuesta," said he, with a stiffening of formal-ity, "know some Engleesh, but only a little. She desire that I spik the Engleesh for her to you. I obey the Señorita de la Cuesta." He turned with an air of expectancy to the girl. Thenceforward his manner was detached, automatic. The flush lingered on his cheeks.

"She say to tell you she understand perfectly," he said, after listening for a moment. "She have watch and she have been mortify that men of her peoples are so estupid. She says this: That if she were a man, she would not stay with peoples that act so. No man like to be led in and show off like a horse or a bull——"

"*Como un' oso*," interposed the girl swiftly.

"Like the bear," said Ramon. "And," he continued conscientiously, "she say if someone do these thing to her, she go away also."

"I say, too," the Doña Conchita added slowly and carefully, "that for my rancho and for my peoples I am sorree."

She inclined her head with a pretty dignity. Nifty stared at her. He was utterly bewildered by all this, could not make head or tail of it. While Ramon was talking, he had merely taken it, with impotent resentment, as a mockery too subtle for his comprehension. They'd have their amusement at his plight, and then—— But somehow, when the Doña Conchita spoke and he had turned toward her, and the slow sweet smile of her, the resentment had died and given place to a profound puzzlement; for there was no mockery in this girl; and with the puzzlement something new, something uneasy that Nifty had never experienced before. Ramon was speaking again, but Nifty could not keep his eyes off the girl.

"If I do that which she say," said Ramon, "it is not that I mean such a discourtesy. No, no, no! It is only that I am proud of my so brave a fighter, and I wish all to see him and be proud of him also. All is friendly in my heart. I had hope—when I return to the hacienda, which is in the valley of the Salinas—that it might be you would wish to go also. Many time the *marinero americano* who leave his ship stay with us and mak' the good *californio*. Of such is Don Juan Gilroy, who was *marinero*. I apol-o-gize, señor." He motioned to the *vaquero*, who had long since rejoined the party. To the latter he handed the lead rope of the spare horse. "You wish to go to Monterey, señor. There is there, I understan', a ship—not the ship from which you come—another. That is what you wish? This man, Ricardo, will ride with you to show the way. He will bring back the horse. *Vaya con Dios, señor*."

He raised his hand with a dignified gesture, which was repeated by Don Justo. The girl, Conchita, smiled gravely and inclined her head.

"*Adiós, señor*," she said softly.

"*Adiós*." Nifty heard himself say that, but the word was an automatic reflex. He stared after the three, his mouth open, his eyes vacant of intelligence. The mounted *vaquero* waited like a bronze statue.

Suddenly Nifty started forward, staggering and stumbling like a blind man through the tufts of the fragrant artemisia.

"Hi! Hi! Hi! Wait!" he choked over and over in a strangled voice. His hands were fumbling his clothing as he ran. When he came to the three, he stopped for a moment, gasping, then began to thrust upon Ramon the gold from his pockets.

"I swiped it! I stole it!" gasped Nifty. "It's yours! From the pot! Here, take it!" He held out his cupped and brimming hands imploringly, the doubloons spilling.

Ramon stared down for a moment, with the air of one speechless with surprise.

"But, *amigo*," he said at length gently, "what talk is this of stealing? How can that be? Is not this *el oro del huésped*, guest's gold, for your journey?"

Nifty remained looking after them, as they again rode away. After a few moments, the *vaquero* brought up the led horse. He mounted, after his awkward fashion, and the two set off in the direction of Monterey.

The two young men, Ramon Rivera and Justo de la Cuesta, made their stately and formalized devoirs to the Doña Conchita at the conclusion of this morning's ride. They stood together looking at the door after it had closed behind her.

Justo turned upon Ramon accusingly.

"Even I, who have not had your advantages in the world, who am a simple *ranchero*, know that this one is not of the *gente de razón*, even among the *americanos*. It is useless to tell me that you do not know this."

"I do not tell you that," said Ramon. "I will say even more: That I have seen many of his kind during my residence among the *americanos* in Philadelphia, when in pursuit of what education I possess, and it is more than probable that not only is he not of the *gente de razón* but he may have sprung from the criminal classes.

Nevertheless," added Ramon, "he is a brave man and a most excellent fighter. My statement to him that I had hoped he would accompany me to the hacienda was sincere. For a time I cherished that desire, for such a one can be a faithful man to one he would consent to serve freely."

"For a time, you said," observed Justo keenly.

Ramon made a gesture in acknowledgment of his friend's shrewdness.

"He is hardened—perhaps by his nature, perhaps by life. He is what *los americanos* call *tieso*—a tough one."

"That is a good phrase," said Justo admiringly.

"Only a miracle softens such a one. And I," Ramon shrugged, "am not a holy saint."

Justo laughed. "I should never accuse you of that," he agreed, "but in your serious moods I find you surprisingly *sabio*."

"But they are rare," pleaded Ramon in mock alarm.

"Very rare," conceded Justo dryly. "So rare that I must take advantage of this one. Why, then, in this affair have you talked so grandly of *el oro del huésped*, and sent him on his way as you would a true hidalgo? You know well he stole that gold."

"I am myself hidalgo," Ramon pointed out simply, "and it is necessary that I act as one."

Justo digested this statement as Ramon watched him, his eyes dancing. After a moment, he laid his hand on the other's arm.

"*Amigo*," said he, "have you forgotten the words the Doña Conchita caused me to say on her behalf to this one? You and I know the world, alas, but what is a handful or so of gold against the shattering of so beautiful a faith in humankind?"

At this exalted sentiment Justo choked, then laughed.

"Your pardon, *amigo*." He sobered as he saw Ramon's face. "Come, *veledor*; you must not be offended. But you see I am only her brother."

"She is a saint from heaven!" cried Ramon.

Justo still looked amused, but he made no reply.

The interchange was at this moment interrupted by the appearance around the corner of the ranch house of two horsemen. One was the *vaquero*; the other was Nifty Barnes. The latter slid clumsily from his saddle. He stood before the two young men. He stared at Ramon's feet.

"I been thinking it over," he mumbled after a moment—"what you said. I really got no strings to me. I'd like to stay, if you still want me." He looked up suddenly. "I'm strong and I learn fast," said he. "You've treated me white. You'll want a good man—you and the young lady—if she wants me," he concluded awkwardly.

"*Hola!*" shouted Ramon. He turned on Don Justo, his face alight. He explained rapidly. "You or I would have had this man in the *carcel*," he told Don Justo, "but she—she knew better than that! She is wiser than you or me, *amigo!* You see?"

At Ramon's expression, Justo erased from his face the fraternal skepticism. But he could not keep a faint irony from his voice. "Undoubtedly," said he dryly, "my sister, in this affair, has displayed an extraordinary wisdom."

Ramon's high spirits, however, were unabashed.

"That is true," said he stoutly. "You and I, *amigo*, are *sabio*—we have wisdom. But it is a wisdom of the head. She has the wisdom of the heart."

Justo grinned.

"I perceive, señor," he observed with a mocking false formality, "that you do indeed love my sister very deeply."

"A fact, señor," Ramon reminded him, a trifle sulky, "which I have not troubled to conceal."

Nifty Barnes, neglected, recalled himself to their attention by clearing his throat.

"Maybe you'd better put this back in that pot," said he, proffering the gold doubloons. "I ain't really got no call on it now."

FAST GUN

by *Robert Patrick Wilmot*

My grandfather told me Matt Howard's story, and he had good reason to know the details of it well, even though Matt arrived in Dragoon Springs before my grandfather was born.

Matt came alone, and he came on foot. He had neither hat nor boots nor britches, and a Chiricahua arrow, with its shaft broken off short, was buried in the muscles of his chest. It had been a day of intermittent sleet storms and harsh, cold sunlight; of lowering clouds and galelike winds. The single street of Dragoon Springs was as empty as the day before the world began when the wounded man lurched into Secondino Garcia's door. Matt was as dirty as a man could ever get without trying, and in his flapping, long-tailed shirt and cotton drawers, he must have looked like a bedraggled ghost.

Secondino Garcia, who owned the Dragoon Springs livery stable, did not believe in ghosts, at least until full dark. When Matt staggered in out of the cold blue dusk, the Mexican was engaged in praying for a small miracle in the way of increased business for his stable, and a tramp without a mount was scarcely the answer to his prayer. He was about to reflect upon several matters, including Matt's probable ancestry, when he saw the crimson stain that spread darkly across the stranger's shirt. A moment later he caught Matt as the newcomer pitched forward in a dead faint.

Garcia's shouts, directed at Mort Beggs' First and Last Chance Saloon, brought forth three cowmen who were sober enough to walk, and one sheepman who was sober enough to run. The latter was sent to fetch Doc Applegate, while the former, assisted by Secondino, carried the wounded man into Mike Corbett's Emerald Hotel. They put Matt into Mike's own bed, and stanched his bleeding with a tight bandage made from a torn-up sheet, and forced a glass of whisky between his teeth while they waited for the doctor to arrive.

My grandfather said the old-timers told him they had quite a wait. Doc Applegate wasn't an inhumane man, but he was suffering from whisky sickness himself that evening, and the sheepman had a difficult time getting the physician out of his shack, which was near the Dragoon Springs cemetery, and a fine, isolated place in which to wage a private war against John Barleycorn. Even when he finally reached Matt's bedside, the doc had to swill a lot of black coffee to steady his eyes, and a judicious amount of whisky to steady his hands, and a full hour had passed before he got around to removing the barb from Matt Howard's chest.

Matt lay patiently all the while, staring at the ceiling with blue eyes that were about the only feature recognizable as such in a face that was a mask of caked dust from hairline to nose, and a tangled mat of wiry reddish beard from upper lip to chin. There was no fear in the blue eyes, nor did they register an unseemly amount of pain when Doc Applegate cut the arrowhead out, and stitched together the wound his surgery had made.

The physician had no ether, the Chiricahua Apaches having ambushed and burned the stage upon which he depended for supplies, and Matt was fed a considerable amount of raw whisky during the ordeal of knife and needle. He was a sick man the next day—as sick as anybody might have been who had dodged Chiricahua bucks in his shirttail for sixteen hours, and been twanged by an arrow, and then cut and sewed by a surgeon who prescribed rotgut for his patient as well as himself.

Matt had little knowledge of what occurred during the next twenty-four hours, and he was only vaguely aware of a girl who washed his face, and spooned broth into him, and held him down when he shouted his intention of going forth to slay the entire Apache nation, by hand. But he slept fairly well on his second night in Dragoon Springs, and awoke refreshed and reasonably clear in his mind, although he thought for a moment that he was dreaming when he saw Kathleen Corbett sitting beside his bed.

Kathleen was Mike Corbett's niece, eighteen years old, and less than twelve months away from her native Donegal. Matt had never seen anyone like her before, nor never would again, because after he'd met Kathleen, Matt Howard never really looked at any other woman at all.

The wounded man sat bolt upright at first sight of her, staring at a figure that had the bold lines of a Grecian statue, at gray-black eyes, at thick and curling hair that was as dark as one of Mr. Harriman's railroad tunnels at three o'clock in the morning. The girl's face was flawless, too, barring a decided tilt to the nose, and her complexion was a thing of peaches and cream and rose petals as well; and looking at her, Matt knew his heart was lost more irretrievably than his britches and his boots.

"Be easy!" Kathleen said, pushing him back against the pillows, and speaking with a brogue that made Matt think of honey and of birds in flight. "You're far too weak to be sitting up yet. Lie back now, and rest, and I'll feed you some broth."

"It isn't broth I want," Matt Howard said, amazed at his own boldness, but reveling in it too. "Not broth, nor rest, either. What I want is fiddle music, and it playing at our wedding. Our wedding. It will be a fine affair, in a church, with all the fixings, and something old and something new and something borrowed and something blue. It will have to wait, of course, until I can earn some money, because my poke was in the jeans that I lost. But we could at least set the date."

"I like a man who gets straight on with things," the girl said demurely, "but not a man who grasps time by the forelock and boots it from behind, all at once. And speaking of something old, I'm thinking it won't be yourself if you go on running about a country swarming with red Indians. My Uncle Michael says you're lucky you didn't lose your hair." A smile touched the corners of her mouth and then disappeared. "Along with your breeches."

"Speaking of hair," Matt Howard said, "I've never seen any as beautiful as yours."

"Speaking of hair yourself," Kathleen answered, "if it's scarcely beautiful, it's at least abundant. If those savages had clipped you, as well as scalped you, they'd have had enough to stuff three mattresses. And now, may I ask an embarrassing question?"

"Ask me anything!" Matt Howard said. "Just so it keeps you talking."

"Well, then!" Kathleen said, with the smile playing about her lips again. "How was it that you came here in such a state of undress? It couldn't have been that the Apaches caught you bathing or washing your clothes, because by the look and the smell of you, you've no use for such practices."

Matt grinned at her. "I'd been three weeks in the saddle," he said, "and it's well-known fact that a horse doesn't perfume any man. Out where I was, I had a hard time finding enough water to drink, let alone to bathe in, and that war party jumped me just at daybreak and didn't give me time to get into my jeans. Now that I've answered your impertinent question, girl, when will we be married? The sooner the better, so that we can start raising a family?"

Kathleen rose to her feet, the color climbing high in smooth young cheeks. "I told you I didn't mind a forward man," she said. "But by your manner of speech, I'm thinking you would always be a few paces in advance of forward—and trampling on your own heels." She put the bowl of broth she'd been holding into Matt's hands. "Give yourself the soup, buckeen! A man with strength enough to think such thoughts needs no spoon-feeding from me!"

"But you'll come back, won't you?" Matt cried after her as she moved toward the door.

"I will not," Kathleen Corbett said firmly. "I've more work below than I could do if there were three of me, what with waiting the tables and helping the cook. There's far more need of me downstairs than there is here, and, anyway, I couldn't be two places, barring I were a bird."

But Matt looked so downhearted that Kathleen smiled at him from the door, and her voice was gentle as she spoke again. "Get yourself well, man," she said. "Mend yourself, and then we'll speak of marriage, if you are still so immortally ruled by the idea. Although I've made up my mind to remain a spinster, in a wild, lawless country such as this, where a girl could become a widow before she was even a bride."

"You," Matt Howard said, "are a mentally left-handed Irishwoman who makes no sense in her speech whatever. But I love you anyway, and in no time at all I'll be the wellest man in the entire territory of Arizona."

Doc Applegate, a cynic who had no great belief in love or in lesser miracles, gave his own professional skill credit for Matt's rapid recovery; but Kathleen Corbett understood how it was that her wounded admirer was up and about before most men would have been able to leave their beds.

Matt ate a beefsteak breakfast on the morning of the day that he arose, bathed in Mike Corbett's tin tub and shaved himself with his own hand. He walked with a reasonably steady step when, decently dressed in some of Doc Applegate's spare clothing, he went downstairs to the lobby of the hotel.

Kathleen, who was there with her uncle, saw that Matt was a pleasantly good-looking young man with a square jaw and a humorous mouth; a young man neither large nor small, but compactly made, with heavy shoulders and no hips worth speaking of, and a horseman's strong thighs. Kathleen liked what she saw, but then, Kathleen would have liked Matt's appearance had he been anything less ugly than a chuckwalla, because Mike Corbett's niece had already half lost her heart to Matt Howard's blue eyes.

Corbett had offered to give him credit until Matt Howard could find work, and when the hotelkeeper put the register before him, Matt signed it with a flourish. But the newcomer didn't put down his own true name. He signed the register "W. H. Bonney," for reasons of his own, in handwriting as legible as print.

Corbett gave the name Matt had written a thoughtful stare, and then looked him over from head to toe. The big Irishman's dark face was gravely impassive when he spoke.

"Welcome to Dragoon Springs, Mr. Bonney," he said. "Concerning the matter of employment, I'm thinking it will be hard to find you a situation, at present. There's little active ranching, with the Apaches up, and most of the mines have been shut down. But the post of town marshal is open, if you'd care to become a peace officer."

"I would not care to, thank you, sir," Matt answered politely. "I would much rather remain among the living."

Corbett sighed, bent his dark gaze at the register again and laid a thick forefinger on the name that Matt had set down. "Any man who writes so well must own some education," Mike said. "We've presently no one to teach our school either. Perhaps you could teach to earn your board and keep."

"It would perhaps be only fair, Uncle Michael," Kathleen said, "if we were to tell Mr. Bonney that the last schoolmaster was after hanging himself."

"Hold your whisht, girl!" Mike Corbett roared. "Any man with a spark of authority in him could make the small ones behave! Keeping the school in order should be child's play for Mr. Bonney."

Matt was about to say that he almost preferred to take his chances with the Chiricahuas again, but Kathleen put a soft hand on his arm, and when she spoke, her voice not only lilted, but dripped with immortal feminine guile.

"Exasperating though the children may be," she said, "I cannot think of a more wonderful work than to be sowing the seeds of knowledge throughout this barren wilderness." Corbett's niece gave Matt a lingering, sidelong look, and then the long lashes modestly veiled her eyes. "Surely, no decent man or woman would wish to bring children into the world in a territory where there's no learning at all."

"I," Matt Howard said, "have apparently become a schoolmaster, although there are probably scholars in the school who know more than I do. If so, I'll learn the king's English from them."

"Let there be no talk of the king's English here," Mike Corbett said. "And having seen the little darlings in our school, I've no great fear any of them will outshine the master. The important thing, you've agreed. Since my thirst tells me it's time for the first of the morning, let us now step into the saloon and seal the bargain."

They took leave of Kathleen and went next door to the First and Last Chance. Mort Beggs himself was tending bar, a sallow, cadaverous man with his oiled front curls reflected on the damp mahogany and the balding back of his head reflected in the gilt-framed mirror behind him. Always a melancholy-appearing man, Mort looked even sadder as Mike and Matt came in, and it wasn't because he didn't like Mike or didn't want his and Matt's custom. The truth was, Mort was worried over the presence of a man they called Salinas, who was drinking alone.

Salinas was a towering, black-bearded thug with an upper body as round and thick as a keg, a gorilla's reach of arm, and shoulders like sides of beef. He had been a border ruffian during the late unpleasantness between the states, and he was presently suspected of using his shack on the outskirts of town as a base for outlaw forays into Mexico.

That morning in Mort's place, Salinas was nursing a hang-over that would have filled two Conestoga wagons, and his small, mean eyes were red and matterated over the black dirt grained into the furrows that wind and weather had slashed into his leathery cheeks. The giant wore a .44, slung low on his left hip, with the holster tied down.

Mort Beggs was worried because he knew that Salinas coveted Kathleen Corbett, and knew the former bushwhacker had been inflamed with jealous rage ever since he'd learned that Mike's niece had nursed the wounded man. The saloonkeeper expected trouble, and the situation immediately shaped up to meet his expectations. Salinas took one glaring, baleful look at Matt, heaved out an explosive grunt and shifted the chaw of plug tobacco that was tucked into one of his bearded cheeks. A brown stream crackled suddenly against the toe of Matt's right boot as Salinas spat across eight feet of space that seemed greater because of the ominous silence that filled the saloon.

Salinas himself broke the silence, and he had a voice that sounded like a thunderstorm on a mountaintop. "Look what's here!" he roared. "If it ain't the sock-foot hero of the one-man Injun war! I heerd you warn't very big, but it could be you wore yore laigs down some, shirttailing it away from them bow-an'-arrow bucks."

Mike Corbett stabbed Salinas with a level, contemptuous glance, and spoke to Matt in a deliberate voice. "Pray take no notice of this specimen," he said. "What you see before you is a two-legged polecat who has been thwarted in lust. He looked with lecherous eye upon my niece, until she closed his eye with a copper pot one night when he followed her out into the kitchen."

Salinas made a growling noise deep in his throat, and reached for his gun. Mike was in his shirt sleeves, and obviously without a weapon, and Salinas' black-furred hand moved slowly into a cross-body draw, as though the giant found pleasure in pulling his gun upon an unarmed man. The .44 wasn't clear of its holster when

Matt Howard pushed forward and looked up into the burly ruffian's face.

"I'll ask no man to take up a quarrel for me," Matt said quietly. "It was plainly me you meant to insult, and if you're bound to gun someone, let it be me." Matt's face, pale from the illness of his wound, was set and dead-white as his low voice went on, "I've got no idea what I've done to rile you, but maybe you'd better empty your craw. I don't know who you are, but my name is Bonney."

Salinas' jaw fell suddenly slack as Matt spoke the name that wasn't rightly his, and the big man seemed to grow suddenly less in size. His fingers moved away from the .44 as though the butt of the weapon were scalding hot, and he took a shuffling step backward and stared at Matt with fear in his bloodshot eyes.

"Did you say 'Bonney?'" he asked, and his voice fluted up as he spoke.

"I said 'Bonney'," Matt answered. "What about it, mister?"

Salinas' whisky glass clattered and rolled on the bar as the big man knocked it over with his elbow, taking another backward step. "I reckon I had no call to ack like I did," he mumbled. "I'm licked up some, as you can see, an' I guess I just warn't thinkin' when I spit. Don't take no offense because of it, Mr. Bonney. I got no quarrel with you."

Mort Beggs fairly gaped with astonishment as Salinas turned suddenly on his heel and lurched out through the front door of the saloon. "Well, I'll be hawg-tied!" Mort exclaimed. "So somebody finally made that big bully turn tail an' skedaddle! Whoever you are, Mr. Bonney, I ought to hire you—at least until I get my mirrors paid for."

But Mike Corbett, mopping his face with a handkerchief, looked at Matt with a wry smile. "It's thankful I am that you are wearing Doc Applegate's jacket," Mike said fervently, "else that scut would have seen you've no weapon at all. I think it may be, lad, that both of us pushed our luck a little far this day. Let us have our drink now, and blot out the memory of our own folly."

Kathleen Corbett's heart was cold with fear when she heard of Matt's run-in with Salinas, and she begged him to be wary lest the one-time guerrilla shoot him in the back. But Matt said that he didn't think Salinas would dry-gulch him, and Mike Corbett swore that he'd have revenge if the gun slinger did.

Matt went to bed happy that night, warmed by Kathleen's concern for him, and when he reopened the school the next morning, he was as cheerful as any man might have been who had to face thirty-five pupils, including several who were as large as himself.

Matt held class in a one-room adobe building that had lost part of its roof. The last schoolmaster—he who had hanged himself— had burned the textbooks during the fit of despondency that had preceded his self-destruction, and discipline was sorely lacking too. Matt acted promptly to remedy both deficiencies. He borrowed a Bible from George Turner, the blacksmith, and used the gospel for a text, declaring that what had been good enough for countless saints was certainly good enough for the juvenile sinners of Dragoon Springs.

On the first morning of his second week as master, before his wound had completely healed, Matt thrashed both of the Tolliver twins, the man-sized seventeen-year-olds who were the ringleaders of the unruly element in the class. Matt was aware that even with discipline restored, his teaching left considerable to be desired, but he did the best that he could, and refrained from carrying his problems outside the classroom. His evenings, thus, were reasonably serene, and he was free to court Kathleen Corbett.

Matt literally courted her with a dish towel in his hands. Kathleen, among her other duties, had to wash up after the evening meal in the hotel dining room, and Matt reached for a towel when Kathleen said that no true man would sit and watch a woman work, even if it was woman's work the man would be doing if he helped her. Mike Corbett teased Matt unmercifully about his part-time employment in the kitchen, but Matt persevered in his dish drying and persisted in his wooing, and on Christmas Eve, Kathleen consented to become his wife. It was then that Matt told her he'd been using an alias, but when he began an explanation, the girl said that she wouldn't have cared if his name had been Geronimo or Magnus Colorado. Kathleen was in Matt's arms at the moment, and names seemed scarcely important.

The young lovers decided to be married as soon as Matt had

found steady employment and had saved enough for the wedding. Mike Corbett, torn between his reluctance to lose his niece and his conviction that an institution of learning must be maintained in Dragoon Springs at all costs, finally decided that Matt—as at least a temporary member of a noble profession—was good enough for his brother's daughter. The Irishman brutally chivied the parents of Matt's pupils when he passed a hat among them at the end of Matt's first month of teaching. The hotelkeeper announced darkly that if his young friend were not sufficiently rewarded for his services, he himself would take over the vacant post of town marshal, and would personally see to it that the children were confined to their own houses or dooryards, every hour of the day. Matt was amazed to find, when Mike gave him the sum collected, that he had earned more than a top ranch hand could earn in a month, and he reckoned that he'd have enough saved to set up housekeeping by the first of May.

It was a long winter for two lovers who wanted to be married as much as Matt and Kathleen did, but the season was short for Mike Corbett, who had reached an age when time was a bird with a rapid wing. In late February a column of Federal cavalry trotted through Dragoon Springs, and the weary troopers returned two weeks later, herding a score of sullen Chiricahua braves, with the body of their dead chief slung like an empty sack over the back of his own horse. Stage and telegraphic communications were restored, and Mike, encouraged by these tokens of peace and stability, bullied his neighbors into helping him put a new roof on the building that housed the school. They finished the work as the winter ended, and it was on the first day of spring that the runty stranger came to town.

The old-timers told my grandfather that the sun went down as red as blood that day, and most of the inhabitants of Dragoon Springs were in the street observing the phenomenon when the newcomer rode in from the east. Matt Howard, standing near Mike Corbett in front of the Emerald Hotel, heard the drumming of hoofs on the dried mud of the street, and looked away from the flaming sky and saw an undersized youth on a shaggy pony that was lathered from running hard. He might not have given the insignificant figure a second glance had it not been for the boy's eyes.

The eyes were pale and cold and gray as a winter cloud, and they caught the light the way thin ice does when it glitters on the surface of a barely frozen pond. They were deep-set in a sharp-boned face that had a hard jaw and a hard mouth, but the stranger's cheeks were still soft with youth, and the blond stubble that covered them was more a matter of silken down than of adult beard. Unkempt pale hair bushed out under the wide brim of a disreputable flat-crowned hat, and the sleeve of a torn jacket flapped about one of the boy's broomstick arms. Looking at the newcomer, Matt Howard saw no weapon of any kind.

The shaggy pony on which the boy sat was sway-backed and hammerheaded. Salinas, who was standing in front of the First and Last Chance, let out a bellow of laughter as the undersized stranger drew rein. Salinas had just returned from one of his forays, and he had Ab Powell with him, and a Mohave breed who was called Charlie One. Powell was a gaunt, tall gun slinger who looked like a weasel on stilts, and Charlie One was dark and cat-eyed, with a pistol on each hip, and he was reputed to have killed four men in California state. They were both of the same stripe as Salinas, as the saying was, and like him they had drunk enough whisky that day to make them quarrelsome-mean.

"Well, look at this here *caballero!*" Salinas hooted derisively. "Is it a horse he's riding, or what? It could be a horse, seein' as how it's got four laigs an' hair, but, on the other hand, it could be a billygoat with its horns sawed off too."

The blond youth swung the pony in toward Salinas, and spoke in a soft voice. "A friend of mine told me once about a book he read," the boy said, "a book about a sword fighter in France. And somebody laughed at his horse, and this sword fella says anybody laughs at his horse laughs at him too." The undersized stranger suddenly touched a spur to the pony's flank; the ugly beast plunged forward, and the hammer head rammed into Salinas' chest. "That goes for me, too, *amigo*," the boy's soft voice said.

Salinas' lips twisted into a snarl as he reached out and caught the stranger by one of his thin arms and yanked him clear out of the saddle. The youth's boots clumped down hard on the earth, and then rose free of it as Salinas clamped on a vicious hammer lock that lifted him off the ground. Matt Howard, pushing his way through the crowd, saw that there were tears of pain and humiliation in the stripling's eyes, but no sound came from his tightly compressed lips.

"I'll bust your arm, you smart little squirt!" Salinas rasped, but he dropped the boy like a hot brick when Matt reached over the newcomer's shoulder and hit him, Salinas, across the mouth.

My grandfather said that, when he was a boy, men talked almost as much of the fist fight as they did of the events that followed. Salinas must have thought that he could whip Matt easily or he would have gunned him, then and there. Grinning a wolfish, confident grin, Salinas unbuckled his gun belt, passed it to Ab Powell, and flung himself at Matt with his great arms swinging like flails.

Matt met his rush with a right uppercut to the face and a left to the body, and Salinas grunted and spat blood as another right smashed into his mouth. The giant reeled under a succession of trip-hammer blows, and sought desperately to close with Matt, but the smaller man was as slippery as a barrel of eels, as fast as light.

As good as he was, however, Matt could neither block nor side-step all of Salinas' sledging blows, and the big man bloodied his face, and closed his left eye, and knocked him down twice as the savage battle raged on. There were terrible moments in which Matt lay on the ground with Salinas' boots stamping at his face, but he managed to roll away from the trampling feet, and to rise and resume the brutal work at hand. Salinas fought with wasteful fury, and fought at a pace he could not hold, and when Matt finally drove a fist wrist-deep into his flabby stomach, the towering man went down. He sprawled on his face, retching and gasping, and made no effort to regain his feet.

Matt Howard turned away without another look at his defeated opponent, and walked toward the First and Last Chance. He didn't want Kathleen to see him with his face covered with blood and dirt, and he meant to wash himself in the back of the saloon. As he went, he saw that the ungainly pony stood in the middle of the street, but the blond youth was nowhere to be seen. Matt was too tired even to wonder where the boy had gone.

He had washed his face and was having a drink from the pail of fresh water that stood on the end of the bar, when Mike Corbett came in. Mike walked straight to where Matt stood, and although the Irishman's face was pale beneath its tan, his voice was steady when he spoke.

"They're coming, lad," he said, "the three of them—and us without weapons! Well, if we're lucky, maybe we'll take Salinas' big popgun off him and have a trial shot into his ear! Barring we couldn't shoot through the dirt!"

Salinas came first, with Charlie One and Ab Powell close behind him. The battered giant staggered as he walked, and his panting breath made hoarse, whistling noises in his throat, but the beating had sobered him, and there was cold murder in his eyes. He lurched along the bar and halted six feet away from Matt, and his two companions moved alongside him and then stepped briskly away from each other, like troopers deploying in the field.

"You had it over me with your fist!" Salinas panted, his eyes glaring at Matt. "Now let's see what you can do with an iron! I was buffaloed some when you first come to town, you tellin' me your name was Bonney, an' me knowin' a sprout name of Bonney was the fastest draw in all New Mexico Territory. It's too bad for you the stage driver told me this morning' that the real Bonney—the gun slinger—is in jail over in San Juan. So, I'm callin' you, four-flusher, callin' you hard!"

The big man made a gesture at Charlie One. The breed grinned an evil grin, drew one of the two pistols he wore, and sent it sliding along the floor toward Matt. The weapon spun around and made a metallic clatter that echoed in the silent barroom, and came to rest against one of Matt's boots. Death was looking at Kathleen Corbett's betrothed out of three pairs of eyes, but Matt owned the fierce unbending pride of youth, and it swelled up stronger than his fears or his regrets. He was stooping to pick up Charlie One's pistol when he saw the blond youth.

The boy had come in on tiptoe, cat-footing his way through the saloon, and stopped so close to Ab Powell that he might have almost touched the skinny man with his hand. The slight stranger had shed his torn jacket, and slung on one of his flat hips was a .38 that he had filched from Amos Tolliver's shop while Amos, the town gunsmith, was watching the fight between Salinas and Matt. The kid's pale, stubbled face was almost expressionless, but Matt never forgot the terrible gleam in the gray eyes.

"Just one minute, big man," the soft voice drawled as the mad eyes fixed themselves upon Salinas' face. "I think maybe you better deal me a hand too."

The three men were fast, but the boy was faster. He drew the .38 with the sort of motion a man makes tossing a ball, but so swiftly an eye could scarcely follow the movement of his hand. The lancing flame of the gun burst like crimson lightning before either Salinas or Ab or Charlie had drawn their weapons, and the saloon echoed with the roar of another shot before Salinas had his .44 clear of its holster.

The boy got Ab Powell first, moving a quick step to one side as he plugged the skinny gun slinger between the eyes. Charlie, when he fired, fired wildly, forced to shoot across Salinas' shoulder. The kid smashed Charlie's hip with a precise shot, and then sent two bullets tearing into Salinas as the breed fell against the giant. Mike Corbett said afterward that it was like shooting fish in a barrel, and of the three men, only Charlie One survived.

The kid quietly sheathed his gun when the affair was over, and looked at Matt with eyes from which the crazy gleam had gone, and when he spoke, it was in the polite tone of a well-mannered boy addressing an elder. "Now, mister, please," he said, "maybe you'll tell me how you come to be using the name of Bonney? Reckon I got a right to ask, seeing as how it's my name."

Matt, his ears still ringing with the sounds of violence, lifted a shocked face and looked at the boy through smoke that hung like a dark veil before his eyes.

"I killed a man in a fist fight," he said wearily. "Last year, in Kansas. I didn't know he had a bad heart, but I might have avoided the quarrel if I'd controlled my temper. Afterward, I swore I'd never fight again, if I could help it. I rode through Alamogordo last fall, and heard about you. I thought if I could pass myself off as Bonney over here, I'd be feared enough to be let alone. I thought everybody'd know Will Bonney is the real name of Billy the Kid."

The boy smiled, a bleak, brief smile. "I was in jail in San Juan," he said, "and I heard about some *hombre* passing himself off as me. I broke jail and lit out for here on the first mount I could find, without even a gun. I said to myself, 'Billy, if you're really way over there in Arizona Territory, you surely owe it to yourself to see what you're doing there."

As Matt stared at him, the blond youth stooped, picked up Salinas' .44, tucked it into the waistband of his jeans and swaggered toward the door. Nearly all of the inhabitants of Dragoon Springs had crowded into the saloon by then, but they made way, and promptly, to let Billy the Kid pass. The boy halted at the door, looked back at Matt and smiled again.

"You surely do handle your fists good," the mild voice said, "and I'm plumb envious. If I was you, I wouldn't fret too much about that fella in Kansas. Things got a way of working out. If you hadn't killed a man who didn't deserve it, I wouldn't have got a chance to plug two no-good jaspers who'd have probably gunned a lot of good people if I hadn't got them. So long, *amigo*. Take care of yourself!"

All of it happened a long time ago. Kathleen had been married a year, and was nursing her first-born, when she heard that Pat Garrett had killed Billy the Kid in Fort Sumner; and even though he had been an outlaw, Kathleen wept for the youth who had saved Matt from death. She and Matt lived long and fruitful lives, and Kathleen always said that there was some good even in the worst of men, and said that God indeed moves in strange ways His wonders to perform. My grandfather, who was Kathleen's seventh son, taught me to believe in these things, too, and I believe in them still.

THE GIFT HORSE
by *Owen Wister*

I sat high up amid white Winter and looked far down where
Autumn stayed, looked at Wind River shrunk to map-size at the
mountain's feet, a basking valley, a drowsy country, tawny and
warm, winding southeastward away to the tawny plain, and there
dissolving with air and earth in one great hazy, golden sleep. Somewhere in that slumberous haze beyond the buttes and utmost foothills, and burrowed in the vast unfeatured level, lay my problem,
Still Hunt Spring.

I had inquired much about Still Hunt Spring. It was a place that
every man seemed to know of, but never any man you talked with
had been to. Scipio I except; Scipio assured me he had been once
to it. It was no easy spot to find; a man might pass it close and
come back and pass it on the other side, yet never guess it was at
his elbow: so they said. The Indians believed it was not there every
day, few of them would talk readily about it; but it was they who
had showed it first to the white man. And because they repeated of
a valley two hundred feet deep, a mile long and a quarter-mile
wide at its widest, this haunted legend of presence and absence, its
name now possessed my mind. Like a fragment of music it recurred
in my thoughts each day of my November hunting in the mountains of Wind River. Still Hunt Spring—down there, somewhere in
that drowsy distance out from the mountains in the plain it lay.
One trail alone led down into its bottom; from one end to the
other—they said—grew a single file of trees so lank and tall it was as
if they stood on stilts to see out over the top, and at the farther
end was a spring, small, cold and sweet; though it welled up in
the midst of the sage-brush desert, there was no alkali—they said—
in that water. Still Hunt Spring!

One night suddenly, at supper, I announced to my two camp

companions my new project: next summer I should see Still Hunt Spring for myself.

"Alone?" Scipio inquired.

"Not if you will come."

"It is no tenderfoot's trail."

"Then if I find it I shall cease to be a tenderfoot."

"Go on," said Scipio with indulgence. "We'll not let you stay lost."

"It is no tenderfoot's place," the cook now muttered.

"Then you have been there?" I asked him.

He shook his head. "I am in this country for my health," he drawled. On this a certain look passed between my companions, and a certain laugh. A sudden suspicion came to me, which I kept to myself until next afternoon when we had broken this camp where no game save health seemed plentiful, and were down the mountains at Horse Creek and Wind River.

"I don't believe there is any such place as Still Hunt Spring."

This I said sitting with a company in the cabin known later on the Postal Route map as Dubois. The nearest post-office then was seventy-five miles away. No one spoke until a minute after that, I suppose, when a man slowly remarked: "Some call that Blind Spring."

He was presently followed by another, speaking equally slowly: "I've heard it called Arapaho Spring."

"Still Hunt Spring is right." This was a heavy, rosy-faced man, of hearty and capable appearance. His clothes were strong and good, made of whipcord, but his maroon-colored straw hat was what one most remarked at this season. His voice asserted itself, having in it something of authority, if not of threat. "Some claim there's such a place," he continued, eying me steadily and curiously, "and some claim there's not." Here he made a pause. "But I tell you there is."

Were these men concerted to practice on tenderfoot credulity, or what was it? I was framing a retort when sounds of trouble came from outside.

"Man down in the corral," said somebody. "It's that wild horse."

Scipio met us, running. "No doctor here?" he began. "McDonough has bruck his leg, looks like." But the doctor was seventy-five miles away, like the post-office.

"Who's McDonough?" inquired the rosy-faced man with the straw hat.

A young fellow from Colorado, they told him, a new settler on Wind River this summer. He had taken up a ranch on North Fork and built him a cabin. Hard luck if he had broken his leg; he had a bunch of horses; was going to raise horses; he had good horses. Hard luck!

We found young McDonough lying in the corral, propped against a neighbor's kindly knees. The wild horse was snorting and showing us red nostrils and white eyes in a far corner; he had reared and fallen backward while being roped, and the bars had prevented dodging in time. Dirt was ground into McDonough's flaxen hair, the skin was tight on his cheeks, and his lips were as white as his large, thick nails; but he smiled at us, and his strange blue eyes twinkled with the full spark of humor undaunted.

"Ain't I a son of a gun?" he began, and shook his head over himself and his clumsiness. Further speech was stopped by violent vomiting, and I am enough of a doctor to have feared then that this augured worse hurt than a leg broken. But no blood came up, and soon he was talking to us again, applying to himself sundry jocular epithets which were very well in that rough corral, but which must stay there.

He was lifted to the only bed in the cabin, no sound escaping him, though his lips remained white, and when he thought himself unwatched he shut his eyes; but he kept them open and twinkling at any one's approach. They were singular, perplexed eyes, evidently very large, but deep-set, their lids screwed together; later that evening I noticed that he held his playing-cards close up to them, and slightly to one side. Scipio called him "skewbald," but I could see no defect answering to this. He was not injured internally, it proved later, but his right leg, as all of us could see, was broken above the ankle. We had to cut his boot off, so swollen already was the limb. The heavy man with the straw hat advised getting him to the hospital at the post without delay, and regretted he himself had not come up the river in his wagon; he could have given the patient a lift. With this he departed upon a tall roan horse, with an air about him of business and dispatch uncommon in these parts. Wind River horsemen mostly managed to look as if there was no such thing as being behind time, because there was no such thing as time.

"Who is he?" I asked, looking after the broad back of whipcord and the unseasonable straw hat.

All were surprised. Did I not know Lem Speed, the biggest cattle-man in the country, with a store and a bank in Lander, and a house in Salt Lake, and a wife in Los Angeles, and a son at Yale?

"Up here looking after his interests?" I pursued.

"Up here looking after his interests." My exact words were given back to me in that particular tone which showed I was again being left out of something.

"What's the matter with my questions?" I asked.

"What's the matter with our answers?" said a man. Truly, mine had been a tenderfoot speech, and I sat silent.

McDonough's white lips regained no color that night, and the skin drew tighter over the bones of his face as the hours wore on. He was proof against complaining, but no stoic endurance could hide such pain as he was in. Beneath the sunburn on his thick hand the flesh was blanched, yet never did he ask once if the hay wagon was not come for him. They had expected to get him off in it by seven, but it did not arrive until ten minutes before midnight; they had found it fifteen miles up the river, instead of two. Sitting up twisted uncomfortably, he played cards until one of the company, with that lovable tact of the frontier, took the cards from him, re-marking, "You'll lose all you've got," and, with his consent, played his hand and made his bets for him. McDonough then sank flat, watching the game with his perplexed, half-shut eyes.

What I could do for him I did, but it was little. Finding his leg burning and his hand cold I got my brandy—their whisky was too doubtful—and I laid wet rags on the leg, keeping them wet. He accepted my offices and my brandy without a sign. Laudanum alone among my few drugs seemed applicable, and he took twenty drops of this with dumb acquiescence, but it brought him neither sleep nor doze. More I was afraid in my ignorance to give him, and so he bore, unpalliated, what must have become well-nigh agony by midnight, when we lifted him into the wagon. So useless had I been, and his screwed-up eyes with their valiant sparkle, and his stoic restraint, made me feel so sorry for him, that while they were making his traveling bed as soft as they could I scrawled a message to the army surgeon at the Post. "Do everything you can for him," I wrote, "and as I doubt if he has five dollars to his name, hold me responsible." This I gave McDonough without telling him its contents, and Scipio thus summed up the seventy-five miles the patient had before him: "I don't expect he'll improve any on the road."

In new camps among other mountains I now tried my luck, through deeper snow, thicker ice and colder days, coming out at length lean and limber, and ravenous for every good that flesh is heir to, yet reluctant to turn eastward to that city life which would unfailingly tarnish the hard, bright steel of my health. Of Still Hunt Spring I said no more, but thought often, and with plans to visit it undiscouraged. I mentioned it but once again. Old Washakie, chief of the Shoshone tribe, did me the honor to dine with me at the military post which bore his name. Words cannot tell the face and presence of that old man; ragged clothes took nothing from his dignity. A past like the world's beginning looked out of his eyes; his jaw and long white hair made you feel as tall mountains make you feel. After we had dined and I had made him presents, he drew pictures in the sand for me with his finger. Not as I expected—almost to my disappointment—this Indian betrayed no mystery concerning the object of my quest.

"Hé!" he said (it was like a shrug). "No hard find. You want see him? Water pretty good, yes. Trees heap big. You make ranch maybe?"

When he heard my desire was merely to see Still Hunt Spring I am not certain he understood me, or if so, believed me. "Hé!" he exclaimed again, and laughed because I laughed. "You go this way," he said, beginning to trace a groove in the sand. "So." He laid a match here and there and pinched up little hillocks, and presently he had it all. I tore off a piece of wrapping-paper from the store and copied the map carefully, with his comments. The place was less distant than I had thought. I thanked him, spoke of returning "after one snow" to see him and Still Hunt Spring. "Hé!" he repeated. Then he mounted and rode off without any "good-by," Indian fashion. I felt I had got a treasure from him.

McDonough's leg had knit well, and I met him on crutches crossing the parade ground. He was discharged from hospital, and (I confess it) his mere nod of greeting seemed somewhat too scant acknowledgment of the good will I had certainly tried to show him. Yet his smile was very pleasant, and while I noted his face no longer embrowned with sun and riding, but pale from confinement, I noted also the eternal twinkle in his perplexed eyes. Why should I need thanks? As he hobbled away with his yellow hair sticking out in a cowlick under his hat behind, I smiled at my smallness.

The doctor, a hospitable acquaintance I had made on first coming through the Post this year, would not listen to my paying him anything for his services to McDonough. Army surgeons, he said, were expected to render what aid they could to civilians, as well as to soldiers, in the hospital; he good-humoredly forbade all remonstrance I attempted. When civilians could pay him themselves he let them do so according to their power; it was just as well that the surrounding country should not grow accustomed to treating "Uncle Sam" as a purely charitable institution. McDonough had offered to pay, when he could, what he could afford. The doctor had thought it due to me to let him know the contents of my note, and that no such arrangement could be allowed.

"And what said he to that?" I asked.

"Nothing, as usual."

"Disgusted, perhaps?"

"Not in the least. His myopic eyes were just as cheerful then as they were the second before he fainted away under my surgical attentions. He scorned ether."

"Poor fellow! He's a good fellow!" I exclaimed.

"Mm," went the doctor doubtfully.

"Know anything against him?" I asked.

"Know his kind. All the way from Assiniboin to Lowell Barracks."

"It has made you hard to please," I declared.

"Mm," went the doctor again.

"Think he'll not pay you?"

"May. May not."

"Well, good-by, Cynic."

"Good-by, Tenderfoot."

The next morning, had there been time to see the doctor, I could have proved to him that he was hard to please. At the moment of my stepping into the early departing stage I had a surprise. McDonough had been at breakfast at the hotel, and had said nothing to me there; a nod sufficed him as usual—it was as much social intercourse as was customary at these breakfasts. The stage rattled up as I sat, and I, its only passenger, rose and spoke a farewell syllable to McDonough, who repeated his scanty nod. My next few minutes were spent in paying a bill, seeing my baggage roped behind the stage, and bidding Scipio good-by. One foot was up to get into the vehicle when a voice behind said, "So you're going."

There was McDonough, hobbled out after me to the fence. He stood awkwardly at the open gate, smiling his pleasant smile. I told him yes, and still he stood.

"Coming next year?"

Again I told him yes, and again he stood silent, smiling and awkward. Then it was uttered; the difficult word which shyness had choked: "If you come you shall have the best horse on the river."

Before I could answer him he was hobbling back to the hotel. Thus from his heart his untrained lips at last had spoken.

I drove away, triumphing over the doctor, and in my thoughts my holiday passed in review—my camps, and Scipio, and Still Hunt Spring, and most of all this fellow with his broken leg and his perplexed eyes.

At Lander they said, had I come two days earlier, I should have had the company of Lem Speed. So he and his maroon straw hat came into my thoughts too. He had started for California, I heard from the driver, whose company I sought on the box. He assured me that Lem Speed was rich, but that I carried better whisky. Trouble was "due" in this country, he said (after more of my whisky), "pretty near" the sort of trouble they were having on Powder River. Yes, trouble was "sure due"; what brought Lem Speed up here so long after the beef round-up? Still, he "guessed" he hadn't told Lem Speed anything that would hurt a poor fellow. No, sir; the big cattlemen were going to demonstrate over here as they had on the Dry Cheyenne and Box Elder. I perceived "demonstration" to be the driver's word for the sudden hanging of somebody without due process of law, and I expressed a doubt as to its being needed here; I had heard nothing of cattle or horses being stolen. This he received in silence, presently repeating that Lem Speed hadn't got anything from *him*. We left this subject for mines, and after mines we touched on more and more subjects, until I confided to him the story of McDonough.

"Of course I should never accept the horse," I finished.

"Why not?"

"Well—well—it would scarcely be suitable."

"Please yourself," said the driver shortly, and looking away. "Such treatment would not please me."

"You mean, 'never look a gift horse in the mouth,' as we say?"

"I don't know as I ever said that." A steep gully in the road caused him to put on the brake and release it before he continued: "I'd not consider I had the right to do a man a good turn if I wasn't willing for him to do me one."

"But I really did nothing for him."

"Please yourself. Maybe folks are different East."

"Well!" I cried, laughing, "I understand you, and am not the hopeless snob I sound like, and I'll take his horse next summer if you will take a drink now."

We finished our journey in amity.

The intervening months, whatever drafts they made upon my Rocky Mountain health, weakened my designs not a whit; late June found me again in the stage-coach, taking with eagerness that drive of thirty-two jolting hours. Roped behind were my camp belongings, and treasured in my pocket was Chief Washakie's trail to Still Hunt Spring. My friend, the driver, was on the down stage, and so to my regret we could not take up our talk where we had left it; but I entered at once again that atmosphere of unspoken doings and misdoings which had encompassed me as I went out of the country. At the station called Crook's Gap I ran upon new rumors of Lem Speed, and asked if he had come about his interests again.

"You and him acquainted?" inquired a man on a horse. And, on my answering that I was not, he cursed Lem Speed slow and long, looking about for contradiction; then, as none present took it up, he rode sullenly away, leaving silence behind him.

When I alighted next afternoon at the Washakie post-traders' store and walked back to the private office of the building where I was wont always to repair, what I saw in that private room, through a sort of lattice which fenced it off from the general area, was a close-drawn knot of men round a table, and on a chair a maroon-colored straw hat! Rather hastily the post-trader came out and, shaking my hand warmly, drew me away from the lattice. After a few cordial questions he said: "Come back this evening."

"Does he never get a new hat?" I asked.

"Hat? Who? What? Oh; yes, to be sure!" laughed the post-trader. "I'll tell him he ought to."

I sought out the doctor, soon learning from him that McDonough had paid him for his services. But this had not modified his opinion of the young fellow, though he had heard nothing against him, nor even any mention of his name; he repeated his formula that he had known McDonough's kind all the way from Assiniboin to Lowell Barracks, upon which I again called him "cynic," and he retorted with "tenderfoot," and thus amicably I left him for my postponed gossip with the post-trader. Him I found hospitable, but preoccupied, holding a long cigar unlighted between his taciturn lips. Each topic that I started soon died away: my Eastern news; my summer plans to ramble with Scipio across the Divide on Gros Ventre and Snake; the proposed extension of the Yellowstone Park —everything failed.

"That was quite a company you had this afternoon," I said, reaching the end of my resources.

"Yes. Nice gentlemen. Yes." And he rolled the long, unlighted cigar between his lips.

"Cattlemen, I suppose?"

"Cattlemen. Yes."

"Business all right, I hope?"

"Well, no worse than usual."

Here again we came to an end, and I rose to go.

"Seen your friend McDonough yet?" said he.

"Why, how do you know he's a friend of mine?"

"Says so every time he comes into the Post."

"Well, the doctor's all wrong about him!" I exclaimed, and gave my views. The post-trader watched me in his tilted chair, with a half-whimsical smile, rolling his eternal cigar, and I finished with the story of the horse. Then the smile left his face. He got up slowly and slowly took a number of turns round his office, pottered with some papers on his desk, and finally looked at me again.

"Tell me if he does," he said.

"Offer the horse? I shall not remind him—and I should only take it as a loan."

"You tell me if he does," repeated the post-trader, now smiling again, and so we parted.

"I wonder what he didn't say?" I thought as I proceeded to the hotel. At breakfast next morning, one of the invariable characters at such breakfasts, an unshaven person in tattered overalls, with rope-scarred fists and grimy knuckles, to me unknown, said:

"Figure on meeting your friend McDonough?"

"Not if he doesn't figure on meeting me."

They all took quiet turns at looking at me until some one remarked:

"He ain't been in town lately."

"I'm glad his leg's all right," I said.

"Oh, his leg's all right."

The tone of this caused me to look at them. "Well, I hope he's *all* all right!"

Not immediately came the answer: "By latest reports he was enjoying good health."

Truly they were a desperate people to get anything direct from.

That afternoon I drove myself and my camp things out of town in a "buggy"—very different from the Eastern vehicle which bears this name—and the next afternoon between Dinwiddie and Red Creek, on a waste stretch high above the river, who should join me but McDonough. He was riding down the mountains apparently from nowhere, and my pleasure at seeing him was keen. His words were few and halting, as I remembered them, and, in his pleasant round face the blue eyes twinkled, screwed up and perplexed as ever. I abstained from more than glancing at the fine sorrel that he rode, lest I should seem to be hinting.

"Water pretty low for this season," he said.

"Was there not much snow?"

"Next to none, and went early."

I turned from my direct course and camped at his cabin.

"What's your hurry?" he said next morning when I was preparing to go.

There was no hurry indeed, those days had no hurry in them, and I bless their memory for that. I sat on a stump, smoking a "Missouri meerschaum," and telling him my plans. To the geography of my route he listened quite intently.

"So you're going to keep over the other side the mountains?" he said.

"Even to Idaho," I answered; "and home that way."

"Not back this way?"

"Not this year."

"You're settled as to that?" he said after a pause.

"Quite."

He seemed to think this over, and then gave an awkward jerk with his head toward the corral. "Like him?" he inquired gruffly. It was the sorrel horse, which I perceived was standing saddled.

"Looks good to me," I replied, adopting his gruffness.

He rose and brought the horse to me. "Get on."

"Hulloa! You've got my saddle on him."

"Get on. He ain't the one that bruck my leg."

I obeyed. Thus was the gift offered and accepted. I rode the horse down and up the level river bottom. "How shall I get him back to you?" I then asked.

McDonough's face fell. "He'll be all right in the East," he protested.

I smiled. "No, my good friend. Not that. Let me send him back with the outfit."

We compromised on this and caught white fish for the rest of the day, also shooting some young sage chickens. The sorrel proved a fine animal. Again McDonough delayed my departure. "I can broil those chickens fine," he said, "and—and you'll not be back this way."

He would not look at me as he said this, but busied with his fire. Dense doctor! I reflected, not to have been warmed by this nature. But later this lonely fellow touched my heart more acutely. A fine thought had come to me during the evening: to leave my wagon here, to leave a note for Scipio at the E A outfit, to descend Wind River to the Sand Gulch, strike Washakie's trail to the northeast of Crow Heart Butte, and on my splendid sorrel find Still Hunt Spring by myself. The whole ride need take but two days. I think I must have swelled with pride at the prospect of this secret achievement, to be divulged, when perfected, to an astonished community. But I intended to have the pleasure of divulging it to McDonough at once, and I forthwith composed a jeering note to Scipio Le Moyne.

"Esteemed friend" (this would anger him immediately), "come and find me at Still Hunt Spring if you don't fear getting lost. If you do, avoid the risk, and I will tell you all about it Friday evening. Yours, Tenderfoot."

I pushed this over to McDonough, who was practicing various cuts with a pack of cards. "That will make Scipio jump," I said.

Somewhat to my disappointment it did not have this or any effect upon McDonough. He held the paper close to his eyes, shutting them still more to follow the writing, and handed it back to me, saying merely, "Pretty good."

"I'll leave it over at the E A for him," I explained.

"Yes. Pretty good," said McDonough, as if I was venturing nothing.

I made an early start, tying some food and a kettle and my "slicker" to my saddle. McDonough watched me curiously.

"Leavin' your wagon and truck?" he inquired.

"Why, yes, of course. I'll be back for it. I'm going to the E A now. Are you a poet?" I continued. "I've begun a thing." And I handed him the lines, which I had entitled "At Gift Horse Ranch." "You don't object to that?"

"Object to what?"

"Why the title, 'At Gift Horse Ranch.'"

He took the paper down from his eyes and I saw that his face had turned suddenly scarlet. He stood blinking for a moment, and then he said:

"I'd kind of like to hear it."

"You shall, when it's finished."

Again he stood blinking before he spoke. "I'll not fool you. I can't read or write. Nobody ever taught me nothin'."

"Oh!" I murmured, getting red myself.

"Never had any folks, you see—to know 'em, that is. Well, so long till you're back."

The sorrel had taken a few steps when it came over me that McDonough knew nothing of my project. "Do you think," I called back, laughing, "that your horse can take me to Still Hunt Spring?"

I am sure now that a flash of some totally different expression crossed his face, but at the time I was not sure, for he was instantly smiling. "Take you anywhere," he called. "Take you to Mexico, take you to Hell!"

"Oh, not yet!" I responded. So he thought I would not dare to go alone to Still Hunt Spring! Well and good; they should all believe me by Friday evening.

I reached the E A ranch (where it used to be twenty-five years since) in less than two hours. Leaving my note there for Scipio took but a minute, and now on the level trail down Wind River I made good time, so that before ten o'clock I had crossed back over it above the Blue Holes, skirted by where the Circle fence is to-day, crossed North Fork here, gone up a gulch and dropped down again upon Wind River below its abrupt bend, and reached the desolate Sand Gulch. I nooned at the spring which lies, no bigger than a hat, some seven miles up the Sand Gulch on its north side. This was the starting point of the trail that old Washakie had drawn for me; here I crossed the threshold of the mysterious and the untrodden.

This unfooted country had always looked monotonous from the bluffs of Wind River, but I found no tedium in it; my delicious solitude was thrilled at each new stage of the trail by meeting the successive signs and landmarks which Washakie had bidden me look for. The first was a great dull-red stone, carved rudely by some ancient savage hand to represent a tortoise. Perhaps, in another mood the grim appearance of this monster might have seemed a symbol of menace, but when I came upon it, just where my map indicated that it was to be expected, I hailed it with triumph.

After the tortoise came several guiding signs: a big gash in the soil, cut by a cloudburst; an old corral where I turned sharp left; a pile of white buffalo bones five miles onward; until at length I passed through a belt of low hills, bare and baked and colored, some pink, and others magenta, and entered a more level region covered with sparse grass and sage-brush. Great white patches of alkali, acres in extent, lay upon this plain. There was no water (Washakie had told me there would be none), and the gleamy waste stretched away on all sides; endlessly in front, and right and left to long lines of distant mountains, full of light and silence. Let the reader who is susceptible to tone combinations listen to the following measures, played slowly over and over:

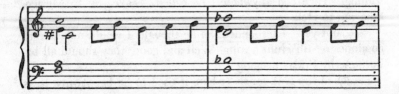

for they will picture that landscape better than any words I could write. I think it was really a very mournful landscape, grand and grave with suggestion of ages unknown, of huge eras when the sea was not where it is now, and animals never seen by man wandered over the half-made world. Earth did not seem one's own here, but alien and aloof, as if through some sudden translation one had fallen upon another planet, which was perhaps a dying one. Yet during these hours of nearing my goal no such melancholy fancies overtook me; I rode forward like some explorer, and I tried to carry out the verses which I had begun at McDonough's:

> Would I might prison in my speech,
> And so keep with me all the year
> Some portion of that wilderness
> Of freedom that I walk in here.

But nothing resulted from this unless the surprisingly swift flight of time. I was aware all at once that day was gone, that the rose and saffron heaven would soon be a great field of stars. I had watched one by one the signs on my map with the realities around me, and now had reached the map's last word; I was to stop when I found myself on a line between a hollow dip in the mountains to the left and a circular patch of forest high up on those to the right. On this line I was to travel to the right "a little way," said Washakie. This I began to do, wondering if the twilight would last, and for the first time anxious. After "a little way" I found nothing new— the plain, the sage-brush, the dry ground—no more; and again a little farther it was the same, while the twilight was sinking and disquiet grew within me. Lost I could not well be, but I could fail; food would give out, and, before that, the sorrel and I must retrace our way to water at the Sand Gulch, seven hours behind us. The twilight deepened. Had I passed it? Should I ride in a circle? Rueful thoughts of a "dry camp" began to assert themselves, and my demoralized hand grew doubtful on the reins, when I discovered that the sorrel knew where he was going.

Before this extraordinary fact became a certainty to me the chasm opened at my feet; the sorrel was trotting quickly along the brink of Still Hunt Spring. In broad day I should have seen it a moment sooner, and the manner in which, in the semi-obscurity, it had leaped into my view close beside me produced a startling impression. The Indian magic legend was easy to account for; indeed, I have met often enough, among our unlettered and rustic white population, with minds that would have been ready to believe, after such a shock as I had just received, that they had beheld the earth open supernaturally. The sorrel's trot had become a canter as we continued to skirt the brink. Looking down I discovered in shadowy form the line of tall cottonwoods, spindled from their usual shape to the gaunt figures described as being on stilts, and then the horse turned into the entrance. This steep and narrow trail was barred at a suitable place by a barrier of brush, which I replaced after passing it. A haunting uneasiness caused me to regret the departure of day, but this I presently overcame. Before we reached the bottom I saw a number of horses grazing down among the trees, and they set up a great running about and kicking their heels upon my arrival among them. There must have been twenty or thirty.

Lassitude and satisfaction now divided my sensations as I made my way to the spring, whose cool, sweet water fulfilled all expectancy. My good map served me to the last, for with it I lighted my cooking-fire, addressing it aloud as I did so. "Burn!" I said, "your work is done." I needed no map to go back! I had mastered the trail! In my complacency I quite forgot how much I owed to the sorrel. While picking up dry sticks I stumbled upon what turned out to be a number of branding irons, which was quite consistent with the presence of the horses and the barrier at the entrance. Evidently the place sometimes served as a natural pasture and corral to owners of stock gathered on the round-up far strayed from where they belonged. Perhaps some one was camping here now. I shouted several times; but my unanswered voice merely made the silence more extreme, and the influence of the magic legend returned upon me for a while. With this my fancy played not unpleasantly while the kettle—or rather the coffee-pot—was boiling. What stories could be made about this place by a skillful writer! The lost traveler stumbles upon it, enters, suspects himself to be not alone, calls out, and immediately the haunted walls close and he is shut in the bowels of the earth. How release him? There would be the story. Or—the lost traveler, well-nigh dead of thirst, hastens to the spring amid the frolicsome gambols of the horses. No sooner has he drunk than he becomes a horse himself, and all the others neigh loud greetings to a brother victim. Then a giant red man appears and brands him. How release all the horses from the spell?

As I lay by my little cooking-fire in the warm night, after some bacon and several cups of good tea made in the coffee-pot, I was too contented to do aught in the way of exploration, and I continued to recline, hearing no sound but the grazing horses, and seeing nothing but the nearer trees, the dark sides of the valley, and the open piece of sky with its stars. My saddle blanket and "slicker" served me for what bed I needed, the saddle with my coat did for a pillow, and the cups of tea could not keep me from immediate and deep slumber.

I opened my eyes in sunlight, and the first object that they rested upon was a maroon-colored straw hat. With the mental confusion that frequently attends a traveler upon first waking in a new place, I lay considering the hat and wondering where I was, until at a sound I turned to see the hat's owner stooping to the spring. Instantly Lem Speed, cattleman and owner of a store and bank in Lander, a house in Salt Lake, a wife in Los Angeles, and a son at Yale, covered me with a rifle.

"Stay still," was the remark.

I smiled. "I could not hurt you if I wished to."

"You will never hurt me any more."

Another voice then added: "He is not going to hurt any of us any more."

"Stay still!" sharply commented Lem Speed, for I had half-risen.

"For whom do you take me?" I asked.

"For one of the people we want."

I continued to be amused. "I'll be glad to know what you want me for. I'll be glad to know what damage I've done. I'll be happy to make it good. I came over here last night for——"

"Go on. What did you come for?"

"Nothing. Simply to see this place. I've wanted to see it for a year. I wanted to see if I could find it by myself." And I told them who I was and where I lived.

"That's a good one, ain't it?" said a third man to Lem Speed.

"And so," said he, "you, claiming you're an Eastern tenderfoot, found this place, first trip, all by yourself across fifty miles of country old-timers get lost in?"

"No. Washakie gave me a map."

"Let's see your map."

"I lighted my fire with it."

Somebody laughed. There were now five or six of them standing round me.

"If some of you gentlemen will condescend to tell me what you think my name is, and what you think I have done——"

"We don't know what your name is, and we don't care. As to what you've done, that's as well known to you as it is to us, and you've got gall to ask, when we've caught you right on the spot, branding irons and all."

"Well, I'm beginning to understand. You think you've caught a cattle thief."

"Horse thief," corrected one.

"Both, probably," added another.

"I'll not ask you to believe me any more," I now said. "Don't I see the post-trader over there among those horses?"

"No."

"Very well, take me to him at Washakie. He has known me for years. I demand it."

"We'll not take you anywhere. We're going to leave you here."

And now the truth, the appalling, incredible truth, which my brain had totally failed to take in hitherto, burst like a blast of heat or ice over my whole being, penetrating the innermost recesses of my spirit with a blinding glare. They intended to put me to death at once; their minds were as stone vaults closed against all explanation on my part. Here in this hidden crack of the wilderness my body would be left hanging, and far away my family and friends would never know by what hideous outrage I had perished. Slowly they would become anxious at getting no news of me; there would be an inquiry, a mystery, then sorrow, and finally acceptance of my unknown fate. Broken visions of home, incongruous minglings of loved faces and commonplace objects, like my room with its table and chairs, rushed upon me. Had I not been seated I must have fallen in the first shock of this stroke. They stood watching me.

"But," I began, feeling that my very appearance was telling against me, while my own voice sounded guilty to my ears—"But it's not true."

"What's the use in him talking any more to us?" said a man to
Lem Speed.

Lem Speed addressed me. "You claim this: You're an Eastern
traveler. You come here for curiosity. You risk getting lost in the
hardest country around here—for curiosity. But you come all
straight because an Indian's map guides you, only you've burnt it.
And you're a stranger, ignorant that this is a *cache* for rustlers.
That's what you claim. It don't sound like much against these facts:
Last year you and another man that's wanted in several places and
that we're after now—you and him was known to be thick. You
offered to pay his doctor's bill. You come back to the country where
he's been operating right along, and first thing you do you come
over to this *cache* when he's got stolen horses right in it, and you
ride a stolen horse that's known to have been in his possession, and
that's got on it now the brand of the outfit this gentleman here
represents—all for curiosity."

"We've just found six more of our stock in here," said the gentleman indicated by Speed.

I repeated my story in a raised voice—I had not yet had time to
regain composure. I accounted for each of my movements from the
beginning until now, vehemently reasserting my ignorance and
innocence. But I saw that they were not even attending to me any
longer; they looked at me only now and then, they spoke low to
each other, pointing to the other end of the valley, and turned,
while I was still talking, to receive the report of another man, who
came from among the stolen horses.

Then I fell silent. I sat by my saddle, locking my hands round
my knees, and turning my eyes first upon the men, and then upon
the whole place. A strange crystal desolation descended upon me,
quiet and cold. The early sunlight showed every object in an
extraordinary and delicate distinctness; the stones high up the
sides of the valley; the separate leaves on the small high branches
of the cottonwoods; the interstices on the bark on lower trunks some
distance away; the fine sand and grass of the valley's level bottom,
with little wild rose-bushes, here and there—all these things I noticed, and more, and then my eyes came back to my little dead fire,
and the blackened coffee-pot in which I had made the tea. "Your
friend McDonough," they had said to me at Washakie, and I had
wondered what was behind their reticence when I inquired about

him. They were always ready, I bitterly reflected, to feed lies to a tenderfoot, but a piece of truth about McDonough's suspected honesty, a word which would have saved me from this, they were unwilling to speak. It was natural, of course; everything was natural. I saw also why McDonough had been so particular in asking which way I expected to travel. Over on Snake River, and in Idaho, the horse was in no danger of identification, and therefore I should be safe. But even with the whole chain of evidence: the doctor's bill, the sorrel, my unlucky tale of a map, and the branding irons with which they believed I was going to alter the legitimate brands—what right had they to deny me a chance?

The last two of them now came from the horses to make their report: "Five brands. Thirty-two head. N lazy Y, Bar Circle Zee, Goose Egg, Seventy-Six and V R."

"Not one of you," I broke out, "knows a word against me, except some appearances which the post-trader will set right in one minute. I demand to be taken to him."

"Ain't we better be getting along, Lem?" said one.

"Most eight o'clock," said another, looking at his watch.

"Stand up," said Lem Speed.

Upon being thus ordered, like a felon, my utterance was suddenly choked, and it was with difficulty that I mastered the tears which surged hotly to my eyes.

"Any message you want to write——"

"No!" I shouted.

"Then let's be getting along," said the first man.

"Any message I wrote you would not deliver, for it would put a rope round your neck, too. And, Mr. Lem Speed, with your store, and bank, and house, and wife, and son, I hope you will live to see them come to the worst ruin and disgrace that the world knows."

A horse was led to me and I got on by myself, a man on each side of me. Memory after that records nothing. We must have been some time—for I think we walked—in reaching the other end of the valley, yet I cannot say what was spoken around me, or if anything was spoken; I can recall only the sides of the valley passing, and the warmer sense of the sun on my shoulders. What firmness or lack of firmness I might have displayed at the very end I can never know, for before we halted at the tree of my proposed execution, and while the rage I had been flung into was still sustaining me, a noise of rattling stones caused us all to look upward, and there, galloping down the steep trail and wildly waving and calling to us, was Scipio Le Moyne. It reeled through me that I was saved.

He rode into our midst at breakneck speed, drew up so short that his horse slid, and burst out furiously—not to my captors but to me. "You need a nurse!" he cried hoarsely. "Any traveling you do should be in a baby coach."

Breath failed him; he sat in his saddle, bowed over and panting, his hand shaking, his face dripping with sweat, his shirt drenched with it, as was the trembling horse he rode. After a minute he looked at Speed. "So I'm in time! I've ridden all night. I'd have been here an hour sooner only I forgot about the turn at the corral. Here. That's the way I knowed it."

He handed over my letter, left for him at the E A ranch. This, with a few words from him, cleared me. All that I had said was verified; they saw what they had been about to do.

"Well, now, well!" exclaimed one.

"To think of us getting fooled that way!" another remarked.

"But it's all right now," said a third.

"That's so!" a fourth agreed. "No harm done. But we had a close shave, didn't we?"

Lem Speed approached me. "No hard feelings," he said, and he held out his hand.

I turned to Scipio. "Tell this man that anything he wishes to say to me he will say through you."

Speed flushed darkly. Had he kept his temper he could easily have turned my speech to ridicule. But such a manner of meeting him was new to a man used to having his brutal way wherever he went, and he was disconcerted. He spoke loudly and with bluster:

"You said some things about my wife and son that don't go now."

This delivered him into my hands. Again I addressed Scipio. "Say that I wish his family no misfortune; they have enough in having him for husband and father."

I think he would have attacked me, but the others were now laughing. "He's called the turn on you, Lem. Leave him be. He's been annoyed some this morning."

They now made ready to depart with their recovered property.

"You and your friend will come along with us?" one said to Scipio.

"Thank you," I answered; "I have seen all that I ever wish to see of any of you."

I had not known—I had felt so quiet and cool—how great was the reaction taking place in my nerves; at this moment I slid from the horse and lost consciousness.

They had gone when I waked; Scipio and I were the only human tenants of the valley. He sat watching me, and I nodded to him, and then silently shook my head at his question if I wanted anything. I lay looking at the rocks and trees—the tall trees, with their leaves gently shaking. It was a beautiful, serene place, and I gazed upon it with those feelings of languid pleasure a man has who is recovering his strength after a serious illness. We began to talk presently, and I learned that the sorrel had been left at my complete disposal. But I would accept no amends from that party; I would ride the sorrel back to Wind River, and then I would send a check to the proper person, as if I had hired the horse. This intention I may say at once I duly carried out. Scipio upbraided me for the spirit I was showing; they had meant no harm to *me*, he argued; they were doing their best now—but I turned upon him.

"Don't get any warped Western notions of slipshod good nature in a thing like this," I said. "I know lynching must be where there is no other law. But look what it does to those who practice it. They were so sure of themselves that they shut me off from the post-trader—one of their own secret faction! I don't complain of anything else; appearances were against me; but that was not even 'natural justice.'"

To this Scipio could find no answer, but he remained unconvinced, muttering that "tenderfeet shouldn't monkey with this country by themselves"; and in this sentiment I heartily concurred.

We spent the day and night at Still Hunt Spring. There was nothing to call us away, and I found my physical powers more ready for rest than for a long ride. Scipio dried out his clothes at the spring, and refreshed his lank body from the perspiration and dust which had covered it. He narrated how it had been whispered that the cattlemen were on the eve of "demonstration"; how McDonough's practices and associates had been gradually ascertained; how it was known that Still Hunt Spring had become a hiding-place for stolen stock. So my letter, designed to be a joke, had quite failed of its design. He had not found it until evening, and had set forth after dark, with no precise knowledge of my danger, but only a general fear for my safety.

This night I slept more soundly and long even than on its predecessor. Scipio, after his night ride, slept like me; we did not wake until the sun was high and warm. After breakfast—it was the last morsel we had between us—I took a final drink at the gentle and lovely pool where I had undergone such terrible emotions, and we rode slowly and silently down the long line of trees toward the exit of the valley. Suddenly the sorrel swerved violently. There, from the tree which was to have been my doom, hung the corpse of McDonough. They had caught him coming to his *cache*, and left him while we slept by the spring at the upper end of the valley.

I recalled his simple, uncomplaining words, when he confessed that he could not read or write, that "nobody had ever taught him nothin'." Poor fellow, with his good-humored face and perplexed eyes! Poor devil! Life had given but a meagre chance to him, and he had lost it.

THE DEVIL IN THE DESERT
by Paul Horgan

One summer morning almost a hundred years ago in the town of Brownsville, near the mouth of the Rio Grande on the Gulf of Mexico, Father Pierre awoke before dawn in great distress.

"Yesterday," he said to himself bitterly; "I should have told him yesterday."

He listened in the dark of his room, whose little window was just showing the first pearly ghost of day over the gulf. Yes, he could hear what he dreaded to hear. Deep in the house were sounds of footsteps moving about. Father Pierre could tell where those steps went, and what their maker was doing. Now he was in the study taking up certain printed materials—a breviary, a missal, a handful of ornately printed blanks for baptisms, marriages and First Communions which could be filled in as occasion required. The footsteps receded toward the refectory, and there a battered leather knapsack soon was being filled with a cheese, two loaves of bread, a little sack of dried meal, a flask of red wine and a jug of water. Presently a distant door opened and closed, and the footsteps went across the paved garden to the side door of the sacristy in the church, where another leather case would be stocked with sacred vessels, holy oils, communion wafers and a set of vestments made in France of thin silk from Lyons.

The sacristy door sounded again, and Father Pierre knew that the next stage of all these preparations for a journey would move out beyond the rectory and the church to the ragged field where, in a corral, the two priests of the parish kept their horses. There, he knew, Pancho, the eight-year-old gelding that was the color of rusty weeds along the river, was going to be captured after an absurd moment of delicacy and apprehension, saddled and brought back to the courtyard, where the saddlebags and knapsacks were waiting.

By then it would be light enough outdoors to see where you were going. It would be time to go.

From the sounds which he could hear and the activities which he could imagine, Father Pierre knew all over again something of the formidable man who was getting ready to depart. If those footsteps sounded like those of an old man, trotting and tentative, yet there was in them a stubborn force. There was plain contempt for human comfort in the noise he made before dawn when others might be sleeping; but he seemed to say that if one man could get up to make all that noise in the name of God, then any other should be glad to awaken to it.

Father Pierre knew there was grim joy in the world that morning for his friend and colleague, Father Louis Bellefontaine. He knew also that Father Louis tried to control a capacity for anger which could flare as quickly and as madly as a cat's. In the new stone rectory the two men lived together harmoniously, for the most part. It took much government of their natural temperaments to make this possible, for over everything lay the difficulty that Father Pierre, who was many years the younger, was the pastor; while Father Louis, who had come from France a generation before Father Pierre, was the assistant, and so, subject to the orders of his junior. But they made jokes about this, as they did about Father Pierre's polished education. Father Louis knew only his God, his duties and what he had learned from hard contests with nature. He knew it was proper for a fine gentleman like Father Pierre to be his superior; and he would wrinkle his old face with shrewd estimate and relish of silken details when Father Pierre was busy with narratives about life at home—which meant France, where one day without doubt the younger priest would be consecrated a bishop. But Father Louis never envied his superior anything, for he knew that in his own work he was a great master—a master of the distance, the heat, the fatigue; the menace of time in slow travel; the harsh vegetation of the brush desert and the murderous Indian, whose soul was within him, but not yet formed; the fears, hopes and needs of the Christian families who lived so widely separated along the inland course of the Rio Grande. For thirty years Father Louis had ridden, mostly alone, and twice a year, on his journeys up the river.

He always undertook them with a sense not only of duty but of escape. Nowhere else did he feel so close to God as alone in the hard brush country riding to bring comfort, news and the Sacraments to some family in a jacal hidden by solitude and open to the hot sky. The older he grew, the more Father Louis longed for his escapes from town and parish. The more infirm he became with the years, the stronger was his sense of mission. Father Pierre would see a glow of youth come back over that sunstung, seamed old face as time drew near for Father Louis to make his plans to go on his ride into the upriver country, which would take him from two to three months. If his eyes were dim with age, not so the vision in his mind, which showed him so much of what people wanted of him, and of what he could bring to them. If his hand now trembled so that he could hardly write down the names and the dates on one of his sacramental certificates, he could always joke about it, and assure his families that the deed was recorded in heaven, anyway. If sometimes his heart fluttered like a dusty bird in the cage of his ribs, and made him wonder what was ready to take flight, he could lie down for a few minutes and feel the thing calm down; and however unworldly he may have been, he always clamped his jaws together with sardonic satisfaction that his time had not yet quite come. He had things to do, and would do them.

Much of this was known to Father Pierre by intuition, and he recalled it as he arose this morning. He hastened, for if he was going to catch Father Louis and say to him what should have been said yesterday, and even long before that, he would have to hurry. *Do you suppose it could be,* thought Father Pierre, *that I am afraid of him? Or am I afraid for my dignity? What if he simply will not listen to me? He has pretended before this to be deaf like an old man when he has preferred not to hear me. Or do I not want to see a look of pain in his small old blue eyes? Actually, is there not a possibility that what I must tell him will shock him so that it might make him ill?*

Father Pierre shrugged angrily at his doubts and tried to answer them reasonably:

Nonsense. After all, a letter from the bishop has approved my decision and given me authority to do what is wise. Why must I heed for a second the individual feelings of anyone, myself included, when a duty is to be done? If I have been a coward for days, in spite of all my prayers for strength and enlightenment as to how best to do what needs doing, must I not be doubly strong today?

And yet as he went downstairs and out to the courtyard, where a rosy daylight seemed to emerge from the ocher limestone of the church wall and glow in the very air, Father Pierre was as never before conscious of the difference in years between him and the old man who was at this moment hauling at straps and buckles, with one knee raised against Pancho's belly to brace himself.

It was a picture, as Father Pierre could not help pausing to notice. The horse was laden, ready and patient. His summer coat was nicely brushed. His bridle was of woven horsehair. His saddle was bulky and tall, with some of the leather worn away so that the wooden forms of horn and cantle showed through. That saddle was chair and pillow, living room and cradle and crutch to Father Louis. To it he had attached many ingenious and cranky accessories, among which there was nowhere any provision for carrying a weapon. Father Louis went unarmed.

The old priest was dressed in a long homespun coat and heavy trousers. On his head was a woven-cane hat with a wide brim, under which his face peered around at Father Pierre like a crab apple underneath a shelf. His boots were high, the color of dried clay. Now, in the presence of the younger man, he redoubled his efforts at finishing his preparations. He made extra movements, to show how difficult the job was, and he completed them with a little flourish, to show how easily he overcame all. His breath went fast, making his voice dry and thin when he spoke.

"Well, Pierre, I am just about off. I hoped I'd see you before I went."

Father Pierre laughed. His heart beat. He said to himself, *Now, now, I must tell him now.* But he heard himself reply only, "How did you think anybody could sleep with all your racket?"

"Ha." It was a dry, indifferent comment. And then Father Louis looked sharply into his superior's eyes. What he saw there made him hurry. "Well, I have everything. I'll send word back to you if I meet anybody coming this way."

"Yes, do. But before you go——"

Father Louis began to slap at his breast pockets with sudden dismay.

"Oh, Pierre, think of it. I nearly forgot my sunglasses, the new ones, you know the pair, which my niece sent to me from Vitry-le-François?"

"I have seen them, yes. They have green glass and metal rims, I believe?"

"The ones! Would you be a good angel and just get them for me? They must be in my room."

"You'll wait for me?"

"But of course."

"I'll be right back."

How could it be, and yet it was. Father Pierre, at the very point of discharging his sorry duty, was sent off on an errand by his victim. He shook his head. What did he fear so? The mere rage of Father Louis? The years of unspoken submission of the older man to the younger? The human aches which can invade the hearts even of those promised to God? He didn't know. All he could believe was that the unshaven, knobbled old man waiting down there by his packed horse, with his hands which trembled on a regular slow beat and his old blue eyes, was stronger than he. Father Pierre was tall and slender and chiseled in man's noble likeness. His soutane was always clean. His white face and dark eyes could blaze with the Holy Ghost. He had proper respect for authority, but could not now use his own.

Lifting piles of papers, and putting aside apples which had dried up and mineral specimens blanched by dust, he searched Father Louis' room for the green sunglasses with their oval lenses and tin rims. He smiled at the condition of the room. He did not find the glasses. He returned to the courtyard.

Father Louis was already in the saddle. In his hand he held the sunglasses. "I found them," he said. "I am sorry you had to go for them. Good-by, Pierre. Give me your blessing. I must be getting along now."

Through his thin old voice and his clouded eyes there spoke a boy who was off to a picnic. Father Pierre's heart sank as he looked at him. He knew now that he was not going to tell what it was his duty to tell. Chagrined at his own weakness, he lifted his hand and made the blessing of the cross, to which Father Louis bent his body.

After all these years he had a map in his head. The river came on a long diagonal, so. An old Indian trail went off northwestward at another angle, so. The farther inland, the farther apart they were from each other. There was one kind of country here by the sea-coast. Presently it changed to something else. Finally, in the dis-tance of weeks, where the map would have only faltering scratches of the pen, based on rumor and legend, lay the farthest wilderness of Father Louis' journeys. The natural limits of his endurance were determined by water. His private map had an ✕ for the end of each stage of travel—a settlement, a farm, a creek, a spring, a water hole —and pray it was not dry.

For the first several days, on these journeys, he hardly seemed to have left home. The earth was still low and sandy, and he could read in it how epochs ago the sea itself was here, hauling and grind-ing the stuff of ocean bottoms where now he rode. The air was moist, and little clouds came to be and to vanish almost before his gaze. He could not closely follow the river, for it wandered and turned, in places doubling back upon itself. And so he followed the Indian trail, leaving it only to go to the isolated river farms in turn.

At such a one he might spend the night, or longer, depending upon what he found. Sometimes death approached in the family, and he gave the last Sacraments. Sometimes there were infants to baptize. In the morning under a tree on rough-hewn planks set across a pair of hogsheads he would say Mass and give Communion. He listened to the local news from Mexico across the Rio Grande— there was talk of another war between ranchers of Coahuila and the Mexican troops; it had not rained for a hundred and seventy days; robbers came over the river lately and killed four men here in Texas and stole some cattle and horses and went back across the river; a child was born in the Bolson de Mapimi who spoke, quite clearly, at three days old, of a flood that would come, but who, when further questioned, seemed to have lost the power of speech; and so on.

Father Louis, in his turn, told how things were at Brownsville, and farther up the coast at Corpus Christi and Galveston, and across the sea in France, where, under the new emperor, business was booming, and trade with Mexico was growing, as you could tell by the many ships which came from Marseille and Le Havre into the Gulf of Mexico. And then, after receiving gifts of food from such a family, the rider left the river and returned to the trail, going northwestward once more.

Days later, though the sky did not cool during the daytimes, the quality of the heat changed, and was dry, as the old seacoast plain gave way to a wilderness of rolling country thickly covered with thorny brush. When he encountered it as it wandered, the river bed was rocky, and rock showed through the hard prickly ground. Everywhere he looked he saw only that endless roll of empty land. Here, near to him, it was speckled with the colors of the olive, both green and ripe, but not with any of the grace he remembered from long ago in Southern France, where the olive trees gave a silver sweetness to the landscape. Farther away in the distance, the land rolls swam in glassy heat. Way off at the horizon there was a stripe of hazy blue where the hot white sky met the earth. Nowhere could he see a mountain, either in Mexico or in Texas.

As he rode, the country tried to hold him back. The thorns of the mesquite dragged at his boots and tore his clothes. Pancho was clever at avoiding most of the hazards, but in places they were so thick that all they could do, man and horse, was go slowly and stoutly through them. But this was nothing new. Father Louis had persisted before against the thorns and had prevailed.

As for water, there was always too much or too little. Too little when, after years of drought, certain springs he looked forward to would, as he came upon them, reveal only dried white stones. Too much when, in hot spells so violent that they could be ended only with violence, there would be a cloudburst and the heavens would fall almost solid and bring the first water, which, as it struck the baked earth, actually hissed and made cracking sounds until the desert was slaked enough to receive the water in its fissures and let it run.

When it ran in such quantity, every fingerlike draw became a torrent in which a man and a horse could easily be drowned. If he crossed one in safety, another was waiting to engulf him beyond the next roll. There was no place for shelter. When the rain stopped, the sun came back and dried everything the same day except the running arroyos, which went dry the next day. All too soon there was bitter dust that sparkled in the light and rose with the hot wind. Against it Father Louis tied across his face his great bandanna, which came from New Orleans.

And they went on, making a small shadow of horse and man moving slowly yet certainly across that huge empty map where days apart, each from the other, little clusters of human life and need clung to being and shone in Father Louis' mind and purpose like lanterns in the darkness—which usually was the first image he saw of his destination, when, by his reckoning, he knew it was time to reach another of his families.

Was this a hard journey? Very well, then, it was a hard journey. But so was the life hard which he found at the end of each stage of his travels. He had seen men grow old and die in his visits here, and their sons with their wives bring new souls to this wilderness in turn. They learned severe lessons in isolation, heat and the hostility of the animal and vegetable world. Everyone—the child, the grandfather, the husband, the wife, the youth, the horse, the maiden—worked unceasingly against dust, thorn, ignorance and scarcity from dawn to dark. The great world was but a rumor here, and, by the time it came to brush deserts, mostly wrong. But a world without limits of dimension dwelt behind the eyes of all those parched brown people obedient to the natural terms of their lives. It was the world of the human soul, in which could live promises so beautiful and satisfactions so full of ease that the hardships and the betrayals of impersonal Nature could be survived, if only someone came from time to time with the greatest news in all life.

For Father Louis knew in a simple flatness of fact—fact as hard as a rock, as mysterious as water, as dazzling as light—that without God the richest life in the world was more arid than the desert; and with Him the poorest life was, after all, complete in a harmony which composed all things. To be the agent of such a composition put upon him a duty in the light of which all peril on his journeys became at worst mere inconvenience. Everyone he toiled overland to see needed and deserved that which he, at the moment, under existing circumstances, alone could bring.

In a very practical way he was still awed by the mystery of his office. And as a human being he could never deny himself the joy it gave him to see in their faces what his coming meant to his people in the harsh wilderness. They knew what he had come through. They were proud to be thought worth such labor and danger. They loved him.

His mind was active in the solitude through which he crawled day after day, mounted on Pancho. One of his favorite fancies was this: that a great triangle existed between God in heaven, and any little ranch toward which he rode through the days, and himself. It was an always-changing triangle, for one of its points was not fixed: his own. As he came nearer and nearer to his goal of the moment, the great hypotenuse between himself and God grew shorter and shorter, until at the last, when he arrived, there was a straight line with all in achieved communion. He smiled over this idea, but he respected it, too; and sometimes he would take a piece of charcoal from a fire and draw a series of pictures of what he meant, explaining it to the people he was visiting, and they would murmur and nod, and consult one another, and enjoy the notion with him, marveling.

One day at noon on the present journey, he knew he should soon see what would look like a long thin blade of cloud shadow far ahead on the earth that slowly quivered with wafts of light like those in wavering mirrors. But it was not a cloud shadow, as he had found out nearly thirty years ago. It was the distant gash of a long canyon whose yellow rock walls were stained with great stripes of slate blue. It came from the north, and far away to the south opened into the rocky trough of the Rio Grande. In its bottom were all the signs of a river but running water. Here and there were shallow pools fed by the underground flow which needed storm water to call it continuously to the surface. Father Louis always paused at such a pool for a bath. There were sores on his body from the catch of thorns through which he rode. Sometimes a needle of the brush would break off in his flesh and burrow its way under his skin. For the most part he was unaware of such an affliction, but by its comfort the warm alkaline water of the pool reminded him of the misery he had forgotten to notice.

It was usually midafternoon by the time he reached the canyon after first seeing it. Shadow was already rising up the canyon wall as the sun went lower. The place was like a palace to him, open to the brassy sky. Wrens and hawks came to look at him in their wary turns. To be below the surface of the rolling plain in the canyon was to have for a little while the luxury of privacy, somehow. He bathed, and dozed as he dried, and sat in the shade reading his breviary. He knew when it was just time to gather himself together and resume his ride in order to come by nightfall to the house and the spring of Encarnadino Guerra, where he could spend the night.

This friend was a boy of ten when Father Louis first met him. He was now the father of six children, the husband of a silent, smiling woman named Cipriana, the son of a widowed mother called Doña Luz, who, on his last visit, told Father Louis she would not live to enjoy the next one. He remembered how she sat blinking in the brilliant shade of the desert, bowing to him over and over, while a triumph of patience went over her face, eroded by time and trouble and work and pain, as she said, "At night, when everything is quiet, and I am awake and alone—for I cannot sleep much any more—something speaks to me, and tells me to be ready, and not to make any other plans."

She looked at him with hardly any light in her small eyes, and he knew she was right. When he said Mass for them that time, he thought he saw in her face some powerful, direct understanding of the Holy Sacrifice which during all her pious life had slumbered within her, but at last came clear in her whole, small, withered being.

He wondered whether through any dry, desertlike tenacity she might still be living.

But when he rode up in the arching twilight to the dwelling of the Guerras, almost the first thing they told him after their excited greeting was that Doña Luz had died early in the summer while sitting in the shade of her bench, holding her stick of ocotillo cactus which her hands had shined so smooth.

In the light of the candle lantern the family looked at him and then at one another. They were shocked by how he had changed since last year. He was stooped and he slowly trembled all the time. He had to peer at them to see them, even though he preserved a smile to make nothing of this. Burned by the wind and the sun, his face looked smaller. He breathed shallowly, with his mouth a little open. He seemed to them a very old man, all of a sudden. It was like a secret they must keep from him.

After their first start, they got busy to make his supper. The younger children lost their shyness and came from behind chairs and the edges of tables to see him, and at last climb upon him. He smelled dry and dusty to them, like the earth.

After supper he held lessons in catechism for the younger children, who tomorrow would receive their First Communions. The parents and the two older sons listened also.

After that, there was a little time left for gossip. The family's news was all of the seasons. The priest's was boiled down out of letters and newspapers from France. The Guerras already knew that the earthly love of his life was his native country, which he had not seen for over thirty years, but which still spoke in his darting eyes, his cleverness at description and in the accent with which he spoke Spanish. They listened respectfully while he made picture after picture in his talk of what he loved and missed, but they could not really see with him either the cool green fields, the ancient stone farmhouses, the lanes of poplar trees, the clear rivers; or the proud old towns, or the glorious towering cathedrals, or the silvery web of his dear city of Paris sparkling delicately in daytime, glowing in the long dusk with golden lamps and violent distances.

But they were honored simply to have him here, and stared before his marvels, and held their breath for tomorrow, when he would give them the Sacraments.

In the morning he visited the grave of Doña Luz. Everybody went with him. She was buried a little way off from the adobe house. When he saw how little earth she displaced, he nodded and smiled, as though meeting all over again her modest character which he knew so well. Guerra brought some water in an earthen vessel —not much, but enough. Father Louis took the jug and held it in both hands a moment, and gazed into it. They were all reminded of how precious water was on the earth, how it determined by its presence the very presence of life. Then he blessed it, and they all knew what this meant in terms of their daily struggle. Then, reciting prayers for the dead, he walked around the small mound of the grandmother and sprinkled the holy water upon it, and they knew he was keeping once again a promise made between heaven and earth a long time ago.

After that they returned to the house and he took them one by one and heard them confess their sins, of which, as they were contrite, he relieved them. Then, at an altar improvised against the wall where the old woman used to sit for so many hours, he said Mass, wearing his embroidered French silks and using the pewter chalice that came out of his saddlebag.

The family knelt on the ground in a straight line facing the altar. The famous triangle of Father Louis was brought into a straight line also. God and mankind were made one. As he recited the words during the offertory, "O God, who has established the nature of man in wondrous dignity, and even more wondrously has renewed it——" Father Louis felt behind him the bodily presences of that isolated family, and an almost bitter sense of the dearness of each of their souls humbled him at his altar.

When Mass was over they returned within the house, where, at the raw table polished by countless unnoticed contacts of all the family, Father Louis sat down to fill in certificates of First Communion for the younger children. He had a flask of huisache ink and a German steel pen. Sitting as far back from the documents as he could, the better to read, he began to write. A look of disgust came on to his face as his trembling hand gave him trouble. Exclaiming impatiently, he put his left hand on his right wrist to add strength and steadiness where they were needed, but this did not help much, and when he was done, he pushed the papers toward the head of the family, saying, "Nobody ever can read my writing except God."

They all took him seriously, prouder than before of their papers.

"But that is enough, isn't it?" he demanded fiercely.

They had a merry breakfast, when everyone talked as though they would not soon again have a chance to talk, which was true; everyone except Guerra, who was going to speak of something as soon as he had built up enough silence. Finally he was ready.

"Father," he said, leaning back a trifle in his chair and half closing his eyes to disguise deep feelings, "you won't be going on anywhere else, after us, will you?"

"Oh, yes."

"Where will you go, father?"

"Why, I plan to ride from here over toward the river. I have a couple of families over there, and I may go as far as the town of San Ygnacio, to see if the priests from Mier are making visits there, as they ought to. Why?"

Guerra put his head on one side and shrugged. He did not want to say that the old man was exhausted and ought not to go so far in the pitiless country under the searing sun. It would not be polite to say the old man was older than his years, and he must be seventy anyway. He might be misunderstood if he said that everybody reached a time, after a life of hard work, when he must pause and rest and let stronger people do what needed doing. It would hardly do to show outright that he thought Father Louis should give up, and stay here, and rest a few weeks, and then perhaps Encarnadino Guerra might leave everything here in the hands of his two strong, quiet boys, and just ride with Father Louis until he saw him safely back in Brownsville.

Father Louis peered close to his younger friend and saw enough of these thoughts to stir him up.

"Eh?" he said, rapping hard with his knuckles on Guerra's skull. "What goes on in there?" He was sharp and angry. What were they all thinking? That he was a feeble old man? He knew all there was to know about that, but if anything was to be said about it, he, not they or anyone else, was the one to say it. "Mind your manners, you, boy," he said to Guerra, screwing up his small eyes until all that showed of them were two sharp blue points of light. "Eh? You have opinions, have you? Who told you to think anything! Eh? When I want you to think anything about anybody, I'll tell you. Eh? I got here, didn't I? How many times have I managed to come? And what for? Does anybody tell me to come? Or where to go? Or when? Or why? Then you keep your place, and thank God for your blessings, and for your friends, and understand that it is just as bad to hold an impolite thought as it is to say an impolite thing. Eh?" His whole body shook with passion which he tried to control. "Bad. You'd just better be careful, that's all I have to say, do you hear?"

The family was appalled at this burst of feeling. They sat with downcast eyes, fearing that it would be disrespectful to look upon Father Louis in his rage. But they had little glimpses of his un-shaven face whitened with anger, and they could hear how pulse-shaken his voice was. Guerra was more Indian than anything else, and his countenance became fixed. He leaned back and took his dressing down without response. He was not even hurt by it. He knew why it came to him. He knew how much it proved him right in his concern. He admired the flare of spirit in the old man. He was at peace with himself for trying what he had tried.

The youngest child, not understanding what had taken place, now, belatedly, felt the emotion among all the older ones, and turning up her little clay-doll face she burst into wails of misery and fear, bringing her tiny creature paws to her howling mouth until

she resembled the small sculptured masks of earth buried with the
dead centuries ago deep in Mexico.

Father Louis roughly took her upon his lap. He bent his bristly
face close to hers, cactus and blossom together, and in barely audible murmurs quieted the child and himself, which took about five
minutes.

This act reclaimed them all for one another. Once again the
visitor was kind and smiling, and the family without fear.

"And so, good-by for this time," said Father Louis, putting the
child down and standing up. "If you will get my horse for me?"

Guerra spoke to one of the boys, who went to fetch Pancho.
They all met him outside. Cipriana brought some tortillas for the
saddlebag. Everyone knelt down to be blessed. The hot sunlight
smote them. They had lingered long over their breakfast. It was
late. Father Louis, mounted and ready, blessed them three times,
and then turned and rode off to the south. After a while he looked
back. They were still kneeling. The next time he looked back it was
hard to see them, for at even a little distance they made the same
shadow as the scrubby bushes which grew on the caked earth, and
seemed just as eternally rooted there.

He had a bad morning. The sun seemed hotter to him than before. The savage brush seemed animated with spite as it clawed at
his legs going by. Pancho, after all these years and a lifetime in the
brush country, took it into his head to be terrified of familiar things,
and from time to time without warning executed a rapid dance
step to one side while throwing his head back and rolling his eyes
at his rider.

"Hush, you fool!" Father Louis exclaimed at such times. "You
fool!"

But he addressed himself as much as he did the horse. For the
first few hours of that day's ride, he reviewed many times the loss of
his temper at Guerra, and developed a masterly case, closely
reasoned, lucid as only a French argument can be, compassionate
with a largeness of heart, yet as logical as music in its progression,
as to why it had been not only natural but actually necessary to
reprove Guerra for having presumed to hold views about him. Reprove? Perhaps actually more of a scolding. Scolding? Thinking it
over, possibly even a tongue-lashing. And the knuckles? The furious

raps on the head? Still, how else could he be made to understand? But understand what?

It was no good. As he always did, in the end, he lost the argument with himself. He knew that after hours of exhausting search for conclusions which would excuse him for what he had done, he would at last come to the truth, which was that he had offended God and man through his lifelong besetting sins of pride, self-esteem and attempted condonement of his own shortcomings; and that there would be nothing left to do but go down upon his knees and admit how wrong he had been, and pray to be forgiven and to be granted strength once more to conquer himself.

He began his penance with a resolve not to eat or drink until nightfall.

By midafternoon, the brush grew thicker. Only occasionally did he come to a little clearing between the mesquite bushes, which rose higher than himself mounted on Pancho. In spite of his green sunglasses, the ground sparkled and glared enough to hurt his eyes. He watched for but he could not see the long pale blur which would tell him that another canyon lay ahead which he would follow until it took him, after several days, to the Rio Grande. He kept the sun on his right, for it was declining to the west in the white sky and he was going south. The day was still.

But how was this? He thought he heard a singing wind, but when he tried to notice whether he could feel the air stirring or see dust rising ahead of him, there was no sign of wind. He halted Pancho. What did he hear, then? He turned his head. Yes, he could hear something, now far ahead, now here in his very ear. He searched the undulating horizon, but he saw nothing except the wavering image of glassy heat where the white sky met the dusty earth.

As he rode on, the singing in the air became louder. It sounded like the voice of the desert heat. He shook his head, resentful of natural conditions which hid behind mystery. And then suddenly he knew, and scornfully rebuked himself for taking so long about it.

He was riding into a swarm of cicadas, and now he could see the first ones, clinging to the mesquite as they raised their shrieking song of the heat. The farther he rode, the louder they became. He bent his head under their stinging assault upon his hearing. There were thousands and millions of them. Blindly they fulfilled their natures in their collective scream of response to the sun and the desert. The very atmosphere seemed to be in flames, and the sound of the stridulating insects added to the illusion.

Father Louis had touched the desert often enough. He had smelled it. He had tasted it when its dust rose on the wind. He had seen it in every state. But never before in so real a sense had he heard it.

He was suddenly exhausted. In a clearing, a little lake of baked dust a few yards in diameter, he halted and dismounted, tying Pancho to a stout mesquite branch. Disturbed, a cloud of cicadas rose on crackling threads of flight and found another bush. The ringing song rose all about him. He could not even hear the sound of Pancho stamping his foot to shake off flies. He clapped his hands, but made barely a sound against the strident song in the air. He felt removed from himself. All desert natures combined to render him impersonal. Here, humbled not only from within but from without, he could find real contrition. He knelt down to pray.

The sunlight was brilliant in the center of the clearing, a little open room hidden by time, distance and mesquite clumps. At the west side of it there was lacy shade, cast by tall bushes. But Father Louis rejected it and knelt in the plain sunlight. He bent his head under the beat of his spirit and of the insect scream which seemed to invoke the zenith. He prayed to be forgiven for his miserable anger. He always prayed in French, the language through which he had first met God.

He was not long now at his contritions, for he knew that prayer was not so often a matter of length as of depth. Much sobered, even saddened, by his intense self-discovery, he arose wearily from his knees and went over to the shade to lie down. He went as deeply into the under boughs of the thorny mesquite as he could. He closed his eyes. At once he felt cooler, just to have the hot light shaded from his sight. Ah, this was delicious, just to lie for a few moments and gather strength to go on for the remaining hours of daylight. He felt how his limbs all went heavy on the earth as he let himself drift off to sleep.

Little coins of light fell over him through the intricate branches. Where he lay, he made solid shadow himself under the mesquite tree. He was as quiet and substantial as a rock. And if he used Nature, it in turn used him without his knowing, for he was asleep.

He did not see, or smell, or feel what came in slow inquiry along the trackless ground, striving forward in orderly, powerful progress, flowing in a dry glitter and advancing through always-new and always-repeated thrust of form from side to side and yet ahead. It was a diamondback rattlesnake in search of shade and the cool. It came from deep in the scattered brush, and it found the heavy-sleeping man under the bushy tree. With what seemed almost conscious caution against awakening the sleeper, the snake drew closer and closer in infinite delicacy, until it lay heavily at rest in the shade of Father Louis' right shoulder, its length doubled back and forth in inert splendor.

The sleepers did not stir for a while and then Father Louis grew tense in dream, his mouth fell open and, awakening with a jerk, he sat up, lost in forgetfulness of where he was or how he came there. He stared at the white sky.

The thick snake, at the first quiver of motion beside it, drew instantly into its coil and shook its dozen rattles. Their song could not be heard over the general din of the cicadas.

"Ah, yes," sighed Father Louis, as he discovered where he was, and why, and whither he was going. He put his hand to his brow and sank roughly back to the earth to take a few more minutes of rest. The snake struck him in the shoulder, and struck him again. Its coils turned dust into liquid light as they lashed. The strikes came like blows made by the thick, powerful arm of a young man.

"What then?" said Father Louis at the sudden stabbing pain, and the blows that shook him. He first thought of mesquite thorns on a springy branch; they were long and, as he had often said, sharp as fangs, and they could fester if not treated. It occurred to him that this would be troublesome now, as he could hardly reach his own shoulder to wash, cut open the skin and dig out the thorns if they had broken to stay in the flesh.

But he turned to see the branch which had attacked him, and saw the snake instead. The snake was retreating. He could see its eye with its glaring drop of light. His heart began to beat hard. He had a surge of rage. He wanted to kill the snake, and actually rose to one knee and scraped the ground with his hands for something to attack with—a rock, a club of dead wood, anything—but he could find nothing. He sank down again, and out of habit in any

crisis brought his hands flat together with crossed thumbs in the
attitude of prayer.

"No, no; no anger," he beseeched of himself with his eyes shut.
He had just endured and come through the storm of his own pride,
and he must not now create another. He opened his eyes and looked
after the snake, and saw it where it paused half in, half out of the
dappled shade of the next bush.

"Go," he said to it.

What he meant by this came to be more and more clear through
calm and struggle in the next hour or so. The snake, as though it
heard him, resumed in infinite slowness the gliding flow of its retreat until it was lost to sight among the hot thickets where the
insects still sang and sang.

"Yes, go," he repeated bitterly; and was ashamed to discover that
he was weeping. It was the humanity in him which wept because
death was coming. He fell over upon his face and put his cracked
and dusty hands over his eyes. His mouth was open and took into
itself the loose acid earth with his breath. His tears ran down his
fingers. His heart was pounding rapidly upon the ground. It seemed
to shake the earth. It told Father Louis that he was afraid.

Afraid? Of what? he thought. *Afraid of death? But I have dealt
with it all my life and I have robbed it of its terrors for those who
knew how to die. Is death the only victory of life? Or do we have
to defeat life in its own terms? That depends. It depends upon
whether sin is ever outside oneself or always within. Yes, this is a
very interesting matter.*

He made himself lie quietly without thought for a moment. If
perhaps he conserved his energy he might by natural vitality, by
pure goodness, defeat the murder which had been dealt him by the
desert. He forced himself to relax, and promised that in a little
while his head would be clearer, his heart would calm itself, and
moving with infinite caution he would arise, mount his horse and
go slowly, steadily, cleverly, toward the long evening, and come to
the canyon where there must be a familiar trickle of water. A cool
night with much prayer, a stout will, and tomorrow he would go
forward and by the end of the day come to friends who would
know how to make poultices and feed him and recover him to the
use and enjoyment of many more years of duty, work and acquired
merit.

But the poison worked rapidly, and he felt it charging his mind with throbbing pain which confused him. Shining blades went across his vision behind his eyes like spokes of a great wheel. He was dazzled by their power. When he raised his head they took it with them, rolling and rolling until he fell down again upon the ground with his cheek cut by little pebbles of gypsum. He tried to speak and to say, "Let me not live for vanity, though, Lord."

Questions now became academic, for he went blind in his inner vision, and lay trembling involuntarily as the terrible message which had been stricken into him traveled the course of his blood and reached him everywhere within.

Tied to his mesquite tree, Pancho stamped and waited. Presently Father Louis believed that he awoke.

His mind was working sharply and with, it seemed to him, exquisite new ease and clarity. He saw all his thoughts in crystal depths of cold fresh water. He knew he was in the mesquite thicket, and what had happened to him, and he possessed this knowledge with a beauty of feeling which all his life he had known in the state of grace, after receiving or administering the Sacraments. It was more than mere physical well-being. It was a sense of delivery from the ordinary guilt of his own clay, and the exasperating weight of the world. It was the real meaning of communion with all that lay beyond himself. In such a state, truth needed no seeking and no definition. It was here, within, and it was there, without. It was everywhere. When all was known, there could be no astonishment.

He was therefore not astonished now when right before him, lying at ease in the light of the sun, was the snake, gazing at him with piercing sweetness.

He spoke to it. "I do not hate you. It is enough that I recognize you."

The snake replied, "That is my damnation."

"Yes," said Father Louis, "for when evil is recognized, all other powers move together to defeat it."

"And yet they never do defeat it, do they? How do you explain that?"

"Ah. You and I do not see it in quite the same way. You conceive of the possible death of evil as being one final end, after which only goodness will survive."

"I do."

"That is your vanity. For the fact is that evil must be done to death over and over again, with every act of life. One might even say that this repeated act is a very condition for the survival of life itself. For only by acts of growth can more life be made, and if all evil, all acts of death, were ended once and for all, there would be nothing left for the soul to triumph over in repeated acts of growth."

The snake sighed despondently and said, "Do you not permit me a comparable purpose and privilege? That is, of triumphing repeatedly over all acts of good—that is, of life—until only I remain?"

"I permit you your established role, but I do not admit the possibility of your triumphing repeatedly over all acts of life. I must point out that, historically, your premise is untenable."

"And yet I have played a part in every human life."

"Oh, admittedly. We are not discussing the fact that your powers exist; only the fact that they have their limits."

The snake smiled. "This? From you?" it asked with ironic politeness.

"What do you mean, sir?"

"If my powers have their limits, then how is it that I have killed you? What greater power is there than that?"

Father Louis passed his hand across his face to hide his amusement. "You have betrayed the weakness of your whole position," he replied. "For it appears to be impossible for you to know that the death of matter is of no importance, except to other matter. The materialist can see only destruction as the logical end of his powers. I, and my brothers, and my children, know that beyond matter lies spirit, and that it is there where answers are found, and truths become commonplace, and such efforts as yours, so restless, so ingenious, so full of torturing vanity, are seen for what they really are."

The snake frowned for a moment, but then shook off its irritation and said, again with politeness, even with charm and appeal, which Father Louis was the first to admit, "Everyone must do that which his nature dictates."

"There again," said Father Louis with assumed gravity, "there is much behind the formation of that nature which you do not take into account."

"Oh, come. After all, I am a snake, I came from snakes, I do a snake's work. How could I behave like anything but a snake?"

"The outer form is hardly the point. You can assume any form you choose, I believe?"

The snake hesitated before answering. A gleam of admiration went through its expression, and it marveled frankly for a moment at the astuteness of Father Louis.

"I must say, even if we are enemies, you force me to admire and like you," it said.

"Thank you," said Father Louis. "Viewed abstractly, you have great and beautiful qualities of your own."

"Do you really think so?"

"Oh, yes, I do. But I must add that they seem to me less important, in the end, than they do to you."

"You can also be very rude, you know."

"I do not think of it that way," said Father Louis mildly. "Finally, it doesn't matter how things are said or done, it is what things are said or done. For example, I really believe you can do things far more expertly than I can. But when we come to what things, there I have you."

The snake looked far from pleased.

Father Louis resumed, "I can't assume any form, for example, as you can. I remain always what I am, a man, an old man, a dirty old man when water is scarce or I am busy, an old man full of pride and sin and vanity and all the rest of it; but nobody is ever in doubt as to what I mean or as to what I think life means, and with all my mistakes in style and good form, the garden I scratch keeps growing."

"And I?"

"And you, sometimes you are a snake, and sometimes a whisper, and again, a daydream, a lump in the blood, a sweet face, an ambition, a scheme for making money, a task for an army. Sometimes you can even be a man and disarm everyone entirely who cannot see your heart. But someone there is who always sees. Goodness is often performed without the slightest knowledge of its doing. But evil is always known."

"Yes, I think more people know me than the other thing."

"But don't congratulate yourself upon that," said Father Louis, "for it means always one of your uncountable defeats when you are known."

Father Louis saw that the snake would have to grow angry unless the subject was changed. The snake changed it. "I wonder," it mused, "why I ever came to you today."

Father Louis shrugged. "Sooner or later, we would have come together," he said.

"Did you expect me?"

"I've been expecting you all my life; though not exactly in this particular guise. You came to me in my sleep, like an evil dream."

"All I wanted was a little comfort. It was so hot. So dry."

Father Louis smiled in delight. "You see? For comfort, even you have to appeal to the powers of goodness."

"Why did you let me go?"

"I had no weapon."

"You could have stamped upon me."

"I do not believe in killing."

"Yet I am your enemy."

"Yes, you are. But I believe there are greater ways to dispose of you than in revenge."

"You do not have much time left, you know. Just think of all the time you would have left if I had not come to you. If you had seen me and killed me first."

"Yes, I have thought of that. But you speak as though time were my property. It is not. How can I count it? Or know how much of it is my share?"

The snake scowled and looked from side to side evasively. Unwillingly, against its own comfort, it asked, "Who else can decide your share? Where do you get it? What do you refer to?"

The snake began uneasily to bring its coils together. There was anguish in its movement, slow as it was. It seemed to be obeying desire which was hurtful and yet impossible to deny.

"You do not really want to hear," said Father Louis tenderly.

"Oh, yes, I do; tell me," said the snake with broken breath, already suffering under the answer which it demanded.

Father Louis bent over the snake with compassion. There was torture in the creature, as with glittering sweet power it besought Father Louis to answer.

"Very well, my poor sinner," said Father Louis gravely. "I, and all creatures, draw our share of time in this life from God, our Father in heaven."

At these words the snake, with the speed of lightning, knew convulsion in its dread coils, and with mouth wide open and fangs exposed, struck again and again at the earth, where the dust rose like particles of gold and silver. Father Louis regarded it with pity as its paroxysm of hatred and chagrin spent itself.

At last, gasping softly and stretched out in exhaustion, the snake said sorrowfully, "And so it is not by my will that you die now?"

"No."

"I was only the means?"

"Only the means."

"Your hour was designated elsewhere?"

Father Louis looked upward. His face was radiant. "My hour was fixed by our Heavenly Father."

The snake closed its eyes and shuddered reminiscently. Then it said, "And my hour?"

"You will die in your bodily form by His will."

"I do not want to die."

"But you will live in your quality of evil by His will."

"You're sure?"

"Yes. But you will live only on earth, no matter what form you assume."

The snake grew pale. "Oh, no."

"Yes," said Father Louis as his argument drew to its close, "for there can be no evil in heaven."

The snake lay with its mouth open, its tongue like a little tongue of fire, flickering in despair, its eyes staring without sight. It was vanquished, destroyed, made trivial. Father Louis shook his head over it and wished it might not have suffered. Then he felt his brow, where the diamondlike lucidity of the past quarter of an hour seemed to be clouding over. His skull was cracking under blows that beat and beat there. How could he feel so bad after feeling so well?

"And now you must excuse me," he said uncertainly to the snake. "I have things to do, and, actually, I do not feel too well. Thank you, if you will just go now," and he looked to see if the snake was leaving, but the snake was already gone.

The battering pains in his head brought Father Louis from vision to consciousness.

"Oh, my God, my God," he said devoutly and with much effort, even with modesty, representing his trouble to Him whose suffering he had dwelt upon so deeply in a lifetime.

He looked around. The air seemed entirely silent. This was because there was a ringing in his head so bewildering that he could no longer hear the myriad insects at their screaming celebration of the heat.

He saw Pancho tied to the tree. "No, you must not stay with me," he said, and tried to stand up. He could hardly stand, for his legs were weak as paralysis crept into them. And so he crawled across the open place among the thickets until he could hold to his stirrup, haul himself up and lean with his head on the saddle for a moment.

"You need not die here, tied to a tree," he said. "Let me get my things, and you may go."

He fumbled with the buckles and straps until he was able to haul the saddle off the horse. It fell to the ground. He worked at the bridle until he had freed it enough to pull it off over Pancho's head. The horsehair bridle hung from the thorny tree and trailed in the dust.

"Huya! Huya!" cried Father Louis, waving his hand at Pancho to make him trot away, as so often he had done after unsaddling the horse at the corral at Brownsville. But Pancho simply stood and regarded him.

"Very well, very well; in your own time, then," he said, and went down to his hands and knees, fondling a pouch on the saddle. Out of it into his hands came the objects he wished to hold once more. Holding them to his breast, he crawled back to his fatal shade across the clearing. The sun was almost down.

"My soul doth magnify the Lord," he murmured in Latin while pains like blades pierced him through and through. Even the heavy washing waves of death could not erase entirely from his foundering mind the terrible privilege of knowing in a final hour what saints might have endured. "And my spirit has rejoiced in God my savior," he said, without knowing he spoke. But he brought a lifetime of prayer with him to death's door, and in a little while it entered there with him.

Pancho late the next evening finished finding his way through the brush back to the house of Encarnadino Guerra. The family saw that he was without his saddle and bridle. Guerra and his big sons went searching, and, though they persevered for days, found nothing in that wilderness of repeated clump and glaring shadow and lost sameness. They had to give up. Later that year, when surveyors from an expedition of the United States Army came by his place on their way to Brownsville, Guerra told them the news, and asked them to see that it reached the proper authorities, along with the horse Pancho which he hoped they would take with them.

And then one day eight years afterward, Guerra was on his way to San Ygnacio on the Rio Grande to see his new grandson, born to the household of his oldest boy, who now lived there. Coming into a small clearing in the brush, he found quite by accident what he had looked for long ago. There was not much left, for the desert earth and sky were voracious. Coyotes and blowing sand, vultures and beating sunlight and wind had worked with the years on flesh and leather, French silk, parchment and homespun. Reverently Guerra took up the few bones that had not been scattered, and the few hard things that still stayed by them: the pewter chalice, a rosary of small sea shells, three American silver dollars, the pair of green sunglasses, and, from a mesquite tree where it hung now off the ground, the horsehair bridle.

When he could, he made the journey to Brownsville, bringing the relics of his old friend with him. He found his way to Father Pierre Arnoud.

"How these things speak to us!" said Father Pierre, after hearing the end of the story that had begun eight years before. He looked at Guerra and saw that this was a man who had lost a dear friend, who would understand anything said to him in the name of Father Louis. He added, "I am leaving soon for France. Do you know where that is?"

"Yes. He used to tell us much about it."

Father Pierre was making ready to obey a summons to return home to receive the dignity of bishop of a French diocese.

"I am going there to assume new work," he said. "These things, this sacrifice," he said, indicating what Guerra had brought, "will help me to do it better."

Guerra nodded.

"We will bury him here in the churchyard," continued Father Pierre, "and you must be present. As you were his friend, and have served him so well, now I would like to ask your permission to keep this."

He held up the little string of sea shells.

"Yes," said Guerra, accepting with simplicity the power to dispose.

"I wonder how he died," murmured Father Pierre. "Indians? A heart attack?"

"Not Indians."

"Why not?"

"They would not have let the horse go."

"True. What then?"

Guerra made a gesture with his mouth, putting his lips forward as though he would point to a place far from there and long ago. He saw the clearing in the thorny brush again, and he knew its nature, all of it.

"I think I know."

"How could you possibly?"

"He did not die suddenly."

"No?"

"No. He had time to free his horse."

"True."

"If he thought he could have saved himself, he would have come with the horse."

"Undoubtedly."

"But he did not come. He stayed. That means he knew there wasn't any use."

"Yes?"

"Where I found him was just like the place where it would happen."

"What would happen?"

With his hand Guerra made in the air a slow, sinuous motion from side to side in an unmistakable imitation.

"No!" said Father Pierre. "A snake?"

Guerra nodded. "I think so," he said.

Father Pierre shuddered at the nature of that fate, and then presently he kindled at the memory of an old weakness and an old strength.

"Do you know? I will tell you something," he said. "Our dear friend was an old man, tired and ill, when he went on that last journey. For days before he left, I was supposed to tell him that he could not go. I tried and I tried. But I could not tell him. Even on the last morning I could not give the order." Father Pierre put his hands together in emotion. "What could I have saved him from? From dying at his work? That is how we—all of us—want to die when our time comes."

He looked earnestly at Guerra, but if he thought he would find the abstract pardon of life there, he was mistaken. Guerra simply looked back at him with the impersonal judgment of the world.

"No, I could not give the order," resumed Father Pierre. "And do you know? I am sure he knew what I had to say. He would not let me say it. He gave the orders. Just to prove it, he even sent me upstairs to find his green sunglasses. I went, and I did not find them. When I came down again, there they were; he had them all the time."

Guerra laughed out loud at the crankiness this recalled, and what it meant. He bent over, took up the pair of green glass spectacles with their rusted tin rims and, with a gleam of meaning, handed them to Father Pierre.

"Then keep these also," he said.

"Thank you," said the bishop-elect soberly.

SMOKE OVER THE PRAIRIE

by Conrad Richter

It is ground into dust now like Mobeetie and Tascosa, swallowed up by the grass and desert along with split ox shoes, shaggy buffalo trails and the crude cap-and-ball rifle. And how can I say it so that you who were not there may see it as I did, rolling, surging, fermenting under the brazen territorial sun, that vanished rude empire of which my father was a baron, a land as feudal as old England, larger than the British Isles, with lords and freemen, savages and peons, most of them on horseback, all here in America a little more than half a century ago, and yet in another world and another age that was just then—although we didn't know it—drawing to a violent close?

I remember, as a small boy, climbing up our roof ladder in the shadowy blot after sunset and telling myself that five days' journey west across the territory the sun was still shining on flocks of my father's hundred thousand sheep. And I can remember the cavelike darkness of some early-morning waking between blankets tossed over tanned buffalo hides on my huge bed and thinking that a thousand miles east on one of my father's mule or bull trains the sun was already shining.

And today I would give a great deal just to glimpse that same sun warming the walls of my father's house, known from Fort Dodge to the Old Pueblo as Gant's Mansion, a squat palace of adobe standing on the San Blas plain, and to see again its wide hall trooping with a grave procession of princely territorial governors and hook-nosed judges, of Indian agents like blue-eyed foxes, of brass-buttoned Army officers, Federal officials, Mexican dons and *ricos*, and the hungry, grunting chiefs of the Utes, the Apaches and the Navajos.

But even then a cloud no bigger than your hand was beginning to cast a shadow over those adobe walls that stood thick enough to entomb horses. The smoke of the native cedar is blue and fragrant, and melts into the air. This cloud on the eastern horizon was a smoke tamed by man, black, foreign, smelling of the pit, and had never hung over this wild land before.

I knew it was important that day my mother called to me in the hall. She sat massively in her armchair in her rooms, not a stout woman, but wrapped, even in summer, in shawls and overskirts, her eyes, dark and bright like a bird's, in a quilted face which even then looked incredibly older than it was. All week I had been conscious of the clamp of her lip and the faint white spots, like touches of alkali, in my sister Juliana's cheeks.

"Go and ask your papa if he can spare the time from his business to talk to me," she said bitterly. "And you come with him."

I knew then that my father had not greeted her, although he had been back several hours from ten days among his sheep in the Canyon Bonito country. I had seen his dust-covered buggy pull up to the store, both horses lathered to the mane, as always when my father held the lines. I found him gone from the store, and I looked for him in his wholesale warehouses sprawling near by, a kind of Ali Baba caves in barred windows, dim and odorous, and heaped with inciting boxes, fat hogsheads, bulging bales, mountains of plump sacks, grain bins, piles of hides to the roof, monstrous sacks of unwashed wool and poisonous-looking copper ingots.

He wasn't there, and I went in turn to the clanging blacksmith shop, to the stables, where his late-driven horses stood in a kind of stupor, and to the wheelwright shop, choked with felloes and rims, blocks and shavings and the dismembered bodies of wagons that knew every ford and pitch hole on the Santa Fe trail.

Only one place remained where he might be, and I reproached myself that I hadn't gone there before—what we called the mansion office, a bare sweep of room with an adobe floor and little furniture except a battered desk whose drawers no one dared to touch. The place was empty, but a guttural of voices drifted from the bedroom beyond.

"Come in!" my father's voice called at my rap.

I lifted the iron latch and for an uncomfortable moment stood in the doorway.

A fire of piñon logs blazed in the bedroom fireplace, and on the floor with his back to it sat Guero, the Mescalero Apache chief, huge and greasy, with the eyes, nose and talons of an eagle, his red blanket thrown back from his shoulders, and bared in his rawhide belt a long American trade knife and the forbidden revolver.

And coolly talking to him from where he stood in a white bowl on the floor, washing himself from a second bowl on the marble top of the washstand, unclothed, unarmed and unconcerned, stood my father, a powerful naked figure, not tall but herculean, in a black beard that twisted and stood out from his chin and cheeks like fine wire. And I noticed that the same stubborn, black, invincible growth curled from his chest and the hard cylinders of his legs.

So far, he had not even glanced at the open door, and now he looked up with some impatience.

"Come in, come in!" he barked, and I stepped hastily into the room, dimly realizing that he had not known who was knocking, that it might have been one of the Mexican women servants with, perhaps, the governor and his lady behind her, but that my father did not care. His unforgettable eyes fixed themselves upon me. "You know Chief Guero," he commanded sternly. "Go up, shake hands and ask him in Spanish about his family."

When my father had pulled on clean linen and fresh black broadcloth, he summed up his long talk to Guero:

"Tell your people this: Tell them there is no danger from the railroad. It will bring no white people here to take away your rights. It makes big promises. It talks big words. Today it boasts. Tomorrow it is forgotten."

He left Guero sitting on the earthen floor of the office, bent voraciously over a huge bowl of steaming mutton stew.

"Now," he said to me in the hall, "You say your mother wants to see me?" For a moment or two as he stood there he reminded me of the male blackbirds I had often seen in the tules, drawing in their brilliant scarlet shoulder straps and soberly ruffling their feathers until their strut and sheen had vanished and they looked subdued and brown. Then I accompanied him in silence to my mother's door. He knocked, and without waiting for an answer, formally entered.

"Nettie!" He bowed gravely, and in that single word still in my ear I can detect greeting, irony, dignity, indulgence and uncomfortable expectation of what was to come.

My mother made no answer except the further clamp of her lip and the faint, unaccustomed rose in her cheeks. She motioned me to come and sit beside her, which I did, painfully conscious that it was an ignoble role I was to play, like the favorite child in Ten Nights in a Barroom, by whom the regeneration of the father was to be made.

My mother's quarters, which she seldom left, seemed perpetually compressed with a stale and heavy air, the musty scent of Eastern carpets, stuffed chests and wardrobes, soaps, medicines and moth balls, all very distasteful to a boy. But today I felt that the sluggish air had been charged with sharp and potent currents. And when I looked at the golden-brown shawl which hung like a vestment about my mother's shoulders, there was almost the play of lightning upon it.

"Must I speak of it?" my mother began bitterly. "I should think you'd confess it yourself with shame!"

No step was audible outside the door, but the latch lifted and drew our eyes. Slowly the door opened. It was Juliana. I can see her today, framed in that massive doorway with the light like a nimbus behind her, quiet, grave-faced, a girlish figure in her full skirts and snug bodice, both of them dove-colored, and over the latter the gold chain and heart-shaped locket in which I knew she carried the picture of her father.

"John is here. Can't I stay?" she asked, and closed the door. With the hushed step of a young woman late to church, she crossed the room to a chair, and the appeal in her eyes as for a moment she glanced up at my father might almost have been at God.

My mother's eyes burned with maternal satisfaction at Juliana's presence.

"People are saying," she went on scathingly to my father, "that Mr. Rutherford has disappeared like other enemies of the high-handed interests in this territory."

I fancied I saw a hidden stain through the beard on my father's cheeks, and my mind traveled with a sort of horror to Vance Rutherford, tall, fine-looking and gentlemanly, whom Juliana had met at the Coddoms' in Capitan. Up until the last ten days he had kept driving to the mansion in a livery rig to pay her attentions, and I had wondered what had become of his narrow-brim hat and the invariable desert marigold in his buttonhole.

"People say many things, Nettie; many things," my father said.

"Is he dead?" my mother demanded in a blunt voice, and I saw the locket hang motionless for a moment on Juliana's breast.

"No-o," my father said blandly. "Not that I know of." And the locket resumed its silent rise and fall.

"Then you warned him to leave the territory?" my mother accused.

"I may have"—my father lifted a square hand—"seen that he heard certain discreet things."

"You had nothing against him, Frank Gant, except that he's chief engineer for the railroad!" my mother challenged hotly. "Where can you find another young man in such a high position? Do you want your daughter to marry a cowboy or buffalo hunter who rides and kills and gambles and soaks himself in the whisky you sell like coffee and sugar over your counters?"

My father prudently said nothing. The color gathered in my mother's face.

"You're prejudiced against the railroad! I say, thank God for the railroad. It's the finest thing that could happen to this lawless land. It will bring schools and churches."

"They're not building it to bring schools and churches," my father reminded mildly. "They're building it to make it pay. They want to lay down eight hundred miles west and south in the territory. It's to cost eighteen thousand dollars a mile or more. That's fourteen million dollars." He ran his hand over his unruly black beard. "Fourteen million dollars when we already have trails that cost nothing and freighters who've built up their trains to more than five thousand steers and mules."

"Steers and mules!" My mother's eyes were blazing. "Have steers and mules ever civilized this country? How many shooting scrapes does the Capitan Enterprise print every week? Murders, they should be called—cold-blooded murders! And that doesn't count the lynchings and men who disappear and the women and children scalped by your friends, the Apaches! Is it any wonder that good people refuse to come to this barbarous country?"

My father looked very humble.

"Aren't you confusing it, Nettie, with farming country like Kansas?" he asked. "That's a new country. This is old. White people have been here for hundreds of years, but they never got very far with farming. I've heard you say yourself it's only a desert. But this

young promoter, Rutherford"—I saw Juliana's eyelashes quiver—
"wants to spend fourteen million dollars to give the desert a railroad. He tells our towns to go in debt with bonds and buy railroad
stock with the money. He tells them the railroad will some day be
one of the biggest in the country."

I saw that my mother was staggered despite herself by the un-
answerable facts and figures. She leaned forward appealingly.

"When one of your Mexican herders' relatives gets into trouble,
Frank, you always feel sorry and help him out. Can't you feel sorry
for an American who isn't much more than a boy, who works for
the railroad company and believes what the higher officials tell
him?"

"No," my father said slowly, and it was the first hardness I had
heard in his voice since he had entered the room. I saw that he had
straightened. "I have sympathy, Nettie, for a man who knows he
is gambling and loses, and for a man who knows he may get hung
for stealing a horse and steals it. But I have none for anyone who
throws away other people's hard-earned money; who's gullible
enough to swallow a wild dream like a fourteen-million-dollar railroad on the desert." He looked straight at my mother and went on,
drawing in his bearded lips with great force: "Such a waster will
never become a member of my house—not while I'm alive!"

There were streaks of chalk in my mother's cheeks, but what is
hard to forget is Juliana. Quiet, the locket still moving gently on
her dove-colored bodice, she sat on her chair, and her face was no
paler than when she had come in. But the eyes that stared at my
father were the eyes of a dead person. I was aware of my mother
laying her ringed fingers, as if for divine strength, on the gilded
covers of the thick family Bible that lay on the table beside her.

"God will punish you, Frank Gant!" she said.

Now that he had taken his position, my father had become his
old self again, firm, robust, Atlantean, almost like a Nubian lion
in his black beard and broadcloth, standing there with such living
power that I felt that words, shafts, bullets and even the hand of
God must glance off from him.

"Perhaps Julie feels badly now," he went on confidently, "but
she'll get over it till I get back. My early clip's started to move East,
and I'm leaving for St. Louis in the morning to sell it."

The plains had deepened in grass to my pony's knees until my father returned. He always remembered me from the St. Louis shops, with something not easily obtainable in his store—a boy's light rifle or silver spurs. Usually his gifts for Juliana were slighter —a sterling napkin ring engraved with her name, a golden-leather album with the photographs of President and Mrs. Hayes in front, and once a mahogany lap secretary. I know that secretly he was very fond of her, but she was only a girl, an heir who would never carry on his name or smoke heavy cigars while making contracts with Kansas City jobbers or colonels of the quartermaster's department, or drive a buggy over a region half as large as New England, overseeing the lambing of a vast number of ewes and sleeping among the herders in all kinds of spring weather.

But no one could predict my father. When, hale, lusty and radiating vitality, he left the mansion for the store, after greeting us on his return far ahead of his mule train, Trinidad brought in two canvas valises from the boot of a new buggy.

There were, I remember, taffetas and alpacas for my mother, but most of it, I glimpsed at once, was for Juliana. My mother held them up to her, one after the other, but all I can recall are a blue velvet riding dress with an extraordinarily long skirt and a black, lathlike sheath dress, a style none of us had ever seen before, and in which, my mother promptly declared, no self-respecting girl would show her figure or could walk across the room if she did.

When I ran to the store with my new, silver-mounted bridle that was on the bottom of the second valise, my father glanced at me sharply.

"What did Juliana say?" he questioned. "Did she try on the dresses?"

I felt a faint chill up my spine, but one look at his eyes convinced me that I must tell the truth. No one today has eyes like his, blue-green in his black beard, leaping at times with a gusto that would stop at nothing, burning again with a deadly green flame and as quickly freezing to blue ice.

"I don't reckon she was feeling good, papa," I stammered. "She just went to her room and didn't say anything."

Al Sleeper, the head clerk, turned quickly to rearrange the wooden boot boxes that stood in a pile on the floor, and the faces of the listening men stiffened as if someone had suddenly brushed them all with varnish. But my father's face did not change, neither then nor day after day when I saw him look up with a steeled expression to see what Juliana was wearing, only to find her monotonously, almost disrespectfully, in the dove-colored gray.

Something had happened to Juliana. There was a spring in a *cañada* of the San Blas plain that the Mexicans called El Olvidado. The grass was never so green as there, with a fringe of tules and red-winged blackbirds and the living water welling up cool and clear. My pony and I had often drunk there. But the last year something strange had come to the place. The tules were still there and the red-winged blackbirds and the grass still looked green, but there was no water to drink.

It was like that with Juliana. She had the same clear skin and straight white path running back along the center of her smoothly parted, dark hair, and the heart-shaped locket still stirred to her breathing, but something clear and living had vanished. Her custom-made side saddle gathered gritty plains dust in the harness room, and her cream-colored buckskin mare grew wild on the range. Most of the time she spent quietly in her room, and when I came in, she would be sitting on the edge of her bed, a two-months-old copy of the New York Ledger or Saturday Night in her fingers, but her eyes would be gazing over the top of the pages and out of the deep window to the plain that already, in August, was a gray, imprisoning sea.

People in the territory were not different from people anywhere else, and I knew they were talking. Whenever Juliana was called into my mother's rooms to greet visitors, I saw them exchange guarded glances. And when she crossed to the store to match yarn for my mother's tireless bone needles, seeing almost no one, walking with open eyes like one asleep, customers watched her furtively, and Mexican women murmured sympathetically, "*Pobrecita*," after she had gone. My father never murmured in his life, and his full-charged, indomitable figure remained as always, but more than once when my mother was not looking, I watched him glance characteristically at Juliana. And although his bearded face remained adamant, I fancied I could see a kind of Spartan pain afterward in his eyes.

Looking back now, I can understand perfectly, and everything falls into its place like the letters of the alphabet. But I was only a boy on my pony that day in Capitan when Lawyer Henry Coddom asked me to come into his house. In the parlor a man was pacing up and down, and, even in that dim room so soon after the bright sunlight, I saw at once that it was Vance Rutherford, tall, perhaps a little older, his cheekbones faintly haggard, a fresh desert marigold as always in the buttonhole of his high Eastern coat, and the familiar far-away look in his eyes which to me had never seemed to belong to the long fighting lines of his face.

I stiffened at the sight of him, but Vance Rutherford bowed in his impersonal, gentlemanly manner.

"Good morning, Johnnie," he said gravely, and asked me to sit down on the black horsehair sofa, where, for a time, like a pair of grown men, we spoke formally on trivial subjects, none of which touched the railroad or my family.

"Johnnie," he said quietly after a little, "will you take a letter to your sister and not let anyone else see it?"

He did not try to urge me. I thought of Juliana walking with mute eyes around the mansion, and I told myself that I didn't like to be the one to keep a letter from her.

"I don't care," I said, meaning I would do it, and he brought it out, and without either of us saying another word, I slipped it into a pocket.

The letter burned like a live coal all the way back on the saddle to Gant's, and I felt relieved that my father was in the Merino Valley and that I did not have to smuggle the letter past him like an Indian stalking out of the store with one of our butcher knives under his blanket. All afternoon I watched the men shovel the new crop of barley and corn into the dusty warehouse bins, and when I put my saddle and bridle away in the harness room in the last golden, stabbing rays of the sun, I found, with surprise, that Juliana's side saddle was missing. She did not come to the table for supper, and when I heard the long doleful bugle of a prairie wolf after nightfall, I went to my mother.

"It's all right, John," she said, and I think she knew about the letter then. "Someone will see Juliana home or she'll stay all night at the Hudspeths'."

It was during the heavy hours of the night that I was awakened by the feel of a kiss on my cheek. I twisted my head on the bolster, and there was Juliana with a lighted candlestick in her hand. She didn't say a word, just stood there looking down at me, and there was in her face a shining something I had never seen before. It wasn't altogether real—the late hour, her illuminated figure against the blackness of the huge room, the strange luminosity in her eyes and her appearance in the stunning blue velvet riding dress my father had brought her. I had the singular impression that it was a dream, but when I reached out to see if I could touch her, she squeezed my fingers and I found her hand substantial and throbbing with warmth.

I thought it strange that she was not at breakfast, and when I looked into her room, the smoothness of the bright, quilted counterpane told me that her bed had not been slept in. Lupita and Piedad, two of the Mexican servants, professed to know nothing about it, but I knew, by the impassive restraint in which they moved away, that a feeling of excitement pervaded the house. And as I passed my mother's open door, I saw her wiping her eyes.

That afternoon my father drove home in time for supper. His beard was roan from the trail and his eyes glinted through it like pieces of turquoise in the dust. As a rule, my mother took her meals in her rooms, where she ate in lone state from a massive silver tray covered with hammered dots. And I felt the keen import tonight when her full taffeta skirts came rustling to the dining room.

I think my father sensed it too. Twice I saw him glance deliberately at the empty chair standing with such silent power at the table. And before he spoke, his bearded lips tightened.

"Where's Juliana?" he asked, and the brown face of Lupita, the table girl, grew thin with emotion. But my mother's eyes burned with a triumphant light across the table.

"She's gone!" she told him, as if she had waited long for this moment. "She was married to Vance Rutherford at the Coddoms' last evening. They're halfway to Kansas by now."

I did not dare look at my father. Sitting there with my dark antelope steak smoking on the plate before me, I suddenly knew why Juliana had come in during the night to kiss me. And for a long, vivid moment I could see her in her blue velvet and Vance Rutherford with a fresh desert marigold in his buttonhole sitting close together in the bridal coach as they swept northeast across the territory, followed by a golden whirlwind of earthy cloud. And now, hours after they had left, it was as if I could still see their dust lying over the plain in the calm October sunlight like a long, motionless finger pointing out to my father the direction they had gone.

Every second I expected to hear him push back his chair and call for Trinidad to hitch Prince and Custer, his fastest buggy team. When at last I looked up, he had regained his indomitable control. But his face was like the faint grayness of winter snow through the heavy growth of black spruce on lone, powerful Mount Jeddo.

He did not speak during the rest of the supper. Lupita tiptoed around the table. The meal lasted interminably. For all of my father's lack of hunger, he did not allow himself to eat a mouthful less than customary. When he rose to go to the store, which always stayed open till ten o'clock, he must have been aware that every clerk and customer would by this time probably know. His beard and shoulders up, the deep smoldering fire in his eyes warning everyone he met, he walked steadily across the trail in the dusk.

Juliana wrote to my mother, letters filled with bright pictures of her new life. She and Vance lived in a beautiful brick house with a marble doorstep in Kansas City. She had bought a stunning maroon cheviot suit with pearl buttons and a bonnet with plumes to match. Every Sunday morning she and Vance attended church, and already at weekday breakfast she knew the day's news of the world. Her letters closed, "Give my dearest love to papa and Johnnie. Your affectionate daughter, Juliana." But if my mother ever ventured to give it, I never heard her.

All winter I did not mention her name to my father and never heard him speak it. I doubted if he ever would. When, sometimes, I would see him walking silently and rigidly about the place, it was as if he were trying by sheer force of will to erase her ghostlike presence from our hall and rooms, from the aisles of the store and even from the territory. By the following spring it almost seemed as if she might never have been there. But once my mother read aloud from the Enterprise that Mr. and Mrs. Henry Coddom had been to Kansas City, and when she came to the words, "they called on Mrs. Vance Rutherford, the former Juliana Gant," something wrenched open in my mind and Juliana was back in the mansion with us as real as she had ever been in the flesh.

It was only in this way she came that windy day in April when the dust was flying in yellow sheets across the plain. A private coach had stopped to buy grain for the horses at our feed corral. Someone walked into the mansion courtyard, and old Piedad came hurrying back through the hall with a kind of consternation on her wrinkled face. Rather curiously, I went to the door, and for a moment had the feeling that Juliana had come. It was Vance Rutherford, a little heavier and more mature, his face solid and squarer, with a reddish mustache and a marigold as always in his buttonhole.

I stood uncomfortably in the doorway, not knowing quite what to do or say, but Piedad had gone on to my mother's rooms, and now my mother came with loud sibilations of taffeta skirts, seized both of Vance Rutherford's hands in hers, kissed him as if he were my brother and poured out a dozen questions about Juliana.

"Juliana's fine," he said. "She wanted to come along, but I'm on business." His face sobered. "I've got to see Mr. Gant in the store and then hurry back, but I promised to see you first, so I could tell her how you all looked."

At the mention of my father, the bright, birdlike glint came into my mother's eyes. I saw that she itched to know the cause of his visit, but he did not offer to tell her, and when he left for the store, she feverishly insisted that I go along, as if my companionship might in some mysterious brotherly manner ingratiate him into my father's good graces.

It was the last place in the world that I wanted to be at the moment, and I kicked grimly at every bone and horn I met in the dust to the wide store steps. Through the open door I could see my father standing in a circle of respectfully listening men, his back and clasped hands to the cold, fat-bellied, unblacked stove. Then I stepped discreetly aside to let Vance Rutherford enter first.

It could not have been possible for more than a few of our customers to know Vance Rutherford by sight; yet when he stepped past the pile of carriage blankets at the door, something was in the air of the big store room that wasn't there before. Ike Roehl, halfway up a stepladder, soundlessly dropped an armful of ladies' zephyrs to the counter. Over by the sugar barrels, a clerk and customer stopped talking. In the silence that followed I could hear the windows rattling and the fine sand sifting across the small panes. And suspended on their nails along the ceiling, the rows of wooden buckets kept swinging silently in the draft.

"Could I see you a few minutes in your office, Mr. Gant?" Vance Rutherford asked.

I expected to see rushing into my father's face that volcanic violence from which I had often watched men shrink. Instead, he seemed to be seized by some strange perversity. Not long before, he had come in from overseeing the loading of fleeces on one of his eastbound wagon trains. The rolling brim of his hat was gray with dust. Wisps of wool clung to his broadcloth and buttons. And now he stood with his chin half sunken on his chest and his eyes half closed, as if warding off someone he intensely disliked with a kind of ponderous lethargy.

"Anything you have to say, you can say it here," he rumbled.

Vance Rutherford stood very straight, but I saw him bite his lip.

"I wanted to talk to you in private, sir," he flushed, "so you'd be free to act as you thought best in the matter." He waited a few moments. "If you force me to make it public property, I'll do it." He waited again, and when my father made neither movement nor further expression, his face grew longer and harder, and I saw that it had not lost any of its fighting lines. "The railroad is coming into the territory, sir!" he announced tensely. "We're starting to lay track across the line in May."

None of the listening men moved so much as a finger, but I could feel a wave of something electric sweep over the room. Only my father seemed immune to it. He still stood like a dozing buffalo bull, only partly aware of what might be going on around him.

"You're coming as far as Capitan?" he grunted.

"We'll have trains running into Capitan in a year," Vance Rutherford promised.

My father lifted his massive head, and I saw his deep smoldering eyes.

"You still have railroad stock for sale?"

"We have, Mr. Gant," the younger man said simply. "It takes money to build a railroad."

"I understand," my father rumbled on, "that you figure on spending millions in the territory?"

"Millions!" Vance Rutherford agreed. "But it will all come back to us, once we're in operation." He leaned forward earnestly. "Mr. Gant, you've been a pioneer in this country. You've had to deal with savages and outlaws, but those days are nearly over. The territory is on the threshold of prosperity. A flood of people are coming with the railroad. Schools and churches will spring up everywhere. It's going to be an empire, the Southwestern empire, sir. I can see the railroad a few years from now hauling great train after train of passengers and rich freight all that vast distance from the Mississippi to the Pacific!"

I was fascinated by his eloquence. There was something magically convincing in his voice and enthusiasm, and for the moment I could actually see a railroad train sweeping triumphantly across our San Blas plain and the Indians and Mexicans fleeing from it in terror. And, looking into the staring eyes of grizzled old teamsters, I believed they could see it too.

Vance Rutherford seemed to feel his power. He went on appealingly.

"Mr. Gant, you're one of the biggest freighters in the country. You know your business, and if you do, you must know that the day of mule and bull trains is past. You've seen what happened along the Santa Fe trail in Kansas. You know what will happen to the wagon business in this territory as soon as we have trains running into Capitan. Don't you agree, sir, that it's good business for a freighter to sell his wagons and mules while there's a demand and put his money into the railroad?"

I heard a sound like a deep mutter that could be no longer withheld, and before I looked I knew that my father had thrown up his massive head and was standing there, rude and immovable, his shaggy beard throwing off defiance, and green fire like the dog star in his eyes.

"No!" he bellowed, and I heard the tinware on the shelves murmur his decree after him. "My only interest in your stock, young man, was to find out whether I could trust you and your fourteen-million-dollar-railroad officials to horse feed when they came through!"

I saw Al Sleeper open his mouth in a soundless laugh and a rancher from the Tres Ritos bring one hand down silently on his denim thigh. The spell of the railroad was irreparably broken. Customers and loafers nudged one another, and Vance Rutherford looked as if he had been struck across the face. His temples twitched, but he stood his ground.

"I think, Mr. Gant," he said, with a great effort at dignity, "if the railroad ever asks it, your feed corral would be justified in extending credit."

I expected him to go, but for a long moment the two men continued to face each other—both iron-willed and unyielding; one, young in years, gentlemanly, with a flower in his buttonhole; the other, older, powerful, with streaks of wool and dust on his clothing; one of the new age, one of the old. Then the younger man turned silently and went out.

News of the coming of the railroad spread like a gold strike through the territory. Stories reached the store by stage and wagon train, by buckboard and carriage. The railroad was awarding contracts for grading, ties, bridge timbers and telegraph poles. The railroad contractors were buying herds of horses and mules. The railroad was blasting tunnels through the San Dimas Mountains. The railroad was crossing the mountains on the old wagon trail. All summer and fall the railroad expected to lay from one to two miles of track a day.

By Christmas the byword among the teamsters returning from the iron rails was, "Look out for the locomotive!" They reported the sleepy old Mexican village of La Luz booming since the railroad had arrived. The Capitan Enterprise announced with pride that Baldwin's were building a new, huge, eighty-ton locomotive for use in the territory and that it would be "in charge of men fully competent to handle the monster." And it added that Vance Rutherford, engineer for the railroad, had promised Lawyer Henry Coddom that he was pushing construction with every resource at his command and that trains would be running into Capitan by the Fourth of July.

In the very next issue of the Enterprise, Capitan stores advertised in tall type that no new merchandise would come from the East until it arrived more cheaply and safely by steam train. My mother had always abhorred the trail, its clouds of dust, the shouts and curses of its drivers, the crack of whips and report of linchpins, and the snail-like drag of long files of chained steers. Ever since I could remember, she had shut it out with heavy brown hangings. But now she began to draw them back and sit at her knitting where she could see, at last, traffic slowly but steadily fading like late afternoon on the old trail. It seemed to give her a satisfaction as if the railroad were just over the rise, ruthlessly pushing the creaking freight wagons out of the way.

I knew that every vanished wagon sheet and silent wheel was a secret growing cancer in the heart of my father. He never alluded to it, but when I rode along in his buggy to Capitan I could see the steely glitter in his eyes at sight of the copper ingots, which his trains formerly freighted to Kansas, piling up in great mounds at the proposed site of the new depot. And his eyes looked straight ahead when we passed teams unloading wool and hides into adobe warehouses that had sprung up like molehills where Henry Coddom had sold the railroad a tract of land for the new Capitan townsite and which, already, people were calling Newtown.

There was actually no more railroad to be seen in Capitan than out on the sand hills, but every day now rigs began passing our store on their way to Capitan to trade. Cowboys nightly celebrated the railroad by shooting up the town. There was talk of the Enterprise becoming a daily after the telegraph had arrived. I saw where Strome Brothers had torn down their old wooden hitching rack and set up individual posts with citified snap chains. And the Enterprise boasted that there wasn't a vacant house in the town.

Up to this time I had never seen a railroad in my young life, and it seemed that our store and trail were being blighted by some mysterious and invisible weapon in Vance Rutherford's hand. This morning I noticed my father throw up his head to gaze at the northeast. When I looked, there it hung like a black dust cloud over the green of the prairie, the railroad at last. And as my father stared at the smoke funneling up persistently on the distant horizon, I saw the same wild defiance come into his bearded face as it had that day at his sheep camp along the Rio Cedro when we had watched a Comanche or Kiowa smoke signal from the hills.

Every morning after this the smoke was there, and I came to think of it as the powerful black breath of Vance Rutherford, moving steadily, silently, inexorably southwest toward Capitan. Now it passed the red mesa, and now for a few days it changed rugged Mount Jeddo into an active volcano. And one day when it had reached some miles abreast of us, I could not resist galloping my pony secretly across the plain to a grassy swell from which I could see a whole bank being sliced away like cake. The prairie there seemed to boil with men and teams, with wagons, plows and drags.

The air was filled with the flash of moving picks and shovels and the ring of iron hammers. And creeping back and forward in the background, hissing, sometimes outshrieking any mountain lion, glided one of Vance Rutherford's tamed iron monsters.

I was only a boy, but I could tell, as I rode thoughtfully homeward, that in this thing my mother called civilization there was no quarter, no compromise, no pity. It was not like your grazing pony that, after tiring you for an hour, would let you catch it, or like a wagon train that welcomed you with a blanket, food and the red warmth of a camp fire. This was something of another kidney, of another and newer age.

After that initial challenging scrutiny, I never saw my father acknowledge the black smoke's presence. When he entered the store, the subject changed. Only once I heard him refer again to the railroad. A passenger on the halted stage boasted that a Mississippi-Pacific train had done twenty-five miles an hour crossing the plains. My father turned with heavy deliberation and stared him into confusion.

"Sir, I can do as much with one of my Kentucky buggy teams!" he scorned. "And if the trail is uphill, I have gold to wager that I can soundly whip your train!"

But some hours after the stage had gone, I saw him silent and solitary behind our warehouse, pacing measuredly around what none of us had ever seen before—a corral of his stilled freight wagons. Mute, deserted and depressing, they stood there, an unforgettable reminder of what had been. And late that evening when my mother sent me to take the St. Louis paper back to his office, I don't think he knew I was there, for I heard from his bedroom deep incredible sounds, like a man praying, which instantly riveted me to the floor. I couldn't understand a word he said, but the shock of hearing my strong father give way like that in secret shook me to my foundations.

Next morning at breakfast he was stanch and powerful as always, and I told myself that I must have been mistaken. And that afternoon I felt sure of it. I was counting twenty, ten and five dollar gold pieces, silver dollars, halves and quarters—there was nothing smaller—on his battered desk in the mansion office when through the window I saw Lawyer Henry Coddom climb determinedly out of his phaeton in the courtyard. The two men had not met since

Juliana had been married in the Coddom parlor, and now, with Henry Coddom appointed attorney for the railroad in the territory, I could feel the clouds gather and thicken. When Piedad brought the visitor to the office door, he asked to speak with my father in private, and I was sent away.

Twenty minutes later Henry Coddom came out like a cuffed schoolboy, hat in his hand, his face crimson. And when my father stepped into the hall to order me back to my counting, there were still pitchforks in his eyes and I had never seen him more absolute and unconquerable. Then he became aware of my mother standing in the doorway to her rooms, color in her quilted cheeks and a newspaper in her hand.

"Nettie"—he inclined his head.

"Frank!" she begged him. "You didn't throw away your invitation?"

"Invitation?" His uncompromising eyes bored her.

"It's in the Enterprise!" my mother went on feverishly. "They're running the first train into Capitan the Fourth of July. The whole territory's going to celebrate. They expect crowds from every county. The governor and judges and politicos and all the big men of the territory will get on the train at La Luz and ride into Capitan. The governor of Kansas and his wife will be on the train and a Kansas band. They've telegraphed an invitation to President Hayes."

Granite had come into my father's face.

"I got no invitation," he answered harshly. "Henry Coddom came to tell me the railroad wants to build to California." His eyes blazed. "They want eighty miles of my land. They want to build through the Canyon Bonito. They want to blacken my grass, plow trains through my sheep, dump squatters along the Bonito all the way from Big Flat to Gant's Valley."

I am not sure that my mother heard him.

"Frank," she went on desperately, "it's to be the biggest thing that ever happened in the territory. The railroad's giving a banquet at the Wooton House. There'll be dancing till morning. And all the railroad officials and their wives will be there!"

It was almost as if my mother had mentioned Vance Rutherford and Juliana by name. With a titanic effort to control himself, my father turned without a word into the mansion office. And all the

time my fingers kept building up fat piles of white and yellow coins,
I could feel the raw emotion working in him. And from the next
issue of the Enterprise we found that the railroad company was
daring to drag him soon, like some petty thief or cattle rustler, into
court in Bonito County, whose vast spaces he half owned, to show
why eighty miles of his choicest river pasture land should not be
condemned for the railroad right of way.

For days afterward he remained around home, silent and impla-
cable, waiting for the case to be called. And when I saw the dull
fire leaping in his eyes, I knew he was forging the bolts of lightning
he would let loose in that small adobe courtroom at Bonito. Of
course Mr. Stryker, his lawyer, would be with him, but it was my
father who would dominate the court.

"No judge in this territory," Al Sleeper declared, "can look Frank
Gant in the eye and turn over his land to Henry Coddom and a
Kansas railroad."

For weeks my father waited while the railroad pushed its mailed
arm into Capitan, while June grew closer to July, and Juliana's
cream-colored mare had a second colt that Juliana had never seen.
And all the time I could see in my mother's eyes the hope that the
case had not yet been called in Judge Tatum's court at Bonito, because he and Vance Rutherford expected to come to my father
privately and settle the differences out of court in time to get him
to the celebration. I knew that if anybody could reason with my
father it was Judge Tatum, whom I had often seen slouched in the
mansion office, an extraordinarily long figure with a face like a sorrel
horse, his long legs up on the battered desk, a thick tumbler and
jug of my father's whisky beside him, and my father laughing
indulgently through his beard at what the judge was saying.

Then all hope of my father going to the celebration faded from
my mother's eyes. One of his old herders, Gil Jaramillo, arrived in
the mansion courtyard on a spent horse. Tall and cadaverous, his
eyes rolling with the mad light of so many men who spend their
lives with the sheep, he called out, "Amo!" with excitement as soon
as he was at the door. And when my father had come into the hall,
he stammered out in Spanish that the Cross V's, whose cattle ranch
adjoined my father's Rio Cedro pastures, were warring on his
sheep, driving some of them into the river, scattering the rest to be

preyed upon by coyotes and wolves, and badly beating up the *caporal* and herders.

I expected to see the anger flame on my father's face. Instead it grew calmer than for weeks, as if news of violence and bloodshed was almost a welcome relief from this petty waiting for a summons to court. Within the hour he drove off for the Rio Cedro, sitting his buggy like a king, Trinidad brown and solid beside him, and a change of horses galloping through the dust behind. And long after he had gone I could see him in my mind, whipping his team across a region half as wide as France, the goats leaping with flying beards from in front of the horses, the cedar branches whipping the buggy from both sides of the narrow trail, himself staying the night in some humble *placita* and, if there was a bed in the village, sleeping in it, and finally matching his strength against his enemies, who had always been putty in his hands.

I was glad he had gone that evening when the deputy from Bonito County arrived apologetically with the summons. But the gray glance of Al Sleeper held a queer light, and under his mustache, jutting out from his face like the waterfall of a roily mountain stream, his mouth looked forbidding. He spoke to my mother and early next morning sent the summons with a Mexican rider after my father, but I knew it was like a desert finch trying to catch an eagle.

The mansion seemed like a convent with my father gone. Our native villagers kept asking if we were not to ride with the governor on the bunting-trimmed train. I told them we didn't like crowds, that we had plenty of bunting in the mansion and that we intended to wait until there was room in Capitan to breathe. They nodded solemnly, polite Mexicans that they were, but they knew as well as I why we weren't going.

And now from morning till night the migration toward Capitan began passing our door—American ranchers and miners on the saddle, buggy and buckboard; officers' families from Fort Gates in Army ambulances with the side curtains rolled up for air; but mostly natives who had never seen the iron horse—Mexican families in heavy wagons, in a few private carriages and on endless saddles; Ute Indians decked with bright ribbons, their bony ponies packed for trade; and aloof Navajos in red calicos and blue velvets and clinking silver.

By noon of the Fourth all had passed. The last trip the stage would ever make by our door took place about one, the westbound coach crowded with passengers. It threw off our leather bag of mail, but failed to stop. And after it had gone and the trail lay quiet again, I suddenly realized that it looked different than I had ever seen it, old, tired, abandoned, almost like the ruins of an ancient *camino* winding desolately over the plain.

About two o'clock I glimpsed a distant smudge of dust to the northeast, a smudge that swirled rapidly nearer, and finally I could make out our bay team plunging wearily toward home, my father driving and Trinidad still beside him, but only one horse galloping behind. My father swerved the foaming, bulging-eyed team into the mansion courtyard. As I slipped back into the hall, he said something to Trinidad, who at once drove away. Then I saw through my mother's doorway that she had stiffened in her chair and bent her face defensively over her knitting.

My father scarcely tossed a glance at me as he came in, haggard and grim, his hat, beard and broadcloth layered with dust. He halted in the center of the hall from where his eyes could flash turbulently into my mother's room.

"Was Stryker here to see me?"

My mother's rigid needles kept moving.

"Yesterday, Frank," she answered.

"Well?" he breathed heavily.

"Judge Tatum appointed commissioners to condemn the land." My mother's lips were tight bands. "He told Mr. Stryker that no individual could stand in the way of progress and the railroad."

My father hadn't moved. My mother tried to leave the subject: "Did you settle the trouble with the Cross V's?"

"There was," my father answered harshly, "no trouble to settle."

"What do you mean?" For the first time she looked up at him.

"I mean," my father said, and now that he had started, the words poured out in a wild torrent, "that progress isn't above using the tricks of a black-leg gambler!" The green lightning had leaped from his eyes and at each successive sentence the bolt seemed to hurl itself again, as I had often watched it in a distant cloud, traversing over and over the same forked path. "There wasn't any sheep war. Nobody had beaten a herder. I didn't find a ewe touched. Somebody paid Gil Jaramillo to come here. They bribed him to lie to me. They had me drive hundreds of miles in a buggy and kill one of my best horses to keep me away from Judge Tatum's court!" Then he turned and went into his office.

I thought I could hear him moving about in his bedroom. There was a purr of wheels in the courtyard, and through the pane at the side of the door I saw Trinidad drive up in the red-wheeled buggy without a top.

My father came out almost immediately. He had changed his clothes, but the dust still clung to his beard and eyebrows. In his hand was the black-snake whip with which he had once whipped a herder for the arch crime of deserting his sheep, and I saw that the lash was still caked with dried particles of red.

"Frank!" my mother cried. She had run to her doorway. "Where are you going?"

He paid her utterly no attention. I don't think he knew she was there.

"Frank!" she screamed after him. "Whoever bribed Gil Jaramillo, it wasn't Vance Rutherford or the railroad! They wouldn't stoop to a thing like that!"

He went on out of the door. Never had I seen my mother move so rapidly. Her full skirts seemed to whisper in terror as they glided over the floor. Her hands seized my shoulder.

"Get him to take you with him!" she begged me. "He never does those violent things when you're along!" She pushed me out of the doorway and I saw the sun glinting on the sleek flanks of the dancing Kentucky team.

I ran to the right side, where the springs had already deeply settled.

"I want to go along, papa!" I shouted at him.

He looked down at me.

"You're sure you want to go along?" he asked, and at his mad eyes a chill ran down my spine, but I nodded. He told the impassive Trinidad to step out, and I climbed in beside him. Prince and Custer were crazy to be off. They had not been driven for days. One hand of my father pulled them back, rearing.

"Easy, boys," he said through his teeth and beard. "We'll have plenty time when we get there."

Crouching on the cushion, I told myself I couldn't see how trouble could happen on a day like this. The sky was a blue bowl and I could smell the freshness of last night's shower in the bunch grass all around us. Horned larks flushed in front of the horses. A road runner clowned at us, his crest and long tail rising and falling comically. But I did not laugh. Ahead, like a bed of mushrooms sprung up on the prairie, I could see the buildings of Capitan.

Halfway across the prairie something ran shining through the grass—the twin iron bands of the railroad. From here to Capitan they had built straight as an arrow, close beside the trail, as if to ridicule the earthy ruts, crude windings and arroyo dips of the sprawling old overland route. Here the railroad cut insolently over the trail and the light buggy pitched on the rough planks of the crossing, but my father gave no sign that the railroad was there— not even when a wailing cry drifted over the prairie behind us and I knew without turning my head that the horizon must be stormy with smoke.

Within a mile or two, the rails only a few yards from the trail were crackling. Our Kentucky buggy horses had grown uneasy and were trying to throw frightened looks over their shoulders, but my father held their heads with an iron hand. Twisting in my seat, I could see the afternoon sun sparkling on something that moved behind us, pursuing us, not galloping up and down like a buffalo but gliding through the grass like a snake. The bulging smokestack was as high as the neck of a camel, the boiler as big as the belly of a horse, and below it a cowcatcher, long and pointed like Judge Tatum's nose, ran on its own pony wheels. A man rode in the cab that was as high off the ground as a buggy, and behind him streamed the coaches of the territory's celebration train.

I could hear a brass band in the cars now. It was playing Dixie. Everything on the train was gaiety as it pulled beside us. Red, white and blue bunting fluttered from headlight, smokestack and whistle. The bell rang triumphantly. The small pony wheels spun. The black-and-gold driving shafts shot backward and forward. Faces pressed at the small, square windows, and on the open platforms of the short, boxlike coaches a few male passengers stood holding to iron railings and brake wheels. But for all the attention my father gave it, the train might not have been there.

So far the railroad and trail had been slightly downhill. Now the train reached the foot of the steady prairie grade up to Capitan. The engine began to puff valiantly, and a cloud of cinders came flying back into our faces. Suddenly I realized that, although my father still sat like a bearded statue beside me, his thewlike fingers had let out some slack on the lines, and the long-denied horses were leaping.

I told myself it couldn't be a race, because my father wasn't racing. He just sat there deaf and unapproachable, but now I know that of all the matches between horseflesh and the iron horse that were to follow on the same rude course, this was the most intense and deadly in earnest. Heads began to appear out of the open car windows. Passengers waved, jeered and challenged. But the train no longer was moving faster than the buggy.

Suddenly something inside of me seemed to stand still. Peering around my father, I had caught a glimpse of a face at a car window. It was more of a lady's face than I had remembered, but the eyes under the nodding plumes were unchanged. They were fixed on my father with a look that I shall never forget, almost the look they had given him that day she had tiptoed into my mother's room two years before, a straining look of appeal that might almost have been at God. Only a matter of thirty or forty feet separated her from my father, but it might as well have been the width of Kansas. He did not turn. The horses raced on, and when I looked again, all I could see in the glass was the blurred reflection of prairie sky, and the face of Juliana had gone.

I had to keep bracing myself on the rocking cushion. The train beside us rode smoothly enough, almost contemptuously, over its new roadbed, but the buggy plunged from rut to pitch hole, and yet, window by window and now coach by coach, the buggy was gaining. Directly ahead I could make out a dense frieze of men's hats and ladies' parasols around the new depot. Nearer, on both sides of the railroad, the green plain blossomed with visiting tents and camp wagons. And now the trail just in front of us began to teem with American, Mexican and Indian spectators, who fell back whooping and shooting as we tore by.

I can still see Prince and Custer running, their heads outstretched, their manes wildly flinging, and at every jump the fine muscles on their hips appearing and disappearing like so many fingered hands. With both horses bent into shying half arcs, we breasted the laboring engine, passed it, left its bright flutter of bunting definitely behind us. And I told myself exultantly that my father

had whipped the celebration train, humbled the railroad in front of
half the territory. Then I saw ahead where the trail swerved sharply,
and remembered that we had another crossing in store.

There was no necessity for my father to take it. He might have
turned off the trail on the unfenced prairie. But my father never
turned off the trail for anything, God or the devil, cruelty or mercy;
so long as it lay squarely in his path, he knew no other justice.
Leaning far to the side for the curve, he snatched the whip from
its socket and the buggy reeled on two wheels for the crossing.

Through the din of the train I could hear the band playing mag-
nificently. It sounded like Columbia, the Gem of the Ocean. High
above it shrieked the voice of the engine whistling down brakes for
the station. It seemed far enough away when it started, grew
steadily louder, louder, till the sound seemed to split my ear. I saw
my father drop the reins and felt him swing me up in his arms.
There was a sound like chair legs crashing, and the blurred earth,
engine and the white faces of the engineer and frontier crowd
turned over like the markings on a grindstone.

It wasn't exactly a pain in my back. I felt benumbed, as if an
arrow pinned me down. My eyes seemed to be ground shut with
dust and sand, and when I forced them open, I could see nothing
but the dude hats of men who had come from the train and the
gaily trimmed bonnets of the ladies all swimming around me in a
kind of leisurely whirlwind.

Only one of the bonnets looked familiar. It was very near,
fashioned with drooping plumes, and I knew that somewhere I had
seen it before.

A portly man in a long coat with a velvet collar thrust a flask to
my lips. I sputtered and strangled, but when I could breathe again,
I felt better.

"Where's my father?" I asked them.

They all just stood there looking at me. I twisted my head and
saw Vance Rutherford. He was close to me, a flower in his buttonhole, comforting Juliana, who was bitterly crying. When I closed my
eyes I could still see my father sitting in the buggy beside me, aloof,
powerful, absolute, his black beard turned stubbornly in the wind,
the reins in his thewlike fingers. All these men from the train
looked white and soft in comparison. They couldn't, I told myself,
whip the bloody back of a herder who had broken the trust to his

sheep. I wanted my father. One bark from his bearded lips, and most of this crowd would scurry like prairie dogs.

"Where'd he go?" I cried, and struggled to sit up. Vance Rutherford and the portly man helped me. The crowd fell back slightly. All I could see between tailored trousers and gayly flounced dresses were the iron bands of the railroad running triumphantly westward and glinting like mottled silver in the sun.